I0581139

Bloodline

More Books by Anne MacReynold

The Creations Saga:
Red Sand
Golden Light

2021 International Best Indie Book Award Winner

2021 American Fiction Awards Finalist in Fantasy

"An engrossing tale of desire, passion, trials, and triumphs that is sure to keep readers turning the pages from cover to cover. I would certainly recommend Golden Light to fans of highly atmospheric descriptions, intense interpersonal drama, and mythos and magic enthusiasts everywhere."

"Undoubtedly fascinating and complex. 5 Stars."

-Readers' Favorite

"A fascinating fantasy world."

"The characters feel very real and very raw."

-NINA Productions

"Beautiful. Adventurous. Mystical. An amazing journey."

-Goodreads

Bloodline

Anne MacReynold

Enchanted Publishing House

Enchanted Publishing House

Bloodline Copyright © 2021 Anne MacReynold

Book Design by Brandon Rice

Manuscript Editing by Enchanted Edits
www.EnchantedEdits.com

Original Cover Photo: © Ermess/Dreamstime.com
All Things Bright and Beautiful © Cecil Frances Alexander
in *Hymns for Little Children* 1848
Going Home © William Arms Fisher 1922

All rights reserved. This book, and parts thereof, may not be reproduced in any form without permission.

LCCN: 2021923272
Paperback ISBN: 978-1-7371218-3-1
E-Book ISBN: 978-1-7371218-5-5
Hardback ISBN: 978-1-7371218-4-8

Printed in the United States of America

Dedicated to Conner

A brother worth living for

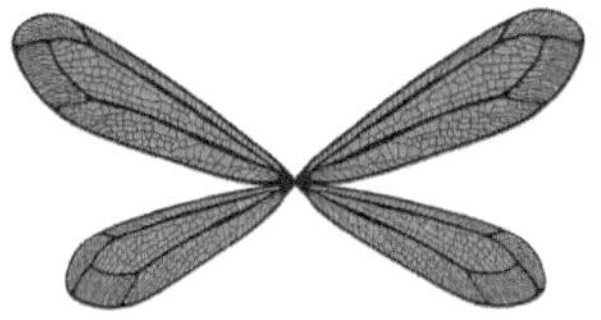

Yvaine

# Prologue

My brother was about to die.

It wasn't right. He was only four years old.

The man held a knife in his hand, but there was a gun a short distance from him. I was so close, but I couldn't move. The man had drugged me, and I lay there paralyzed. I couldn't remember when or how he did it. I was helpless. The knife was against my brother's throat now.

I had to get up.

I tried to force my body to obey. To fight for my brother.

But what if I wasn't strong enough? What if I failed and he died?

All because I was too weak.

He cried out in pain as the blood poured from him; the man was taking his time. I was powerless, but I felt every nerve in my body fighting, reaching for freedom. I felt the muscles burn, the bones groan in agony, yet despite this, I heard the screaming voice in my head that begged me to give up. To die.

But something broke. A barrier that had forced me to lay helpless, a fear that had taken root, now snapped and crumbled. The burning adrenaline coursed through my blood, working its way through my young body. Control. I was in control.

The man had set a bowl below my sibling's throat where he lay bleeding on the floor. It was nearly full of the red liquid. The man didn't hear me when I stood. I reached for the small pistol on the table. The man still held the ancient knife to my brother's throat, slowly widening the wound and speeding the flow of his blood.

The pistol's grip rested comfortably in my hand, and I raised it so he would finally notice the threat beside him. He stopped cutting and turned his head in my direction. The look on his face gave me a jolt of confidence. He was angry. Good.

Although I had the better weapon, he still had the knife against my brother's skin, ready to end him at moment's notice. The man caught my subtle glance toward the blade. This made him smile.

"Let my brother go."

"Why don't you put the gun down, like a good girl, and I'll let you live." We both knew he was lying. He wouldn't let me go. As soon as I put down the gun, he'd finish my brother and go for me next.

Slowly, I answered, "No." This time, he didn't argue. He just stared at me, measuring my expression. And what he saw there worried him. I didn't know what he was seeing. Numbness had overtaken me—it was the only way to get through this.

The man slowly pulled the knife away. I motioned for him to move, and he wisely obeyed. I walked with him, so I stood between the dying child and the monster before me. Lugh was still paralyzed, as I had been, but the pain must have freed him in a way, allowing him to scream.

Once I was sure he couldn't harm my brother, I cocked the pistol. I hadn't wanted to fire early, and with the adrenaline pumping through me, I would have.

But now that Lugh was safe...

The man's expression changed. He had been wary before, but he'd clung to his arrogance. He never thought a man such as him would be defeated by a young girl. But now, he was frightened, and I was glad. He dropped the knife, and its tip stuck in the wood floor. Without a shred of remorse, I said, "I hope hell exists." I pulled the trigger, but soon realized that we were the ones in hell, and he had just escaped the pit that was this life.

Yvaine

Anyone who has common sense will remember
that the bewilderments of the eyes are of two kinds,
and arise from two causes, either from coming out of
the light or from going into the light.

—Plato: The Allegory of the Cave, from The Republic

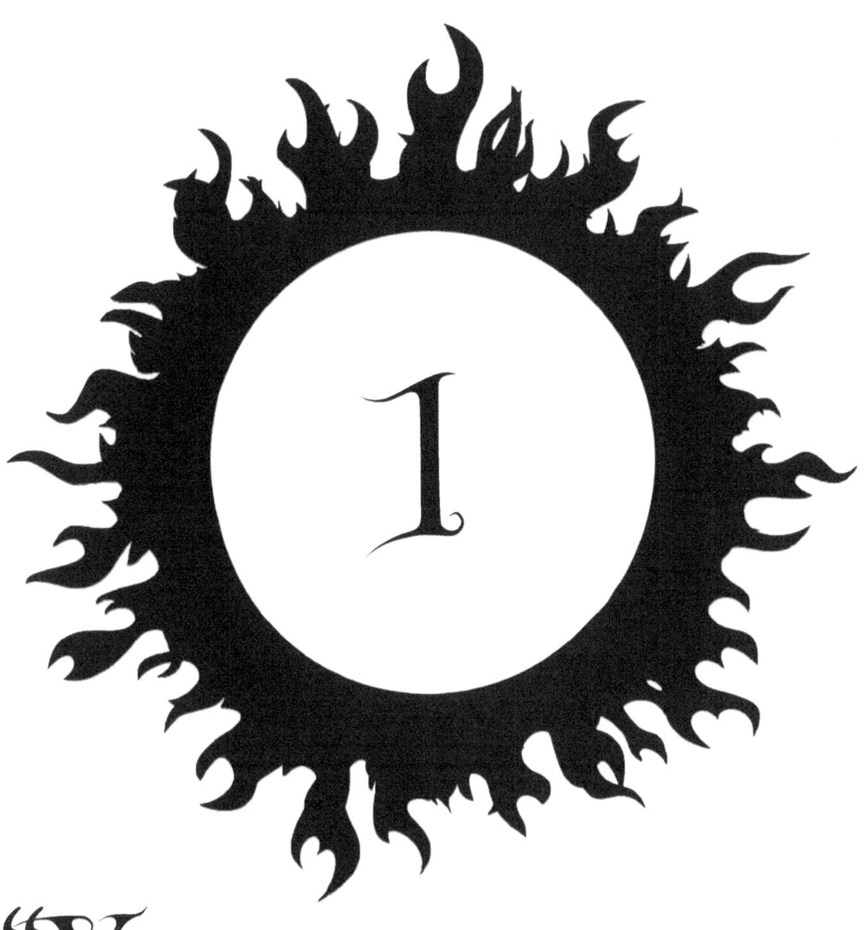

"Yvaine! Behind you!" I turned to find a monster peering into the shadows I hid in. Its golden eyes pierced my own, but it would not take me. I refused to allow it. Someone else needed me to live.

I raised the ancient dagger and plunged it into its phantom-like body, knowing it was one of the few weapons on the planet that could kill it. Though there was no flesh and bone to damage, I could feel its essence convulse in pain as I twisted the blade. The surge of power burned my arm, as it always did when I used the dagger. The same one that had nearly killed my brother thirteen years ago. I thanked that murderous man every day for delivering such a useful weapon into our hands. If it hadn't been for the dagger, we would have perished along with the rest of humanity.

The monster—we called the Guise—dissipated, leaving nothing behind of its existence. The sun was shining bright. A perfect day for the monster to hunt, while humans and Fae alike were forced to hide in the shadows and hoped that the darkness was black enough to keep the creatures at bay.

"You're getting sloppy. That was too close for comfort, Yvaine," my brother scolded. Though Lugh spent much of his time in the darkness, like the rest of us, the scar on his neck was stark white compared to his pallid complexion, forever reminding me how close I had come to failing him.

"Relax." Raising the blade to eye level, I continued, "As long as we have this, they cannot hurt us."

"That blade doesn't make you immortal."

"I don't need to be immortal. I just need to live longer than you," I joked.

Lugh's face pinched in exasperation. *Always so serious.*

"That thing didn't ruin your appetite, did it? If it did, I'd be glad to eat your half." I reached for the gnome he clutched in his hand. It was still bleeding out from the arrow Lugh had shot into its gut. Which was most likely how the Guise had found us; it could scent blood from oceans away.

Yanking the pathetic Fae creature away, he said, "No way! I'm the one who killed him. If anything, you should give me *your* half." Lugh's blonde hair fell into his eyes, giving me just enough time to retrieve the meal from his loose grip.

Dangling it in front of him, I said, "Well, I killed the Guise. So, let's just split it as planned." I smiled at the annoyed set of his jaw.

"Fine."

"Fine."

We retreated into the abandoned tunnel of the dead city, hoping that there was enough firewood to spare and that the Fae had not found a home within its walls while we were away.

The smell of the tunnel was nauseating, but it was comforting at the same time. Places like these dank, damp caverns kept us safe from the monsters that roamed the lands. The Guise were created by humans experimenting with things they shouldn't have. Although we didn't know it at the time of the Collapse, humans were incapable of wielding magic. Any time one of them tried it would backfire. And they tried one time too many, taking the whole world with it.

Now, monsters made of light hunted us, feasting on our bodies, minds, and souls. Our one defense was the darkness. But we hid within the blackness only to discover that there were others hiding there, too. *The Fae.* They had stayed hidden among us for millennia, content to stay concealed if it meant it would keep the peace between our peoples.

But humans screwed that up, too.

The Fae hated us. They hated our greed and ignorance. And they hated that they were hunted alongside us, forced to stay in the shadows permanently.

The dagger hanging at my side glowed a pale amethyst hue, guiding us through the winding underground pathways. No, humans could not wield magic, but they could use weapons that were endowed with magic. Such as this blade: a long, thick dirk with a pearl handle and runes etched into the metal. I didn't know what the runes meant, but they kept us safe—that was all I asked for.

"Do you remember Mother's garden? Her flowers were so tall, we could play hide and seek in them," I recalled.

My brother took his time answering, "No."

"What *do* you remember?" I had asked him before, but perhaps if I kept trying, he would eventually remember something from our childhood.

"Nothing."

"That can't be true. You were young, but not a babe." The water rose the farther we walked down the tunnel, soaking our feet.

"Guess, I'm just lucky."

"Lucky to forget our parents? Home?"

"It's better than remembering and regretting that I don't have it anymore. At least this way, I don't have anything to compare this life to." Lugh adjusted his quiver, shaking out whatever emotion was festering beneath the indifferent mask.

Maybe he was right. Maybe it was better to know nothing else. That way, there's nothing to mourn.

Especially the end.

Lugh held up his hand in warning, the other clutched our meal tightly. I stopped and unsheathed the dirk, waiting.

An arrow shot through the blackness, but it was not my brother's. It flew between us. *A warning.* Lugh immediately returned fire, however, it was impossible to see what he was shooting at. I placed my hand on his arm and said, "Don't waste the arrows." The blade in my hand obeyed without effort. The light went out, and we were all blind.

I pushed Lugh flat against the west wall and felt my way forward. The blade pulsed in warning, but it was not urgent. I listened for footsteps, for breathing, for any sign of what lurked ahead. The fact that an arrow had been used against us eliminated many of the Fae species. Most of them didn't need weapons due to their *natural talents*, and many were too small for the size of arrow that passed by. And humans were so rare, I doubted we'd happened upon one, even near a city. Not that I was complaining.

Water splashed behind me. I spun, leading with the dirk. I made contact with warm flesh. Fresh blood coated my blade, dimming the light that reignited at my command. A male's cry echoed down the tunnel, and I worried that he would bring more of his kind our way if they heard him.

"Quiet," I said. Bringing my blade up to his throat, I was able to discern the elf's features. He was a head taller than me, pale skin, sharp features, green eyes, and black hair. A typical male elf. They were beautiful, yes, but beauty was worthless when the inside was as ugly as a goblin. And elves were the worst of all the Fae people.

The elf clutched his side. The bow had been dropped to the wet ground, but the arrows were still in his quiver. "Do it then," he panted. "End me. Anything would be better than this darkness anyway."

At his words, I paused. I was ready to slice into his skin without a second thought. I had become so numb to the carnage of this chaotic world that I had forgotten a very important thing. I lowered my blade. "Are there more of you?" I asked.

The elf eyed my knife, but said, "No."

"Why did you attack us?"

"I'm alone in a dark tunnel. It's better to be safe than sorry. Though I'm certainly sorry now." The elf fell to his knees, consciousness fading. He was losing too much blood. I thought of my brother in that moment, when he had been the one bleeding on the ground.

"Yvaine, leave him. Let's go," Lugh pushed. He picked up his used arrow from where it had lain on the ground beside us. I acknowledged that he had come close to hitting his target.

The elf sank to his side, and the water beneath him darkened. "No," I said.

"No? Are you insane? It's him or us. I prefer us." Lugh was right of course, but I couldn't help but empathize with the elf. *Anything would be better than this darkness.*

"Grab a side. He's coming with us."

"Yvaine—"

"Now," I ordered. Lugh may have been a capable hunter, but he was still young—only sixteen years old. A near decade more didn't make me a sage, but I'd learned to listen to my instincts early on. And they were screaming at me to help this Fae. With the hem of my shirt, I retrieved the elf's bow from the stone ground and placed it over my free shoulder, refusing to touch it with my bare skin for fear of magical repercussions. Many elves placed curses on their weapons, so their enemies would suffer even after the true owner had been killed.

Lugh grumbled but obeyed, his thin build struggling to lift the heavier-than-he-looked elf. I had been training for years with a blade, so I could wield powerful blows against my opponents. I was strong. I would not falter, and I could carry my brother's half if I was forced to. Our camp was not far. There, I would be able to mend the Fae's wound and set him free without having to add another tick mark to my long list of sins.

"This is unlike you." Lugh sat opposite of me, roasting the Fae over the fire. Gnomes were small beings with oversized ears and noses, tiny feet and hands, and had coarse grey hair from the time of their birth to their death. They also had the worst temperaments, similar to vultures.

I didn't respond to my brother. What was there to say? I knew it was idiotic. Suicidal even. But I was tired of the killing, and the fact that the Fae had *wanted* to die had torn down the wall I'd built to protect myself. I looked to the elf where he lay wrapped in bandages and furs. His breathing was even, and his fever had broken over the course of the day. He was going to live. I smiled until I saw Lugh's disapproving face, and it disappeared.

"The Fae are masters of magic. Are you sure he didn't do something to you? An obedience spell? You know the rumors: most victims don't know it's happened to them, and sometimes they even enjoy it." Lugh's eyes darted back and forth between us, gaging how much he should be concerned.

"I'm not under a spell, jackass." *Was I?* We had waited to eat until night had fallen, and the things hiding in the tunnels left to hunt so we could dine in peace. During that time, I had mended the elf's wound and bandaged him as well as I could with the fabrics we had. It was a long day, listening to his hitched breathing and wondering if he was going to last each hour that passed.

"If you say so," he muttered. The gnome was done roasting, and I reached to tear a leg off when the elf stirred in the corner.

"Where am I?" the elf asked. He tried to sit up, but... "Untie me!" he demanded.

"No," I said. His eyes flitted around the small space we camped in, searching for something.

"The plan is to kill me slow, huh?" The elf watched as I tore the leg from the roasting gnome. "No, you're going to eat me. Of course. Why waste a good meal?" He continued to mutter unintelligible things, but I caught, "What a way to go. Eaten by humans, and I thought it couldn't get much worse."

My brother and I looked to one another and laughed so hard that I spit out my meal. Lugh teared up from the howling. We hadn't laughed that hard in a long time. Lugh never smiled, and I was grateful for the elf, even if all he gave us was this moment in time.

"You find this funny? Humans are sick." The elf tried to turn over but yelled out when he put pressure on his wound.

"Stop squirming, or you'll ruin all my hard work," I scolded.

"Why did you mend me if you're just going to kill me anyway?"

"Because we're not going to kill you. Even though you attacked us first." I took another savory bite of food. "Give yourself a couple days to heal, and you'll be released." The elf's shocked face nearly made me spit up the food again. "For a price, naturally."

"And there it is. Humans always want something in return. They can never just give. Only take." He didn't have to remind us of this. We knew our species was the cause of the Collapse, but we lived in a world where *taking* was the only way to survive.

"Yeah, yeah. Get over it, elf. Time to move on," Lugh said around bites of his own meal. But there was a sadness in his eyes, an emotion only I could see.

"My name is not *elf*." He stopped struggling against the ropes and relaxed, accepting his fate.

"What would you like to be called then, elf?" Lugh asked.

"My name is Coilleach."

Lugh laughed again. "That's a mouthful. I'm going to call you Cole instead."

Cole grimaced. "My name is Yvaine and that is my brother, Lugh," I offered, stopping the fight I could feel coming. Cole met my gaze, and I stopped breathing. Elves *were* beautiful.

Lugh cleared his throat and said, "So, to pay for your freedom, we want a spell. One that will protect us during the day."

Cole released his hold on me and gave Lugh a tired expression. "You're joking? If I could give you that then why would I be in the tunnels at all? I am just as powerless as you."

"Whatever, we know elves have magic. We've watched them disappear into a cloud of darkness when the Guise are near." Lugh nodded his head toward me. "We want that. A permanent one."

Cole considered for a long moment. "Deal. When you release me, I will give you the spell."

"No, we want it now," Lugh demanded.

Cole said, "When you release me, I will give you the spell. Protect me until I am healed, and I will cast the spell myself." The elf wasn't going to give in. He had been ready to die only a few hours earlier. The Fae had no reason to barter to begin with.

Lugh opened his mouth to argue when I said, "Deal." Before the elf could meet my eyes, I looked down to the leg bone in my hand. I could feel his gaze on me, a trail of fire burned up my body and finally rested on my face.

"Yvaine," Lugh warned.

"It's a fair exchange, Lugh. Now, get him some food before he starves and is no use to us." I tossed the leg bone into a dank corner. Our camp was at the end of a side tunnel, one that was left unfinished.

Rolling his eyes, Lugh stood and took a chunk of meat to Cole, who said, "You're going to have to untie my hands, unless you want to feed me yourself." I looked to the elf while he was distracted and saw the mischievous glint in his eye. Pointed ears peeked through the ebony hair.

"No way, *Cole*. Trust is earned. You're just going to have to starve." But Lugh knew that we had to feed him one way or another.

"Give it here, jackass. Get some sleep. I'll take the first watch." Making my way to the elf, I took the meat from Lugh and sat as close as I dared to Cole. Without further argument, Lugh laid down to sleep and was snoring in a matter of moments. I smiled at his peaceful face.

"How long have you been alone?" Cole asked, his deep voice soothing.

"Never. I've always had Lugh." I tore the meat into small pieces and fed him a bite. He ate with fervor, surprisingly. From what I knew of elves, they were herbivores. But this elf was different.

Cole looked to Lugh, then me, marking the age difference. "How long?"

Reluctantly, I answered, "Since the Collapse. You?"

"Longer." I fed him another bite, and his green eyes gleamed in the light of the fire.

"Sorry." I didn't ask if he had family or what happened to them.

He shrugged. "At least you have your brother."

My brother's breathing was long and deep while he rested. "Lugh gives me a reason to keep moving. To live." I stiffened. *Why did I say that?*

Cole was about to say something else when he spotted the dirk strapped to my side. "What is that?" Black hair fell into his eyes, and I clenched my hands to keep myself from sweeping it away.

Defensive, I turned so he couldn't see the runes. "A knife."

"That's an endowed weapon, isn't it?" He shifted so he could peer around me, but cringed, due to the pain.

"Stop moving, or you'll rip your stitches," I said.

"Where did you get it?"

"The thread for your stitches? An old shirt." Nonchalantly, I inched away, putting as much space as I could between us.

"The dagger," he said, annoyed.

"I took it."

He contemplated asking where but changed his mind. "The light. That was what I saw in the tunnel, wasn't it? How did you get it to work?"

"I don't 'get it to work.' It just listens. Isn't that how all endowed weapons are?" The band holding my hair snapped and blonde strands fell into my eyes. "Damn it. That was my last one."

Cole watched as I finger-brushed my long, wavy locks and said, "For a select few, yes."

Frustrated with the bird's nest that was my hair, I flung it over my shoulder. "Lucky me."

"Yes, you are." I allowed myself a peek at his eyes again; they had darkened.

"Well, I am sure wielding a magic blade is nothing compared to what you can do. Elves are full of magic." I twisted so I was facing him; there was no need to hide the blade now that he knew.

"Are you going to feed or interrogate me?" Cole's voice was rough, and he fidgeted in his bonds.

Embarrassed, I said, "Rest up. The faster you heal, the faster we can get the spell and you can leave." I shoved the remainder of the gnome into his mouth and went to the opposite side of the tunnel to finish my watch.

Cole choked down the meat without another word and fell into a fitful sleep. As I watched him twitch and twist, I couldn't help but feel guilty. Humans had destroyed this world. Humans had destroyed themselves. It felt wrong to add to it.

I shoved the guilt down deep, knowing there was nothing I could do about it. The decision was an easy one to make. I would choose Lugh every time. No matter who or what it cost.

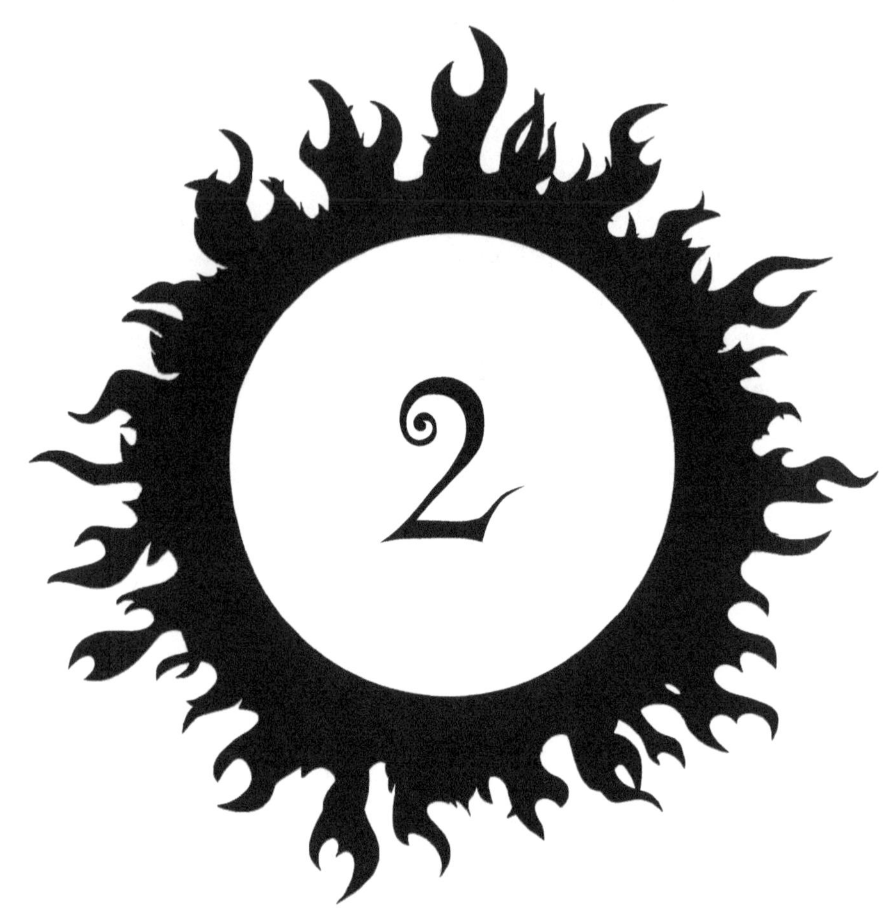

Her screams were intense. I covered my ears in hopes to drown out her pain, but it was there in my mind and memory. The man had already killed Father. He lay at the front door, eyes open, with a gaping hole in his forehead, the bullet now embedded in his skull. Mother fought against the man, her grief obvious, but she looked back to her children where they huddled in the corner of the room, and the fire returned to her eyes.

The man had her pinned to the ground, her throat slit with a familiar knife. She let go of her open throat and grabbed onto his. He dropped the blade, surprised at her strength. The man's face turned red, unable to breathe. Mother's blood poured onto the floor. There's too much blood. Too much. She's going to die.

"Mother!" I called out, worried for her. She turned her head toward me, opening her throat farther. That's when the man grabbed the blade from the floor and plunged it into her heart. "No!" I screamed. Lugh was tucked beneath my arm. He didn't see. He didn't know what had happened, but I could feel his body shaking anyway.

The man was angry and abandoned Mother. He stood slowly, taking deep, greedy breaths. He looked to the children hiding in the corner. I couldn't move. I couldn't take my eyes off the bodies. I heard his approach, but still, I did not move. My brother sobbed, not understanding, or perhaps understanding too much.

Get up. Move. Fight.

The man pulled a bottle from his pocket and poured the liquid onto a rag. He placed it over my mouth. Still, I did not move. Not as I scented the sickly-sweet rag or even as the man took Lugh from my arms. I did nothing.

Then, there was nothing.

Mother's screams began again, but I was blind. There was only darkness.

"Where are you?" I cried.

"Yvaine, wake up!"

Mother kept screaming.

"Yvaine!" Someone slapped me.

My eyes opened, and the dirk woke with me, illuminating the small space. But the screams didn't stop.

"Untie me now! I can fight!" a stranger's voice said.

"Lugh?" I asked.

"A banshee. She's almost here. We have to move now!" my brother said.

I unsheathed the dagger and looked down the tunnel. A white silhouette approached, beckoned by the stench of death. Her gaping jaw released a scream of pure torment. I looked to the elf and confirmed that he had survived the night.

What drew her here?

The discarded gnome bones in the corner gave me an answer.

Stupid! Sloppy!

"Untie me!" Cole repeated.

"Yvaine?" Lugh asked, his voice trembling.

"No, he stays bound. We can take care of ourselves." I took a few steps forward. "Once I have her distracted, take the elf and run past her. Make for the exit. We don't know how many are in here with us." Banshees traveled in packs, hunting for rotting flesh. Though, one didn't have to be dead to attract them, near it would suffice.

"You're going to need my help," Lugh said.

"Stop doubting me and move!" I ordered, placing the elf's quiver and bow over my brother's clothed shoulder beside his own; my hands tingled.

Lugh hesitated but did as I asked. He helped Cole to his feet, only untying the rope at his ankles. I ran forward with the dagger lighting my way. I charged her head on, and she screamed louder. At the last moment, I ran by her, slicing her arm with the blade. She spun to face me and lashed out with her long, poisonous claws. Her body was covered in lizard-like scales, and her tangled white hair hanged past her naked breasts. The banshee's eyes were white and useless—blind. Their sense of smell was terrifying.

"Go!" Lugh pushed Cole past the creature while I sliced her other arm. I met Cole's gaze for a brief moment and swore that I saw concern there. But all I cared about was Lugh, and I hoped that the elf wouldn't hurt him while I was distracted. "Run!" I shouted, attracting the attention of the Fae monster.

Once their footsteps were out of earshot, I began the true fight. The banshee had stopped screaming long enough to listen for me. My steps were silent against the stone tunnel, sure in my placement. The glow of the dirk allowed me an advantage, as I could see every move the Fae made. Her nostrils opened wide, scenting me. Taking my time, I picked up a rock and threw it behind her. She turned and lunged at the sound. The knife was in her back before she could scream again. She fell, and the smell of death was immediate. *More would come.*

The scales that had clung to her skin molted. The black poison dripped from her claws and teeth, discoloring the water below. I stepped out of the water, worried that the toxins would reach me through the boots.

"Yvaine?" I whipped around and saw the faint outline of my brother at the end of the tunnel. And another one behind him. Before I could warn him, the banshee shot forward, knocking Lugh to the ground. He splashed in the water, struggling to escape, but the Fae had trapped him.

I sprinted forward. *Not again. Not again. Not again.*

She lifted her claw to pierce him. Another silhouette appeared in the darkness.

We're going to die. I can't fight both. Maybe I could buy him time...

The second silhouette plunged an arrow into the banshee who trapped Lugh. She screamed and collapsed onto my brother, dead. "Lugh!" Finally reaching the end of the tunnel, I pushed the banshee aside and lifted my brother to his feet. The elf stood before us, unbound and armed.

I waited for his decision: attack or move aside.

The elf did neither. Cole went to Lugh's other side, throwing his arm around him. "Let's get out of here," he said calmly. I stared at the Fae a moment, fascinated. Lugh groaned in pain, leaning his full body weight on me. I nodded in agreement.

Taking a tired step forward, I said, "Stay with me, Lugh. Stay awake."

My brother's answer never came, and his head sagged.

My stomach clenched and my heart pounded from fear, but I clutched his unconscious body tight, knowing there was nothing I could do until we were in the light.

The trek was long. Every sound and smell had me looking behind us, preparing for the worst. Then, we found the exit with the sun shining down on it. The elf and I paused, looking to one another. Without a word, we stepped out and into the sun, praying that the Guise hunted elsewhere.

The sun was warm on my too-pale skin. I would burn if I stayed in it too long, but with the Guise swarming the land, it wasn't an issue. I raised my face to the sky, selfishly enjoying the moment. I suspected that it would be the last bit of joy I would ever have.

"The sun feels good." Cole had stopped to enjoy the light, too. Seeing him clearly, I couldn't help that my heart fluttered at his beauty. His ebony hair shined, and his forest-green eyes sparkled. Like me, his skin was too pale, and his body was under-fed. Yet, he managed to capture my attention anyway.

It was when I realized that he was staring at me, too, that I quickly turned away. Lugh was resting against a tree in the shade, unconscious. I hadn't had the nerve to check his wound yet, knowing what I would find. "Do you want me to?" Cole asked, following my stare.

I was about to say, "Yes, I'm not strong enough." But instead, what came out was, "What do you want?"

Perplexed, Cole responded, "Nothing. I just want to help." He clutched his wounded side, cringing at the pain movement caused.

"Why? And why did you save us in the tunnel? What's in it for you?"

"Unlike humans, Fae give, asking nothing in return. I know that's a hard concept for you to understand, but it's the truth," Cole spat. I had hit a nerve, but so did he.

"Don't preach about *giving* to me. I saved your life!"

Cole expelled a bitter laugh. "Oh, yeah, thanks for stabbing me and then threatening to kill me afterward if I didn't give you what you wanted. You have a twisted definition of 'saved.'"

"I only stabbed you because you shot at Lugh! I was defending us." Blonde strands fell into my eyes for the hundredth time since waking, and I flipped my hair back aggressively.

Our glares could have cut a Guise in two.

Lugh groaned in his sleep. I rushed to him. *I had to do it.*

I lifted his torn shirt and found a long bleeding scratch along his chest. Black puss oozed from the wound, and I gasped. *She poisoned him.* I held back a sob. There was no cure for a banshee's poison, except... "Heal him." I whispered.

Cole stood close behind me. "Come again?"

"I don't want the darkness spell anymore. Just heal him, and your debt is paid." My hands shook while I put Lugh's shirt back in place.

"I can't."

"Please, I'll do anything. What do you want?" I begged.

"I said that I can't," Cole said, his voice callous.

"I can hunt for your meals, I can find you jewels, I can..." I stopped. *Do it for Lugh.* "I can give you my body."

Cole took a step back. "What did you say?"

"You heard me. I said I will do anything. If that is what you want, I'll do it. Just heal him!" I turned to face the elf, tears streaming down my face. The sun blinded me, and I closed my eyes.

"Stop," he whispered.

"Am I not enough? I can find others—"

"I don't have magic!" Cole bellowed.

I opened my eyes to find the elf standing farther away. "What? How?" I accused.

"I was born without it." He turned toward the forest.

"But all elves have magic. All Fae have magic. How—"

"I'm half human," he spat. "Apparently, the human side of me dominates because I have never been able to use magic. Why do you think I'm alone? I'm shunned by my own people."

All hope was lost. There would not be another who would be willing to help us.

We were alone.

I turned back to Lugh. "That's it then. He's going to die." The tears stopped flowing, and a familiar numbness washed over me. "Leave us."

"What are you going to do?" he asked, wary.

"That's not your concern. Just leave." The only way to save Lugh was magic, and only Fae had magic. Even if I found another elf—the masters of magic—I couldn't force them to help us. They were too powerful. Even if I struck a bargain, it would be too late by then. There was nothing I could do. But I would not let my brother die alone.

"Yvaine—"

"Leave!" I roared, turning back to him. I stood and pointed north. "Get out of here unless you want to be taken by the Guise." I was sure that there were ones on their way, considering all the noise we were making. *Good.*

I refused to acknowledge the pity in his eyes. I listened as he left us, his footsteps light on the leaf-covered ground. When I looked up, he had completely disappeared into the shadows. Alone, I thought that I would cry or scream, but the numbness was there, keeping me sane.

I straightened Lugh's clothing and brushed his shaggy hair back. I laid beside him, against the trunk of the tree, and rested my head on his shoulder. His breathing was shallow. The sun had moved and now cast its rays on us, keeping us warm.

At least we weren't going to die in the dark.

I waited. Waited for the Guise to find us and end our short lives.

Hours passed. The sun was setting. I wondered if we were going to have to wait until morning to end the misery when I thought, *The Fae would finish us. Night was the time to hunt, and we were fair game.*

I remembered the first time I'd seen a Fae. I'd overheard whispers of the strange new species wandering the land from the other humans, not that they knew I was listening. They described monsters worse than even the Guise. Massive predators with claws and teeth that were deadlier than any weapon, and what was worse, they had intelligence. And a thing called magic.

When they spoke of magic, I thought of wands and flying brooms. The cartoons I'd watched over and over again fascinated me so much that I was excited to see real magic for myself. I'd waited and watched the trees while a four-year-old Lugh played in the shed we sheltered in. I'd made sure to pick a place near the edge of the woods, so I'd have a better chance of seeing one of the elusive Fae.

One night, a bird flew down from the canopy. Starving, I'd slowly approached the animal. The closer I got, the hungrier I was. And the more guilty. But I did what needed to be done to feed my brother.

Once I was only a few feet away from the bird, it turned. The moonlight cast dim rays down on us, and I gasped. It was a small bird-like woman with butterfly wings. Her eyes glowed in the darkness like a cat. "Are you a fairy?" I'd asked. Honey-colored light shined from the magical being.

The Fae didn't speak, but she flew up and into my waiting hand. It seemed that the fairy tales had been true. There was magic and beauty in the world, even at the end times.

Then, she smiled and bit into my palm with sharp teeth. Her wings fluttered wildly, dragging me into the forest. I screamed but that only attracted more. Fairies swarmed my body, biting and tearing at my flesh. I was never sure if that was their true nature or if the Collapse had changed them, too.

Soon, I was being beaten. Child's hands wailed against my tender skin, smashing the Fae until they either flew away or died trying to eat. I had thought to draw the dagger, but there had been no way to harm the fairies without stabbing myself along with them.

Soon, I was laying in the grass crying with my little brother huddled in my lap. He was unable to do anything but be there for me, as I realized that fairy tales didn't exist, and magic was merely another weapon to wield.

The last of the warmth seeped from my bones, as I rested beside my dying brother. I had hoped to die in the sunlight, but at least we'd enjoyed it while we could. My skin was warm, and I would have probably woken with a burn in the morning if death wasn't so near. I straightened Lugh's limp body. He would die with dignity, unlike the sister who'd failed him.

The last of the sun's rays lay upon us. Everything else was in shadow. The air was chilled, and the dying leaves fell silently to the ground. I heard movement behind the tree. *The Fae had found us already.* My heart sped, but I was glad it would be over soon.

A glowing monster followed the sun as it moved across our tree. Its golden eyes and long, delicate limbs moved with grace. A hungry Guise had found us after all, hunting until the very end of the day. Once the light disappeared, they would cease to exist and appear again in the morning, starving. There were mere moments left. *Please, make it quick.*

I clutched Lugh's hand in mine and closed my eyes.

The Guise reached toward us. Its energy was powerful, resonating in my bones. Yet, it brought me no peace, because all I could feel was the fear.

The monster screamed. I reluctantly opened my eyes. An arrow passed through its transparent form. It wouldn't kill the monster, but it would hurt it. The sun was lowering behind the hillside. Another arrow flew. Cole appeared from the shadows.

"What are you doing?" I said.

"Saving your life. You need to see how it's done." The elf had the nerve to send a mischievous smile my way. His bow was larger than Lugh's. The string was thick and tight, but his arms didn't tire as he shot arrow after arrow at the monster.

"Who the hell do you think you are?" The numbness faded and anger replaced it. I cursed him for stealing away the calm.

The elf chuckled. "Cole, apparently." He danced with the monster until the sun faded, and the Guise disappeared from existence with a shriek.

"Why did you do that?" I asked, numb again.

"You're welcome," the elf said, as he gathered the unbloodied arrows back into his quiver.

"Why would I thank you? That death was better than having one of your kind find us!" I stood, frustrated. I unsheathed the dagger and pointed it at the elf. "Are you so cruel that you would rob us of a quick death?" I looked back at Lugh. "He's going to suffer longer than he needs to now."

Returning the anger, he said, "Quick? What do you think happens when the Guise takes you? How could you want that fate for your brother?" He paused. "And yourself?"

"I don't..." Honestly, I didn't know what happened. I only knew what I'd heard from human whispers. I'd never stuck around long enough to watch the Guise feed.

Realizing that I truly hadn't known, he said, "You become one of them."

The guilt was instantaneous. I had been blind to the truth. To exist for eternity full of fear would be the worst fate of all. *Was it any different from now?* "It doesn't change anything. My brother is still dying, and there's nothing I can do." I sheathed the dagger.

The elf raised his hand toward me but dropped it after hearing a rustle in the trees. "I brought someone who can help," Cole said gently.

As night fell and the moon rose, I worried that it would be bright enough to summon the Guise again. But it was not full, and it only cast enough light for us to see shadows. I peered through the darkness to find who the elf had spoken of; a spriggan stood just outside of the tree line. His branch-like body blended with the surroundings, and his eyes reflected in the darkness, casting a green hue that displayed the powerful sight it possessed. If it were a fight between us in the dark, it would win.

"There is no need to fear. Coilleach has explained your need for magic," the spriggan assured.

"What do you want in return?" I asked, suspicious.

"Again with this? What is wrong with you?" the elf began, but the spriggan held up his leaf-covered hand.

"There is no need, my friend. This human merely wants to balance the scales." He walked to me, his trunks begging to take root in the soil. "After what humanity has done, perhaps we should let her."

I bowed my head in shame. I knew that I had not personally caused the Collapse, but I felt responsible, nonetheless. "What can I offer you?"

The spriggan looked to Cole before answering, "A strand of your hair."

"That's it? What do you want it for?" Even Cole looked confused by the request.

"For a collection of mine. I will say no more about it." The spriggan smiled, revealing a baby owl sleeping in his throat, a soft nest surrounding it.

"And you can cure my brother of the banshee's poison?" I said.

"No, but I can slow its curse, giving you enough time to find the true cure."

I looked to Cole; he no longer held his side in pain. "You healed *him*, why not my brother?"

"Unlike the banshee, my magic is similar to what lies in your blade, so I was able to help. But your sibling is a different situation entirely." The spriggan shifted, ripping baby roots from the soil.

Abandoning the argument, I said, "Where is the true cure?" It was a chore to stand still and speak to the Fae calmly. My instincts said to draw the weapon, but I would do this for Lugh.

"Within the Cairngorm Mountains lies a circle of stones. They can concentrate an elf's magic long enough to cast the spell of banishment. This should rid your brother of the curse in his blood." The baby owl woke and looked at me with bright yellow eyes.

"Should?"

"There are no guarantees when it comes to magic. We do not rule over it. It rules us," the Fae explained.

"That's great, but where am I going to find an elf willing to help us? This isn't going to work," I said, disheartened.

"I'll go with you, and I'll cast the spell." Cole cast his green gaze on me, and I shuddered under its power.

"You don't have magic. How are you supposed to help?" I whispered to him, the spriggan forgotten.

"I am half elf. If there is magic in me, the stones will reveal it. It's your only chance." Cole tightened his fists. "*My* only chance. I owe you a debt after all." He smiled to reassure me, but it didn't work.

I looked to Lugh; his chest barely rose with breath. *My brother was almost gone.* "Deal." I plucked a strand of blonde hair from my temple and laid it in the spriggan's leaves.

The spriggan walked slowly to Lugh and knelt at his side. He opened my brother's mouth, plucked a leaf from his own brow, and placed it on

Lugh's tongue while saying something in an unfamiliar language—the tongue of the Fae. With an old, rough voice, he explained, "As long as the leaf stays green, your brother will live. If you take it out or if it loses health, he will die."

"How long do we have?" I went to Lugh and checked his heartbeat—it was strong again.

"With good fortune, until the cold season is upon us. But you must make haste. Magic is fickle and can change its mind on a whim. I wish you luck, human." The spriggan stepped into the tree line and melted into its surroundings, leaving me unsure if he had truly departed.

"There's color in his cheeks again," Cole said. There was genuine relief in his tone.

"Why are you really doing this?" I asked, as I stroked Lugh's hair, grateful for the additional time we had together.

"This is as much for me as it is for you. I have been shunned by the elves my whole life. If the stones work, I will wake the magic in me and finally live among them." The elf stepped closer.

"Why would you want to if they treat you so poorly? Isn't the world terrible enough without family abandoning one another?" I zipped Lugh's jacket and adjusted his hood.

"It is the way of our people. Magic is sacred, and if it deems us unworthy, then we are worthless." A rehearsed line. One, I was sure, that was told to him over and over again by his people. And himself.

"You think you're worthless?" I asked, unable to ignore his troubling allure.

"The same way you feel about yourself," the elf said.

"I never said that I was worthless." I wiped my face clean of emotion and concentrated on monitoring Lugh's breathing.

"You said it when you chose to die with your brother instead of living for him."

My heart sank. *I'd failed Lugh again.*

Beyond the tunnel, the abandoned city loomed in the distance. Its crumbling structures taunting every human who was nearby. I turned away from the reminder. "Let's go while it's still night. It's a long way to the mountains and winter is only weeks away." I lifted Lugh onto my back; his bow and quiver was already in the elf's possession. Cole extended his hand to help, but I moved out of his reach. "I can do it myself."

"I know, but you don't have to," Cole said, pity staining his eyes once more.

Looking to the north star, I said, "Yes, I do." Without another word, we began our journey north, where magic stirred with awareness and judgment.

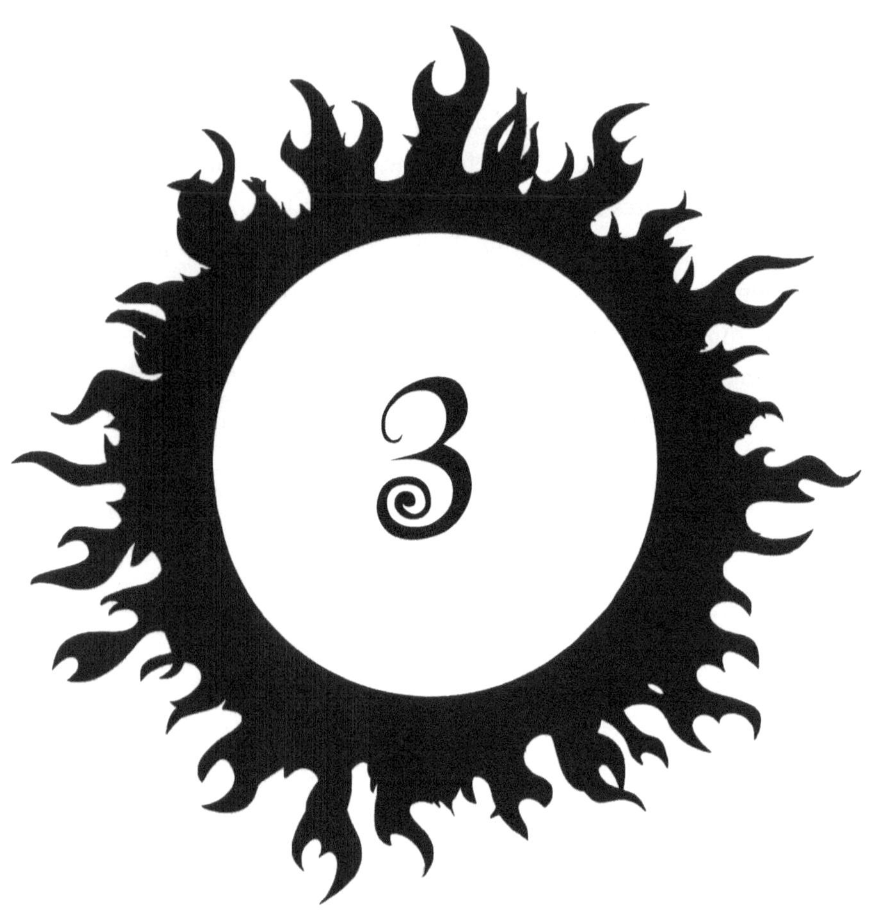

The night was long. Lugh grew heavier by the moment, and the light that shone from the dagger flickered in time with my will power. Every time it went dark, Cole would reach his hand out, preparing for my fall, but that only gave me another burst of strength. *I was not weak.*

The waxing moon was disappearing into the navy-blue sky. Morning was coming. The sound of running water was music to my ears. Through the bramble, I spotted the river, and its sound increased tenfold after passing the wall of plants. I rushed to its side. My mouth was dry. I rested Lugh on his back, propping his head on my knees, and cupped the fresh water in my hands. I opened his mouth and saw that the spriggan's leaf was still there. I was afraid that the water would wash the spriggan's spell away as I poured it down his throat, but the leaf seemed to be sowed to his tongue.

Cole plunged his face into the river and drank greedily, not bothering to boil it first. But of course, I hadn't either. I didn't have the energy or resources at the moment. When he rose, his hair was wet and darker than it had been before—absolute midnight. He proceeded to wash his hands and neck while I tended to Lugh. The elf moved close to us—too close. "Let me watch him while you clean up. You've carried him all night."

"No, thanks."

"Yvaine," the elf said my name in such a way that I raised my eyes to his, "let me help."

"Why should I?" I asked, mesmerized by his tender voice.

In the same painstakingly wonderful tone, he answered, "Because you stink."

The trance was broken, and I burst with laughter. The elf smiled his mischievous smile. "I suppose that's reason enough. Can't risk insulting your delicate nose."

"And the forest for that matter. Didn't you see the trail of destruction you left behind? All the flowers wilted as you passed by," he teased, winking.

I punched Cole in the arm, but he didn't flinch. "Fine. But don't leave his side. Do you understand?" I said this while resting my hand on the blade's pearl handle.

Cole's glance was quick, but he received the message. "Deal." Without another word, Cole gently lifted Lugh and placed him over his shoulder, his knees didn't give out or shake. The elf, though lean and tall, was strong. I wondered if it was the human part of him that gave him strength.

Once I was sure that the elf had gone deep into the foliage, I stripped my soiled clothes and washed them in the river's current. I hanged them from a branch and stepped into the icy water. My body recoiled, but I forced myself forward until I was deep enough to lower my head and wash my matted hair. I had soap in my bag, but that bag was deserted in the tunnel with the dead banshees.

The nights were growing colder, so I was grateful for the dawn's presence. Navy-blue was blooming into purple and saffron sky, which made the yellowed tree leaves glow with warmth. The sun had not made an appearance yet, as the clouds were hovering overhead.

Frustrated with the blonde tresses, I stared at my reflection. I had barely seen it since I was twelve. I remembered our house had mirrors in every room. Our mother hadn't been vain, but loved to collect old, beautiful things. The mirrors were framed in gold and silver, or painted with blacks, greens, and purples. Sometimes, as a young girl, I would stare into the mirrors and wonder if something stared back.

A young woman stared back at me now. Almost unrecognizable. Her once roundish cheeks had thinned and sharpened; her previously innocent, wide blue eyes were now guarded and dark, the blue almost matching the waning night's navy blue; her nose was pixyish, while her lips were thin and pinched in frustration; her forehead was creased with worry for her brother, the lines leaving marks even while relaxed; and her ears were rounded, marking her as a human. Her skin was red from basking in the sun the day before. *While she'd waited for death.*

I huffed and lifted my gaze to the sky, breathing in the cold air. Just as I was about to take another deep breath, I was pulled under water. I clawed at the river's floor, begging to find a grip. Forcing my eyes open, I looked to what clutched my ankle, and there, swam a selkie. She was half-formed; her tail kept the original seal shape, while the top half was of a woman. She must have been starving if she found herself all the way up the river; they dwelled in salt-water areas.

I kicked her sharp teeth, shattering a few fangs, but it came at the cost of my heel. Blood floated in the water, sending her into a frenzy. I reached for the dagger, but it was on the shoreline. All I had wanted was one moment of relief. One moment where I didn't feel like I had to carry the weight on me. And look where it got me—dead.

The selkie dragged me across the riverbed, and toward the center of the river where I would be too weak to fight the strong current. The webbed hands crushed my ankle as she pulled. Her powerful fin easily maneuvered the water. My lungs were empty. Blackness spotted my vision.

Keep fighting.

I was blind. I breathed in the cold water. Still, my limbs flailed in hopes of causing damage. I silently begged Cole to take care of Lugh after I was gone. Perhaps his need for magic would drive him to do so.

I'm sorry Lugh. I wasn't strong enough.

Numbness overtook me. The pain in my ankle disappeared. I floated without worry. Strangely, my life didn't flash before my eyes as people said it did in this moment. I didn't see or feel anything. I breathed in the ice-water with a sense of relief, knowing I wouldn't have to fight anymore. The darkness had protected me for most of my life, perhaps it would in death, too.

A slight pressure was under my arms, ruining my bliss. The water flowed around me, and soon, my head broke its surface. Lips were pressed against my own; they were soft and warm. Air was forced down my raw throat, and I lurched upward, expelling the river from my lungs. The sun peered through the clouds, attempting to warm me. The selkie floated down the river, an arrow through her eye. "Keep breathing," a soothing voice said.

Clutching shivering knees to my chest, I looked to my savior. The elf was drenched, and his eyes were panicked despite the calm voice. "How?" I asked, my voice shaking.

"I came to check on you. You weren't here. I thought you had left to look for us when I heard you scream." Cole glanced to the water. With the sun now shining, it was easier to see into its depths.

"I screamed?" I wondered mostly to myself. Looking to the side, I saw the bows had been abandoned in the grass.

"Good thing you did. It saved your life." Some primal instinct had taken over, using my last pocket of air to call out for help. *Because I had been too weak to help myself.*

"Where's Lugh?" I stood and collapsed, my ankle was swollen, and my heel was bleeding.

"He's just behind the thicket. Lay down, you're hurt."

I took another pain-filled step and realized that I was bare for the world to see—for the elf to see. "Get Lugh and bring him to me." The demand in my voice was not as strong as I had intended. My cheeks turned pink, and my arms held close to my chest, doing what I could to hide the scars. My gaze stayed far away from the elf's.

Cole realized quickly why my demeanor had changed, and he grinned. "No need to hide, I've already seen all there is to see."

"Get my brother!"

The elf held up his hands in surrender, his body still dripping river water. "Fine, fine." Cole disappeared into the trees, weapon in hand again. I made my way to the branch holding my clothes and forced the partially dry material over my wet body. It clung shamelessly to my skin, revealing my shape. I usually wrapped my chest in binding but there was no time, and I stuffed the long fabric into my pocket. The dagger hung at my side again, comfortable in its black leather sheathe. My long hair tangled in the strap, making the day so much worse.

While I waited for Cole, I wrapped my heel in a piece of the chest binding fabric, and the bleeding stopped. *What was taking him so long?* Just when I was about to walk into the forest to find Lugh myself, Cole appeared, a grim expression on his face. "Where is he?" I said.

"The coblynau took him."

"The what?" I bellowed.

"They're like the gnome you ate the other night, but the good thing is that they're much nicer. Your brother has a chance. I can track them. They were headed west." Cole was stiff as he explained, waiting for my response.

"Let's go." I bent and picked up Lugh's bow and quiver.

Confused, he said, "That's it?"

"What would you like me to say? That you had one job and failed? That I won't ever trust you again? Because those things go without saying." I stomped west.

"It doesn't make a difference that I saved your life, does it?"

"No."

"Why?" he asked.

"Because you've spent enough time with me by now to know that my brother's life is more important than my own. If you were trying to impress me, you've failed miserably." I could feel his fierce gaze on my back, but I didn't have it in me to meet his stare.

I heard him take a step, and a herd of reindeer came barreling through the trees on the other side of the river. They leapt into the water, desperate to cross. Some were lost in the current, but most made it to our side, still frightened for their lives. "Yvaine," Cole warned.

Guise appeared at the shoreline, dozens of them chasing after the reindeer. The Guise had no need to swim the river; it passed right through their bodies. I took a step backward, Cole's hand on my shoulder. Together, we inched toward the darkness of the trees while the reindeer ran by. The sun was shining bright and broke through the canopy, but it was our only chance.

Three Guise turned their eerie heads in our direction, sensing fear.

"Run," Cole whispered. He grabbed my hand, and we leapt into the trees with the reindeer. We weren't as fast, but they would distract the Guise long enough for us to find a place to hide. Antlers prodded me and hooves kicked my calves. I was about to be trampled when Cole put his arm around my waist and yanked us to the side. We dove into a hollow, most likely some animal's den, but whatever we would disturb was better than the monster that chased us now.

We tucked ourselves tight into the crevice, the earth entrance eroding. Thankfully, it was not enough to trap us, but it was hard to breathe. Cole's arm was over my head, protecting me from the possible cave-in. The reindeer ran over us, the soil just strong enough to hold the den together.

Minutes that felt like years passed us by. We slowly relaxed, listening. The reindeer were gone, and I was about to suggest that we take a look outside when an agonizing moan sounded. The Guise were still hunting. "Damn it." Tears wanted to escape, but I wouldn't let them, not in front of the elf.

"We'll wait until nightfall and then go for your brother. He will survive long enough for us to find him, Yvaine." Cole's arms were still around me, and I shoved him off, so angry I could have killed him right then and there if he wasn't vital to healing Lugh.

"How are you supposed to follow his trail now? The reindeer all but obliterated it." I pushed Lugh's bow angrily against the wall, begging for more room. Cole's was strategically placed along his spine with the quiver.

"I don't need the trail. I know where the nests are." The den was small, so we were pressed against each other with nowhere to go.

"How do you know so much about the forest? First the spriggan, now the coblynau. For someone who's shunned, you sure know a lot about your people." I curled into a ball on my side, my knees tucked and pressed against Cole's hip.

The Fae turned toward me, so my knees rested against his lean stomach. "Not all Fae are kin, you know. It's like saying humans and reindeer are the same people. Typical *Common* mentality." The elf rolled his eyes.

"Common?"

"You didn't think that the Fae had a name for your kind, too? The non-magic folk," he sneered.

"Just never heard it said before, but I guess I haven't spent much time around live Fae." I returned the cruel smile.

"Figures. Though, I suppose your kind should be called the Uncommon now." It was true, humans were a dying species and the animals we had known before the Collapse were, as well, unable to avoid the growing number of Guise. Magic was an important defense against them. Without it, we wouldn't survive long. Seeing the look on my numb face, he continued, "And I know these things about the Fae *because* I'm shunned. Not much else to do except watch and learn."

"Hmph."

"No rude comment to add? C'mon, you know you have one in you," he goaded.

"Too tired, I suppose." My ankle throbbed in response to the words.

"You've had a busy morning," he said thoughtfully.

"I don't think 'busy' is the right word." My hip cramped, and I straightened my legs, giving Cole room to breathe. The dagger lit, and its pale amethyst glow illuminated our faces.

"How can you do that so easily? You didn't say an incantation or even touch it." Cole reached for the dagger.

Slapping his hand away, I responded, "Don't know. It's always listened."

"You mean, since you took it?" the elf said, remembering what I had told him in the tunnels.

"Yes."

"Who did you take it from?" he asked.

"Never learned his name. He was too busy killing my parents and bleeding out my brother." My eyes darted to the entrance, wishing for an escape.

Cole stiffened. "Where did he bleed him from?"

"Does it matter?" I snapped, meeting his stare.

"Well, some spells require blood to come from certain parts of the body." He looked to the dagger again. "If he was using an endowed knife, I can only assume that's what he was doing."

All these years, I had never considered that the man could have been trying to perform a spell. To me, he was just some psycho who broke into our home, taking advantage of the chaos the Collapse had caused. "The neck," I answered.

Cole nodded. "Yes, powerful spells require the blood to come from the throat. It's been touched by the voice, a spellcaster's most useful tool. But honestly, only those who are desperate or naive to the amount of magic needed risk it."

"But why did he want us?" I whispered. "Why did he need *our* blood?"

Cole's green gaze glanced to the entrance as mine had. "I don't know."

"I doubt we ever will."

"I'm sorry you had to do that at such a young age," he said, sympathetic.

"Do what?" I asked.

"Take a life." The elf was quick, I'd give him that.

"I didn't have a choice." I shoved my matted hair aside, the wash from that morning ruined.

"No, you didn't. But it doesn't make the pain hurt any less."

"Get some sleep. You'll need it if we're going to find my brother. Because we're not stopping until we do." I carefully turned away from the elf, wary of the earth walls. I heard him do the same.

The day crawled, and other than the occasional moan from the Guise, the only noise was Cole's breathing. Though, I suspected he slept about as much as I did. All I could do was concentrate on the star's rotation and wait for night to fall. *I'm coming for you Lugh.*

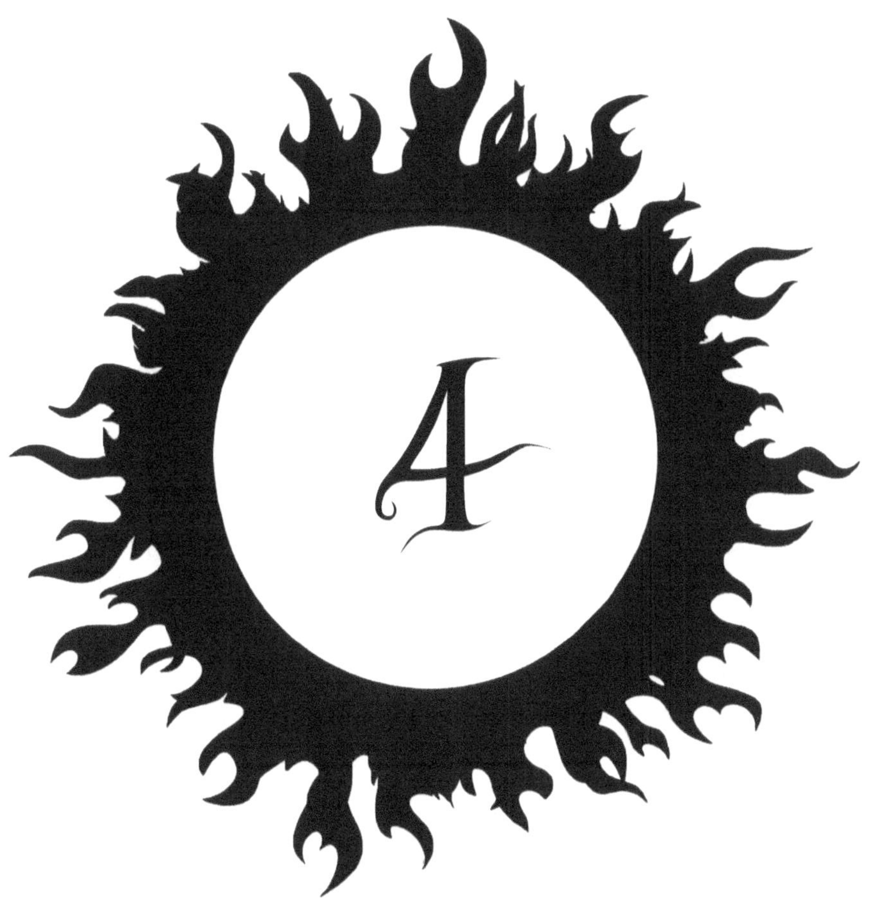

I shoved my hand through the collapsed entrance and felt the night's chill. It was damp and dark, so much, it made me wonder if the darkness was a physical thing that we could touch, not just see. Without waiting for Cole's opinion, I crawled out of the hollow. The Guise were gone for now. But if we stayed, they could reappear at any moment. All it took was the moon to shine too bright or the flames from a fire to summon them.

"Which way?" I asked, as Cole stood and brushed the soil from his clothes; they were mostly leather.

"The closest nest is west. That's the direction they were headed, so let's start there."

I nodded and we began our journey. "Why do you wear leathers and eat meat? Aren't elves herbivores?" The mention of meat made my stomach ache with emptiness. The gnome had been the last meal I had.

The thought of food caused Cole to clutch his middle absently. "Another perk of being half human, I suppose," he said dryly.

"How can you hate humans when you are one?" I wondered, stepping over a protruding root.

"I'm not human," Cole's tone dropped, and his eyes sliced me open.

"Half. Sorry," I responded, refusing to acknowledge his outburst.

The elf sighed. "I've only ever known humans as selfish, greedy beings. They ruined this world because they were power-hungry, and I have to live with that every day."

"Everyone does."

"Yvaine, they didn't just take my home. They took a part of me. I have to live a magicless life because my human father decided to rape my elf mother." He stopped walking. "You don't know what it's like to look your mother in the eye every day of your childhood and see hatred." He straightened his back. "Humans can only take. I refuse to become like them. Like *him*." The elf started forward again without waiting for a response.

As I walked behind him through the dense greenery, I said, "Thank you for saving me."

Cole chuckled. "Which time?"

With tight fists, I muttered, "Both."

The elf stopped again and met my stare. "You're welcome. Thank you for not finishing what you started in the tunnels." We both remembered what he'd said, which was what had stopped me to begin with: *Anything would be better than this darkness.*

What would have happened if I hadn't shown mercy? Would Lugh and I even be alive? Would the banshees have overrun us? I didn't like the answer, but knowing it made it much easier to be near the elf. "Don't think I still won't. If you don't find my brother, there will be hell to pay."

"Understood." Cole grinned, but I could see the determination in his eyes.

"Tell me about the coblynau. Why haven't I heard of them before?" My pace sped the more I thought of the Fae who stole my brother. What were they doing to him? Was he a meal? A plaything? A sacrifice?

"They tend to keep to themselves. They have gentle natures. And before you ask, yes, they are herbivores." The elf pushed the long ebony hair out of his eyes.

"So, why would they take Lugh?" I said, entranced.

"Curiosity, most likely. They like to take things. They're hoarders by nature. The nests they build are not just made of twigs and grass, but of random things they find lying about." Cole matched my pace easily; his legs were much longer than mine.

"But Lugh isn't a 'thing.' He's a living being."

"If their treasures don't attack, the coblynau don't care. They are thieves, not fighters. Show force, and the creatures will run." Cole pushed aside some branches in my path. I marched past, ignoring the gesture.

The dirk glowed at my side, lighting the way. And confident that we were well away from the Guise. "We will have to show force then." Cole glanced in my direction. I could feel the displeasure without looking at him. "What?" I groaned.

"There's really no need. We should try asking for him back first. They would trade him for something that would contribute to their nest."

"They *stole* my brother. I'm not going to politely ask for him back." The clouds were clearing above, allowing the stars to shine down on us. It was difficult not to glance over my shoulder every second to see if they shone too bright.

"Just wait until you see them before you make a decision. Will you do that for me?" Cole's green eyes sparkled in the starlight, and the fear of the Guise disappeared for a split second.

"Why would I do anything for you? You're the one who lost him to begin with," I said, frustrated with my distracting thoughts.

"Because of the moment we shared by the river. Did it mean nothing to you?" Cole's face was a mock impersonation of a wounded lover.

"We shared nothing by the river! I was drowning, pervert!"

"C'mon, don't tell me that you didn't feel anything. It's been so long since I've taken a lover, and to know that it wasn't as good for you… It would damage my male pride." Cole held onto the fake facade, but the corners of his mouth were turning upward.

Giving in, I said, "Well, if a little kiss on the lips is all it takes to satisfy you, no wonder the females haven't been interested lately." This conversation was ridiculous, but strangely, I found myself smiling, too.

We came upon dense trees with only enough room for one of us to pass through at a time. Cole parted the branches hanging in its path so I could cross, but when I stepped forward, he blocked me. "And what would it take to satisfy *you*?"

We had been close in the hollow, hiding from the Guise, but this felt different; an emotion I'd never experienced before. Though we were inches apart, his breath near enough to send shivers down my spine, I wanted to be closer.

I stepped back.

"That's not for you to worry about." I looked down until he stepped aside, and I could pass through the narrow gap.

Following, Cole said, "Sorry, I didn't realize."

"Realize what?" My pace quickened.

"You haven't been with anyone."

I stopped in my tracks, and Cole ran into me from behind, but I did not waver. "I didn't say that, and it's none of your business anyway." I started walking again. *Would this journey ever end?*

"No human catch your eye?" he asked, genuinely curious, despite his mocking tone.

"Lugh and I haven't had much human interaction lately. They died off mostly, and those we have encountered only wanted to hurt us. So, no. No *man* has caught my eye," I said bitterly. I told myself long ago that I was content without that kind of relationship. Sibling comradery would have to do. *It was what I had counted on.*

In a painfully sultry voice, he said, "Well, perhaps a man isn't what you need."

"Oh yeah? You think I need to look past my own species? Will romantic relations with a Fae solve all my problems?" I tripped over a vine, and my face heated.

"Well, it would solve one of them," the elf chuckled.

I turned my glare on him. Cole stopped moving and looked toward a circle of small trees. "What's wrong?" I asked.

"Don't look now, but I think that I've found you some suitors." Stepping closer to the circle, I peered into the space between them and saw piles and piles of *things*. From brambles to human garbage to bones to dulled weapons. It was the *Lost and Found* of the forest. Tiny feet scuffled about, organizing and mending the nest. Their bodies were smaller than gnomes, but I could see what Cole meant when he said they were similar. Coblynau had the same large nose and ears and coarse grey hair. But they were gentler somehow. Their movements weren't sharp and greedy but soft and tentative.

And there, in the midst of the chaotic nest, was my brother lying unconscious on a pile of old, moldy blankets. "Back me up if they get handsy," I told Cole. Then I stepped into the circle of trees to politely ask for my stolen brother back.

The Fae were busy with their nest as I snuck over to Lugh, staying hidden in the shadows. Reaching him, I checked his pulse—it was strong. I opened his mouth and saw that the leaf was still there. I was afraid they had stolen that from us, as well, but we'd made it to my brother in time. Just as Cole promised. Though, his shoes were missing.

"Hey!" The little Fae stomped over to where I knelt beside Lugh. "That ours! Get your own!"

"Yours?" I bellowed. "This is my brother! You stole him from me!"

"No! He alone. We save him. Now he ours. Bad sister." The short, clipped speech of the coblynau was irritating, especially the part about me being a bad sister. Because he was right.

"I won't be a bad sister anymore. I can take him with me, and he'll be mine." I clutched Lugh's arm tight.

The Fae considered a moment. "What you give us for him?" The dagger lit, casting its light upon us. "Oh, yes! We take knife. Brother yours."

Damn it.

As I struggled to explain why I couldn't give him the dirk, Cole appeared beside me. "I have something better." He held up a rope, the same one I had tied him with in the tunnels.

"Not as shiny. Want knife."

"But a knife can't do this." Cole pinched the end of a single thread, and it parted from the thick braid. He peeled several more for the Fae before the coblynau approached and grabbed the rope from the elf's hands.

"Brother and knife yours. Rope ours."

I exhaled a sigh of relief. I hadn't wanted to kill such defenseless Fae.

But I would have if they hadn't agreed. "Thank you," I whispered to Cole.

He winked and placed something in my hand. "For your hair," he said.

A long thread from the rope had been twisted and braided into an intricate hairband. "When did you do this?" I asked.

"You didn't think I was sleeping in that den, did you? Especially while you were in there with me." Cole's fierce gaze was on me, gaging my reaction.

I was at a loss for words. Besides the random things Lugh and I scavenged for each other, the last gift I had been given was from my mother; a silver hairbrush that matched one of the mirrors I'd enjoyed staring into.

Luckily, the coblynau saved me from a response. "Eat. Sleep." The Fae then placed some red berries in front of us and scuttled away to share the new treasure with his kin.

"Are they safe to eat?" I hadn't been much of a gatherer since the Collapse due to my fear of being poisoned.

The elf popped one in his mouth. I squeaked in panic. But this was not my brother, who knew about as much as me when it came to foraging. "Well, I'm not dead. So, I think yes."

I punched his arm in frustration.

"Keep that up, and you'll eventually leave a bruise." The Fae grabbed a handful of berries and shoved them into his mouth, starving.

Berries were shoved down my throat next. My stomach rumbled in response, unsure of the new food, but was glad to be filled. I glanced at Lugh, who slept peacefully from what I could see. "How am I going to feed him?" Anything I put in his mouth would cause him to choke.

"I don't think you need to. The spell should take care of that. Just give him water to nourish the leaf." He wiped his lips with the back of his sleeve and red juice smeared across his cheek.

I chuckled. "Here, let me help." I licked my thumb and wiped his face clean. By the time I was done, he was smirking. I quickly removed my hand. "Well, this place is as good as any to camp. The sun rises soon. Let's get some sleep." I laid down with Lugh on our bed of saffron leaves and rested my head on his shoulder. "Sleep well," I said to both of them.

"Sleep well, Yvaine."

The last sound I heard were the coblynau settling down for the coming day, their soft voices murmuring happy dreams to one another. I clutched the braided band tightly in my hand and drifted.

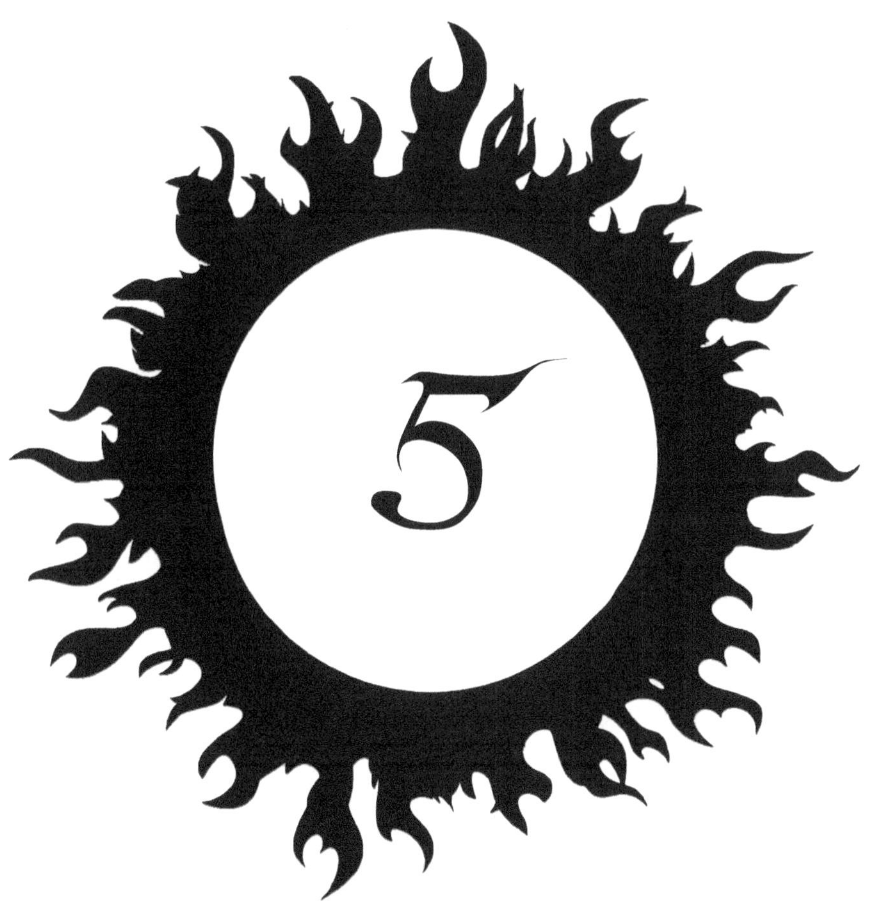

The day slipped by in our dark cocoon under the trees. Not one Guise disturbed our rest. I hadn't slept so peacefully in years. The caring nature of the coblynau was welcomed, and the presence of Cole was, as well. I surprised myself awake at the thought.

Stop now, before it's too late.

"Yvaine," Cole whispered. I shifted to find him pressed against my back, his arm wrapped around my waist.

"Yes?" I responded.

"Stop that," he mumbled.

"What?"

"That tickles." Cole held me tighter, laughing under his breath. And so obviously dreaming about something he shouldn't have.

"Oh, get off me!" I rolled back and over him to get away—Lugh blocked my other side.

Cole caught me before I could stand and drew me to his chest, I flipped over so I could punch him, but his eyes opened, the green gaze shrouded with dreamy content. "Yvaine, I didn't know you could be so forward." His fingers tightened around my hips.

"Enough, elf!" Cole released me upon hearing the name "elf." I knew it would hurt, but it had to be done.

"Fine." Cole didn't waste any time pushing me aside and standing. "I'm going to get more berries." His back was stiff as he walked away from me. The elf was getting too comfortable if that comment hurt so much. *I'd have to change that.*

I crawled to Lugh's side, and beside him was a glass of water. The cup read: *Sparkle Like A Unicorn.*

I took a sip, silently thanking the coblynau people. The last half was given to my brother. His leaf was still deep green. "A lot has happened these past few days, hasn't it, Lugh?" I finger-combed his tangled blonde hair while I spoke. "We're going to find the stones, and Cole is going to heal you. I know, why am I trusting the elf, right? Well, he hasn't betrayed us so far, and he's had plenty of opportunities." I looked up and watched Cole interact with the other Fae, he was kind and open, the small hurt long forgotten. "The last time we trusted someone it almost got us killed. But we are stronger now." I straightened Lugh's cotton clothes. Sneakily, I plucked his stolen shoes and a heavy jacket from the nest, maneuvering my brother into them. I left my shoelaces as payment.

"That should keep you warm for now." I paused to stare at my teenage brother. He was so young and had lived through too much. "I'll be right back. I doubt anyone will try to steal you from here. You're already in the hoarders' nest." I chuckled to myself, amazed at the discovery of kind Fae.

Past the dense trees, I found a patch of waning sun to warm myself in. A cursory glance told me that there were no Guise in the area. I pulled out my chest bindings and was ready to remove my shirt when Cole came running through the trees. "Seriously," I whined.

"Quiet," he warned.

"What's happening?"

"Humans are raiding the nest." Cole put his arm around my shoulders, leading me in the opposite direction.

"Wait, my brother is still in there. I have to go back," I said, instantly frightened for him.

"He's human and unconscious. They'll leave him be."

"And the coblynau?" Cole's gaze was grim. "They're already gone," I acknowledged.

With a nod, he said, "That's why I can't be seen. They're Fae haters. They'll kill me just for existing too close to them."

"Fine, stay here. I'll get Lugh myself." I took a step, and he grabbed my arm.

"No way am I letting you near them." The green of his eyes had darkened. *He was afraid.*

Placing my hand over where his rested on my arm, I explained, "Either it's safe enough for humans, and I can get my brother without trouble. Or it's too dangerous for anyone, and I have to go fight for my brother. Which one is it?"

Cole sighed, a sadness in his eyes. "Fine, but I'm coming with you."

"Not like that you're not." The chest binding still in my hand, I pulled Cole down so I could reach far enough to wrap his head in the fake bandage, hiding his ears. I picked some of the red berries from a nearby bush and spotted them along the white fabric.

"What are you doing?" he asked.

"They can't know you're Fae. This way, they won't question you." I picked up some dirt and rubbed his face in attempt to hide his sharp features. "Try not to make eye contact. Your bright eyes will give you away. Hopefully, these humans haven't spent too much time around elves to notice the difference."

"What difference?"

"Your eyes are much prettier than ours. The color is clear and bright." I caught on too late, and said, "But you already knew that didn't you, Coilleach?"

"Strange, I've always thought the opposite." He smiled. "And call me Cole. The name has grown on me."

"Noted." *How could he make me feel so light in this heavy situation?* "Let's go," I said, eager to be on our way to the mountains.

The last of the sunrays gone, we were cast into darkness. But I couldn't light the endowed weapon. If one of the humans saw the glow, it would be the end of us. They would stop at nothing to obtain it, and I would stop at nothing to protect it—it's the only thing that kept us alive.

Blades were swinging and cutting down anything that moved. No gunshots were heard; ammunition had run low quickly after the Collapse and noise only attracted the Guise. I peeked through the brush and saw my brother still lying where I left him.

"Hey, over here! There's a kid."

I tensed.

"Is he dead?" a second male voice asked.

"No, he's still breathing." The first man crouched down and placed his fingers under Lugh's nose to feel his breath. He tried patting his cheek to rouse him, but when that didn't work, he started prodding him, searching for injuries. "Kid got a nasty scratch on his chest. Looks like a banshee attack. Damn, those gnomes were going to make a meal out of the poor guy."

"We should put him out of his misery. There's no cure for banshee poison." Once the first man nodded, the second one raised his axe, ready to end Lugh's life.

"Wait! That's my brother!" I cried. I lurched out of the tree line with the knife still sheathed.

The two men readied their weapons but relaxed upon seeing a woman. My hair was tied back with the hairband Cole had made for me, and my human ears lay bare. "Sorry to hear that, miss, but you're only prolonging his suffering at this point," the first man said.

"Please, don't hurt him. I've found a treatment that works." I put on my innocent face, knowing they would listen.

"There is no treatment for a banshee's mark." The second man looked to the first one. "Except magic. Do you have magic?"

"No, of course not. I'm human, I can't use magic." I swallowed, my mouth dry.

"Then what are you using?" he asked.

"Herbs," I blurted. "Yes, I came across an old book with medicinal herbs listed in it, particularly ones that fight against poisons. I took a shot in the dark, and it's working. Please, please, don't hurt him." I clasped my hands together, begging them to listen.

"Where's this book?" the first man asked, eager for the knowledge I had.

"The gnomes stole it." I pointed to the corpses that decorated the nest. I had flexibility with these humans, they didn't even know the difference between gnomes and the peaceful Fae that lay dead before us. "They took my brother and the book while I was foraging. I just found him now. Thank you for saving him from the Fae." I spat in the direction of the coblynau for good measure.

Egos boosted, the first man said, "It was no trouble, miss." He exchanged another look with his partner. "Why don't you both come with us? We can keep you safe while he recovers, and you can share what you learned from that book."

"Oh, we couldn't. You have done so much already. I'll just take my brother and get out of your way." A quick glance told me that the rest of the men were gathering the nest's treasures.

"What's that you got there?" the second man asked.

Playing dumb, I said, "What do you mean?"

"The knife hanging at your side. Looks like a nice one. Can I take a look?" He stepped forward, eager for a new toy.

Fingering the sheathe, I said, "It's really nothing. Just an old, dull blade I found in a city tunnel."

"Then you won't mind if I take it, will you?" the second man held out his hand, expectant. I reached for the blade. And it wasn't because I was going to give it to him.

The men's eyes widened. A warm body pressed against my side. The knife was held outward in the hands of another. "Of course she wouldn't mind. It's the least we could do after you saved Lugh." I pinched the elf's side, irritated and unable to fight him for the dagger.

"Who are you?" the second man asked as he took the endowed dirk from Cole's hand.

"He's my brother," I said. The elf raised his dirt-covered brows. "My other brother, I mean."

"Any more of you going to pop out of nowhere?" the first man asked, suspicious.

"No, it's just us," I assured, fighting against the urge to stare at the knife in his friend's hand. "This is Cole."

Cole wrapped his arm around my shoulders and pulled me tight against him. "And this is my little sister, Yvaine." He shook me a little, and I realized that if I wanted him to let go, he'd have to do it willingly. *How could an elf be so strong?*

The first man said, "I'm Brody. This is Donal." Brody nodded toward

Donal. "We're nearly finished here. Gather what you can and follow us."

"Will do," Cole said. Brody left and started packing his backpack full of treasure from the nest.

"What happened to you?" Donal asked the elf.

I discreetly glanced to Lugh's bow where it rested beside him. Cole had ditched his bow and quiver in the trees; it had Fae writings etched on it. I only hoped that Donal wouldn't notice the same writing on mine. "Gnomes got the best of me when they took Lugh. Attacked me while I slept," Cole lied smoothly.

"Sorry to hear that." Donal searched the pile of items near Lugh and bent down. "Looks like they got your shoelaces while they were at it." The man picked up the purple laces that I had traded for Lugh's coat and shoes and handed them to me, nodding toward my laceless black combat boots.

"Thank you," I muttered, wrapping the laces around my fist.

Donal nodded once, knowingly. He moved on, removing the old, chipped knife from his sheathe and replacing it with mine. His weapon now rusted away in the nest with the rest of the undesired items. I could have sworn the empty sheathe at my side had a heartbeat, and it was racing out of control.

"What the hell was that?" I angrily whispered to Cole.

"They would have figured out it was endowed if you fought them for it, and then you would have been dead or worse." The elf hadn't let go of me. The inward battle raged while I considered staying within his protective embrace.

Frustrated, I turned my back on the elf and knelt to check Lugh. *The same as before.* "Lugh, don't worry. I'll get us out of this."

"Let's go now, while they're distracted." Cole stood close behind me. I could feel his body heat, and it warmed my chilled skin. The sun had completely faded now.

"I can't leave the knife with them."

"Yvaine, no matter the power, it's just a knife. It's not worth all of our lives," he argued, desperate to get away from the Fae killers.

My brother's eyelids twitched. "Lugh? Can you hear us?" I asked.

No response.

With sympathy in his voice, Cole said, "He's in a deep sleep. Your brother's not going to wake until the spell is done." I knew he was right, but I couldn't help but wish my brother was still with us, listening. *But that would be cruel.* No, it was better that he couldn't hear what was happening around him—to him.

"Take Lugh and run. I'll find you later after I've stolen the knife back." I zipped Lugh's jacket up and laced his shoes.

"You know, how about I take off this fake bandage and ask them if they'd like elf for dinner instead of gnome? Also, I need to correct the specist bastards." Cole reached for the wrappings on his head.

I lurched up and grabbed his hands. "Why would you do that?" I said, panicked.

"That's what I was going to say to you, but you needed to be shown how stupid your idea was first. It's suicide, and you know it." Cole removed my hands from his ears but kept them in his grasp. "If the knife is that important to you, I'm going with you."

"But Lugh—"

"Lugh would do the same exact thing. And he will, just not conscious."

Donal glanced up from his work to check on us, and I sent him a small, friendly smile. I could have vomited right then and there, knowing what we were about to do. "Damn you," I whispered.

"It's all or nothing. Choose wisely." Cole's thumbs gently ran over the back of my hands. The numbness returned as it always did when a difficult choice needed to be made.

"All."

"So be it," he sighed.

I pulled my hands from the elf's and re-laced my boots. Even if we had all run, the humans would have caught us. Humans were greedy and stubborn. They wouldn't be easy to ditch, and even more difficult to steal from. It was smarter to stay together, even if it was in the midst of predators.

Brody called out, "Time to go." A few coblynau hung from his grasp—dinner.

I nodded and went to lift Lugh. "Let me," Cole said. I opened my mouth to argue, but he interrupted before I could. "I'm a man now, aren't I? It would look bad if I let my little sister carry a nearly full-grown human while I twiddled my thumbs."

"Fine, but watch your words. Humans don't call other humans 'human.'"

"Noted." I nearly smiled, but the men surrounding us made it disappear. "Play along, but we stay together. If they separate us, we're finished." I sifted through the nest quickly and found two more warm jackets. One for each of us.

Cole put his on before swinging Lugh onto his shoulder. It was black leather with silver zippers. With his ears covered and the square shape of the jacket, he did look human. I found myself missing the original version.

With a concerned face, Cole whispered, "What's wrong?"

"Nothing." The numbness washed over me again, blanking my face expression. I simply picked up Lugh's bow and quiver and stepped past the circle of trees that had given us sanctuary. Now, it was just a graveyard.

The humans stalked through the dark forest, their fires dim to keep the Guise from awakening. There were more than I had predicted. At least thirty men surrounded our small trio, guiding us to their den of horrors.

Lugh and I may not have been a part of humanity anymore, but we'd had encounters with them. None had been pleasant. They were dark, desperate beings who had no magic or morals. The removal of government only set them free. They thieved, pillaged, and raped when they pleased. The last thought made the numbness heavy. So much, it became hard to walk.

Cole slowed his pace with me, but the men behind us were moving quickly. The elf grabbed my hand and pulled me forward while still carrying my brother. "Keep moving, Yvaine."

I tried and failed.

"If you stop, I'm leaving Lugh here."

I ripped my hand out of his. "So much for being a *man*," I spat. Walking ahead of Cole, I took a deep inhale of forest air and shivered, grateful for the new leather jacket. Cole didn't say another word but kept close enough that I could hear both his and Lugh's breathing in the quiet night.

It was nearly sunrise when we reached the human's hideout. It was a cavern, south of where we'd been. Not a man-made one like the city tunnels, but a natural one that had stalactites hanging from the ceiling. Chain fencing blocked the entrance, not that it would stop the Guise if there was enough light to enter, but it would deter mindless animals. Though, there were a lot less of those than we assumed.

"Hand over your weapon." Brody had walked behind us the entire night, acting as our *escort*.

"Why?" I demanded.

"Newcomers have to earn their weapons. Prove your worth, and you'll get it back." The man scratched his thick red beard nonchalantly.

"You mean, trust you and leave us defenseless?" I corrected.

"Look at it anyway you like, girly. You're going to hand it over one way or another." Brody took a step closer, standing over me. He was a large man, but he was slow.

"Give him the weapon, Yvaine. What good will it do anyway? If they wanted to hurt us, they would have done it already." Cole's expression was unfazed, and he merely switched Lugh to his other shoulder.

"I'm glad that one of you has some sense." Brody held out his hand. I relinquished the bow and quiver, refusing to open my mouth. Because whatever would come out would surely get us killed. "Follow me." Brody led us past the metal barrier and into the dark cave just as the sun shone down on its entrance. The men piled their findings inside, assumingly to be sorted later. Lugh's bow was tossed onto the pile. I held back a frustrated scream.

Once we were farther in, where the sun could never touch, torches lined the walls and guided us down the pathway. Soon, we came upon a fork in the tunnel. We were herded to the left, leaving me curious and suspicious of the other tunnel; no torches were lit in that direction. Cole tried to take my hand, but I moved it out of the way just in time. I heard a snicker from behind and hoped it wasn't because of us. He was supposed to be my brother after all.

At the end of the tunnel, the walls widened dramatically, opening into a massive space. "Welcome to the City of Inscius. It's small, but we're growing. Always looking for folks to join and help provide." Brody was proud.

"Who named the city *inscius?*" Cole asked, a small smile on his lips.

"Our founder. As soon as we settled, he passed away. A damn shame, to do all that work and not get to enjoy the spoils." Brody gazed out at his community, comforted by its presence.

"Do you know what *inscius* means?" Cole forced a blank expression as he asked this. I was wondering why he cared so much.

Irritated, the leader said, "No, we assumed he just made it up. Why?

Do you know what it means?"

"Not at all. I was just curious." Cole turned his head into Lugh's side, pretending to wipe the dirt from his face, but I could see his shoulders shaking slightly. *Was he laughing?*

"Anyway, the women's quarters are over there." He pointed to a large tent at the west end of the cavern. "The men's over there." To the east. "And the medical tent is there." To the north. "Rest for a few hours, but we want to hear all about that book you found. We didn't find anything like it at the nest, so we're going to have to rely on your memory, girly."

"We're staying together," I said, annoyed with the nickname he'd given me. I scanned the other tents in the towering cavern. A few had people coming and going, hauling boxes of supplies; canned and packaged food leftover from before the Collapse. There was also fresh meat roasting on spits by the entrance. One tent stored weapons of every kind; it was clear that there was a weapons smith among them due to the gleam and sharpness of the metals. Other shelters had old, ratty clothing hanging to dry after their wash, and another had furs piled on tables, both Common and Fae. All in all, it wasn't a bad setup, but I wouldn't call it a "city."

"No way. If you start mixing rest areas, the other men will want to do the same. And if you want any semblance of privacy and respect, don't tempt fate. It's hard enough as it is." A few of the passing men grumbled after overhearing his words, and he turned his glare on them.

"But they're my brothers."

Brody glanced between Cole and me, and I was sure, at our complete lack of similarities. "Be that as it may, I don't feel like dealing with it. Stay in your designated tents during rest time. And that's the last thing I'm going to say about it."

I felt a gaze. When I turned, Donal was staring at me, and it took every ounce of self-control I had to keep my stare fixed on his eyes and not the dagger. "Fine, but I'm taking Lugh to the medical tent first."

Brody agreed and we went on our way with Donal at our backs. Instead of keeping his head down like he should have, Cole examined every man's face that passed us by, challenging. "Are you trying to start a fight?" I whispered to him.

"Just looking," he responded. The elf didn't explain what he was looking for, but with Donal so close, I didn't dare push the issue.

Reaching the large tent, I found three women tending to the beds and those who slept there. Some men had been wounded from hunting nymphs and satyrs; they were both very aggressive species, despite looking friendly. Their tactic was to lure prey into one of their traps and devour them slowly. The gouge marks on the men's skin were evidence enough—completely shredded.

I sighed, seeing the hate that was shared between the humans and Fae. I didn't personally blame the magic folk for humanity's mistakes, but it would've been nice if the Fae had stepped in to help before we messed things up.

Cole laid Lugh on one of the cots. There was a pitcher of water already at its side table. I sat under Lugh with his head on my lap and parted his mouth just enough to pour the water down his throat. The leaf was still there, but the interaction had been so quick, I wondered if I hadn't seen yellow on the leaf's edge. I didn't dare open his mouth wider to check. Not with spectators.

One of the women approached. "I'm Helen. I'm one of the many nurses here. I'll take good care of..."

"Lugh, my brother. I'm Yvaine and this is Cole." I nodded to the dirty elf who stood too close to my side. "Lugh was poisoned by a banshee. I've found a treatment and it's working. I will be the one giving him his medicine. All I ask is that you watch over him while he sleeps."

"Of course. I'll take good care of him." The woman smiled a practiced smile, catering to a concerned family member.

"No. I mean it. Don't even give him food and water. The treatment is very specific. If one thing is done wrong, he will die. *Do not touch him.*" I bore my eyes into the woman's skull, willing her to listen.

The nurse's eyes widened with fear. *Good.*

"All right, sis. Time for bed. Helen will watch over him while we rest." Cole placed his hand under my arm and guided me from the bed. Helen grabbed a blanket and placed it over Lugh. When she looked over and saw my glare, she left to tend to another patient.

"Would you like *your* wound looked at?" Another nurse approached. This one was younger, most likely a trainee.

"Thank you, but I'm fine. I just need some rest," Cole responded.

"And you?" She looked toward me.

"Me?"

"You're limping," she said.

I peered down at my boot and to the swollen ankle beneath. The selkie had done a number on it, but honestly, I had forgotten about it as soon as I learned Lugh had been taken. "No." She nodded and left us alone. I pulled Cole to the side, keeping my eye on Donal where he stood at the tent's entrance.

"Meet me here in an hour after everyone's asleep. We can talk more then." I moved to leave when Cole wrapped his arms around me, forcing me into his strong chest.

"Rest well, sister. Don't worry about Lugh. These people will take good care of him." He squeezed me tight, and his hands roamed from my shoulders down to my hips. *Very unbrotherly.*

"Okay, you too, bro." I shoved him away and punched him in the arm.

We definitely weren't actors. The others didn't seem to notice the strange interaction though, so I exited the tent and made for the women's quarters. There, I was able eat, wash, change into clean clothing, and rebandage my ankle. The women greeted me but weren't particularly interested in my presence. They were most likely used to newcomers if what Brody said was true.

Before long, the voices inside and outside the tent quieted, and there was only the dim glow of stalactites in the cavern. I had planned to stay awake until my meeting with Cole, but exhaustion won, and darkness greeted me kindly.

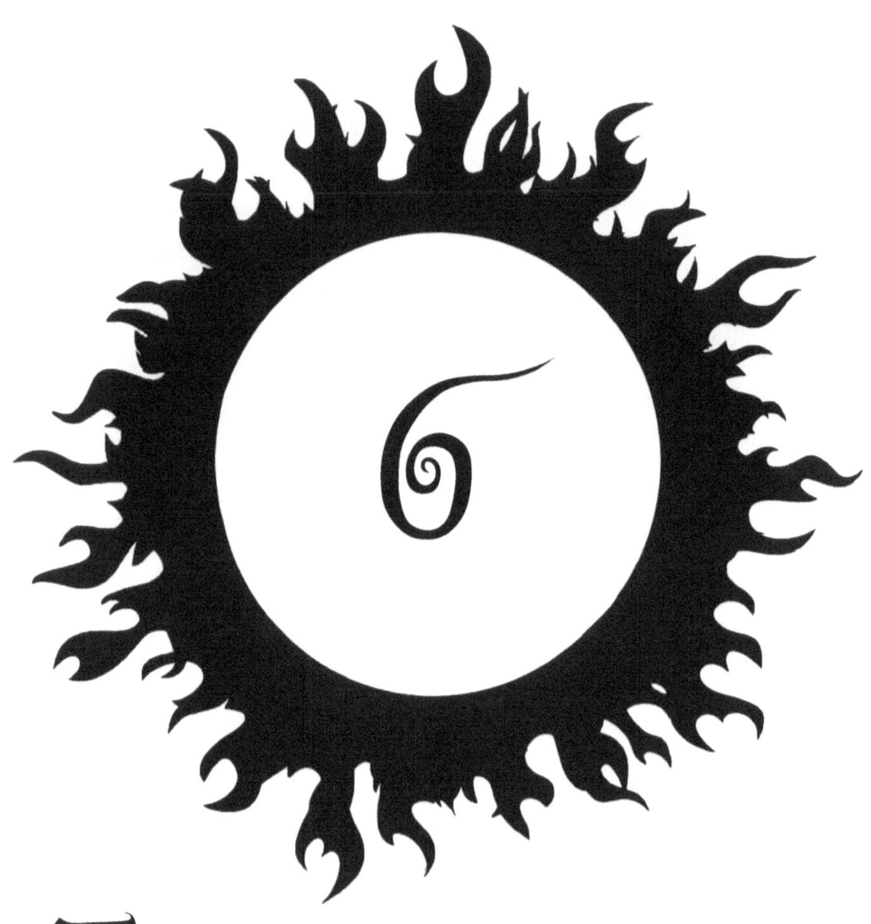

There was a hand around my ankle where it rested under the sheets. I jerked my leg up and away from whatever touched me and gasped.

"Cole, what are you doing?"

"You need to take better care of yourself. This wrapping is atrocious." The elf reached for my ankle again only to be disappointed.

"Get out of here, you're going to get caught," I pressed.

With a small smile, he said, "Doubtful. Half of the men snuck over here after the lights went out. I just blended in with the testosterone-filled shadows."

Despite everything, I chuckled. "So much for privacy and respect."

I relaxed my leg and allowed Cole to rebandage my swollen ankle. He wrapped his cold hands around the injury, and I was grateful. The agitated beat of the bruise slowed, but when I looked into his green eyes, my heartbeat leapt, sending heat everywhere.

The tent was large enough that each woman had her own space, blocked by furs hanging around them. Still, it didn't stop the noise from drifting in. "Have you checked on Lugh?" I asked, distracting myself from the neighbors.

"Yes, and the nurse still fears you. So, don't worry. I think your attitude will buy us some time." Cole scooted closer and placed my leg on his lap. I tensed.

"My attitude?"

The twinkle in his eye was undeniable. "Oh, I'm sorry. I meant to say your bubbly, outgoing personality."

Too tired to argue, I said nothing and merely enjoyed the elf's touch. That alone had me worried. I tried to look past the Common and Fae furs to the men lurking in the shadows.

"What happened to you when we left the nest?" Cole unwrapped his fake bandages, allowing his angled ears to peer out from between midnight strands.

"What do you mean?" I refused to meet his curious gaze.

"You were gone. The light left your eyes." His hand tightened around my calf. "Were you afraid?"

Strangely, I found myself telling the truth, unable to keep it buried inside. "Yes."

"Why? You weren't that scared with the banshee or the selkie or even the Guise. I've only seen it once when you realized that your brother was..."

"Dying?"

"Yes," he said.

"Because I knew that if I didn't survive, Lugh wouldn't either. I wouldn't make it to the stones and cure him." I pulled the blanket close to myself, unwilling to reveal any more of my fears.

"That's not it."

"What?" I spat, shooting him a glare.

"Well, that's part of it. But what's the real reason? What is it about humans that scare you? You're one of them." There was shuffling outside my room. The furs rustled, but after a few moments it was quiet again.

Trapped in bed with the elf, I realized that my only way out was to tell the truth. "I haven't had great experiences with men."

"So, it's not humans. It's romantic issues?" The elf held back a laugh, keeping his smirk contained.

"It could hardly be considered romantic." I clutched the blanket tighter.

"Then what?" Cole inadvertently moved his hand up my leg. My body both warmed with pleasure and trembled with fear. Why was he doing this to me? Wasn't I under enough stress with Lugh?

"You shouldn't be so clueless since your own mother was hurt by one," I whispered.

Cole stiffened, and his eyes turned into blazing green fires. "You were—"

"Almost," I interrupted. "I don't want to talk about it."

"Did you kill him?" Cole slowly stood, placing my feet back on the cot. He had his back to me, and he peeked between the fur doorways.

"No," I hissed. "But he's dead." Cole turned and opened his mouth to speak when I said, "Tomorrow, you're going to have to take Brody into the woods and amaze him with your knowledge of herbs."

Surprised by my change in topic, he said, "I'm not leaving you here alone."

Even though I'd been afraid of being trapped alone with a man again, I didn't want Cole to leave. Something about his presence both calmed and excited me. It was different from anything I'd felt before. But, I couldn't afford another obstacle. *That's all he was.* "Well, I can't show him. I don't know anything about plants. And someone needs to look for the knife."

"There's no looking for the knife, Yvaine. Donal has it strapped to his side at all times. Trust me, I watched. He went to sleep with it on. We're not getting it back. We should be discussing escape options now." *Escape without the only thing that's kept us alive? Not an option.*

I debated, "Brody isn't going to let us leave unless we show him something. If we can fake a cure, I'm sure he'll let us go. Maybe they'll give the weapon back." *Would he?*

Cole read my face expression. "You don't even believe your own lies, so I'm certainly not going to. You know, as well as I do, that humans are greedy. These *inscius* humans will force us to stay simply for the manual labor."

"What does that word mean?"

Cole laughed darkly. "*Ignorant.* It derives from an ancient Fae language."

"The founder had a sense of humor, apparently."

"Apparently, he knew exactly what humans did to this world and wanted to make a joke of their attempt to rebuild." Cole peered outside the doorway several times, suspicious of any noise.

"Well, maybe if the Fae had stepped in before it was too late, we wouldn't be in this mess," I huffed, flipping my hair aside.

The elf gave me a bewildered expression. "I'm going to pretend you didn't just say that."

"Why? It's true."

"If you haven't figured it out by now, humans aren't responsible with magic. We did our best to hide it from them and keep everyone safe." The elf let the furs fall back into place and stepped toward me.

I threw the blankets aside and stood, my ankle throbbing. "Then humans aren't the only ones who are *inscius*. The truth always comes out. No matter how hard you try to hide it."

"We weren't the ones who created monsters and forced the world to live in darkness because of them." Cole approached and stood over me, angry.

"You also didn't do anything to stop it. Which one is worse?" I argued.

We glared to no avail. There was no point. What was done was done.

"It doesn't matter now," he said, stepping away.

I nodded, moving on. "You didn't like my plan. Do you have a better one?"

The elf smiled. "People won't look for something they don't know is missing."

"And?"

"That pile of stolen goods at the entrance of the cave should have a similar blade. We can switch it out." The elf paced back and forth in the small space.

"You're kidding? He would notice it's not the same knife." I rolled my eyes.

"Eventually, but all we need is time to run. If we take his knife and disappear at the same time, he'll know. But if we had time..."

"And how are we supposed to get out to begin with? It will be especially hard with Lugh in tow." I imagined the nurses throwing a fit if we tried to take their patient.

"We'll need a distraction." The elf rubbed his hands together, eager.

"Great."

"What's wrong?" he asked.

"Sounds like a lot of sneaking around for two people." I crossed my arms in frustration.

"Don't worry, it can be done. I mean, haven't you been listening in on the other bunks? Two people can sneak around just fine, and they're doing a lot of it." Cole cocked his head in the direction of the sounds, and I blushed.

"That's *much* different." Blonde hair fell into my eyes as I looked down. I had untied it before going to sleep, and the hairband Cole made for me clung tightly to my wrist.

"Not really." Cole took a step toward me. The only light cast was the stalactites glowing outside the tent. "They both require instinct. I've seen you in action, Yvaine. You have what it takes." He winked.

My blood boiled upon hearing his enchanting voice. "Am I a joke to you?"

The twinkle left his eyes. "No, of course not."

"Then stop flirting. I know how you feel about humans. There's no point." The throbbing in my ankle increased, and I returned to the cot.

Cole averted his gaze and rubbed the back of his neck. "I don't feel that way about all humans. Plus, it's not them, it's what they do that I don't like."

"Then know this elf," Cole flinched, "you are nothing but a means to an end. The end of my brother's suffering. After you cast the spell and Lugh is healed, we will part ways. Both of us better for it."

I couldn't stand to see the hurt in Cole's eyes. Even in the darkness, it was clear. "You really are human," he whispered.

"What else would I be?"

Ignoring my question, he said, "I'll take Brody to hunt for the fake cure at sunset. You find a replacement for the knife. We'll go from there. See you tonight." Cole rewrapped his head bandage. Without another mischievous glance in my direction, he stepped into the shadows and disappeared. The words I'd said to him left a cold, empty feeling in my chest, as if I had been poisoned along with my brother.

I awoke at sunset and immediately went to the medical tent, refusing to think about Cole or the risky mission he was on. He was spinning a delicate tapestry of lies, and it would only take one snip to ruin us all.

Soft white candles were lit in the tent, casting a relaxed glow on the patients. They looked better. Maybe the nurses did know what they were doing. I approached the young girl from the previous morning. "Do you have any disinfectant? Cool water?"

The girl was around fourteen with long chestnut hair and a friendly smile. "Of course. Take a seat, and I'll be right over."

I nodded my thanks and took the place beside Lugh. He had been cleaned by one of the nurses. Though I was grateful, it left me unsettled. I watered him again. This time, I took a better look at the magic leaf—it was edged with yellow. *But it had only been a few days. How could it be dying already?*

"Place your foot in here. Be warned, it might sting a bit." The girl had brought a metal bowl full of clear water. I plunged my foot ankle deep and yelped.

"How is it so cold?" The stinging came next. "What did you put in it?"

The girl laughed. "There's a freshwater stream just beyond the cave, and I mixed it with a little alcohol to clean your cuts." She knelt to examine my foot. "Selkie?"

"How'd you know?"

She rolled up her shirt sleeve and revealed a unique scar. "A selkie surprised me in a river a few years ago."

"Same."

"Did you kill yours?" She rolled her sleeve back down.

"No, but Cole did." I thought of how he pulled me out of the water, and how warm his hands were on my skin…and his lips…

"Lucky. Mine got away. Hopefully, it wasn't the same one. I would feel bad." The girl gave me an awkward smile. "I'm Cara, by the way."

"Yvaine. Nice to meet you, officially. Sorry for yesterday. It's been a long...life," I finished, unable to say *week* when it just couldn't explain how tired I was.

"It's okay. He's your brother. I'm sure you're worried about him," she sympathized.

"I am." Inspiration struck. "I was actually going to look for a few of his things that were taken by the gnomes. Am I allowed to search the pile at the entrance?" I gave her my friendliest expression, but worried that I didn't have one anymore.

Cara considered a moment. "I don't see why not. Though, I wouldn't advertise it. The hunters tend to get territorial over their loot."

I looked down, disappointed.

She leaned in and whispered, "I'll cover for you."

"Thank you, Cara. It really means a lot." And it did.

Once my ankle's swelling had gone down and the wounds were finally clean and bandaged, I went in search of the decoy knife, relying on my instincts to sneak through the camp and down the tunnel. I blushed every time I thought of the word *instinct*. Mostly because I heard it in Cole's sultry voice.

I passed by the other tunnel. My gut clenched. *What was down there?*

I forced myself to stay on mission. I only had a limited amount of time, and I needed a knife. The pile was vast, much more than what had been at the nest. I sorted through the weapons area and found an ivory-handled blade that was roughly the same size. It would have to do. There was no sign of Lugh's bow and quiver; someone had already claimed it.

Voices sounded from the tree line outside. *Did Cole bring them back early to spite me?*

I hid behind a mound of furs, clutching the weapon to my chest. It was cold and lifeless and without light. "Dandelion root? That really works?" Brody asked as they passed the gate.

"It has so far. As long as he's given water at certain times." I was relieved to hear Cole's sincere, yet sarcastic tone. There had been a part of me that wondered if he would survive their questions. And another part that worried he would leave us behind.

"Doesn't seem right to me," Donal grumbled.

"We thought that, too, but we were desperate to try anything. And if it works, then it works. The only thing we can do now is wait until he wakes up," Cole explained.

"*If* he wakes up." Donal spit, and it landed beside where I hid out of view.

"*When* he wakes up." I heard Cole shift his feet, and I knew he was facing the rough man. "My brother will wake up. So long as his treatments aren't interrupted." I could hear the threat in his tone and the worry for Lugh in his words. *His acting had improved.*

"Whatever you say, kid." Donal spit again.

Cole took a step toward the brute.

"Now, now. Why don't you prove this treatment works and get the herbs to your sister, eh?" Brody stepped in, sensing the fight.

Cole grunted an acknowledgment, and the other men in the party relaxed, the tension dying with Cole. They sauntered away from the dark entrance, the sky heavy with black outside. I waited until I couldn't hear their steps echo against the cavern walls and strode past the iron gate. The autumn breeze was brisk but welcomed. I breathed deep, enjoying the clean air. The cavern smelled of people, and it wasn't a pleasant scent.

The moon was a sliver of itself, but the stars were bright and clear. I hated how I had come to fear their light, worried it would bring a Guise to life. I hated how I prayed for clouds and gloom. For shadows.

A shadow darted behind a tree. "Who's there?" I raised my blade.

No response.

"Answer or die."

Slowly, a small shape appeared and drifted toward where I stood at the gate. "Please, let my mother go. She hasn't hurt anyone."

I lowered my blade at the sound of a human child's voice. A young kobold stood before me—a shapeshifter. Though they could take the shape of any living thing, they could not age themselves. So, I doubted it was a ruse. Still…"I don't have your mother." I peered into its reflective eyes and what I saw there frightened me—grief.

"But you're one of them," the child said.

Unable to argue, I asked, "When was she taken?"

"One moon ago. I've waited for her to come out, but she hasn't. And I can't go past the door." The child pointed to the iron gate. Some Fae, especially the young, were sensitive to iron, so any attempt to move the gate would have probably burned the poor creature's hands.

"Why did they take her?" I asked.

The child burst into tears. "Because of me." It was difficult to understand the kobold's words through the weeps, but I got the gist. "She told me to hide, but I didn't, and they came. She attacked them so I could run. It's my fault." I sheathed the cold blade, knowing it was made of iron. "But she can't help them. They want banishing and darkness spells, but we're not that kind of Fae. They don't understand. We only have green magic. We can only help plants grow." The child fell to its knees. "Please, give her back."

I approached the child slowly and sat with it in the cold grass. "I'm sorry they took her." I paused, considering my words. "Just like you're scared now, the humans are, too. They think that they need to take to survive."

Sniffling, the child argued, "But she can't help them."

"I know."

"So, why?" The child wiped at its tears, frustrated.

"It's easier to live a life of ignorance than it is to face the truth." I clenched my fists, unable to express my grief for the world any further.

"That's stupid."

I laughed. "I know." The wind howled, and the tree's saffron leaves rustled. "Are you fed?" The shifter seemed healthy, but I didn't know how far their abilities went.

"Yes. Mother taught me how to forage and find clean water."

"Good. Don't try to go inside the cave. It's too dangerous. Stay safe and out of sight." I took a breath, knowing I was promising a lot. "If your mother is in there, I will get her out. But if you haven't seen either of us by the next moon cycle, you need to move on and find a safer place to live. Humans have claimed this area, and it's not good to dwell. Do you understand?"

"I'll never leave her behind." The child's tears stopped, and determination replaced its grief-stricken expression.

Guilt clawed at my insides. "I know the feeling." Leaving the kobold child alone in the dark, I returned to the cave and made my way to the human camp. But I stopped and looked down the adjacent tunnel. Still, there were no fires lit. I looked to the left and stared at the lights that would lead me to Lugh and Cole.

I went right.

I was blind without my dagger, so I clutched the foreign weapon tightly in my hand and relied on my other senses to guide me. The smell changed the farther in I went. While the human camp had smelled of meat, men, and steel, this tunnel smelled of rot. Of death.

I glanced over my shoulder several times throughout the journey, worried I had been followed. But there was no silhouette in the shadows, and no echoes could be heard besides my own footsteps quickening in the cavern. I should have taken one of the torches lining the left tunnel, but I hated being a target.

I stumbled over something on the floor. Reaching down, I felt my way along the cold, damp ground. Fur enveloped my hand, unmoving. That was when the stench intensified.

I moved on, knowing what lay there was long dead.

The tunnel curved and rocks jutted from the walls, stabbing my skin when I moved too fast. Each step was agony, but I needed to know. Making another turn, a glow shone up ahead. I followed that small light, relief drowning out reason as I ran. The tunnel opened wide like a yawning mouth, revealing a nightmare in the fire's shadows.

Fae.

Fae of every kind festered in the cavern. Some were sleeping, some were searching the ground for crumbs, some were mating, and some were just watching. The last one was the worst. Because those were the Fae who saw me first.

My heart thudded so loud I was sure some of them could hear it. I turned to run, but the sound of chains stopped me. The watchers had crawled toward me, dragging the iron restraints with them. Nearest to me was a dearg: a man-rat creature with thick red hair and a long tail. A strange language left his mouth, but it sounded a lot like curses.

Still, I said, "Let me help you."

With a thick Fae accent, he spat, "We'd rather die."

I looked into his large black eyes, searching for any kind of humanity. But, of course, there was barely any humanity in humans anymore. Why would I expect it of anything else? "They aren't going to kill you. They will torture and bleed you out until you have nothing left to give. And then keep going. Do you really want that for yourselves?"

By now, the rest of the Fae had turned their attention to me, all eyes facing the only exit. I noticed a human-looking Fae; every part of her was chained to the wall. The rest of the creatures were chained by the throats and ankles.

"There is a kobold child waiting outside the cave—waiting for its mother. I'm sure she would want to be freed and reunite with her young-ling," I argued, staring at the overly-chained woman.

She hissed at me, using her one inch of allowed movement to do so.

The dearg laughed a deep, primal sound. "Leave, human. We don't want your pity."

"Why? Is your pride really worth that much to you?"

"Pride is for humans. We are Fae. Magic bore us and magic will end us." The cavern filled with growls, shrieks, cries, yowls, and curses. So loud, I was forced to run before my ears bled. Long after the voices quieted, I heard the iron chains rattling.

Much like the Common, Fae were proud and would not bow to their rivals. They would only listen to their own. And the humans weren't going to let anyone leave.

Cole had wanted a distraction. *I found one.*

I hid the knife beneath my shirt and entered the medical tent. Cole was there with Brody, explaining, in great detail, the treatment plan. "Hey, *sis*, back from collecting water so soon?"

Confused, I just nodded.

"Where's the water?" Brody asked.

I looked to Cara, where she tended to a patient in the corner. The girl gave me an apologetic expression. "Damn fairies stole it right from my hands. Took the bucket, too," I lied smoothly.

Brody shook his head in disapproval. "You shouldn't have gone out alone in the first place. Fae aren't to be trusted, even ones as small as fairies. Cara shouldn't have sent you out there." He gave the girl a pointed look.

Cole handed me a cup of water and winked.

Cara responded, "Sorry, Father." I nearly spit the water back into the cup, knowing the leader's daughter had lied for me. *I couldn't risk that again.*

"Take one of the men with you next time, or better yet, don't go outside at all. It's not safe." Brody turned to Cole. "Make sure of it."

"Understood, sir." My jaw dropped at the shear arrogance of these men. I didn't like the human version of Cole, despite it being an act, but I held my tongue and went to Lugh. His breathing was even, and his heart was strong.

"I'll leave you two to tend to your brother. Come, Cara. Give them some privacy." Brody was many things, but family meant something to him. I could see it in his eyes when he looked at his daughter, and when he spared my brother's life at the nest. He knew family was everything.

With only the shallow breaths of patients in the tent, I felt safe enough to tell Cole about the kobold child and prisoners. "Its mother is down there. So are many others. If we set them free, that will give us the distraction we need to get the knife and run." I paused. "And Brody and his people won't be able to come after us."

Refusing to acknowledge my very permanent solution, he asked, "How do you expect to exchange the knives during the chaos? He'll draw it to use against them." Cole felt Lugh's forehead for a fever and straightened his blanket. The act warmed my cold heart, but I looked away before the elf could see it in my eyes.

"No matter what, I don't think an exchange is going to happen. Donal is a warrior. We're not going to be able to sneak around him. But we may be able to take him down if surprise is on our side." I pulled out the knife from beneath my shirt. Its dull blade gleamed in the candle's light.

"You want to take down a warrior with this?" The elf ran his finger along the blade, leaving the edge without blood.

"Yes, because you're forgetting, I'm a warrior, too." I took the blade back from Cole, and my fingers grazed his by accident. But he clutched my hand with the knife between us.

"I'm not going to let you fight him alone."

"Someone has to free the Fae, and they're not going to trust me. You have to do it. Lead them to the weapons at the entrance and tell them to fight. If they don't fight now, the humans will track them down." I thought of the child waiting for its mother outside. I looked to Lugh, slowly dying in his cot. The winter was approaching swiftly. *I would protect him at any cost.*

Rawness in his voice, Cole confessed, "I don't want to be a killer."

"You don't have to be. I already am."

Cole released my hand and blade. "Means to an end, right?" The glint was gone from his green gaze.

I forced myself to look him in those dulled eyes and say, "For Lugh, always."

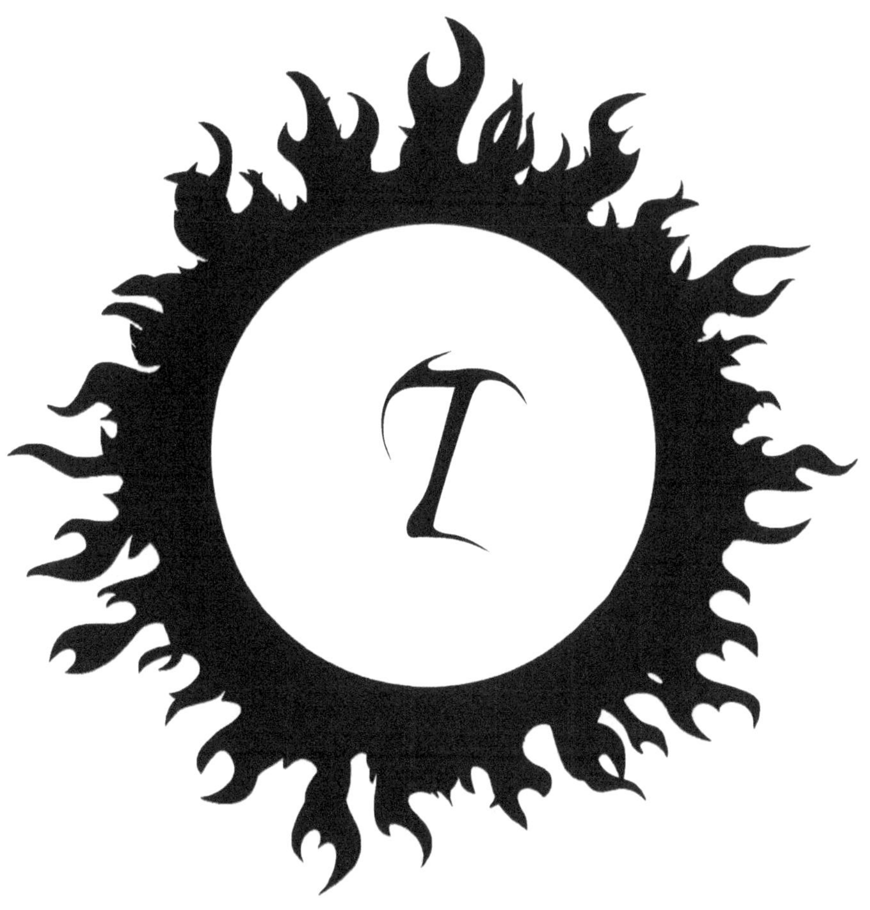

Days passed before we learned Donal's schedule. He was Brody's shadow. He went where the leader went, with the exceptions of eating, sleeping, and shitting. And one other place. Cole had followed him as far as he dared down the tunnel and watched him turn into the adjacent one. Donal personally checked on the prisoners once a day.

There were groups of men who went into the tunnel and came back hours later covered in blood. They were torturing the Fae, trying to force magic out of them. I could see that Cole was disturbed by this and by me, too, most likely. I was willing to cause a massacre of human and Fae lives so I could get my brother out with the only weapon that could protect us.

Some would say I was the monster.

But my mind could not be changed, and the elf knew that. Which was why he only spoke to me when necessary. The question I constantly asked myself was, *Why did he stay?* He could have left at any time—a perk of being a "man." If he wanted to, he could have gone to the stone circle himself and performed a different spell, unlocking his magic without me. *Yet, he stayed.*

The elf must have wanted something from me.

The day was upon us. Though the only lights I could see were the stalactites above, I could feel the heat from the sun shining down on the cavern, and in turn, feeding the Guise who wandered the land. The humans dispersed, resting in their designated sleeping areas. This was Donal's time to check on the Fae, but Cole left just after the fires were put out and before Donal exited the men's quarters.

I hid behind the medical tent, waiting for Donal to leave. I watched man after man abandon their quarters and sneak into the women's. Soon, Donal appeared, took a quick glance around, and began his short journey. Though it was near impossible to see in the darkness, let alone pick out a specific person from the shadows, I could feel the dagger. It called to me, begging to rest in my hand again. I followed the siren call.

My hair was pulled back painfully secure. I had wrapped my ankle tight and let it soak in cold water for so long, it was numb. Weakness would not cost me this fight. As I groped along the cavern's walls, I sent a quiet prayer to Lugh, "Be safe, brother. I'll come back for you."

I was just about to cross from the cavern into the tunnel when a voice whispered, "Yvaine, where are you going?"

I tensed and turned. "Cara, what are you doing out here?"

"You didn't come to bed, so I came to check on you. I saw you leaving the medical tent." She glanced at the dull knife in my grip. "What are you doing with that? You know we're not allowed to have weapons."

"Cara, please, go back to bed. Be mindful of the men sneaking around," I warned.

"Is that why you have that? Did someone threaten you?" Cara was sincerely worried about me, but I couldn't allow myself to care.

"No, but it doesn't hurt to be prepared, does it?" I sheathed the blade, counting the seconds that passed while I dealt with the girl.

"Where are you going?" she asked again.

"I'm going to look for Lugh's scarf. I couldn't find it in the pile last time, and it's getting cold." I watched the men's shadows dance between the tents. It was only a matter of time before they saw mine.

"We have extra blankets. Don't worry about that. And I can't lie to my father again. He was really upset that I let you leave." Cara shifted her weight from one foot to the other, nervous.

"Just pretend you didn't see me and go back to bed." My voice was stern. I was running out of time.

"Come with me. You aren't allowed to leave," she begged, twisting her hair anxiously.

"I'm sorry, Cara."

Before she could ask why, the butt of my knife struck her temple, and she collapsed. I dragged her behind a curtain where food supplies were kept. Maybe she would be safe there during the battle, but I couldn't concern myself with her anymore. I had a job to do.

I ran down the tunnel, my feet silent and practiced in the dark. Reaching the prisoner's side, I listened and heard soft footfalls. I sprinted. I needed to reach him before the prisoners were freed. Surprise was crucial. If he saw what Cole was doing, I would lose my advantage. Numbness enveloped me in its grey blanket.

The footsteps faltered. A pale amethyst light glowed ahead.

The endowed dirk.

"What the hell is this?" Donal said to himself. I threw the dull blade from my hand. It impaled him in the shoulder. *Damn.*

Donal cried out and turned toward his attacker. I willed the dirk at his side to go dark and flattened myself against the rock wall. His eyes would take time to adjust, but I knew exactly where he was, as I was comfortable in the blackness. The dirk's heartbeat was my own. I felt it move in one direction and another, searching for me.

Donal reached behind and yanked out the dull dagger from his shoulder blade; only half the blade had pierced him. Blood poured down his back. "Where are you?" he bellowed, his pain obvious. *Good.*

I stayed silent, biding my time. He shouldn't have pulled out the knife—he was only going to die faster. I circled, eager. The endowed weapon lit upon my approach, giving Donal my position. "You. I knew you were bad news, little bitch."

The man lunged and attacked head on, knowing he was much stronger than me. But I had learned how to fight. I was forced to learn or die. Since I was twelve years old, I had done nothing but fight and survive and protect my brother. This human man was nothing compared to a redcap: a being made of solid muscle and who soaked its clothing in the blood of their live victims; or a dullahan: a massive horse-man creature who decapitates its prey before devouring the organs.

No, this man was not as strong as those Fae monsters.

I avoided his direct attack and landed a hard blow to his kidney, kicked his knee out from under him, and plunged my fingers into his stab wound, widening the hole. I reached for the magic blade, but he lurched forward just before I could, unsheathing it so he held a dagger in each hand. Donal panted, slowly bleeding out. "Why? Is it for the loot? What do you want?"

"You could say that."

"Then take what you can carry and leave," he spat.

Lies. "Giving up the fight already? I thought you were a man, but it's just an act, isn't it? Bark is worse than the bite."

"Bitch."

"Is that the only thing you can bark? Maybe you don't even have that going for you." I needed him angry; his strength would mean nothing if he was sloppy. And I was much faster. Another wave of numbness washed over me, readying for the final blow.

Knives in hand, he ran at me, swiping furiously through the air. Each lunge was countered with grace as I danced around him. Dozens of foot-falls echoed against the walls. "No. How could you…" The man stopped and stared into my night-blue eyes. "Your so-called brother freed them," he accused. "You've just killed us all."

"No," I said. The man turned to run. "Just the *inscius*." His eyes lost me in the darkness that came with the dagger's sleep. Quickly, I kicked the dull blade from his grip and grabbed his other arm, placing it between my two forearms. The snap of his bone was loud in the cavern, but his scream was earth shattering. He dropped the endowed blade, and it glowed anew when I picked it up and sliced his throat.

Glassy eyes stared up at me. Red hair and too-pale skin was what was left of Donal.

I could hear Cole shouting orders to the Fae prisoners. "This way! Grab a weapon and follow me." So, it worked—they had agreed to fight. I willed the numbness to drench me in its dark waters. Nothing could be felt beyond the pounding of my heart and the sharp intake of my breath. I stayed hidden, flattened against the wall as they passed by. Only a few Fae bothered to look at the corpse in their path. They probably assumed Cole had killed him to get to them.

I saw the kobold from before and wondered if it was the child's mother. Her skin was changing shape; fur was growing and teeth were elongated. The iron chains were now gone, and she was finally free to shift.

I followed the chaos, a mere shadow. They grabbed the weapons piled at the entrance and turned down the fire-lit tunnel, ignoring the exit before them. They attacked the men's quarters first. Cole discreetly left for the medical tent, not wanting to attract attention to it. I did the same. Once I was inside, Cole grabbed my hand and pulled me into him. Still on guard, I punched him in the stomach. "Owe!" he complained. The elf's head bandage was gone.

"Let's get out of here." I reached for Lugh.

Cole grabbed my arm. "Are you okay?" The elf looked me up and down, searching for something.

"Yes, let's move."

"I saw Donal. What you did to him," he said.

"I said, move!" I lifted Lugh onto my back and pushed Cole aside when he tried to take him. I didn't know how much longer I could hold myself together. The grey was fading into black. I was going to be blind in this chaos if I didn't hurry.

Not caring if Cole followed, I ran toward the exit, sticking to the walls and shadows so we wouldn't be seen. The wait was excruciating, as I had to hide in between the carnage, unable to fight with Lugh on my back. The dirk stayed dark, hiding us. The stalactites were the only light. Some fell to the ground, unable to withstand the rumbling from below. Humans were forced from their beds, dragged across the cavern floor, beaten, and murdered. The humans who had been armed fought without mercy, slicing into Fae skin, fur, fang, and feather.

Don't look at the bodies. Don't look at the bodies. Don't look at the bodies.

This mantra was my salvation, as I reached the tunnel and ran past the gateway into the sunlight. I saw the kobold child hiding behind a tree, but I didn't stop. I didn't know if its mother was going to live. I didn't know if they would be together again. But I couldn't stop running.

Light steps sounded from behind and I spun, holding the dagger. It was pressed against an elf's throat. "Yvaine, it's me, Cole." I didn't lower the blade. "Yvaine, follow me. I'll get us out of here."

The numbness lightened just a bit, and I nodded. We ran through the forest at a fast pace, worried that the humans would come after us. The sun overhead was daunting, knowing I could be seen. My gaze caught anything that moved. No Guise appeared.

Finally, we stopped. I recognized the tight circle of trees that was now a gravesite for small, innocent creatures—at least those who weren't taken for dinner. "Why are we back here?" My voice felt unfamiliar, dead.

"I needed to get this back before we moved on." The elf unburied his bow and quiver from beneath a rose bush.

"Fine. We need weapons."

"This isn't just any weapon, Yvaine. It's endowed." Cole stood, brushing the dirt from the runes that were carved into the wooden bow.

"And you left it here?" Survival was key. My eyes darted between trees, searching for a lurking threat.

"It was better than having the humans take it. Look how hard it was to get your dagger back. Imagine if we had to get this back, too." The elf clutched the weapon tight before placing it over his shoulders.

"Yeah, I guess." A thought occurred to me, and my heart sped. "Then why didn't it kill the Guise? You shot it with that bow."

"I can't get the magic to awaken."

"But endowed weapons don't need a magic wielder. They are magic. That's why I can use mine." I rushed through the words, eager to be on the move again.

Cole took his time answering, reading my face. "I don't know why." His voice was blank, much like mine was.

Uncaring, I said, "Let's go."

"There's a cave up ahead." We ran again, and I clutched desperately to my sanity.

It was hours before we reached the cave he had spoken of. The small shelter was nestled behind a cluster of hemlocks on a hillside. The sun was fading from the canopy. "Take Lugh."

Unsurprised, Cole took my brother and laid him on the soft ground beneath the dark cover of trees. "We'll wait here." I didn't know how Cole knew, and I didn't stop to ask. I ran into the cave and basked in the darkness there, the safety, the comfort, the disguise. The numbness faded. And I screamed. I screamed for so long, my throat burned, and my voice was all but gone. I cried until I was utterly empty and my eyes were swollen shut, unsure if Cole and my brother had joined me inside the pit or not.

I hid deep in the cave until night had come and gone and the sun mocked me once again.

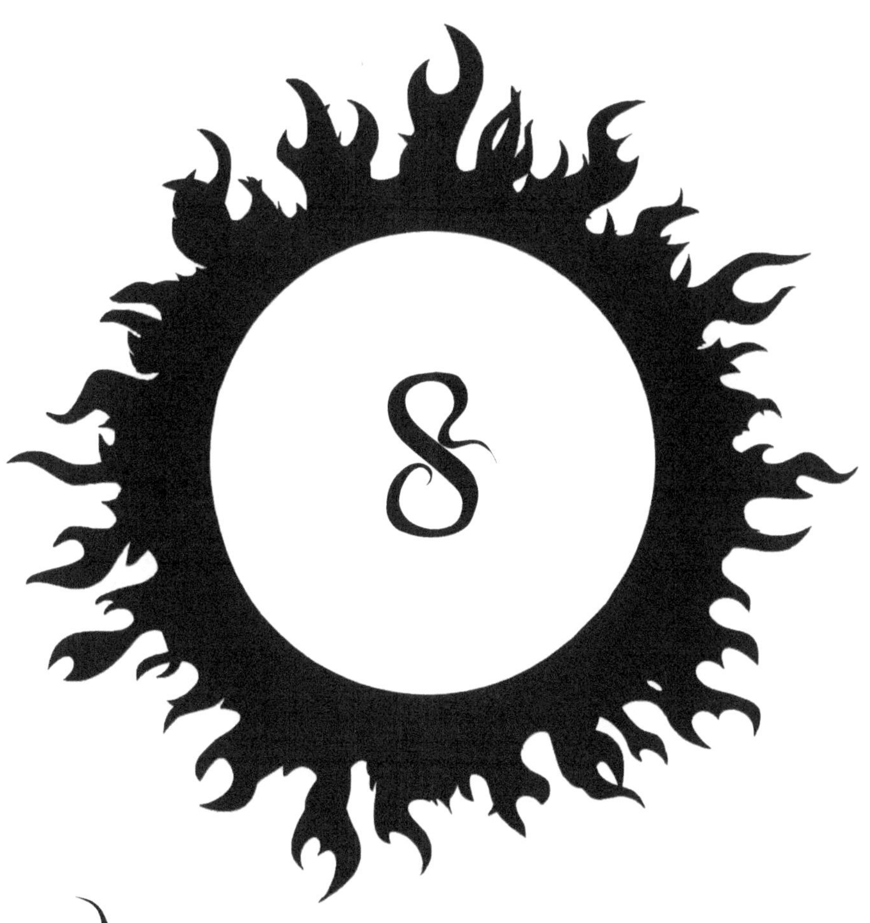

A fire was crackling when I woke. I rose into a sitting position, peeling my eyes open as I did. A damp cloth was put in my hand. When I wiped my eyes clean of salted tears, I saw that it was night, and the stars were shining outside of the cave. I shifted my leg and flinched.

"Don't move. Your ankle is worse. You need to stay off of it." Cole's tone was careful, as if he didn't want to spook a wild animal.

"Shit," I mumbled.

"There she is." Cole stoked the fire, uncaring of its blazing light.

"I don't know what you mean." I laid back down, exhausted.

The cave howled as a breeze passed through. "I think that I'll call the one from yesterday the *other woman*. What do you think?" the elf said.

"Call who the *other woman*?" How long had I been sleeping? How much time had I wasted?

"You, obviously," he taunted.

"Why?"

"For the she-beast you turn into. You sure you're not part werewolf?" Cole put down the stoking stick and met my stare.

"Werewolves aren't real," I commented. The dread was lifting faster than it usually did after I killed. My stomach floated rather than sank.

"Exactly. The *other woman* is so frightening, she comes from a fantasy novel." I peeked my eyes open again and witnessed a small smile lift at the corner of the elf's mouth, but his eyes didn't twinkle with mischief like they usually did.

"Sorry, I must leave when she's here. I don't know much about her. Can you tell me?" I pulled the moss blanket over my shoulder, grateful for the warmth; it felt like it had been under the sun all day. My heart melted just a little, knowing he had gone to the trouble of making it.

Cole broke eye contact as he spoke. "She's fearless, bloodthirsty, and strong." His tone changed to one of worry. "But also blind and reckless." It was odd how Cole saw me as blind during the numbness when I thought the opposite.

"The *other woman* doesn't sound like someone you want to mess with." Though what the *other woman* did frightened me, she still gave me a sense of pride, knowing I could rely on her to get me through anything. No matter how terrifying.

"She's not, that's for certain." Cole was trying to lighten the mood, but he couldn't muster the energy to make it convincing. He ran dirty hands through dark hair and hung his head.

"I'm not sorry that I did it." Lugh was the priority, always. "But I am sorry that I had to." The swelling reduced in my eyes incrementally, and I was able to see Lugh on the other side of the fire, covered in another moss blanket. He was pale, cheeks sunken. I gasped.

"The leaf is dying. I gave him water, but it didn't budge. It seems the magic is being fickle as the spriggan warned. It doesn't know what to do with Lugh."

Tears escaped, and I wiped them away before Cole could turn back to me. "We have to move faster. There can't be any more interruptions."

"Do you think I planned those interruptions? My goodness, Yvaine, you can't control everything." Cole exhaled an angry breath.

"Obviously."

Cole let out another breath, but it was slow and calming. He scooted close to me and placed his arm on my shoulder. "We'll make it in time."

Without warning, another tear fell, and I regretted it as soon as it happened. The shameful expression returned to the elf's face. "Stop pitying me. I hate it." I tried to hide under the moss to no avail.

"It's not pity, Yvaine, it's worry. Don't you know the difference?" he asked, incredulous.

With a sad smile, I said, "No. I haven't had anyone worry about me before."

"I'm sure Lugh worries about you all the time. You're a handful." He squeezed my shoulder tight, and I couldn't help but notice the tremble in his voice. *Was he truly worried about me?*

Sighing, I said, "It's not the same. I've raised him since he was four. I'm basically his mother. It's not his job to worry about me." I attempted to smile but failed. "But that's okay. It's the least I can do for taking away his real mother."

"What do you mean?" Cole stilled, shocked by the confession.

Then it spilled out of me. "We were there when our parents were killed. I kept Lugh from seeing, but I watched it happen. Father was shot before the man stepped through the door. Mother went to him and had her throat cut. The psycho pinned her down." I paused. "And then, she was miraculously winning. She was strong. She was fighting for us." Another tear fell. "I called out to her because I was scared. That was all it took, and he plunged this knife into her heart." I lifted the magic weapon. I could almost see my mother's blood on the blade, despite having cleaned it vigorously several times since. "Because of me, Lugh doesn't have a mother. And you know the worst part?" I wiped my nose, realizing just how much I was weeping.

"What's the worst part?" Cole asked when I didn't say anything.

I whispered, "I didn't do anything. I didn't try to run or hide Lugh. I just sat there and let the monster take us. And I've done nothing but fail my brother since."

"That's not true," he whispered.

"Yes it is."

"Yvaine—"

"You wanted to know how the man died? The one who tried to rape me and failed?" I blurted, unable to keep the guilt inside any longer.

Gently, he said, "Yes."

"Lugh killed him. He saved me. A ten-year-old boy had to save me because I trusted the wrong person." I sat up, unable to hold still. "I couldn't even save my baby brother's childhood. It was taken away the same way mine was." I shoved the swollen eyes into my knees, trying to block out the memory.

There were suddenly warm hands in my hair. "What are you doing?" I asked.

"Birds would appreciate your hair. The twigs and moss tangle together nicely in your curls. They wouldn't hesitate to raise a family in it." The hairband was removed carefully and long, gentle fingers brushed through the tangles.

I giggled, hysterical from exhaustion and trauma and guilt and life.

After a few peaceful moments of hair detangling, he said, "When I was little, I would comb my mother's hair. It was the only time I didn't have to see the hatred in her eyes. When she was faced away from me, I could pretend that she loved me."

"I'm sure that she loved you, Cole. She was just in pain." *I couldn't imagine…*

"Yeah, well, the pain forced her to banish me from home." A knot was carefully undone, and it fell down my back.

"I thought your people did that to you?" I asked, careful with my tone.

"They joined in once my mother suggested it." Cole spoke naturally, as if that part of his life was long behind him, but my gut was telling me that there was more to the story.

I choked on traitorous tears.

"Sorry, did I pull too hard?" His fingers left my hair, and I was suddenly very cold.

"No, just surprised is all."

With a playful tone, he said, "Oh c'mon, you tried to banish me, too, back at the city tunnels. Seems no one wants me around."

I cringed, and a new kind of guilt flooded me. It filled me with so much sadness and shame, I was nauseated. "I was wrong. Where would I be if it weren't for you? Where would Lugh be? Dead." The elf's nimble fingers returned to my hair, and I sighed.

"Would you really have done it? Let the Guise have you?" the elf asked.

"I didn't see another way out," I whispered.

"There's always a way out," Cole whispered back, his breath caressing my ear. My eyes widened. "There, you are no longer a bird's dream home." I pulled my hair forward and felt the intricate braid he had woven; the pattern matched the hairband that gripped the end.

"It's beautiful."

When I turned, he smiled and said, "Only elvish defenders are allowed to braid their hair that way."

"Defenders?"

"Warriors." My stomach clenched. I felt light and heavy at the same time. I was going to throw up. "Are you okay?" he asked.

I just nodded and said, "Thank you." Laying back down, I noticed Cole didn't have a blanket. I considered giving mine to him, but it looked as if it would crumble if I tried to move it. "It's cold. Get under the blanket," I ordered.

"What?" The elf peered at me suspiciously.

I just motioned for him to lay next to me, unable to meet his eyes. He took my offer quicker than I thought he would, especially after seeing the *other woman.* "Face the fire." I turned and faced the wall, so our bodies were barely touching. "Control your dreams this time, or at least don't say them aloud."

"I don't know what you mean. You're the one who groped me. I woke up to you sitting on my lap!" Cole laughed, distracted from the memories of his past.

The dirt shifted on the other side of the fire. I shot up and saw Lugh's arm twitch. "Lugh? Can you hear us?"

No response.

"Goodnight, Lugh." I laid back down.

Cole responded instead, "Goodnight, Yvaine."

"Goodnight, Cole."

With a smile in his voice, he ended the night with, "Have happy dreams."

I kicked him under the blanket.

I kept watch for as long as I could, flinching at every sound I heard from outside. Had the humans tracked us? Were there hungry Fae outside? Common animals? Was there enough light for a Guise to emerge?

Soon, exhaustion won, and I fell into a fitful sleep. A sleep without rest because my imagination was dried up, and there was nothing but haunted memories to replay over and over.

Lugh tried to remove his hand from my grip, but I felt better if I knew where he was. He was ten years old and full of life. I was only eighteen, but I felt one hundred. We scavenged the city for food, staying in the sewers during the day. The knife hung from my side, a constant companion. Its glow was bright—too bright. A Guise appeared below a sewer grate. I pushed Lugh back, his small arrow nocked, but I shook my head.

I lunged before the creature had time to react. Once I was finished, only sunrays were left behind. I stuck my pale hand out and felt the warmth. Lugh joined me. We looked to one another with both happiness and sadness. That was the most sun we'd had in a long while.

The treasured moment faded when a man's voice said, "What you got there, cutie?"

I woke with a gasp, sweat forming around my hairline. Once my heartbeat was under control, I realized how comfortable I was and then how screwed I was. My front was pressed flush against Cole's back, and my arm was wrapped around his stomach.

I inched my arm away and then my body. Slowly, I uncovered myself and laid the moss back down on the elf. I tip toed to Lugh, my ankle screaming, and checked his breathing and heart—strong. I checked the leaf—yellow edges. *Damn.*

I looked to Cole out of habit and found him grinning, eyes open and very much awake.

"Don't say a word."

His grin widened. The elf knew he'd won this battle. And I hated it.

"Food?" I asked, begging to change the impending topic.

"There's not much vegetation to pick from around here. We're going to have to hunt," he explained, rising from beneath the blanket. The elf's clothing was disheveled, and I could see where I had held him because there was a dirty handprint on the bare skin of his stomach.

"I'll go." I reached for Cole's bow, and he leapt up, grabbing the weapon before I could touch it.

"No, I will. You're hurt." The elf clutched the bow as if his life depended on it. All of ours did at the moment.

"Can you even hunt? Aren't elves herbivores?" I could see the coming fight, and I strangely looked forward to it. Cole straightened his clothing, and I pretended not to watch.

Cole opened his mouth to argue, but paused and said, "Nice try. But you won't stall me anymore." He put his boots, jacket, and quiver on and headed toward the sunny entrance.

"Maybe we should wait until nightfall?" I suggested.

"No way. I'm starving. I'll need the energy if I'm going to be dealing with you for the next couple weeks."

"Couple weeks?" I asked.

"That's how long it's going to take to get to the stones. Then you won't have to see me again." He stopped at the entrance, just before the light demarcation. "That's what you want, isn't it?"

Was that what I wanted? I recalled the dream I had last night and answered my own question. "Yes. And I'm sure you feel the same way after getting to know the *other woman*." I tried to laugh, but it came out quiet and small. I shifted my brother so his other side was heated by the flames.

"Yeah," Cole exhaled. He stepped into the light and disappeared behind the trees.

Stoking the fire, I spoke to Lugh, comforted by his presence. "Oh Lugh, I'm sorry your sister is so weak." A spark flew up and landed in the darkest part of the cave. "It seems history is repeating itself, isn't it? You'd think I would learn. But here I am again, trusting another man. Half-man, I guess." I brushed my brother's blonde hair back, combing it like Cole had done to my hair only hours before. I fingered the braid hanging over my shoulder. *Elvish defender—warrior.* I smiled.

"Are you sure he didn't do something to you? An obedience spell? You know the rumors: most victims don't know it's happened to them and sometimes they even enjoy it." Lugh's words echoed in my thoughts. After what happened, how could I ever trust another? How could I risk my brother again?

I held Lugh's wrists, remembering what he had done for me. "Do you think he's lying, Lugh? About not having magic." I waited to see if Lugh would twitch or blink or anything, but I was alone. "I don't know how else to explain what I feel. Maybe you were right in the beginning. Maybe he cast a spell on me, and this whole time, I've been infatuated with him because of a lie. But what does he want?" I felt my ankle and acknowledged the fresh wrappings. "I suppose it's the same thing that the man wanted from us when we were children, what Finley wanted when he attacked, and what the Fae want when they hunt us.

Lugh didn't move.

I sighed. "They want to take. It's as simple as that."

Cole returned that night with a single squirrel.

"So, I was right, you aren't a hunter." I would have laughed if I wasn't so hungry. I should have stolen supplies from the humans—*sloppy*.

"No, I am a very capable hunter. There's just nothing to hunt. The Guise were swarming these woods. We're going to have to move on soon."

The fire's flames flickered in Cole's green eyes, making them dance. He handed me the now-full waterskin he'd taken from the humans during our escape.

"How far did you go?" I asked as I watered Lugh and then myself.

"About five miles north."

"Damn, well we can't turn around. We would lose too much time." I cringed, knowing what I was about to say. "We can look for food in Perth. It's on the way to the mountains and only two days from here if we don't dawdle."

"I know of it. Why does it give you that sour-look though?"

"No reason. Just hungry." As I spoke the words, Cole finished skinning the squirrel and placed it over the fire. A thin stick carefully skewered the Common animal from mouth to end.

"Does killing bother you?" I wondered, searching for answers to questions I didn't know how to ask.

Slowly, he answered, "Yes."

"When were you banished?"

"When I was ten. That's the age when magic awakens in our kind, but when nothing happened..." He turned the squirrel to roast the other side. "Anyway, it's been about twenty years."

My hunger was forgotten. "That's it?"

Appalled, he said, "My goodness, how old do I look to you?" It was strangely satisfying to know that my opinion mattered to him.

"No, that's not what I meant." I stumbled over the words. "I just assumed that you were some outrageous age, even though you look young. But I've been wrong about Fae before. Eavesdropping on humans who know nothing about Fae isn't a good source of information."

"There are some Fae who live long. Like every species, it varies. But elves live just as long as humans. Naturally anyway." The smell of cooked meat filled the cave, and I worried it would attract unwanted visitors.

"Naturally?"

"Well, elves are capable of using many types of magic. One of them being healing and life enhancement. Some manage to live for hundreds of years before passing on." Cole turned the meat over, cooking the other side.

"That's amazing."

"It used to be. But who would want to extend their life sentence nowadays?" Sadness crept into his eyes, and the flames dimmed. The elf's shoulders bowed in resignation.

"Isn't it my job to be negative?" I said, hating that he was so unhappy.

"I apologize." Cole dipped his head sarcastically. "I bow to the queen of darkness."

"As long as you know your place," I retorted.

The elf rolled his eyes but smiled.

Unsure how to begin, I blurted, "Why haven't you tried the stones before?"

His smile disappeared. "The stones are sacred to my people. Only true magic wielders can use them."

"What changed your mind?" I averted my gaze, preparing for the lie.

"Someone needed my help."

"You make me sound like a damsel in distress," I muttered.

"Well, yes, but really it was a *damoiselle* and a *damoiseau*." He looked to Lugh and laughed. The teenager's mouth hung open, drooling.

"Ah, Lugh." I wiped my brother's face clean and closed his mouth, propping his head on my jacket. The leaf's yellow hadn't spread, but it hadn't healed either. I doubted it ever would.

We were running out of time.

"We leave for Perth tonight. Eat and rest for a few hours. I'll wake you when its time."

"You're not going to make it very far on that ankle." Cole pointed to my bandaged injury, and I tucked it beneath my leg.

"We can't afford to wait. If the Guise are as bad as you say, we should travel at night. And we've already lost some dark hours." It was painful to ask, but I did. "Can you carry Lugh? I'll manage if I don't have the extra weight."

"Of course." The elf smirked, triumphant.

"Why are you smiling? You're going to have to carry a nearly full-grown man across miles of forest." Cole was hard to understand, yet I'd never connected with someone so easily before.

"You asked for my help."

"You've helped me plenty. I don't see how this is different." I concentrated on the squirrel as the elf took his skinning knife and cut the creature in half.

"It's different."

"Yeah, well, until I heal, get used to it." I really did need to heal. I hadn't stopped to rest my injury for more than a few hours since it happened. It was so swollen, it could have been another limb growing from me.

"I'll be sure to adjust to the queen's whims." He handed me my half of the meal, and we devoured the squirrel in moments. "Wake me when you're ready." The elf crawled under the moss blanket and was snoring soon after.

The sad thing was, I didn't know if I'd ever be ready for this journey. Perth was not a place I wanted to return to, but as I stared at Cole's sleeping face, I knew we could handle it.

The spell he cast on me was a powerful one it seemed.

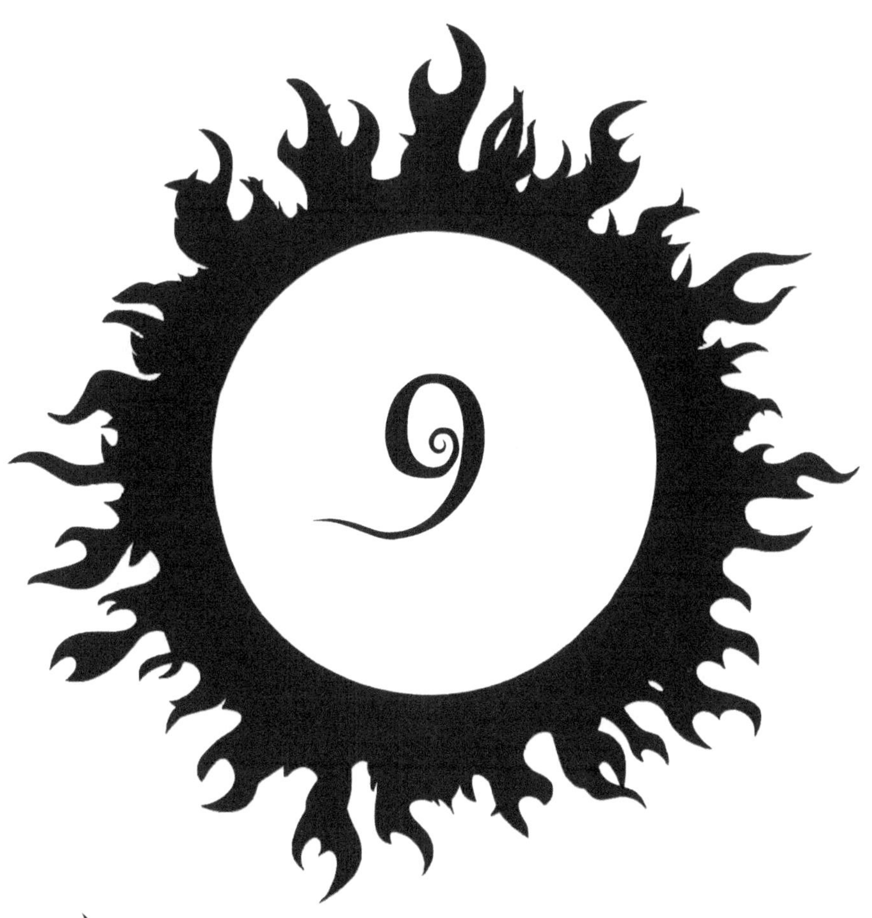

ole had been right. The Guise were everywhere. We barely found shelter in time. One by one, they appeared in front of us. We spent an hour in the sun, hiding behind trees and sneaking across rough terrain, before we found an old bridge to camp under. It sat above a dried-up river and connected to the main road.

"What was it like to drive a car?" Cole asked. He was staring at a wrecked Camaro in the ravine, while we stood in the darkness beneath our only protection. Nature had taken over since the vehicle crashed. The hood had been forced open by a tree, its roots curling around the tires and windshield.

"Frightening. Exhilarating." Perth was where I'd learned to drive, not well, but I managed. Racing and terrorizing the dead city was how I'd coped. I reprimanded myself, remembering how I had risked Lugh's young life by having him in the car with me when I sped down the ruined streets.

"I'd like to try."

"Why haven't you before?" I asked, my heart pounding, imagining the two of us racing down the city roads together.

"Human lands were forbidden to Fae. We had a responsibility to stay hidden, but even after the Collapse and the Fae gave up the facade, it was hard for me to enter the cities." My stomach fluttered at the sound of his voice; the timbre was as gentle as falling leaves, but as strong as the trees from which they fell.

"Because of the iron?" I asked. *Control yourself. He's Fae. He's the enemy.*

"No, the iron was tolerable. I think mostly because I'm only half Fae." He continued to stare at the car while he spoke. "I didn't want to know humans."

"Sorry, I ruined it."

Finally, he looked at me. "You didn't ruin it. You opened my eyes."

"And what do your open eyes see?" I said, curious.

"Humans are much worse than I assumed."

I punched his arm and he laughed. "I'll ignore that comment, considering that I'm part werewolf," I said.

"You're certainly something," Cole whispered, seemingly to himself. I was about to ask him what he meant, but a sound thudded against the wooden bridge. The sun had risen fully now, and the only thing protecting us was the rotting cover above. I could see Guise weaving in and out of trees and wandering down the roadside. Their gold forms were as transparent as light and as beautiful as the sun. Ghostly Gods I'd always thought. Unforgiving Gods.

"Quiet down there," a small voice hushed.

We both stiffened, and Lugh twitched. I searched the top of the bridge between the cracks and saw no one. "Who said that?" I demanded, knife drawn.

"Quiet, or the monsters will hear you."

Cole pointed to a dark corner where the wood met the paved road. A pair of yellow eyes stared back at us. I fell back, surprised. Cole caught me, and I righted myself immediately. "A trow," he stated.

"Never heard of them." I pointed the dagger in its direction, unsure of the threat.

"We'd like to keep it that way. And we will if you ever shut up," the rude trow whispered. It burrowed deep into the wood, and its eyes vanished.

"What are you doing?" I quietly asked, as I approached the corner.

"You think this bridge would last as long as it has without help?" The creature unpeeled itself from the wood plank and revealed its small wood-like body, no bigger than my hand. It walked along the underside of the bridge, its feet rooting itself into the lumber with each step. Silky red hairs sprouted from its head. Its bark skin was smooth and polished, each limb a woodworker's dream. Where it had emerged from was now a rotted hole in the underside of our shelter.

"You keep it together? All alone?" I asked. Dozens of eyes appeared in the darkness, all yellow and glowing from inside the wood planks. "Apparently not."

A strange glimmer surrounded each one as they stepped from their hollow. Cole whispered in my ear; his breath was warm and sent shivers down my spine. "Trows are very hard workers. And very vain. They glamour their true forms."

"Why?" I wondered.

"Because we are ugly. The rotting-wood disease spreads to us when we work," the trow explained. It had very sensitive hearing, too.

"Why care for the bridges then?" I asked.

"It's not just bridges. We mend all trees." The trow looked to its kin. "But the Guise forced us out of our forest. This bridge is the only place dark enough to hide."

"I'm sorry," I whispered, unable to express the guilt I felt, and sheathed the endowed weapon.

"Don't be sorry, just get out. You'll bring them here," the Fae hissed.

"We have nowhere else to go," Cole said.

The trow considered. "What will you give us in return?"

"What do you want?" the elf asked, a smirk forming.

The small creatures looked at each other and made a silent, unanimous decision. "We want a song."

"A song?" I said, baffled. "Won't that attract the Guise even more?"

"No, we can disguise the noise with a spell."

"Then why did you tell us to be quiet?" I asked, angry.

A smile shown on the trow's little face. "We wanted you to leave. We thought that would help you along."

I glared at the tiny Fae.

"You heard them. Sing a song," Cole encouraged, suddenly very serious.

"Me? Why not you?" I backed up, and Cole pushed me forward, leaving his hands on my arms. Lugh was tightly tucked under our jackets in the soft grass beneath the darkest part of the bridge. I wished he was awake, if anything, to make fun of me.

"Whose brother was it that I carried for the past several miles? Oh right, yours." He continued to hold me firmly in place and facing the eager trows.

Surrendering, I asked, "What do you want me to sing?"

"A hymn." The trows danced in delight, excited. *So much pressure.*

"Ummm... All right. Let me think." After a moment, I recalled a time

in church during summertime. Lugh was only two years old. I sang the
song, a hymn that had been buried in my memories.

All things bright and beautiful,
All creatures great and small,
All things wise and wonderful,
'Twas God that made them all.

Each little flower that opens,
Each little bird that sings,
He made their glowing color,
He made their tiny wings.

The purple headed mountains,
The river running by,
The sunset and the morning
That brightens up the sky.

The cold wind in the winter,
The pleasant summer sun,
The ripe fruits in the garden,
He made them every one.

He gave us eyes to see them,
And lips hat we might tell,
How great is the Almighty,
Who has made all things well.

As I sang, Cole released his hold. I couldn't see him from where he
stood behind me, but I could feel his gaze. The trows burrowed into their

hollows again, content for the moment. They continued to hum the song while they worked on the bridge. I looked out to the wandering Guise. None had turned our way. The trows must have cast their silence spell.

"Why did they want a hymn? Do Fae believe in God?" I turned away from my small audience and found the elf staring at me.

"No, we believe in magic. But there's really no difference between the two. Humanity just decided to personify the definition of goodness." Cole considered a moment before continuing, "You have a beautiful voice."

Embarrassed, I blushed. Lugh had been the only one to hear me sing before. "Thank you. Hopefully, it will keep them happy for now."

"Well, it made me happy."

The man's voice echoed down the sewer tunnel, "What you got there, cutie?"

I turned and pushed Lugh behind me. "Get back." I raised the magic blade toward the man before me. He was young, but older than me by a decade. Despite the environment, he managed to look clean and handsome. Two very rare things among men nowadays.

The man lowered his sword and placed it on a damp ledge. "Don't be frightened. My name is Finley. I can help you." He looked to the small boy peering out from behind me. "You look hungry."

"We're fine. Leave now," I demanded.

"Cutie, you're going to starve that poor boy because of your pride. That's no way to act." Finley took a step closer.

I glanced to Lugh. His arrow was nocked once again, ready to defend his sister—a sister who couldn't feed him. His gaunt cheeks and hollow eyes said as much. "What do want in return?"

Finley considered a moment. "That knife of yours would be a great addi-

tion to my collection."

"No." My tone was final and unwavering.

"Then perhaps your company? I've been alone a long time and would enjoy a conversation with a beautiful woman." Woman? The stranger reached into his pocket, the other staying up in surrender, and pulled out a packaged lemon cake. I hadn't seen one since I was small. "Here, for the boy." Finley took another step forward and waited, asking permission. I nodded but didn't lower my blade.

When the stranger was only a step away, Lugh raised his bow high, aiming at the man's chest. "Lugh, it's okay," I said.

"I don't like him," he said, but his hands shook, and the bow string quivered.

"Don't turn down a meal. They don't come along very often. Take it." Lugh lowered his weapon, and although I allowed him to take the cake from the stranger's hand, I never dropped my guard. I scanned Finley, taking in his full, muscled body. He was well fed and strong. I could only imagine how weak I must look to him. How weak I was in comparison. Lugh needed someone like him.

Lugh stuffed the cake in his pocket, never removing his gaze from Finley. "I have a camp at the end of this tunnel and more food. Come with, and you'll be safe there." His eyes bored into mine, willing me to obey.

I nodded.

Finley picked up his sword and passed us, leading us either to our salvation or our doom. But I was too exhausted and starved to care which one it was.

I woke, the sunset's deep hues shining beyond my eyelids. My dreams had taken a turn for the worst, refusing to let go of the memory. I would be haunted by it until it had run its course. As all my nightmares did.

"How'd you sleep?" Cole's voice startled me, and I sat up, the knife out. A quick scan of my red-rimmed eyes, tense body, and readied weapon gave him the answer. "Ah, I see."

Lugh breathed deep beside me. We had all huddled together to keep warm during the day, unable to light a fire with so many Guise nearby. But it was better than if we'd slept in the night. Winter was approaching quickly, and the darkness only made it colder. The only positive aspect was that my ankle's swelling was staying down because of it.

Laying against Lugh's other side, Cole grabbed the waterskin and handed it to me. I propped my brother's head on my knees and opened his mouth. The yellow edges were moving inward. I poured a generous amount of water down his throat and watched the leaf.

"It's not going to heal, Yvaine. We just need to beat it to the finish line," Cole whispered to me, as if he didn't want anyone else to hear.

"I know." I took a small drink of water and gave it back to the elf. His ebony hair was stark against the backdrop of saffron hues. The Guise were slowly disappearing, crying out just before they ceased to exist. I wondered where they went during the dark hours, then decided that I didn't care. My stomach rumbled. "We'll make it to the city by sunrise if we hurry. There will be plenty of cover there."

"Have you spent much time in Perth?" he asked, waiting for the sun to completely fall before moving.

"A few months."

"What did you do there?" he asked.

"Tried to survive. Lugh and I moved from city to city for a long while." I shifted uncomfortably, the topic unwanted.

Surprised, he said, "Why didn't you try living in the forest?"

"I didn't know how to hunt or forage. The Fae were everywhere. It wasn't until Lugh ditched me to go hunt in the woods that we started hanging around there." I laughed. "I guess that he wasn't happy with old canned food and stale crackers."

"I can't imagine the *other woman* handling that well."

"She didn't." I allowed myself the pleasure of staring into Cole's eyes and not searching for a lie. "I learned to track quickly and found Lugh caught in a human's animal trap. I got him out, but he was the one who fed us by killing a deer."

"You must have been proud." Cole sat upright, arms draped over his knees, relaxed. But there was a tightness in his posture that always seemed to be there. Of course, that was only to be expected in a world like ours. Let your guard down and you die.

"I was, but also scared. He was getting older, and I didn't know how much longer I could protect him on my own."

"Yvaine," I looked away, "getting older means that he can protect you, too. Not that he needs *more* protection." Cole's tone was soft but confused.

"The older we get, the less we want help. The less we listen." I stroked Lugh's soft hair. "And that's what gets us killed." The silhouette of Lugh and the banshee in the sewer tunnel brought a tear to my eye, but I blinked it away before Cole or the trows could see. The small Fae were peering down at me now, listening to the conversation.

The sky darkened, and the last of the Guise departed. "Thank you for letting us stay here," I told the trows. I retied my boots and stood to stretch. The hard ground was not ideal for sleeping, but honestly, I hadn't slept in a real bed since the Collapse. It'd been hard-packed ground, stone tunnels, or moldy mattresses. *If I had a real bed, would I even want to sleep in it?*

The Fae cooed in delight and thanked me for the hymn. "They like you," Cole whispered. He was standing now, too. The elf stretched his long, lean limbs, and I couldn't help but stare. Cole was beautiful for an elf, and that was saying something.

"I like them, too. They're beautiful. On the inside and outside."

All the little eyes turned to me. "You haven't seen our true forms."

"I don't need to," I said, preparing Lugh for travel.

"Did you have a sight spell cast on you?" one trow asked.

"No, I just know." Suddenly, all the trows stepped out from their hollows, and the glamour dropped, revealing their true selves. Without skipping a beat, I said, "Beautiful." All the little Fae smiled. Some put their glamour back on, but others decided to show themselves instead.

Cole lifted Lugh onto his shoulder, and I secured my brother's hood so his ears would stay warm. With a final wave to the bridge's caretakers, we were gone and down the road in minutes.

"That was nice, what you said," Cole commented. "A bit strange for you though."

"How so?"

"Let's just say, you don't hand out compliments very often," he said.

"Well, they needed it." I lengthened my stride so Cole didn't have to slow down for me, as he usually did.

Intrigued, he said, "What makes you think so?"

"Because trows are the ugliest people I have ever seen."

With a laugh, Cole said, "There she is."

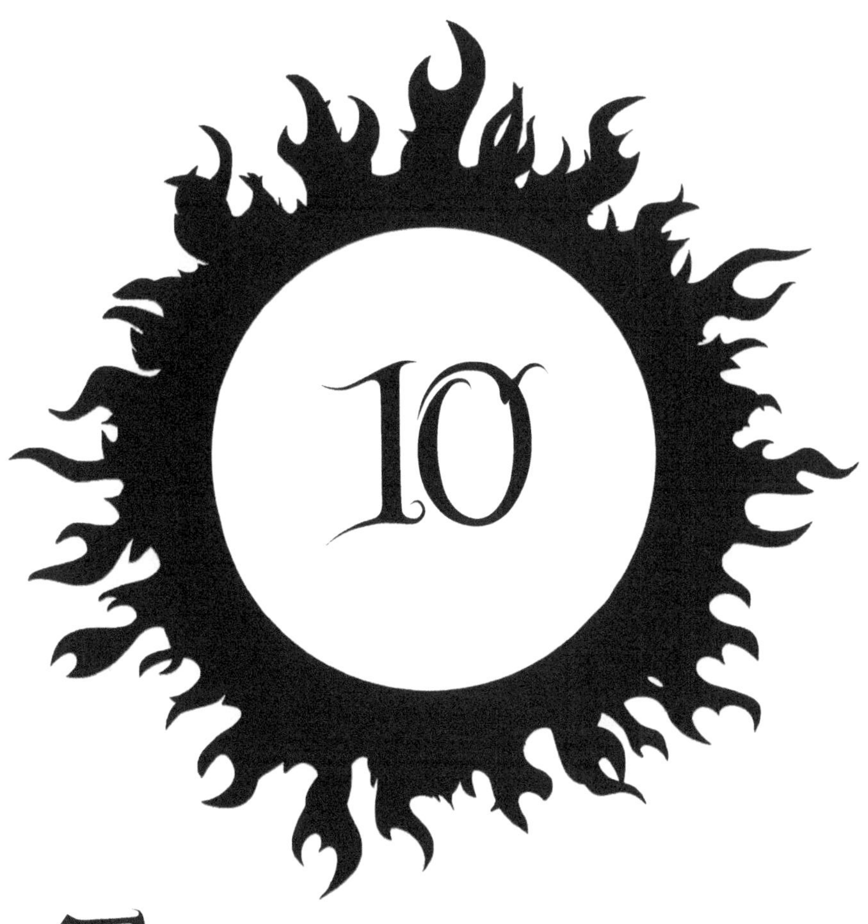

The city was worse than I remembered. The towering buildings were crumbling, and the roads were littered with rusted cars and corpses. The bones of the departed peeked through the gnawed flesh—the Fae who had tried to enter the city, and the Common who couldn't survive it. The only movement was the autumn leaves racing across the pavement.

It wasn't like the cities to the north; they had been destroyed immediately. The military had bombed the place, hoping it would kill the monsters. But the only thing it did was murder all the people who lived there and make it an unlivable piece of land.

Perth, though, flourished in human sickness. The Guise were drawn to it, creating a circle of death around the infected land.

"You wanted to drive. Take your pick. There are trucks, broncos, bugs, and I think there's a corvette hiding under that fallen streetlight." I pointed to a gridlocked intersection. The cars were crammed together in panic. Nature had managed to reach far into the city, its vines crawling through the shattered windows.

The elf cringed.

"You expected something better?" I taunted.

"No, it's just..."

"What is it?" I asked, limping my way along the highway. My ankle had improved during our rest under the bridge, but it ached the more I used it.

"The chaos that caused all this. The humans must have been so scared when the Guise appeared." I followed his gaze, and it led to a small hybrid car crushed between two trucks; the back door was open, and a child's car seat dangled from the seatbelt.

"Yeah, we were."

Cole whipped his head to me, realizing what he had said. "I'm sorry, I didn't mean to bring it up."

"It's fine."

"Where were you when it happened?" he asked softly, worried about my reaction, but too curious to resist.

"At a small bookstore in Glasgow. My mother and I went there every week to pick out a new book." I smiled at the memory. "It was something that only we shared. Father didn't go into the city unless he had to, and Lugh was too young." I listened for Lugh's breath before speaking again. "I tried to teach him to read after the Collapse, but surviving takes up a lot of time, and it's especially hard when you're hiding in the dark."

"Maybe when he's healed you can find someone to cast a language spell on him," Cole suggested.

"A language spell?"

"Yes, each Fae is given the spell when they're born. There's no need to learn to read and write. It's put in their mind already. Every language on Earth, both Common and Fae." Cole carefully stepped over a dog's corpse.

"I always wondered how the Fae could understand me. Now I know, they cheated in school." I smiled at the elf, amazed with the world I had yet to uncover.

He straightened his posture, adjusting Lugh. "Perhaps it would spare the humans some disagreements if they learned that way." The sky wasn't so black anymore, and I could now see the cracks in the pavement. The knife was kept dark as to not attract unwanted attention.

"Probably, but it would rob people like me of the satisfaction of hard work. Of mastering something. Do the Fae cast spells for every skill?" We carefully climbed over a car that blocked our path. I silently prayed that the alarm didn't still work, while Cole pushed Lugh across the hood to me before picking him up again on the other side.

"Mostly, but just like humans, some Fae are better at things than others. Even with the knowledge." The elf's dark hair fell into his eyes; he kept it longer than most human men, though Lugh's was quickly catching up.

"Are you good at anything in particular? Or do you let the magic do it all for you?" I teased, worried that he would hear the strain in my voice.

Cole peeked at me through the ebony strands. "I would tell you, but I'm afraid that you would think I'm flirting. And I don't want to put you through that horror again," he mocked.

With a huff, I said, "Tell me."

"Lovemaking."

I punched his arm. "Tell me," I demanded.

Laughing, he said, "Fine, fine. I've had many skill spells cast on me, but the one I enjoy the most would have to be the flute."

It was difficult to maintain a straight face. "That's wonderful. Very fitting."

"Are you laughing at my skill?" His brows lifted, challenging me.

"No, not at all. It's a very useful skill. It will feed and shelter you when the nights are cold." A giggle finally broke through my thick armor.

"Yes, it will. Just like reading. Tell me, what does that say in the distance? Will it lead us to safety?" Cole gestured to the street sign ahead, beaming from ear to ear.

I knew the elf was teasing me, but I read the sign anyway. "No, but we now know the crosswalk is just ahead. We are doing some major jaywalking right now. We're lucky there's not a cop around to see it." I glanced toward the sign again and caught movement. I pulled Cole and Lugh behind a car and waited.

A gunshot sounded, and the bullet planted itself in the car behind us. "Was that a gun?" Cole asked, his voice both curious and horrified.

"Definitely." Someone had either found a forgotten stash or knew how to make more ammunition. "Let's move. Keep low and behind the cars." I pointed to a sewer cover. "We can hide down there." Quickly and silently, we found ourselves near the cap behind a crushed Kia, but the hole itself wasn't hidden. "The cap is heavy. It's going to take both of us to lift it."

"No, stay here with Lugh. I'll get it."

"I think you're overestimating yourself." A shot landed in the car we were at moments ago. They had lost track of us.

"I can do it. Trust me." I tensed at the request, though he didn't stop for my response.

Praying it was dark enough, I watched as Cole crawled to the manhole and tucked his thin fingers into the small openings in its side. He pulled, but it didn't move. A bullet flew by Cole's head, chipping the sidewalk. "Please, please, be strong enough," I prayed, clutching Lugh tight against me, and ready to leap into the hole at a moment's notice. There was a ladder below. There had to be.

Cole had lifted the cover a few inches when another shot sounded, but I didn't see it land. The elf cried out as he finally lifted and slid the lid aside. "Get in," he ordered. His bow hung over his shoulder, but we both knew it wouldn't do anything against a gun.

Keeping as small as possible, I slid Lugh with me to the opening and lowered myself in. Cole placed Lugh on my shoulder, and it took all my strength to keep a grip on the damp ladder rungs while I descended into the darkness below. Cole followed, but paused to slide the cap into place. Three more shots rang before he was done.

Soon, the cap was closed, and the dim skylight was gone. The endowed weapon lit without instruction. It was a long, slow crawl down. Lugh had never felt so heavy before, and my ankle was screaming. Drops of mysterious liquid dripped onto my face on the way down. *I did not miss the sewers.*

Taking a deep breath, I jumped onto the cement floor below, the ladder nonexistent past my feet. I gripped Lugh's head against my shoulder, and hoped that I didn't break him when I landed. I couldn't help the sob that escaped me while I laid on the ground, my tailbone aching. My ankle was surely broken by now. Lugh's heart sped, but a quick check told me that he had survived the fall.

Cole jumped next and collapsed. "Cole!" I laid Lugh down gently and went to the elf's side. "Are you all right?" I turned him onto his back. That's when I saw the blood.

"It's just a scratch," he whispered, unable to speak any louder. He had been shot in the chest— right above the heart. The magic bow and quiver had been tossed aside.

"Damn it, Cole." The elf raised his hand and stroked my face. Blood dripped down his fingers. "It's yours," I whispered, realizing it had been blood falling on me.

"Good. I'm glad you're safe. Is Lugh?" Cole tried to raise his head to see but winced instead.

"He's fine." I ripped a section of my shirt off and tucked it against the wound. I grabbed Cole's cold hand and placed it there. "Keep pressure on it."

"There's no need to get naked, Yvaine. I don't want pity sex. It's just not the same." Blood seeped from his weak grip, and he coughed.

"Can you ever stop making jokes? It's not the time." I threw my braid over my shoulder, irritated.

"If I stop, that means I'm dead." Pausing my plan for a moment, I stared into the elf's eyes. *Fear.*

"If you think for one second that I would give you any kind of sex, then you haven't been listening." I took my jacket and Lugh's off, and tied each arm together.

"Even if I'm dying, huh? You are ruthless." He choked on the last word, unable to take in a real breath. His strong build shuddered with pain.

"You know it." I looked down the tunnel, trying to recall what street we had been on. "Did you save any of that rope I tied you in?"

"Inside pocket."

I reached into his coat and pulled out more rope than I thought one could fit in a pocket. I needed to get the bullet out of Cole, but whoever shot at us might come looking. And we couldn't be here when they did. "Can you walk?" My voice was calm, no emotion was allowed through my barriers. I would not fall apart again.

Cole nodded, preparing for the terrible journey ahead. I tied the rope under Lugh's arms and around my waist. He was laid on the jackets with the nearest coat arm knotted together with the rope. I couldn't carry Lugh if I was going to help Cole walk. I shoved down the pain in my throbbing ankle and helped Cole to his feet. The elf brought his weapon up with him, his breathing hard and unsteady.

I said, "Steady, deep breaths. We move slow. I know where we can rest." *If the camp was still there. If no one had claimed it. If I could find it.* But it was our only chance for protection.

Trusting me, Cole hung his arm across my shoulders, pressing hard against his wound with the other hand. I hoped it was enough. I supported the elf's weight while he bled, and dragged my brother behind me in the damp sewer.

Finley led us down a narrow path, and away from the main tunnel. I followed, eager to find more food and maybe a fire. I was shivering in the damp cold; Lugh was wearing my sweater over his. Winter was departing, but the chill was still there. It had been a long, cold season, and I was done with it. All of it.

"We're almost there," Finley threw over his shoulder, completely at ease with the strangers at his back. I couldn't blame him. We weren't much of a threat—a half-starved teenager and child. The man's blade gleamed as we passed under grates. The sun was finally fading.

The narrow tunnel ended, and what resided there was a room big enough for a small family. A tarp was draped over the space, protecting the bedding from sewer condensation. There was a small opening, high above. A ladder was placed below it, but at the moment, it rested horizontally. I could barely see the blue bucket outside. "Snow," I said.

He followed my gaze and nodded. "I prefer water that hasn't touched the ground yet."

"Won't someone steal it?"

"It's just a burnt warehouse above us. Doesn't attract many visitors." Finley reached inside a crate, and I raised my blade out of habit. He eyed me, but continued what he was doing. He pulled out three red-brown packages, and my mouth watered.

"Jerky," I exclaimed, too excited to be suspicious.

"What's jerky?" Lugh asked. My excitement disappeared, knowing that he had been too young to enjoy such a treat, and had too weak of a sister to find him any after the Collapse.

"Jerky is dried meat," Finley explained.

"That doesn't sound very good," he responded, still wary of Finley.

"Oh, it is though. It has lots of seasoning, and it'll take away that gnawing in your belly."

Lugh's bow lowered, his arms either gave out or his stomach had. "Go ahead Lugh. It's good," I encouraged.

With that, we both took the offering, ripping the packaging open with our teeth and shoving the meat down our throats. Finley offered us clean water to wash it down with, and it was heaven. "Sleep now. I'll watch over you," he said.

Exhausted, I took Lugh to the corner of the space and laid on one of the sleeping bags there. The knife never left my hand.

"Yvaine, are you going to make it?"

With a jolt of surprise, I was back in reality. *I passed out. Damn it.*

"Yes, just a little farther." I did not get us lost. We didn't have time to be lost. Cole was heavier than before. I looked back and saw that Lugh was slipping out of his binding. "How are you holding up?" I asked. It had been a couple of hours since we left the entrance, but we had not spoken in that time; we were both in too much pain.

"Fine," he said. *He didn't make a joke.*

I pushed us faster, knowing I had to get the bullet out. One hour later, Magic or God answered my prayers, and I saw the gap in the wall where the side tunnel began. The two of us barely squeezed through side-by-side, but we made our way down the long, winding path until we reached the camp.

No one had touched it since we left. Finley was but a skeleton now.

The tarp still hung in place, and the crate still sat in the corner. I lowered Cole down onto the damp, moldy sleeping bag, untied myself from Lugh, and went to the box. I sent one last prayer into the universe before opening it, and for a second time, it was answered.

Packaged treats, jerky, and canned corn beef hash rested there, waiting to be devoured. I tore open a twinkie and shoved it down my throat. Then three more. As I ate, I dug into the chest and found a small emergency kit; it had some bandages and a needle and thread. And two bottles of scotch tucked beneath it.

I turned to the entrance, waiting for someone to come bursting through and attack us, knowing this good luck would not last long. I went to Cole with my findings. Lifting his shirt, I was able to see the wound better, and I swallowed a gasp.

"That bad, huh?" he choked.

"Eat this." I shoved a twinkie in his mouth, begging him to keep quiet during this. "I haven't removed a bullet before, so I'm sorry in advance." I poured the scotch generously over the wound.

Unsheathing my knife, I stared at the tip and wished it to obey me in this endeavor. I gave Cole a sip of the scotch and the rope to bite on. I took a few swigs of the drink to calm my nerves. "Not too much, she-beast. I want to live through this," the elf mumbled around the rope.

"Sadly, for both of us, she isn't here right now." With that said, the tip of my blade entered the wound and searched for the hidden bullet. The elf screamed around his bit, and I worried that people would find us if he continued. I sped my search, feeling every nook and cranny of the torn flesh with my blade and fingers. In the very deepest part of the hole, I felt metal clang against the blade. Removing the narrow-tipped knife, I pinched my thumb and forefinger, and pulled the bullet excruciatingly slow out of him; it was slick with blood, and I didn't want to shock Cole further.

The trophy in hand, I poured the scotch over the opening again, applied pressure, and began the next horrible thing: stitching with a too-small needle and too-thick thread. I gave the elf another swig of scotch and placed the rope back in his mouth. I didn't risk another sip myself, as I was going to pass out from the pressure. Blood and sweat made my hands slick, and my nerves made them shaky. I couldn't thread the needle. I stopped for a moment and took a breath.

"Keep going," Cole said, holding his wound closed with the piece of torn shirt.

I nodded and tried again. This time, Cole supported my needle hand, keeping it still. I forced the string through the small opening and tied it off. "Ready?"

The elf answered by squeezing my hand, then placing his own on my knee. And I let him. We both needed the comfort. After a while, I developed a rhythm, learning how the skin moved under the needle, and whispering prayers I'd heard my mother say before bedtime.

Footsteps echoed outside. I didn't see anything beyond the small opening at the top of the wall, but I stopped stitching and dragged Lugh under the tarp with us and out of sight. I dimmed the dirk as I finished patching Cole's wound, just waiting for the next bad thing to happen.

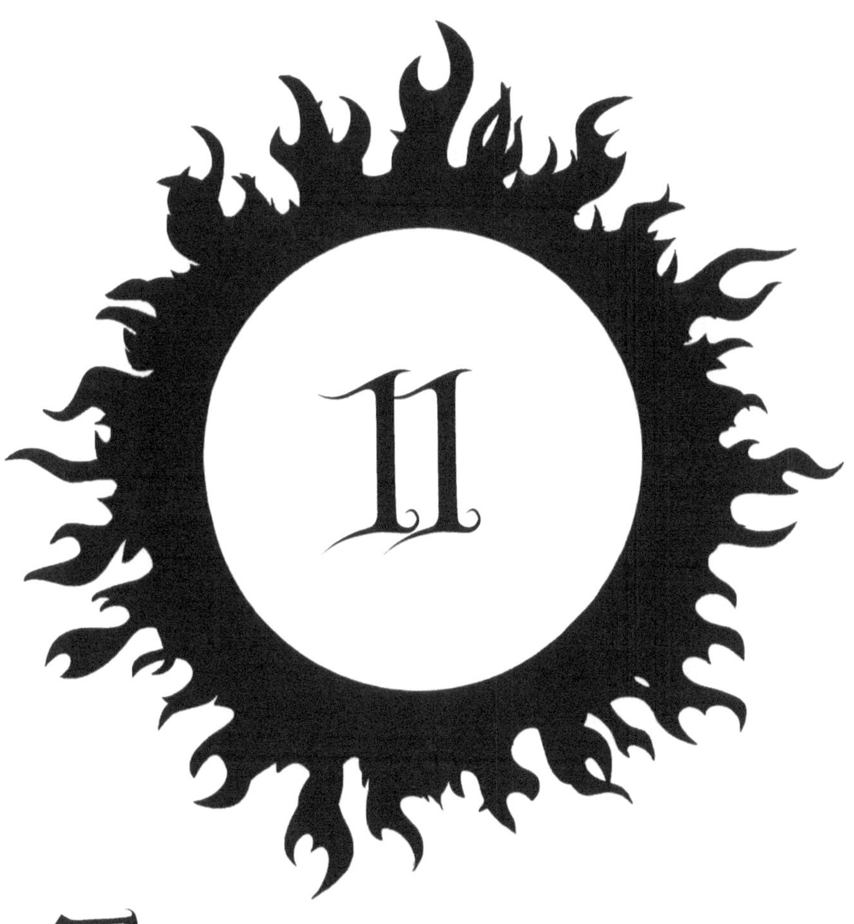

The first thing I did was cover Finley's body with a tarp. Then I recreated the trap he had left behind. One long, thin string hung across the doorway, no higher than the ankle. Out of sight and behind the stone walls, the string was attached to small bells. If someone was going to attack us, we would know about it first.

I stayed awake anyway, the pain in my ankle keeping me alert. Lugh's heart was strong, but the leaf had yellowed farther, so I gave him the remainder of our water. Cole was sleeping now, but his breathing would hitch now and again, as if pain shot through him in intervals.

How were we ever going to make it to the stones?

The footsteps echoed outside again, but I suspected it was a lone dog sniffing around. I could hear it digging in the rubble above, and then sound a sad whine when it didn't find anything. "Are you still awake?" Cole whispered.

It had been silent for so long, I flinched at his voice. "Yes. Someone has to guard you two." I gave him a small smile, trying to show how completely fine I was.

He wasn't buying it. "We're safe. No one has been here in a long time. It's time to rest." Cole handed me the bottle of scotch that he'd been clinging to all day.

I shook my head.

"Yvaine," *damn him and his sultry voice*, "you need to sleep."

"I can't." I looked away, toward the doorway, wishing to escape into the tunnels. But I was trapped. Again.

"Why?" Cole shifted, so he was inclined against a moldy pillow.

With a long, tired sigh, I said, "This is where it happened. Where he tried to hurt me. *Finley.*"

Cole's eyes widened, and he glanced to the covered corpse. "Why did you bring us here?"

"There was nowhere else to go."

The elf took a real look around, assumably for the first time. "These were his supplies?"

"Yes," I answered. Cole offered me the scotch again, and this time, I took it. Inhaling a burning gulp, I said, "Doesn't matter now. He's dead and gone. These supplies belong to us now." I tipped the bottle toward Finley in acknowledgment.

I passed the scotch back to Cole. He drained it and opened the second bottle. "To the dead who keep on giving." He took a blazing sip and passed it to me.

"To the living who keep on taking." The scotch filled my aching stomach, and I slumped against the slimy wall.

Cole unzipped his sleeping bag. "It's cold. Get under the blanket."

I smiled knowingly. I crawled to the beckoning warmth, assured that Lugh was wrapped tightly, and the doorway was secure. The bottle met my lips one last time before I climbed into the bag with Cole and zipped it behind me.

The alcohol and exhaustion muddled my mind, so I wrapped my arms around his torso and said, "Thank you."

"For what?" The elf stiffened, surprised by my touch. But he relaxed and rested his arm along my shoulders, tucking me into his strong but wounded chest.

I retreated. "Shit, your heart."

He pulled me close. "No, it feels better with you here."

Glad to be beside him, I answered his question. "Thank you for staying."

"You've had quite a bit to drink, haven't you?"

"Not enough," I muttered, falling asleep in the elf's arms. My thoughts and body were blissfully numb, as I fell into the abyss. But at the last moment, a truth wormed its way in: *People only help when they want something from you.*

Too late to move from his grasp, I fell asleep, knowing it was only a matter of time before Cole revealed his own truth.

The knife was still in my hand when I woke, but Lugh was nowhere to be seen. "Lugh?" I called, my voice still rough from sleep.

"The boy went to relieve himself. He'll be back soon." Finley's voice surprised me, and I lurched upward. "Calm down, cutie. It's just me." He was sit-

ting beside a small fire. It burned below the wall's opening; the airflow fresh enough to have one. A cat roasted there, and its skin was laid aside to dry. Vomit rose to my throat, burning me. Seeing my gaze, Finley said, "Can't afford to be picky nowadays. You a cat lover?"

I nodded, thinking of my black cat from before the Collapse. I couldn't remember her name, and I didn't know what happened to her after our parents were killed. After I saved my brother and took the endowed knife, we never returned to the house.

"That's a shame. It makes a better meal than lemon cakes and old jerky."

I nodded my agreement. Just because I liked cats, didn't mean I wouldn't resort to eating one to survive. "How long has my brother been gone?"

"Only a minute. No need to worry." Finley's muscles rippled through his tight shirt, as he stood and took the cat off the fire. His brown hair was shaved short, and his eyes saw everything.

"What were you before the Collapse?" I asked.

Surprised, he said, "Military."

"What are you doing here, then? I thought the government hid away somewhere safe while the rest of us were left to suffer." I heard these things when I eavesdropped on other humans, and honestly, it wouldn't surprise me if it were true.

Wary, he answered, "They did. I was left behind."

"Why?"

"I stayed to protect those I could." His eye twitched as he said this, but I chose to ignore it when the smell of cooked meat reached my nose. It had been so long. I set the knife down, glad to be relieved of the weight. Lugh's bow and quiver rested in the opposite corner of the room, along with Finley's sword.

"That's an uncommon trait."

With a grunt, he responded, "Yes, well, not many people agree with my philosophies."

"That's a shame." I fidgeted under his stare but forced myself to calm. He *was here to help. "I should check on Lugh." I stood and made for the exit, planning to return, when Finley stepped in front of the doorway.*

"Don't pester the poor boy. Let him piss in private."

Worried now, I said, "It's been too long. Get out of my way." I fisted my hand, expecting a handle to be there, but the knife was on the bedding behind me.

Finley's eyes darted to where it rested, so quick, I wasn't sure he had. "Stay here, like a good girl, and you won't be hurt." I blanched, remembering when my parent's murderer had called me that.

"What do you want?"

"I want you to sit down and listen to every word I say. You promised me a conversation." He walked over to my bed and picked up the blade. I considered abandoning the weapon and took a step. "Move another inch, and you won't see your brother again."

My body trembled in fear. "Where is he?"

"Alive. That's all you need to know. Now sit." I did as he instructed, powerless. I watched as he cut the meat from the cat's ribs with my knife and ate it painfully slow, his eyes never leaving me. Once he had finished his meal, he said, "Take off your clothes."

A man's hands were around me. I was too warm. My head ached.

I was exhausted.

I felt for the weapon at my side, relieved to find it there. I breathed again. *It was just a dream.* Quietly, I sat up and lifted Cole's bandage. His wound was nearly healed. *I was right!*

I shook him awake and said, "What the hell, Cole? Why are you so much better?" I knew he had been lying. He *did* have magic, and he was hiding it from us the entire time.

Shocked awake, he lurched and clutched his chest. I tumbled out of the sleeping bag, eager to get away from the liar. "What?" he mumbled. The elf felt along his stitching and noted the pink scarring. Wary, he removed the threads. "That's amazing."

"Cole, tell me how you're healed. Now." I gripped the dagger tight, his answer would determine if I used it or not.

The elf met my angry gaze, his green eyes shimmering. "You... I..." He couldn't finish his sentence.

"Cole!"

"A recovery spell. I had it cast on me," he blurted.

"Yeah? Then why didn't you recover that quickly when I stabbed you?" I thought back to the morning we woke to the banshees. He had still been very much injured. The spriggan was the one who had healed him. Or so I thought.

"I had it cast on me afterward. The spriggan healed the stab wound and gave me the spell." Cole rubbed his new scar, intrigued.

"How long is the spell supposed to last?" I questioned.

"For as long as the magic deems me worthy, I suppose." The elf looked worried.

"What did you trade him for it?"

"What do you mean?" Cole averted his gaze, staring at his scar in disbelief.

"I had to give him a hair. What did you have to give him to heal you, twice now?" My fingers itched to aim the dagger at Cole. I knew he was lying. I would not ignore the signs again.

"Nothing, he's my friend."

"Right," I spat.

"What else could it be, Yvaine?" The way he asked the question was strange. As if *I* knew the answer and was the one keeping it from *him*.

If he had me under an obedience spell or even an infatuation spell, he could not know I was aware of it. I would not risk Lugh's life for my pride. "Nothing, I suppose. I was just shocked. I'm glad you're better."

Nodding, Cole motioned to Lugh. "We should find him some water." We both looked outside—it was dark.

"We need to move on anyway. We've lost too much time." I moved through the space, gathering up the supplies and stuffing them into the hiking pack stashed in the corner.

"Sorry for getting shot. I know it was a huge inconvenience for you." I could hear Cole rolling up the bloodied sleeping bag that we'd slept in.

I exhaled a dark laugh. "Just get moving, magic man."

Our jackets had been ruined from dragging Lugh across the slimy sewer ground and Cole's had been torn and bloodied. We used the ones we'd found at Finley's shelter instead. They were warmer and cleaner, but I still hated them. Cole was well enough to carry Lugh again which was bittersweet. It confirmed that Cole was lying about having magic, but I could barely walk, let alone carry another person. Though, I did have to carry a backpack now. I could hear the scotch swishing around in the bottle, as we walked down the dank city tunnel. I wished Cole would give up the pretense and use his magic to heal my ankle. *Did he even need the stones to heal Lugh? Or was it another ruse?*

"Where are we headed?" the elf asked, distracted as we walked.

"We could take our chances and hope to find bottled water at the grocery stores, but I highly doubt we'll find any." A rat ran in front of me, and I tripped, startled. Cole caught me by the waist and righted me; it took all my energy not to push him away.

"Where then?" he asked, his hands lingering for far too long.

"The neighborhoods. The nice ones. Let's hope they have some pressure left in the wells and some water in the pipes." It had saved Lugh and I more times than we could count. People didn't think to run the faucets anymore because of the lack of electricity, but the water from before the Collapse was still underground, waiting to be taken.

"Wouldn't the water be bad by now?"

"Depends. But we'll need to boil it regardless." Lugh's breathing was unsteady, and his face was pale. "Plus, we need to get some fresh air. The sewers are not a great place to be in."

"I can smell that." Cole wrinkled his nose in distaste. "Why didn't humans just bury their waste? Did shitting really have to be such a complicated process?"

"Do you know how many times I've stepped in shit while I was walking in the woods? At least humans tried to hide it by sending it down pipes." The slime along the walls reflected in the dagger's light, and I nearly hurled.

"And where do the pipes go?"

"Into a tank to be treated. And then redistributed." I smiled, knowing the reaction to come.

"Redistributed?"

"To drink," I clarified.

"No," Cole said, disbelief ringing in his voice.

"Except for those with well water, of course. But those who use the city water, yes." I laughed, acknowledging just how disgusting it was.

"Humans," he muttered.

"It's better than no water at all." We turned to the left, down another long tunnel, but I remembered the sewer cap wasn't far.

"It's called a river, stream, creek. You know, running water." Cole slowed his pace, despite the fact that I was speeding up. *I hated being weak.*

"Yeah, well, that can make us sick, too." The stench of the sewers made my eyes water, and I hurried my pace even more, eager for the fresh night air.

Cole shifted Lugh, so my brother's limp limbs flailed. I squeezed my brother's cold hand. "If humans drink their own waste, I don't think a little river water is going to kill them," the elf commented.

A rat ran across my foot, but this time, I kicked it into the water. "You'd be surprised what can kill us, *elf*." I stopped and looked up, searching. "Humans have been known to die from a broken heart, and I'm not talking about a heart attack." Raising the glowing blade, I saw the ladder and its heavenly ascent to freedom.

Cole switched Lugh to his other shoulder and winced. "Spells usually fix things like that."

I looked to the Fae, not with hate or anger, but disappointment. "Not everything can be fixed with magic, Cole."

The elf responded with a look of shame, though I couldn't understand why. "Stay here." Cole put Lugh down, climbed up the rungs, and pushed the cover aside. He stuck his head out, and I half expected another shot to sound, but he returned safely and said, "It's clear." With that, he picked Lugh up and climbed with him to the surface, reaching for me once I was near the top. He lifted me right out of the dank hole and placed me on my feet.

"How are you so strong? Strength spell?" I couldn't hide my curiosity any longer.

With a smirk, he answered, "No, it's all natural."

"Glad something is."

The smirk disappeared. "What's that supposed to mean?"

"Nothing, let's get moving before the sun shines." The elf didn't push for an answer, but he did watch me carefully as we made our way to suburbs.

We found the neighborhoods with only moments of darkness to spare. We searched for the house with the least amount of damage. Lawns were beyond overgrown, but I could still see the smashed windows and broken-down doors. Looters and murders had acted quickly when the Guise arrived. They didn't run and hide like most; all they could think of was taking from those who were frightened, defenseless, and alone. And those who were left of the innocent became scavengers in order to survive, leaving most homes empty of supplies. *Those people weren't innocent anymore.*

I spotted a creek flowing through a patch of trees. I considered taking water directly from it, but there was a decayed human corpse lying at its edge, which forced my decision. Following the soiled water, we found a small, pale house at the end of the street that had only one window busted, its place in the trees keeping it hidden. I nodded in its direction, and Cole agreed silently. There could be anyone around, so it was important that we stayed silent. In the forest, we had to worry about predators, but in the city, it was our own kind. They had become monsters, and I was not going to fall victim to them again.

The paved driveway was cracked, and weeds grew furiously upward. The sky had transformed into pale saffron. If this house didn't have water, we would have to stay anyway. The sun was about to trap us, and once the light was bright enough, the Guise would appear everywhere. It would no longer be a human city, but a light infestation.

The back door was untouched and locked. I wrapped my hand in the sweater I'd tied around my waist. My fist was through the glass square and unlocking the deadbolt before Cole could stop me. "Yvaine, I could have done that. You already have a bad ankle."

"And you got shot yesterday, so what?"

"That's different," he said, exasperated.

"Oh yes, because you can heal yourself. Why don't you spread some of that magic to me, huh?" I twisted the doorknob and stepped into the moldy house. The dust mites must have really enjoyed their rise in power over the last decade.

"I wish I could," Cole whispered, defeated.

Right.

The back door led into a kitchen. The living room was just beyond it, a counter the only thing in between. There was a large cream couch centered with the TV mounted on the wall; the screen was cracked. The wallpaper was the same cream color with pink roses throughout; the paper was peeling. A small fireplace rested in the corner, firewood prepped and ready to use. All in all, very open and homey. I coughed up stale air.

The kitchen sink was full of dishes, but I held my breath against the stench as I turned on the faucet. Water spewed out. First brown, then rust, then clear. *When was our luck going to run out?*

I dug through the pile of dishes for the pot at the bottom. And as I was digging, a bowl, which had rested on top, was knocked aside. Chili residue, and it wasn't dry or molded. The last couple beans that sat in the bottom of the dish looked good enough to eat.

The dirk was in my hand. I motioned to Cole. Lugh was placed under the kitchen table and covered with our gear. The elf nocked an arrow and entered the living room, trailing right, toward a mud room. I took the stairs adjacent to the kitchen, grateful for the silent wooden steps. Pictures hung on the wall, tilted but unharmed. An older couple with children and grandchildren smiled in the photos. A wedding was the first picture I saw; the grandparents and owners of this house. They were married near the ruins of Troy. It was a strange choice, but once I saw more of their ventures in the pictures, I concluded that they were history buffs, and it made sense.

There were three rooms upstairs: a master and guest bedroom, and one bathroom. Quietly, I searched the small bathroom, noting any fresh disturbances. None. Next was the guest bedroom. The sheets were still made, ready for visitors; most likely grandchildren, according to the toys scattered about. I tensed, knowing I was going to have to open the closet, which would surely make noise.

The double door clicked open, and the hinges squeaked. Nothing but spare coats and shoes. We would have to make use of them. They were certainly better than our sewer scented sweaters and shit-covered boots.

The master bedroom wasn't as neat. The bedding had been used recently. The dust was disturbed, and I could see foot impressions in the carpet. A jacket was slung over the bedpost. I reached out and touched the cotton material—it was cold. The closet was empty. The only things left were hangers strewn along the ground. *I hope they'd escaped the city with their family in time.*

Worried about Cole, I hurried down the stairs. *Why did I still care?* Even knowing I was under a spell didn't change the effects. And there was only one way I'd ever be free of it.

Cole met me at the bottom of the stairs. "No one's here."

"They must have moved on," I guessed. "Let's search the kitchen. Maybe they missed something, and we can have some dinner." I thought of the bowl of chili, and my stomach ached.

Weapon sheathed and guard down, I entered the kitchen and froze. "Take another step and he dies." A girl, a few years younger than me, held a hatchet to Lugh's throat. Our bag had been emptied onto the tiled floor, exposing our stash of provisions.

A voice that would scare even death itself rumbled out of me. "If he dies, you will wish that you could trade places with him." I took a step.

The girl was smart enough to look frightened. "Just give me your stash, and I'll leave. No need for *anyone* to get hurt." The hatchet rested against my brother's skin. His eyelids twitched, and I wondered if he was going to wake.

The cupboard door under the kitchen sink was open; that's where she had hidden. If she wanted our food so badly, the place must have been empty. We couldn't afford to waste the measly meals we had. Our energy was waning, and there was much more land to cross before we reached the stones. I took another step. "Fine." I nudged a packaged treat in her direction. "Take it and leave."

The girl slowly removed her weapon from Lugh's throat and reached for the food. I leapt and planted my foot on the hatchet's handle, trapping it against the floor. She raised her head, and I kneed her in the nose. The girl released the weapon and clutched her face. I kicked her in the ribs, and she collapsed on her side, choking. The hatchet slid toward Lugh. I raised my blade, numbness washing over me in this time of need.

"Stop!" Cole rushed to my side and blocked the strike.

"What the hell are you doing? Get out of my way," I demanded. Pushing him aside, I raised the blade again, but he attacked from behind and twisted my arms back, so they were pinned between our bodies. The blade dropped to the floor, chipping the tile. The girl peeked through her blood-soaked fingers at the glowing weapon mere feet from her.

"She's just a girl. You don't have to kill her," Cole breathed in my ear.

I struggled against the elf's hold, but he was too strong. "Let her live, and she will kill *us*." Cole didn't know how the city worked. It wasn't the same as the forest. There, the predators hunted and killed to survive. But the city... People killed not only to survive, but for pleasure. And they did much more than kill when their prey was caught.

"She can't take both of us. Look at her, she's starving." Cole motioned toward the window. "The sun is up, and she has nowhere to go right now. She's under our control. Once night falls, we can all go our separate ways."

"You don't know what you're doing." I clenched my teeth, eager to be rid of the threat.

"And as I said before, the *other woman* is blind. Let me help." The *other woman* was cruel at times, yes. The numbness removed any doubt from my mind and had allowed me to do unspeakable things to survive.

But that part of me wasn't here now. I felt every emotion coursing through me: the anger, fear, and sadness. Every touch Cole gave and every breath that teased my neck was clear in my mind.

And still, my instinct said to kill this girl.

"It's not like I can stop you, is it? Let me go," I spat.

Cole loosened his grip. "I'm trying to do the right thing."

"I'm sure." *Just like he did the right thing by casting this spell on me.*

The elf led me to Lugh's side, and I took the bait, kneeling to examine him. There was a slight cut on his neck beside his scar. It was as deep as a papercut, but the fact that the girl had touched him at all had my insides boiling. I wiped the blood from Lugh's throat and straightened his jacket, tucking the hatchet discreetly into the backpack.

The girl was crying now. Her knees were tucked in, and she had bloody palms covering her mouth. But there was a glint in her eyes—one I was familiar with. Cole picked up my knife and stashed it in his inside jacket pocket. "We won't hurt you. Here, let's get you cleaned up." Cole offered his hand.

After only a small moment of hesitation, the girl took it and stood. The tears came flooding out, and she bawled. I nearly laughed at the over-acting, but then she embraced Cole and said, "Thank you. Thank you. I'm sorry. I was just so scared." She clung to Cole's shirt, and to my instant fury, he wrapped his arms around her.

With a tight jaw, I said, "Watch your hands, girl. You'll cut yourself." Cole seemed to realize what I meant and gently stepped out from her embrace, keeping the knife at a safe distance.

"Please, don't hurt me. I'm alone. All I'm trying to do is find food." She wrapped her arms around the bruised ribs, and I smiled at the broken nose above her lips.

"I'll do much worse than hurt you if you touch my brother again." The smile stayed, and the girl recoiled.

Clearing his throat, Cole offered, "All right, why don't we all sit down and have a…" he looked to the wrapped human food, "something."

"Don't turn your nose up at it now. It's all we got. I'm sure that *hatchet swinger* already scoped out the place." I couldn't calm the rage. *What was wrong with me?*

"Did you?" he asked her, his eyes full of sympathy.

"Yes, there was only one can of chili. The rest had already been taken." She continued to cry but looked to me when Cole was distracted.

I should kill her now. "Make a fire. We need to boil the water." I pulled out the pot and filled it as high as it would go.

"But the smoke will attract others," the girl said.

I looked out the window and into the blue sky and gold sunshine. The Guise swarmed the house. Luckily, most of the windows had dark shades, and they couldn't come inside. I closed the one I looked out of now. "If there are people stupid enough to hunt us on this nice day, they are welcome to it." For once, the Guise were a blessing.

"What's your name?" Cole asked the girl.

"Nessa," she sniffed.

"Nessa, clean yourself up, and I'll prep the fire." The girl nodded and went upstairs to the bathroom. Or to grab a stashed weapon.

"Don't trust her."

Cole stared into my dark-blue gaze for a moment before speaking. "You took a chance on me. What makes her any different?"

That was exactly my point. My eyes lowered. "Well, how can I argue with that?"

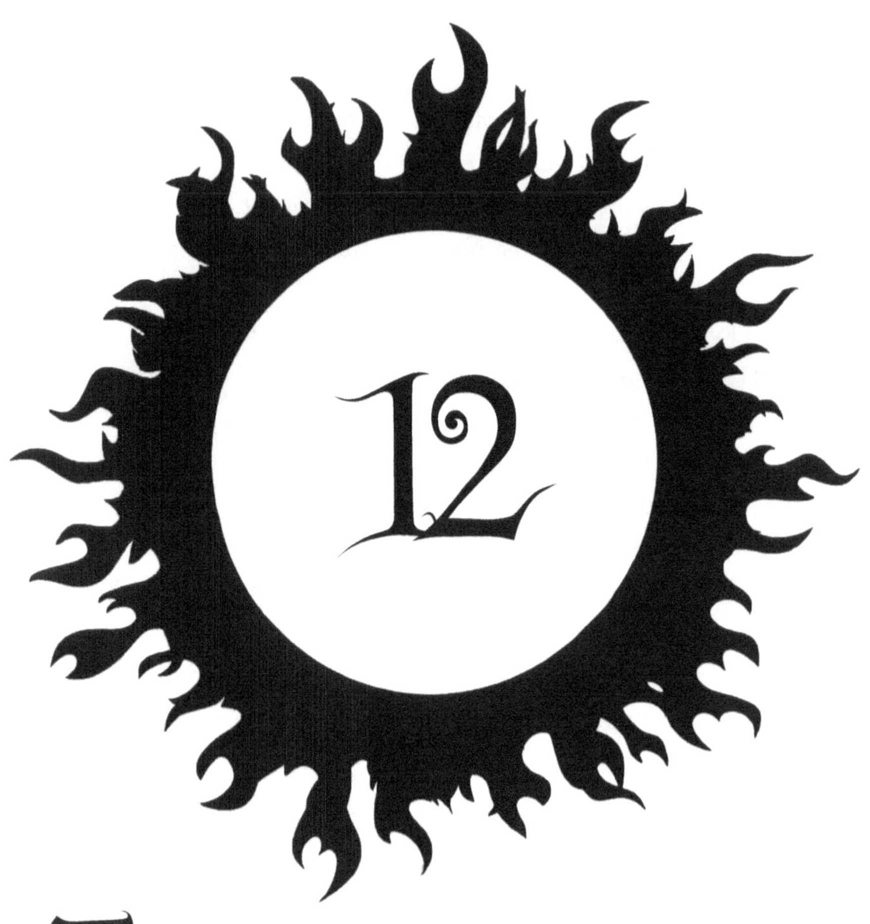

12

The girl, Nessa, sat near the fire. Her nose had been reset, but she couldn't hide the bruising beneath her eyes. She was twitchy and a poor actress, though, Cole gave her his attention anyway. She was short, no more than five-foot two. Her hair was chopped into a pixie cut; the name was ironic because pixies didn't actually have hair at all, but long soft feathers. The girl's eyes were dark, nearly black, and full of immoral thoughts. I had spent enough time around city scavengers to know the look. Because I had been one of them.

"Are you alone, Nessa?" Cole asked. I didn't know why he bothered. Her answer didn't matter. She would lie at every turn.

"Yes. I've been moving from house to house for supplies, but this was the first one that had anything." She took Cole's hand where he sat on the floor beside her. I was in the only chair watching the train wreck of an interaction. "I'm sorry that I ate it all. If I knew you were going to be here, I would have saved some for you." Cole had provided a twinkie for everyone, though they had disappeared quickly.

A chuckle escaped me.

"You find something funny?" she scoffed.

"Yeah, Lugh is drooling again." We all looked to my brother, where he was wrapped in fresh clothes and blankets, his mouth hanging open. The leaf, at least, hadn't yellowed farther. I stood and tended to my helpless sibling.

"What's on his tongue?" The girl tried to approach, but the sound that came out of me could have been compared to a growl. And she didn't seem to like it.

"An herb to ease his pain," I lied. One thing about living among the city folk, my lying skills had been perfected. It was essential to one's survival. One wrong word, and the others would rape you, kill you, or eat you. Or all of those combined, and not necessarily in that order.

"Why let him suffer? It's not like he's going to heal." The scavenger picked at her nails while she said the cruel words.

"How could you possibly know that?" I said, my blood boiling.

"Banshee poison, right? I can see he's pretty far along." She pointed to Lugh's wrist, and I withheld a gasp. His veins had blackened. The poison was spreading, and we were running out of time.

"We have hope that he will pull through," Cole explained.

"You know something that I don't? It takes magic to cure something like that." Her voice was grating on my nerves. The scotch beckoned from my bag, but I was unwilling to share it. The relief would have to wait.

I looked away from Lugh just long enough to see Cole pull his hair back and reveal his elvish heritage. "We're on our way to find some," he said.

"An elf," the girl squeaked.

"Cole, what the hell?" With wide eyes, I said much more, berating him for such a stupid move. I knew I should have covered him up before we entered the city, though, I thought we would be safe with the long hair. But apparently, the elf wanted to advertise himself to a bunch of Fae-hating humans, so my efforts would have been in vain anyway.

"We're headed to the mountains and need help getting through the city. If you navigate us past the dangerous bits, you can come with us." Cole dropped his hair, and it fell over his ears again. I couldn't help but follow the silky strands and trace his sharp face with my eyes.

The girl was staring at me when I looked over. "What do I need magic for? I've got all I need right here in the city." Nessa stared at my ears, wondering if she had wrongly mistaken me for a human, too. The pot boiled over from its place in the hearth. Using oven mitts—an item I hadn't seen since my mother had cooked in our kitchen—I set the scalding water aside to cool.

Despite the stupidity, it was a good idea to have a guide. It had been years since I'd been to Perth. Territory lines had changed and worse humans had taken over. Answering the girl's question, I bitterly said, "Because you're alone and starving. Magic can give you food, beauty, youth, and love. Why would you not want that?"

Considering for only a second, she said, "Prove that you have magic. I ain't a fool."

Opening my mouth to tell her the bad news, Cole said, "Yvaine, show her your knife—the magic knife." I gave the elf a patronizing expression. *Would she really be that stupid?* The elf handed me the blade, and I commanded it to light. The pale-purple glow mesmerized the scavenger; a shiny object that she instinctually wanted. Cole immediately took the blade back, and it took all my strength not to snap his arm before he could.

"You an elf, too?" She looked to my rounded ears again.

"No, but he gave me this magic. We are going to the mountains to renew his powers because he was wounded and needs to recharge." The lie was well delivered, and the girl bought it.

"All right, I'll help."

"Great," Cole and I said simultaneously; one with vigor and the other with disdain. Lugh's eyelids twitched, making me wonder what he was dreaming about.

The sun finally descended after the horribly long day. I was forced to watch Nessa flirt and fawn over Cole. I had to endure her lies and disgusting lust-filled eyes.

I sat up in my chair, unable to sleep for fear of the nightmares returning. Lugh slept peacefully in clean clothes and blankets near the fire. Nessa had gone upstairs to sleep, and insisted that Cole come along because she was frightened of the Guise. I was just grateful I didn't hear anything coming from that direction. *Could Cole have cast a spell on her?* She was deceitful, yes, but lustful for an elf? It didn't seem right. Clearly, I was not enough for the greedy Fae. He wasn't so different from his father after all.

Cole entered the living room, adjusting his new clothes. "Looking good. Did *Nessa* pick those out for you?" I sneered.

"She tried, but no, I picked out my own clothes." The elf paused what he was doing and checked Lugh's pulse. "His heartbeat is strong. We still have time."

"Thank you for the report, Doctor Magic."

"Is there a reason you're being so difficult?" Cole approached and stood before me, while I lounged nonchalantly in the chair. My new boots and jacket were a bit too small for comfort, but it was better than sewer-soaked rags.

"I'm always difficult. Haven't you noticed?" I said, ignoring his piercing stare.

"Yes, but you're different since we entered the city. Is there something you need to tell me?" Cole fiddled with the buttons on his new shirt, confused by the human design.

"I could say the same." I met his green-eyed gaze with ferocity. *Admit it, liar.*

"What do you—"

"We going to head out? Or are both of you comfortable dying here? Someone had to have seen the chimney smoke today." Nessa bounded down the stairs and clung to Cole's side.

"Let's go then," I agreed. At least his spell would keep Nessa in check.

"Yvaine," Cole started. He reached a hand outward to help me up from the chair.

Instead, I held out my own hand and demanded, "Knife." The elf was wary, and his hand retreated. "Assuming that you still have it." I glanced toward the girl.

What looked like hurt flashed in his eyes. "Of course I still have it." He reached into the inside pocket of his leather jacket; the house's owner had good taste. What a shame he had to leave it behind.

The blade came alive upon seeing me, and a warmth filled my bones—one that I hadn't known disappeared. The pearl grip fit in my palm perfectly, as if it was made with me specifically in mind. "For your sake, I'm glad. Now," I sheathed the dagger, and the light dimmed, "let's be on our way."

"How's your ankle?" Cole asked, barring my path to Lugh.

"Fine." It throbbed, but I had found medical tape in one of the cupboards, and it was wrapped securely.

"Why don't I look at it before we go? You're terrible at wrapping." Cole smiled, and most of the time it sent my heart into overdrive, but with Nessa clinging to his side, I just wanted to stab him again.

Maybe he could only concentrate his spell on one girl at a time.

"I'll scout the path while you do that." With that said, the girl dashed out the door with a sly wink to the elf.

"No." I pushed past him, making my way toward Lugh and the backpack full of supplies. I secured the bag tight to my back and reached for Lugh out of habit. Before I could touch him, Cole hurried over and blocked me.

"I have an idea," the elf rushed to explain. He fidgeted in his new clothes, and it irritated me.

"Great, get out of my way."

He held me in place with strong hands that gripped my arms, and I hated how his touch felt—both soothing and frightening. "Try to use the dagger. The magic inside it might be able to help."

I stepped back. "But I'm human."

"I know." The elf glanced past me to the door.

"Then why would you think that I could take that risk? The last human who used magic destroyed the world. I'd rather not follow in their footsteps." What was the elf trying to do?

Cole stared at me for a moment without speaking, and I was lost in his curious gaze. I was about to ask him what he was thinking when Nessa burst through the doorway. "All clear. You guys ready yet?"

"Yes," Cole answered kindly. I stepped around him to get Lugh, but Cole beat me to it and swung my brother onto his shoulder, the endowed bow and quiver already on him.

"Nice try." He looked to the backpack, but knew better than to argue with me about that.

I turned to Nessa. "Where are we headed first? The fastest route to supplies. Then out of the city."

The girl had the decency to look me in the eye while she lied. "I know some people who can get us supplies. They're in downtown. From there, we can follow the road out of the city."

"No people. We can't afford to trust anyone right now."

"Then we're not going to have food for the road. It's all been hoarded by the gangs." The girl's pupils dilated, and for a moment, she had pitch black eyes.

I took inventory of our small stash from the sewers in my head. "Maybe we can make what we have last until we can hunt outside the city limits." I wasn't looking forward to nibbling on stale lemon cakes for the next couple days, but it was better than being taken by the gangs. We had drank our fair share of water and filled the waterskins. Maybe that would stave off the stomach pains.

"No offense, but that's a shit plan. The Guise swarm this city for miles. There's no wildlife to hunt." Nessa picked at her dirty nails.

"Then why do people stay here? The food from before the Collapse can only last so long," Cole asked, pure concern in his voice.

With a quiet, sincere voice, the girl said, "It's all we know. So, we make it work." I knew what "make it work" meant, and it was not good.

"Fine, but you will not tell these people about us. You're on your own getting the food." It was the price she would pay for getting magic—as far as she knew.

"Whatever," she threw at me. I stepped forward, my hand inching toward the blade.

"All right then. Let's get moving while it's still dark," Cole interjected.

With those words, we abandoned the small piece of protection we had and took our chances in the night with monsters that could rival the Guise.

The suburbs disappeared quickly, as we walked down the ruined streets. The surroundings were no longer trees and houses but rotted shacks and crumbling stores. Bones and garbage littered the cement pathways, and though I had lived for years among the filth, it was somehow different. Perhaps my time in the forest had changed my view. This kind of life was no longer acceptable.

My change of perspective was thanks to Lugh. He was the one who made us leave the city. He had hated it there, and wished for fresh meat and water. After he found a bow in the remains of an antique shop, he'd been dedicated to training himself, so we could leave someday without fear of starving in the forest. Even after rejecting him several times, he hadn't listened, and I was grateful for it.

I trailed behind Cole and Nessa. Lugh's hair swung with each stride that the elf took, my brother's face hidden in the blonde locks. I smiled, remembering how much we fought, and I missed it. I missed *him*. With the scavenger and lying elf, I was alone to defend us.

Lugh's pale neck was exposed. As we turned down a narrow street and into the moonlight, blackened veins were revealed. The smile disappeared. "How much longer? We're losing dark hours," I asked again.

"It's just up ahead," Nessa said, her tone was rough, nervous. I peered into every dark crevice of the street; the broken windows, the doorways, the sewer grates, even the cracks in the sidewalk. I looked high and low for a trap of any kind. Despite finding none, adrenaline pumped through my veins, and the dirk begged to light. But now was not the time.

Cole slowed so he was in step beside me. He didn't say anything which was strange for him. "What do you want?" I complained.

"Can't I walk next to you without an ulterior motive?" His green eyes glowed bright in the moon's light. His gaze met my own, and my heart leapt. The elf was taking turns with the infatuation spell. I was his target at the moment.

"Hmph," I grunted, unable to answer honestly.

"We'll get through this, Yvaine. You just have to have faith."

"In what exactly? Magic? God? Whatever rules over us clearly doesn't care. Look around." I motioned toward a small skeleton. There was a rotted doll in its hand; the toy's eyes were open despite it being laid on its back.

Cole did look, and when his eyes returned to me, he said, "There's always good to be found. Even in a place like this." His elf ears peeked out from dark hair, reminding me of *his* goodness.

"Good always comes with a cost." *One I'm not willing to pay.*

When he opened his mouth to speak, Nessa interrupted. And, for once, I was grateful. "We're here." We stopped beside a hardware store; its door was beaten down, and the shelves were emptied.

"Here?" This didn't seem like the ideal hideout for a gang. Despite her secrecy, it was easy to guess who she was looking for.

"No, this is where you'll hide. The base is a block down at a ware-house. If I'm not back an hour, don't bother looking for me." The girl's small fingers cracked and popped, nervous.

"Why didn't you get food from them before? Why scavenge in the neighborhoods?" I questioned. *Why not be part of the gang?*

Looking down, she answered, "These people aren't ones you want to mess with. I didn't want to chance it before. But if a better life means leaving the city, then I'll take that risk." Her voice softened. "Any requests?"

Understanding swelled inside me. "Protein if you can." I unzipped the backpack and pulled out the hatchet. "Here, you'll need this."

The girl took the weapon greedily, and I could see the relief on her face. "I'll do what I can." There were no lusty eyes for Cole now. Only understanding between two scavengers, as she began her journey to the warehouse alone with only a hatchet at her side.

Once she'd turned the corner, I said, "This way."

"She said to wait here," Cole argued.

"I know." That was exactly why I was moving us across the street and into what used to be a bank. Just because I understood the girl, didn't mean I trusted her—that was exactly why I didn't.

The glass protecting the bankers had been shattered, and bullet holes riddled the walls. But the counter was thick and long and would shield us. The bank vault in the back had been opened. There was no damage to the lock. It must have been unlocked by an employee at gunpoint. The man's body still lay beside it, the keys in his hand. I reached down and plucked them from his grip, fingerbones snapping. *Just in case.*

"What is this place?" Cole wondered, stepping inside the vault.

Recalling my past life, I answered, "This is where humans kept their money and valuables."

"All together?"

"Yes, there were guards watching it at all times." I followed the elf into the darkness, watching as he reached out to iron boxes only to retreat before his skin grazed their surface.

"Strange."

"How so?" I asked.

"Humans don't trust anything, especially each other, yet they put their treasures in the hands of others." Cole blew the dust from one of the dangling boxes, revealing a dull shine beneath.

"Yeah, well, humans are hypocrites."

"Or maybe they want to trust, but their pride won't let them," Cole offered, his lips pinched with sadness. He recognized that there were no valuables contained in the iron boxes anymore. No treasure would rest long in one place with humans roaming the land.

Irritated, I said, "It's not pride that won't let them trust."

"Then what?" The elf laid Lugh down on the hard ground within the vault. My brother's eyelids moved, and his fingers twitched, but he did not wake.

"Isn't it obvious? We're not as complex as you make us seem."

"Tell me."

With a sigh, I said, "Fear."

The elf turned from his exploration to look at me. He looked long and hard until I couldn't hold his gaze anymore, and my body began to fidget. "You said that you were at a bookstore when it happened. What was it like?"

"The world collapsing around me? What do you think it was like?" I snapped. I should have never told him anything about myself. But of course, I couldn't have stopped. Just like I couldn't stop now. "It was terrifying."

"How did you and your mother make it home?"

The memory was not something I liked to recall, and bringing it up would only encourage the nightmares to rage the next time I closed my eyes. Still, I said, "It was midday and light was everywhere, so the Guise had free rein over the city. Of course, no one knew that darkness was the only defense against them. They left the lights on in the buildings, letting the monsters right in." I sat down next to Lugh and held his hand in mine; it was cold. Cole stood by the entrance, glancing toward the shattered windows every few moments.

"I remember the screams the most. Mother wouldn't let me see what was happening to the people around us. She covered my eyes, so I just listened as each person was murdered. Or so I thought." Looking to Lugh, I said, "I didn't know they were being transformed. I didn't know it was so much worse than death." I met Cole's gaze, and his eyes shimmered with pity. "I kept my eyes closed long after my parents were gone, and both of us had grown."

"She didn't want you to be scared," he said.

"I know."

"How did she get you out of the bookstore?"

I strangely struggled to remember. It wasn't something I looked back on often, but still… "I remember being taken into the basement and into an underground tunnel. It was dark, so dark that I wasn't sure how she could see where we were going. But eventually, we made it into another building and out the door. We took a car that wasn't ours. Then we were home…" I trailed off, realizing how odd the journey had been. As if I was in a fog the entire time.

"You were in shock. It's normal to forget traumatic things," Cole assured, his eyes quick to catch any moving shadows outside our shelter.

I nodded. But the harder I thought about it, the more difficult it was to remember. I thought to our parents murder, Lugh's torture, and the murders I committed. There was no forgetting those traumatic memories. They were clear and permanent.

What was different about this one?

"You made it home. That's what matters." Cole looked to the windows again, waiting for his other victim to come skipping back to us. Though, he couldn't possibly hold on to the spell while she was so far away. Perhaps she would realize what happened and turn us over to the gang.

"Yeah, but it was only a few weeks before the man showed up at our door, begging for shelter from the Guise. My father was a kind man. Too kind." His generosity killed him and his wife and left his children alone to survive on their own. "I've never stopped being mad at him." Mother had spent hours boarding up the house, and I remembered the fear that shot through me when Father tore down the wood planks from the front door to let the man in.

"Well, that explains a lot."

With a glare, I said, "Explains what?"

"Why you look down on kindness and mercy. You think it will only end with pain." Cole swept the ebony hair back from his alluring face, and my heart stopped.

"That's because it does," I whispered.

"We'll see," he said, though his mischievous smile was nowhere in sight.

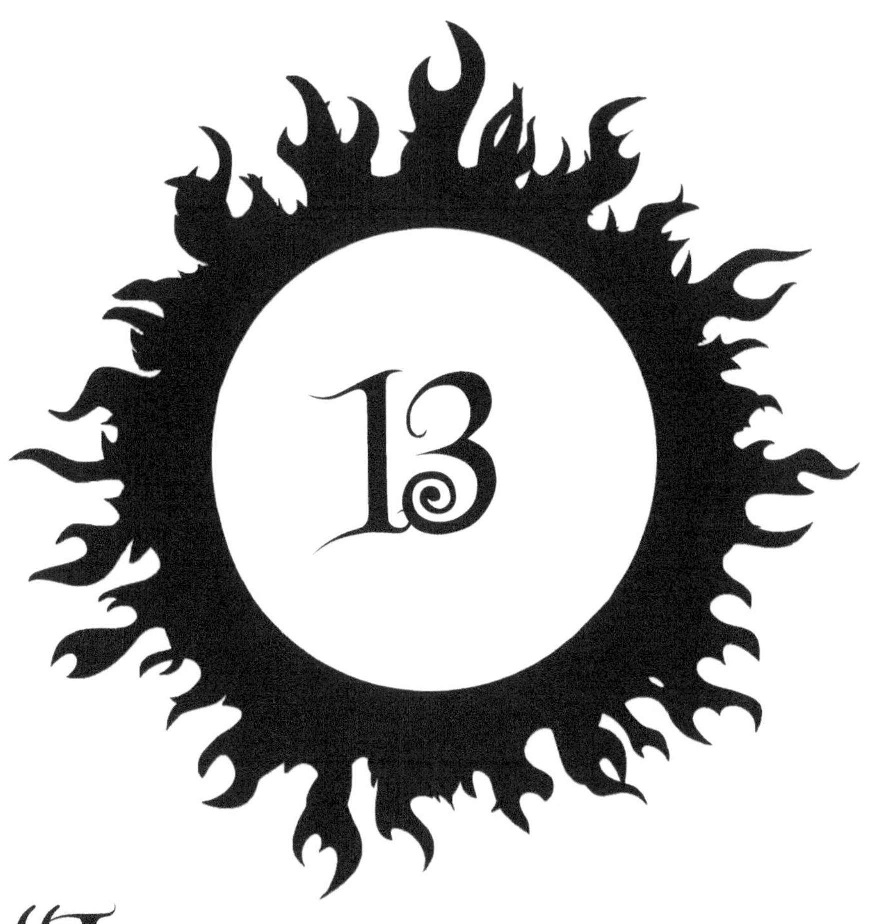

"It's been over an hour. We need to move on," I whispered in Cole's ear by the vault entrance. We hadn't spoken in a long while. There were armed people patrolling the streets now, looking for something or someone. "She gave us up. Our only hope is to run."

"She'll come back."

"Cole—" I started, but he turned his hypnotic gaze on me, and what I saw there was sadness. "Fine, we'll wait another ten minutes."

Cole smiled, and I had to tell myself to breathe. *Damn elf.*

Lugh shifted, and I whipped my head to where he rested in the darkest corner of the vault. His eyelids and fingers were spasming. "Lugh, I'm here." I rushed to him, waterskin in hand. I opened his mouth, allowing the little moonlight from the doorway to shine on his face. The leaf was still there. Beginning on the edges, it was a slim line of brown, sickly yellow, then green at the core. "Lugh, you're going to be okay. Drink, drink." I poured the water down his throat and over the leaf, hoping to revive it yet again. The spasms stopped, but the leaf remained the same. "Stay with me, Lugh. Stay alive for me."

Cole placed his hand on my shoulder. I cringed away from it. I could feel the hurt without looking at him, but he didn't have a right to pain when all he did was take my free will away and prolong Lugh's suffering. "Let's go," the elf said.

Cole bent to pick up Lugh when someone came running through the doorway. The dagger was in my hand before Cole could react. I ran at the intruder, pinning them against the wall—one hand on their mouth to keep them silent and the other with the dirk at their throat, preparing to end their life.

"Wait!" Cole pulled me back. Once again, keeping me from saving our lives.

"She gave us up! She needs to die!" Only the sound of patrolling humans stopped my fight against Cole. We couldn't risk being caught. There were too many.

"I didn't give you up," the girl spat.

"Liar!" Cole restrained me again.

"They wouldn't give me anything, so I had to take it. That's why the Anthros are out. They're looking for me," Nessa explained.

"Anthros?" I questioned, never hearing the name before.

"For anthropophagus, I'm assuming?" Cole asked. Irritated, I shoved the elf away from me, though, my skin ached for his touch as soon as it was gone. *I hated him.*

"I don't know," Nessa said, her eyes on me.

"Are they cannibals?" he asked.

The scavenger nodded, her bruised eyes even darker than they were before.

"How did you know?" I wondered.

"There are human bones hanging from their necks and pierced in their skin." Taking a better look at the humans passing by, I was able to see the bones Cole spoke of, and better yet, their blood-stained mouths.

"Great, there's a whole gang of man-eaters now. When I was here last, it was only random serial killers. Apparently there were more psychos than I thought." I glanced to Lugh out of habit, and my heart sank, imagining his fate ending with the Anthros.

"How did you find us? Did we leave a trail?" I questioned Nessa intensely. I needed to know if they could find us.

Startled, she said, "No, no. I found you by chance. After I saw that you weren't at the hardware store, I ran from building to building to stay out of sight." Catching her breath, she added, "Thanks for that, by the way."

"Get over it. You would have done the same." Our voices had quieted to whispers now, waiting for one of the Anthros to enter the bank. "You said that you took from them. What did you get?"

Nessa released the bag from her shoulder and unzipped it, revealing several cans of meat and fruit and packets of jerky. "Nice work, Nessa," Cole praised, taking the bag from her shaking hands. He quickly added the bounty to my backpack.

Ignoring the fact that he was trusting me with all the supplies, I said, "Yes, but how are we going to get out of here now? They're swarming the streets and sunrise is only a few hours away. They're bound to come in here at some point." I sheathed the dagger only so I could prepare Lugh for travel, tightening his shoelaces and zipping his coat high. I held his hands in mine, hoping to warm him. The black veins had spread all the way to his fingers and below his jaw.

"How far does their territory go, Nessa?" Cole asked in his annoyingly sensual voice, and I almost threw my knife at the back of his head.

Nessa finally turned away from me. "Three blocks north, five south. There's three gangs that make up the city."

"Are the ones to the north cannibals, too?" I asked.

"No, but they're known for taking slaves," Nessa answered, her voice stiff.

"Better than being eaten," I said.

"Agreed." Cole picked up Lugh and waited by the entrance. "They're passing by in waves, using numbers to their advantage. We run after the next one," he said.

"Strangely organized for a man-eating gang," I commented with a sadistic smile. I swung the food-packed bag over my shoulders and secured the straps, leaving Nessa with only her hatchet.

"Didn't you know? Human flesh improves brain capacity. Making one smart *and* deadly," Cole whispered to me. *Just me.*

"You're kidding?" I said, appalled.

"Yes." His breath caressed my neck as I peeked around him, toward the street. The bow hanging from his free shoulder shone in the moonlight, making the runes translucent. I had the urge to run my fingers across the markings but stopped myself. Because I knew where my hands would wander next.

Retreating to the safety of the vault, I punched his arm, and he laughed. Nessa stood a few feet behind us, gawking. Surely she had realized that her traveling companions were insane. *Good.*

"Now," Cole said. The three of us ran silently out of the bank, Lugh hanging over the elf's shoulder. The keys for the vault clanked together only once before I silenced them with a fist. They conspicuously dangled from my sheathe so I tucked them into the hem of my pants as I moved forward.

I could hear the footsteps of the Anthros ahead and behind us, echoing against the crumbling buildings. Ours were silent, all but Nessa's. I signaled to the scavenger to silence her step and she nodded, though, there was only an incremental change. But I couldn't risk correcting her now. If worse came to worse, we'd throw her to the cannibals and run. Luckily, I didn't see any guns in their arsenal, only axes and swords.

My ankle throbbed with a heartbeat of its own. The chilled air kept the swelling down, but sweat poured from my skin with both exertion and fear. I focused on Cole's back as I ran, knowing he was our way out of this. I couldn't make it to the stones without him. I couldn't carry Lugh anymore.

I was too weak.

I begged for the numbness to take over. For the *other woman* to save me. But she wouldn't come out. I was too tired. I was starting to panic. I could feel it budding in my stomach, a slow build of dread. It tightened until a sharp pain shot through my chest. My head raced with horrible thoughts, becoming louder the farther we fled down the decaying road.

There were too many Anthros. Too many gangs. Too many enemies around me. I looked back at Nessa, then forward at Cole. *Enemies that I needed.*

Lugh, you need to wake up! I need help! My brother's answer came in the form of twitches. He was dying slowly, and I couldn't do anything but keep moving painfully forward. *I would save him in time. I had to.*

We were only a block away from the slaver's territory. Cole raised his hand to stop us. He pointed to a nearby door that used to contain a clothing boutique. We ran inside just before a group of Anthros rounded the corner, their faces hideous with fury. "Double back! We must have missed her in one of the buildings," a harsh voice ordered.

We hid beneath clothing racks that held moldy, moth-eaten shirts and dresses. Cole had Lugh with him under his small circle of hangers. Nessa took the one in the back of the store. I took the one beside Cole, refusing to let Lugh out of my sight. The moon was fading overhead, and the sky had lightened ever so slightly. If we didn't find proper shelter soon, we would be monsters by midday. But of course, that applied to the Anthros, too. They couldn't search forever.

My stomach sank, nearly making me fall backward and into the clothing. An Anthros gang member entered the store carrying an axe. It was dripping blood—they had found someone else while they were searching for Nessa. Or it had gotten into a fight with one of its own. Either way, the adrenaline from the kill was still in the man's eye, and it didn't bode well for three tired scavengers and an unconscious boy.

Silently, I unstrapped the backpack and set it on the carpeted floor.

The Anthros hurried through the store, knocking over shelves and racks, knowing the sun was going to rise soon. He passed by Cole's and mine, and I breathed out a rare sigh of relief. Then Lugh began to spasm.

Cole secured Lugh tight in his arms and covered his mouth, but he could not stop the clothes from twitching with Lugh. The man turned to leave when he saw the shirts shifting out of the corner of his eye. He smiled. I unsheathed the dirk.

The glow that came from the weapon was the brightest I had yet seen. I burst from the clothing just before he could swing his axe. The light blinded the man long enough for me to place the blade in his heart, covering his mouth with my hand. But the man wasn't going to die without a fight.

He bit down on my palm, tearing away the flesh there. It took every ounce of strength I had left to stay silent. I twisted the blade in farther, wishing I had the energy to make his death last longer. The land would be a better place without a monster like him living in it.

More Anthros searched the building next door. Despite his bite, I pressed my hand into the monster's mouth, willing him to stay silent. He tried to raise his axe, but my boot had pinned his wrist, and my knee pressed down on his esophagus. He clawed at me with his free hand, but it was weakening. And though this death only took but a few moments, it felt like an eternity as I waited for more to find us. I removed the blade and allowed his blood to flow, his breath finally gone.

There was no hiding us now. *We needed to move.*

"Yvaine," Cole said, lifting me from the corpse.

"We need to move," I said, but my voice was shaking.

"We will. Let's just wait for them to pass."

"They'll see him…" I stuttered, losing control of myself. *What was wrong with me?* I had killed many before, but the *other woman* wasn't with me. *Where was she?*

"They'll see *us* if we leave now." Cole pulled me under the clothing rack with Lugh, quickly wrapping my hand with a moldy shirt. Though it was a tight fit in the hiding place, he made it work. The elf pressed me into his warm chest while I clutched Lugh to mine, his spasms stilling for the moment. The clothes still shook despite this, and I realized too late that it was my own shaking that caused it. Cole whispered in my ear, "You're safe. Lugh is safe. You saved him."

"And you," I breathed.

Surprised, he said with a small smile, "And me."

The Anthros waited until the very last rays of moonlight disappeared and the sky was a navy blue, leaving us defenseless and without shelter. The panic had subsided in Cole's embrace, but it showed its face again when I saw the first rays of sunshine.

"What are we going to do?" I whispered. The store faced east and had wide open windows to let the light in. The moans of the Guise were already echoing down the streets. The nearest sewer cap was too far, and even if we made it, I was sure that we would find Anthros already down there looking for their own way home. We didn't have any options left.

The three of us exited the clothing racks and looked in and around the store, searching for a dark closet, basement, or attic to hide in. Every single room had windows and every single one was curtainless. I was about to start collecting clothes to cover the shattered windows when I came upon a strange wall in the back of the store. It had fresher paint than the rest of the building, not a mark of damage on it. I knocked my good hand against it. *Hollow.*

I stole the axe from the dead Anthros's hand and plunged it into the wall. Nessa joined me with her hatchet. Before long, we had discovered a dark, secluded room. Black-out curtains blocked our view of the secret place beyond the wall. I pulled them aside with vigor, eager to find shelter.

There was a table, two chairs, one bed, and an empty cupboard. There were stairs leading downward, which I assumed led to the elusive basement. And two small skeletons huddled together on the bed. The clothing had molded away, but the remnants of a teddy bear remained between them.

"Where are their parents?" Cole wondered.

"Probably died searching for food." I pointed to the empty cupboards. "They starved to death in here. Alone."

"They weren't alone," Cole said.

"Lot a good it did them," Nessa commented. She marched past us and gathered up the sheets under the skeletons, carrying the remains out of the small space and into the store.

I tore my gaze from the dangling hand that poked from the sheets as she passed by. It reminded me of how Lugh looked now, hanging from Cole's shoulder. *That could have been us.*

Cole went to lay Lugh on the rotting bed, but I said, "Wait." Darting into the store, I plucked a surviving blanket from the shelves. The Guise were beginning to surround the shop, smelling the thickening blood of the Anthros.

All of us within the curtained space, I lit the dagger and laid the blanket across the death mattress. It was about time Lugh had a proper bed, or at least some cushion to sleep on. *He hadn't ever before.*

"Why does the coma patient get the bed?" Nessa barked.

"Go downstairs and search for your own bed," I growled in response. Nessa opened her mouth to argue, but something stopped her. And it wasn't me this time because I didn't waste any energy looking in her direction.

I watered Lugh and sipped on the waterskin after. When I handed it to Cole, he shook his head and said, "We need to treat your hand."

"I'm too tired," I muttered, planning on lying beside Lugh and passing out. But Cole grabbed me before I could and sat me down on the chair instead. "You are so annoying. Let me sleep," I whined.

"Not until I look at that wound. He bit you. We need to know how bad it is." Cole carefully unwrapped the dingy bandage and pieces of flesh came with it. I gasped and would have hurled if it wasn't for my empty stomach. "Looks like the cannibal got a taste for you and liked it."

I grimaced.

"Though, I can't blame him. Who wouldn't want a piece of *you?*" he asked with a playful smile.

"You're such an asshole."

"Oh, lighten up. We've survived the night yet again. That's a cause to celebrate." Cole loosened the straps of the backpack I carried and slid it from my shoulders.

"What are you doing?" I knew what he was going for, and I wasn't willing to give it up to anyone.

Cole held his finger up to quiet me. "We'll keep it hidden." Cole relieved the scotch from the bag and removed the cork with a silent *pop.*

"Hey, you were right! There is a bed down here, and it's much nicer than yours," Nessa called up the stairs.

"Use it then!" I answered.

"Goodnight, Nessa," Cole said politely. "You've earned some peaceful sleep."

The scavenger's response was a grunt and a plop onto a squeaky spring mattress.

"Why are you so nice to her? She'd sell us out for a crumb if she had the chance." I winced when he poured the scotch over the wound, clenching my teeth. Once he was done, I grabbed the bottle and chugged a few gulps.

"You would do worse, yet I'm nice to you," the elf said, a needle and thread already out and ready. The tugging sensation was the worst part. It was slow and disturbing. At least the bite had been so painful I couldn't actually feel the pores of my skin being ripped open one by one.

"I do it to survive."

"So does she," Cole shot back, cutting the string with his teeth.

"She does it for herself."

Cole stopped and looked me in the eye. "It's okay to do things for yourself, Yvaine. It's not selfish or wrong."

"You would think that, wouldn't you?" I took another gulp of scotch, relishing the burn that swam down my throat. Cole took the bottle from my tired fingers and poured it over the wound again. "Don't waste it!"

"I'm not wasting it, Yvaine. The wound has to be taken care of or you'll lose your hand. Speaking of, let me see your ankle." Cole finished wrapping my hand and grabbed my leg, placing it on his lap.

"What's the point if you're not going to use your magic on it anyway? Might as well let me rot away like the pathetic human I am, right?" I hiccuped and my stomach rumbled from hunger, but I just couldn't find it in myself to care.

"You know that we have to wait until the stones for that, Yvaine," Cole said sternly, clearly irritated.

"Whatever, you have magic right now! You just don't want to share. It's some sick game with you. Do you put spells on every girl you meet or just me and the scavenger? Does it help you pass the time in your *extended* life? The least you could do is heal me. Owe!"

Cole squeezed my swollen ankle. "Enough, Yvaine. You've had far too much to drink."

"Not enough! One hundred bottles wouldn't be enough to make me trust you! These feelings are only from the spell you placed on me. They're so infuriating! Take them away," I begged. Tears plummeted to my lap. I took my leg back and placed the tender foot on the ground, causing more tears to fall.

Cole didn't say anything. Finally, I looked up and into his green gaze. Fury stared back. For the first time, I was frightened by it. "Spell? You think that I put a spell on you? After all we've been through. After all I've done to help you and your brother, you still think I would do something like that?" The elf stood and paced the small space, running his hands through dark hair and revealing Fae ears.

"Of course I do! You healed from a gunshot wound to the chest overnight. What else am I supposed to think? You are using Lugh and me for something. I just don't know what yet." I marched over to Cole's elvish bow. "This probably works, too." I picked it up and a light brighter than the dagger's filled the space. The familiar burn of an endowed weapon ran up my arm, filling me with strength. The runes began to swirl and change.

"No!" Cole ripped the weapon from my hand, and the glow died. Guise had found their way to our corner of the store. We waited in the darkness until they left, but my anger lingered.

"Liar," I spat. "You could have used magic all along. Why didn't you use it? It could have saved us so much time. Lugh would be awake by now."

The tears fell again. Though I said that I didn't trust him, there had been a part of me that had. The pain ripped me open, proving my skeptic's side right. "Take the spell off of me now," I threatened. "I'm done feeling this way."

"I didn't put a spell on you, Yvaine. I never did."

"Stop lying!" I raised my hand, and the dagger came with it.

Cole stared down at me calmly. "You're really going to stab me again? Whatever you think, I'm not going to recover this time."

"And why not?"

"Because I don't have my own magic." The elf stared into my eyes while he said this, but I couldn't ignore what my instincts were telling me.

"You're bound and determined to die, aren't you? Tell me the truth." I raised the dirk higher. My ankle and hand didn't hurt anymore. The alcohol had numbed them, but not my emotions.

"The truth is this: the bow is endowed." He threw it to the ground, disgusted. "And I *can't* use it. I am a magicless elf who was shunned by his people. Only the power of another Fae can heal me." He paused. "I can't cast spells on my own. And even if I could, I would never try to control you, Yvaine."

"But the stones—"

"Still might work."

"Then why are you helping us? Do you need sacrifices to get your magic? What is the real reason?" I clutched the knife tight but knew I wouldn't be using it once I saw the expression on his terribly beautiful face.

"If I didn't know better, I would have thought you were the one who cast the spell on me." The glow of the dagger pulsed in time with my heart.

"So, you aren't controlling my feelings?" For the first time, I dropped the knife. The haze from the scotch lifted and left me feeling…embarrassed. I definitely preferred anger. "Oh, no."

"Oh, yes." Cole smiled. I ran to the edge of the curtain, debating if I should step out and into the sunlight. "Are you done with your tantrum?"

"Tantrum?" Anger returned, and I was glad for it.

"The first time you drank too much, you thanked me. The second time, you try to kill me. I can't figure out if I like you drunk or not." Cole took two steps forward which brought him nose to nose with me. The curtain brushed against my backside, and I grabbed it, ready to run.

"I'm not drunk," I muttered under my breath, what little there was of it.

"Then, you're naturally insane?"

"Yes," I responded automatically. "No, I mean." My head was swimming. I couldn't slow my heart. My hair had come undone and was falling into my face. The urge to retie it was strong, but *he* was in my way. I reached back to undo it but found it in a tangled mess.

"Here, let me," Cole said. He gripped my wrists gently and moved them to my sides. Returning to my hair, he moved even closer, so I could smell his tree-sap scent. It cocooned me while his long, gentle fingers unbound my hair. My arms felt useless just dangling beside me, so I placed them innocently on his sides to steady us.

Once he had untangled the mess, he wrapped the hair tie around my wrist and let the hair fall to my waist. "You aren't going to braid it?" I asked quietly.

"There's no need to be a warrior today, Yvaine. It's time to rest." But Cole didn't move from his place. Instead, he rested his hands on my waist, forcing me to move my hold to his chest. The Fae within gave him beauty, but the man gave him strength. And I could feel that strength through his shirt. My hands seemed small and weak in comparison. I spread my fingers, ignoring the pain in my palm and traced the sinews beneath.

The trance was broken when he leaned down and rested his forehead against mine. We were so close, yet it didn't feel close enough. *For someone who hated weakness, I certainly made myself vulnerable.* That thought tightened the muscles that had managed to relax. Cole leaned in, and I froze from fear, but he only pressed his lips against my cheek. That small touch warmed my core, so much, I could have melted into the floor, perfectly content.

Cole withdrew from our embrace but held my good hand tight. Grabbing our discarded weapons, we climbed onto the old bed, Lugh between us. My brother was cold and pale, so I wrapped him in the blankets that rested there and held his hands. The elf and I stared at one another, not saying a word, for what felt like both a second and an eternity. But finally, my eyes closed, and I was drifting away when I remembered that another person shared our shelter.

Had she overheard us? I listened for Nessa, and before long, her soft snores drifted up the stairway. The panic abandoned, I allowed myself to rest, hoping I was too tired for the nightmares to surface.

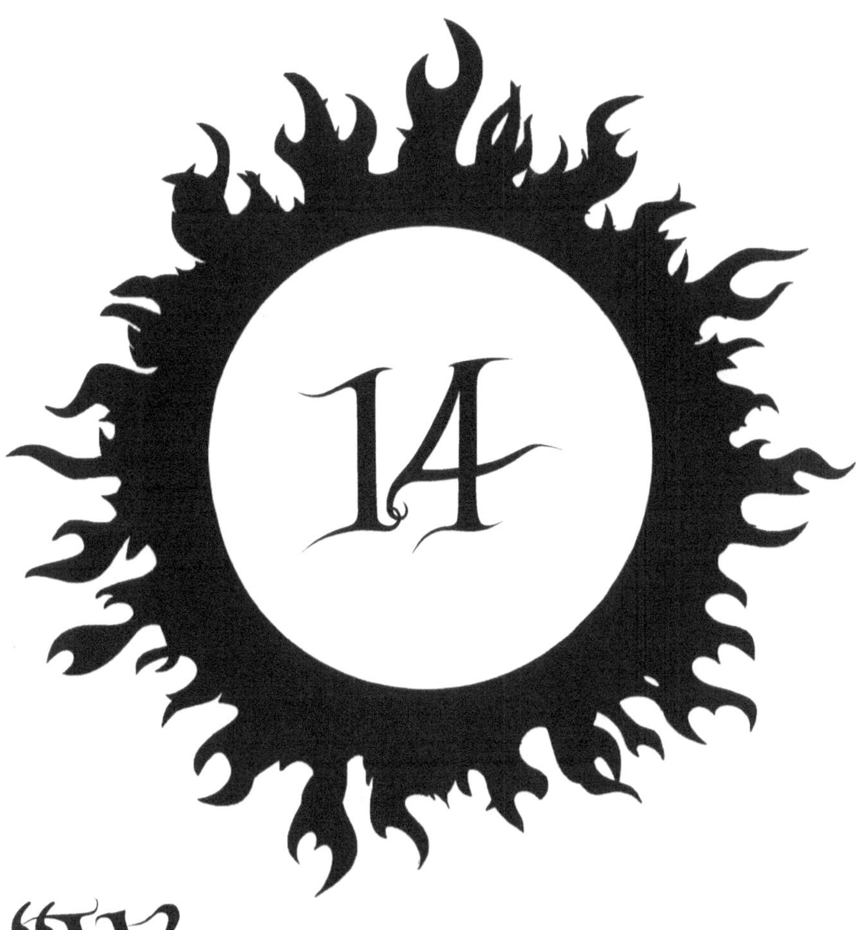

"*What did you do to Lugh?*"

Finley stepped forward, my blade clutched tightly in his hand, though it was still dark. "You'll see your brother later. Do as I say, and take off your clothes." There was no room for argument in his tone. I had been afraid many times before, but the feeling in my gut was indescribable. Complete and utter dread. A dread without hope. There was no saving me. But I could save Lugh. Slowly, I removed my jacket, and it dropped to the floor along with my pride.

You can get through this, Yvaine. Just turn it off. You don't have to feel a thing.

Just as the dread became too much to bear, the numbness returned, and I was grateful. The shake in my hands stilled, and the tears stopped flowing. The smoke from the fire circled me before it rose to the opening in the wall and escaped with the wind. The smell of meat held no meaning to me now; the hunger had gone.

The last of my clothing fell to the ground just as a piece of firewood cracked, the chill from winter in the air. I saw Finley's reaction, both with body and mind. The hunger in his eyes was prominent. He loosened his grip on the blade ever so slightly. The man stepped forward, stalking his prey. Still, I didn't care.

Scrutinizing my vulnerable body, he said, "You'll do. Better than I've had lately." He motioned to a bowl of water by the fire; a rag floated on its surface. "Clean yourself up." Upon command, my feet moved to the fire. I knew the flames were too close to my skin, but I didn't feel them. I just stared at the water. "Clean yourself," he repeated, "or you won't see your brother again. Perhaps I'll sell him as a slave or maybe to the fighting rings. They're always looking for fresh meat, and I'm sure your brother would last all of two seconds before they massacred him, being the little boy that he his."

I picked up the rag and scrubbed my skin hard, until it reddened.

"Don't forget the most important part, cutie."

I scrubbed that delicate area, too, knowing it would never be clean again. Not after him. I threw the rag back into the dirty water and waited, never removing my stare from his dark gaze.

"Where'd you go? Come back and enjoy the fun, cutie. I know you're in there." Finley joined me by the fire, the endowed knife now at my throat. His free hand gripped my breast painfully, twisting the sensitive flesh with anger. When he didn't get a reaction, he put the tip of the knife against my throat, pressing hard as it trailed down my chest and stomach, leaving a line of blood.

I gasped from the pain.

"There you are." He used the knife to part my legs and plunged his unwanted fingers into me. I willed the numbness to envelop me, refusing to feel his vile touch. He would not win. He would not break me. If that meant hiding

until he was gone, so be it.

"Cutie, you're hurting my feelings. Don't you want to feel me inside you?" His touch moved hard and fast, ripping apart what had never bloomed. I withheld a scream, grasping for control, but he stopped, and I recovered before I lost it.

Finley stuck the blood-tipped blade into the fire, waiting. I didn't move. I refused to acknowledge what was about to happen.

Keep Lugh safe. Keep Lugh safe.

The blade glowed, but not its usual pale amethyst. It was red and scorching, yet the metal didn't bend. He placed it on my breast. I screamed and tried to move away, but he held onto me tight. "Scream louder! I want your brother to hear." Finley dragged me to the bed and forced me down, laying his strong, massive body on top of mine. I couldn't stay numb anymore. The instinct to fight was too strong. I struggled and fought, but I could not win. I was too weak. Too tired. Too starved. Too young.

"Stop!" I screamed. The blade was forced deep into my skin. He restrained my hands with his one. The blade moved down my stomach, a scar that would remain with me forever, if I lived after this.

"Oh, cutie, I knew you wouldn't ruin this for me. You just needed some encouragement." The blade was drawn downward.

"Stop! I'll do what you want. Just stop," I begged.

Instead of acknowledging my pain, he moved the blade farther, until it reached the apex of the area I had been forced to wipe clean. He's not going to stop. I'm going to die today, and by the time it happens, I'll be begging for it to be over. The ever-loyal numbness returned, allowing me to still. Allowing me to accept my fate. Lugh would not hear me scream again.

The blade fell into my lap, burning me there too. But I knocked it away, and it clattered to the stone floor. I met Finley's eyes—they bulged with surprise and pain. Blood poured from his mouth and onto my face. An arrowhead protruded from his throat.

Small hands gripped Finley's shoulder and threw him to ground with the blade. The bow was still in the corner of the room with only one arrow missing from the quiver. Lugh picked up the knife and placed it next to me. His wrists were swollen and bruised. My brother's nose was bloodied, and his left eye was black and sealed shut. "Are you okay?" he asked. The young boy reached for my clothes but winced when the weight was added to his grip.

"Am I okay?" I wondered, a bit lost.

"I'm sorry that I didn't get here faster." Lugh glanced to the cuts and burns. Luckily, the blade had cauterized most of the wounds. I took the clothes from my brother's hands. He turned away.

After I was dressed and the knife was secured at my side, I whispered, "I'm so sorry, Lugh." I knelt beside him and gently examined his wrists.

"He chained me to a ladder, but I got out of the cuffs." My little brother broke his wrists and killed someone to save me from my own stupidity. I was a terrible sister. A terrible guardian.

I hugged him tight and said, "Thank you." I looked to where Finley lay bleeding on the ground. "Let's get out of here." We grabbed our weapons and ran, leaving the fire to burn and the corpse to rot.

I opened my eyes to darkness, the dream fading from my conscious mind. Lugh was breathing deep beside me, and Cole sat on his opposite side, staring at the black curtains. The dagger lit, allowing more vision.

"She's gone."

I sat upright. "What?"

"Nessa took the food and left. I went to check on her after I woke, and she wasn't there." The elf stood, his posture stiff.

"That bitch." Running to the curtains, I peered into the store. It was well into the night. The moon was high above us, casting its light through the broken windows of the shop. We'd slept longer than we should have.

Lugh's breathing hitched. The black veins appeared one by one along his jaw. I looked around and said, "She even took the waterskins." Another glance to the table told me that she had taken the remainder of the scotch, too. Thankfully, we had both slept with our weapons. She didn't steal those.

"We'll find her," Cole promised, anger in the set of his shoulders.

"There's no time. We need to move on. It was a bad idea to come here." I searched the shelter for supplies, but of course, there were none.

"We didn't have a choice," Cole reassured.

"And we don't now, either. We need to go. We'll figure something else out once we get away from the city." I didn't bother checking Lugh's leaf. I knew it was worse, but I couldn't do anything about it.

With a sad, disappointed nod, Cole swung my brother over his shoulder along with the magic bow and quiver. Nothing for me to carry, I was able to walk faster though the crumbling building and along the cracked sidewalks, though my ankle continued to scream. No sound could be heard in the city. It was a strange feeling after spending so much time in the forest. At least the birds had sang in the canopies, but there were no trees here. Just death and stone.

We were deep in the slaver's territory when the first sound was heard—footsteps. We turned and ran the opposite direction, searching for a build-ing to hide in. But all the doors on the block had been sealed shut, and it would only make noise if we tried breaking one down.

"Over here!" Nessa called to us from a window across the street. Reaching the building, we realized there was just enough room for one person to squeeze through at a time. I went first, then Lugh, then Cole. Nessa shut the window just as a group of painted men rounded the corner, weapons in hand. The markings were as red as blood, so much so, I was unsure if it was truly paint.

"You're not very smart, are you?" I said, my hand on the dagger's hilt.

"It's not what it looks like, I swear." Nessa raised her hands in defense—empty hands. Cole set Lugh on the floor gently but kept his weapon.

"Where are the supplies?" I growled.

"I *was* going to ditch you guys, but I changed my mind and doubled back. That's when I got attacked." She cringed. "They took the supplies. I'm sorry. But I can get them back," the scavenger insisted.

There wasn't a scratch on her. "How can you get them back?" I asked.

"I followed them. There were only two scavengers. Not a gang. We can get into their hideout and steal it back, no problem." I looked to Cole, and I could see exactly what he was thinking. *This was a trap. But we needed food and water.*

"*We* isn't happening. *You* are going to get our supplies back and fix your mistake." There was no way we were going to walk into a trap. We'd come too far for us to fail now.

"Fine, but could you stay close? It was hell trying to find you guys after the last time," she said, annoyed.

"We'll stay put," Cole agreed. I turned my glare on him, but he didn't meet my stare. He was watching Nessa with new eyes. A new perspective.

"Let's go before the sun shines," I said, distracted by Cole. "Where is it?"

"South, a few blocks down." Nessa fidgeted while she spoke.

I crossed my arms, the bite mark rubbing against the cloth bandage and making me want to scream. "That would make us backtrack. I don't like it."

"It's the only way to get our supplies," Cole said, resigned. The elf placed his hand on my shoulder. "She'll be quick. Right, Nessa?"

With a twinkle in her eye, she said, "Of course." All in agreement, we left the way we came, accepting that the city wouldn't free us without a fight.

We hadn't come across this street on our journey. And I didn't understand why we had to at all. Gang tags were painted on every building, claiming the block as their own. "Why would scavengers choose this place to squat?" I whispered, the darkness both comforting and foreboding.

"I don't know. Maybe they have a way to get food here," Nessa said, strangely calm considering how nervous she had been in Anthros territory.

Cole wrapped his hand around mine. He was strong, yet held me with such gentleness, I didn't pull away. My heart pounded, and I was afraid the gang would hear it echoing down the street. Cole didn't say a word, but instead gave me a triumphant smirk.

I rolled my eyes but smiled back. Rather than search the streets for danger, I stared at Cole, absorbing every detail of his face. The sharp angles, the gleam in his forest-green eyes, the ebony waves that fell to his strong shoulders with only the very tips of his ears peeking through the strands. In that moment, he didn't look like an elf or a human. He looked like *him*.

He looked like home.

My eyes moved to the young man hanging over his shoulder. Tall and lean but malnourished and pale. My brother hadn't eaten in many days, and hadn't soaked in the sun in years, except for the day he was poisoned.

The day I failed him.

I let go of Cole, gesturing to the dark alleys. He nodded in understanding, but the disappointment was there on his face. So, I looked away.

The alleys were quiet while Nessa led us south. Her walk was steady and sure. She knew exactly where she was going. Her brown boots were worn and weathered, a dark liquid staining the soles. The liquid left spots of red as she walked along the pavement.

"So, Nessa, how did you manage to fight off so many scavengers on your own? You said there were five of them, right?" I asked nonchalantly, still scanning the pockets of darkness.

Distracted, she said, "Yeah, but they didn't seem interested in me, just the food. Must have been hungry. Hopefully, we can get some back before they eat it all." The girl continued walking, keeping the red trail alive.

The hatchet swung securely at her side. "They must have been if they forgot to take your weapon, too," the elf commented, seeing the trail of red at last.

Nessa just nodded her head, refusing to say another word.

"So, did they offer you a place in their gang or are you selling us to them out of the goodness of your heart?" I asked calmly, the dirk drawn and dark.

The red trail ended where she stopped ahead of us. She turned and saw the tracks for herself, cursing beneath her breath. "I'm only returning the favor."

"We offer you a way out of this pit, and you return the kindness by killing us? *Nice.*" I took a step, but Cole placed his arm in front of me.

"Why?" he asked the scavenger.

"Don't act so innocent. I heard you upstairs during your lover's spat." Nessa met Cole's stare. "You never had magic. You were just using me like everyone else. Well, it's my turn. I will have power over my own life, and being a part of the Doms will give me that." The hatchet was raised, ready to attack.

"We weren't lying about everything. We are going to have magic, so long as it finds us worthy. Please, there is still time. Come with us." I didn't dare interject, not while she was so close. One swing could have the hatchet in Cole's chest or Lugh's spine.

Nessa didn't swing but shed a tear instead. *This girl was lost and afraid, without a single person to trust.* "Too late, liar. They are going to be here any second. It didn't take much convincing. Once I told them there was an elf in the city, the hunt began. A perfect thing to throw into the fighting cages. You'll be our entertainment until you die, elf."

"You didn't tell them about Yvaine or Lugh?" Cole said, his posture strangely relaxed.

"I didn't need to. You're all they wanted, but I'm sure I'll get extra rations for the pleasure slave and easy meal anyway." Nessa glanced in my direction, watching the dagger in my steady hand. She laughed, the tear now on the pavement.

"I'm sorry," Cole whispered. To whom, I wasn't sure, but the hatchet slipped gracefully from Nessa's fingers and into her throat. The only sound was a wet crunch as it entered and a small whistle as it was removed. The scavenger added to the red trail with her own blood, collapsing. *A quick death.*

Lugh still rested upon Cole's shoulder along with the bow and quiver, yet he had managed to end the girl's life with only a few movements. "Cole…" I started.

"I'm sorry, Yvaine. This is my fault. You were right, we should have killed her in that house. Now…" The hatchet shook in his hand.

I understood then. Cole didn't try to save lives because he was weak. It was because he was strong. He was a skilled killer. *A killer with a good heart.* I reached out and clasped his hand in mine, the hatchet remaining in his palm. "You gave her a chance. That's more than most people get. This was her fault. Not yours."

Cole's eyes left mine and darted down the dark road. "We need to go."

The sound of footsteps reached my ears upon his words, and we ran, leaving Nessa to rot in the street. They would find her soon. And they would know exactly who did it.

We made it only a couple blocks north when the worst thing that could happen happened. I fell.

"Yvaine—"

"I'm fine. Keep moving." I rose and fell again, my ankle giving out. "Damn it, get up!" I told myself. Three more attempts had me exhausted, and I realized just how screwed I was.

"You can't walk anymore." We'd stopped in a grime-filled alley with only shadows to greet us.

"I know." With the last bit of hope I had left, I said, "Please, take Lugh and go. Heal him at the stones. Take this." I held out the life-saving weapon, the glow dim.

"You know I can't do that."

"You can, but you won't. You'd rather sacrifice all of us instead of just one." I raised the knife higher, begging him to take it. "Go."

Lugh spasmed, almost falling from Cole's wide shoulder. "We aren't leaving you, Yvaine. So, put the knife away." He tossed aside Nessa's hatchet, the blood quickly drying on the iron surface.

With a growl, I sheathed the knife and said, "Bastard."

"Hold these, will you?" Cole handed me his bow and quiver, and I took them, confused. "Brace yourself," he warned just before yanking me upward by the arm, bending so that my stomach would land on his shoulder. When I looked over, Lugh was dangling beside me, our hair hanging long and wild down Cole's back. I had yet to tame my blonde waves, and it irritated me more than the Doms hunting us.

"I never agreed to this," I mumbled.

Cole reached out for the bow and quiver, and I placed them in his hand, hanging them beside me on his shoulder. "That's why I didn't ask. You know, it's not fun for me either. You're heavier than you look." His hand rested on the back of my thighs to keep me steady.

"Just watch where you put your hands." The blush blossomed on my face, but of course, it could have been because I was hanging upside down.

"I intend to," Cole chuckled, but there was a strain in his mischievous tone.

The sound of hunters echoed against the alley's walls.

"What's the plan now? You can't run with both of us." I reached over and grabbed Lugh's limp hand and clasped it tight. He was cold.

"I don't need to run." Cole's tone was dark, frightened even.

"What do you mea—" My voice disappeared at the same moment my head dropped beside Lugh's. The tight grip I had on my brother disappeared. I was in pain before, but this was utter agony. My entire body ached from its own weight. The heaviness trapped me in stillness, so much so, I could only move my eyes toward the alley entrance where the Doms now stood, staring right at us.

"I heard voices," the man in the front said. The red paint appeared black in the shadows. His hair was long and tangled and filled with filth. The sword in his hand was broad but chipped and weak.

The men stared into the alley a moment more before another Dom said, "You can't tell the difference between real voices and the ones in your head anymore." He smiled wide, revealing rotted teeth.

The Doms burst with laughter, pushing each other back and forth, enjoying their hunt. With a grunt, the first man took a few steps forward, eyeing the ground beside us. "They're close." He raised Nessa's hatchet in the air. The breeze from the movement caressing my cheek. Yet, he did not see the three people he hunted before him.

We listened until the men's voices faded, and I could no longer withstand the stillness. Being paralyzed was agony. I could see and hear and feel everything, yet the strength to move evaded me. It brought back a memory I wished to repress.

Please, God or Magic, tell me that Lugh is asleep and can't feel this.

"It's going to be okay, Yvaine. Just wait a little longer." Cole said this as he entered the street and ran as quickly as he could while carrying two people. I didn't know what was happening, but there was nothing I could do about it. So, I put my trust in Cole and hoped that he would bring us to safety.

Reaching the end of the road, I could see from my limited vision that there were no open doorways. They had all been boarded up, and with the Doms near, noise was not an option. "Co…" I breathed, unable to form the name on my lips. "Co…"

"Save your strength, Yvaine. Let me do this for you," Cole whispered. Strangely, even though I was in agony and we were being hunted, I felt safe. And that worried me.

Cole approached the brick wall of a building that used to be a gun shop. The sign dangled above the entrance, the pistol artwork faded and forgotten. The windows and doorways were blocked just like the rest of the street.

My heart pounded as the elf stepped into the bricks, bracing for the impact. But there wasn't one. The three of us faded into the wall. The beams, insulation, and electrical wires passed through our bodies, as if we were ghosts. And I wondered if the Doms had actually found us in the alley and killed us.

Gravity pressed down on me as Cole moved, worsening by the second. The air itself was suffocating me, similar to how it felt to drown. My lungs wouldn't work anymore. I tried to cry out, but no sound escaped.

Then, we were in the building, and Cole set me down on the hardwood floor, along with Lugh. My lungs finally expanded, allowing the musty air in. Cole had fallen beside me, struggling for breath as I was.

Lugh spasmed, but his breathing was normal.

"Wha…" I tried. "What…was…that?" I wheezed, the strength slowly returned. But only enough that I could lift my head and look into the elf's tired eyes.

"I'm sorry. I didn't want to have to do that. You were already too weak." The elf turned onto his side and moved the hair that had fallen into my eyes.

"Do what?" I asked, wary.

Cole cringed. "I didn't lie when I said that I didn't have my own magic," he said, already building a defense.

I didn't say a word, I merely watched the play of emotions on his face as he debated what he was going to say.

"Discovering this ability was what forced my kind to banish me. It is a 'sickness' a 'deformity' they told me." Tears swelled in his eyes, but they did not spill. "I cannot produce magic of my own, but I can take another's."

He waited for my reaction. But I didn't have one. Numbness teased at the borders of my mind, ready to protect the already traumatized thoughts.

"Yvaine?"

"Why didn't you tell me? Withholding information is also lying. We could have used this so many times…" I stopped, realizing what he had said. "Where did you get the magic, Cole?" Anger and panic coursed through my body, and I was able to raise my upper half. In a sitting a position, I could glare down at the mischievous elf. My hands shook from fatigue.

Cole stared at my trembling limbs, then met my hateful stare. "The dagger. There was magic left in it from the previous owner. I took it, and because you have used it so many times, it must have affected you somehow. I'm sorry for that. I didn't want you to get hurt."

The sincerity in his words caught me off guard. He meant what he said. *So why did I feel so suspicious?* Chalking it up to a lifetime of bad luck,

I said, "Thank you for saving us. Again." I gave a small smile, but it disappeared quickly. "But no more secrets."

Fear flashed across his beautiful face, but it was gone before I could decide what it meant. I tried to stand and fell once again. "Don't move." Cole stood, fully recovered, and explored the shop we were trapped in.

"This was a place for weapons?" he wondered.

"Yes. The same as the one that shot you."

He cringed and rubbed his chest, remembering. The advertisements on the walls were all that remained of the thing he feared. The store had been ravaged, the shelves emptied and thrown aside.

"There's nothing here. It's been cleaned out." I pulled myself closer to Lugh and did what I had been procrastinating. I parted his lips and peered at the leaf. The center was still green, but the yellowed edges had turned brown and curled in on itself. I closed Lugh's mouth, brushed the hair from his face, and straightened his clothing. "Can you use the dagger to help Lugh?" I asked, desperate for a way out of this situation.

Cole abandoned his exploration and knelt beside Lugh, across from me. "I can't give back what I take. I'm sorry." He paused, thinking, and stared at the black veins that had spread across Lugh's pale face. "Weapons are loyal to their masters. Maybe, if you asked, it would give some of itself to your brother," he suggested, revisiting a previous conversation.

"Ask? Are you saying it's alive?"

"In a way."

"But I'm just a human… The last time my people messed with magic, it destroyed the world." I drew the dagger and held it in my hands. The iron blade gleamed despite the darkness of the store, and the pearl handle's curve was smooth against my skin.

"Yes, but I bet that they didn't ask nicely." Cole's smile lightened my heart and gave me hope. It was an effort not to cringe away from the emotion—an emotion that had led me astray many times.

Do it for Lugh.

The thought came naturally. It was only ever in these words that I found strength and the will to continue. I raised the dirk and laid the knife on Lugh's chest, my hand still holding the smooth grip. "Heal my brother." I waited. I couldn't even make the glow appear. The dagger had become as weak as me. *Useless.*

I tossed the dirk across the room, and it clattered from the wall to the floor, scratching the wood finish.

"I said to ask it nicely," Cole remarked. He stood and retrieved the weapon but held onto it.

"How are we going to get out of here? I can't walk. The dagger is dead. And Lugh doesn't have much longer. Even if we started running for the stones now, we wouldn't make it." A sob broke over the last two words, but there were no tears—I was dehydrated. My broken ankle throbbed, and my stomach groaned in pain, along with the rest of my body.

I was broken. Dying.

"Don't say that. You're going to make it, Yvaine. You are the strongest person I know. And I'm not just talking about humans." Cole laid the dirk back on my brother's chest and squeezed his shoulder with sympathy. "Lugh is lucky to have you as a sister. He knows you will save him. That's why he has lasted this long. He's fighting, too."

Another sob sounded from my throat when I looked at my young brother, so near adulthood. Would he ever make it to my age? Would either of us make it to tomorrow?

Lugh's fingers twitched as I asked myself this. The movement spread up the arm nearest to me. "I'm here, Lugh. I'm here." With my eyes closed, I clutched his cold hand tight, willing what little strength I had left into him. "Keep fighting," I whispered to him.

"You are stronger than you know, Yvaine, remember that." When I moved my gaze to Cole, an amethyst glow was there, casting shadows across his face and sharpening his already sharp features. He never looked more like an elf than in that moment.

The glow emanated from my brother's chest where the dirk rested. The light had been there before when I fought in the darkness, but this was different. The light took on a form of its own, almost as if it had transformed into smoke, but thicker, heavier. A burn could be felt where I touched the blade.

The magic swirled in the air and back down into Lugh. I parted his lips again and watched as the dead edges of the leaf uncurled. The brown became yellow again, but no green returned. Even as I gripped the pearl handle and silently pleaded with the weapon to continue. The glow dimmed gradually in my hand. I nearly threw it across the room again, but the black veins receded from Lugh's face, and I was grateful that the dagger had helped at all.

For once, I gave a genuine smile. *There was hope.*

I reached out to where Cole's hand still clutched my brother's shoulder, but I retreated when I heard banging on the outside wall. "What was that?" I said.

Cole stood and ran up the stairs silently, where there was sure to be a window. He was only gone a few seconds, but they were agony as I sat helpless beside my sleeping brother. "The Doms are searching the buildings now, they're breaking down the doors." The elf's face was resigned.

"Didn't you just tell me to keep fighting? Help me up. We have to leave." I got to my knees before Cole pushed me back down.

"There's nowhere to run." He placed his hands on either side of my face.

"You can take more magic—"

He stopped me with a shake of his head. "I can't keep using your magic. It will kill you, Yvaine."

"It's not mine. Just take it. Damn it, Cole. What else are we going to do?"

Despite the situation, Cole looked… happy. "Let me do this for you." His words from earlier filled my stomach with dread.

"Co—" I was interrupted again, except this time I didn't mind. Cole's lips were soft and moved gently against mine. My worries were forgotten as I gripped his shoulders, the sting of the bite mark on my hand was dull in comparison to his warmth. His hands found their way into my knotted hair, wishing to be closer, just as I was.

The banging on the wall was louder than before, but I didn't care. If these were my last moments alive, this was what I wanted to do. *I wanted to stay with Cole.*

Cole ran his fingers down my arms, finding where my hands clutched his shoulders and neck, and gently removed them. "Don't go," I whispered.

The elf kissed me once more and said, "You never needed me to begin with. You are capable of saving Lugh all on your own. Just look inward and use the dagger."

"How can you say that? I'll always need you." I was surprised by the truth that came tumbling out of my mouth. I clutched his strong hands, refusing to let go, but they were shaking. I had been so distracted with my own pain, I hadn't realized how tired and worn Cole had become. I immediately wanted to help him.

"Heal yourself, find the stones, and save Lugh. Remember to use the dagger, Yvaine. It's important." Reality was a hard thing to accept, but Cole left me no choice when I fell limp to the floor. The elf caught me before I hit the hardwood, slowly laying me down. And I finally realized what he was doing. "Keep the bow, I won't be needing it."

I struggled to move, to fight, as Cole approached the wall. I managed to lift my arms and pull myself in his direction, but not far. "Wai…" I gasped.

At the wall, he turned and whispered, "Live," before stepping into the bricks and disappearing.

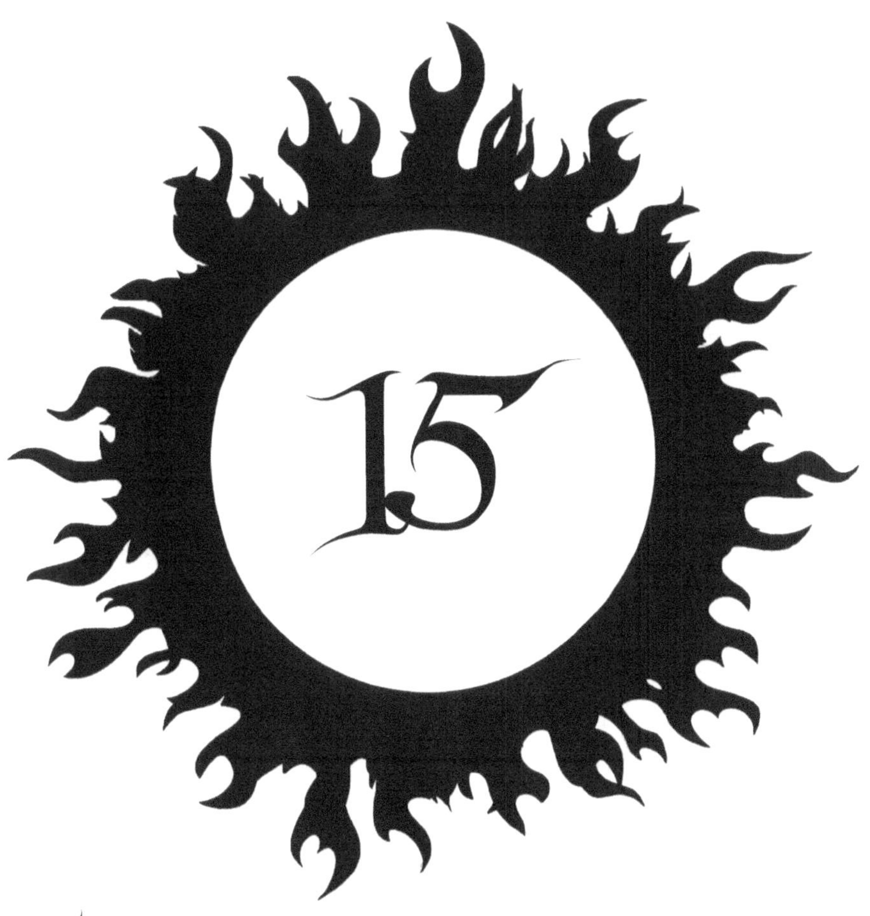

I wanted to scream, to cry out for him, but I couldn't find my voice. He had taken it with him, along with enough magic to phase through the wall again. To *them*. The Doms.

"Once I told them there was an elf in the city, the hunt began. A perfect thing to throw into the fighting cages. You'll be our entertainment until you die, elf," Nessa had said.

"You didn't tell them about Yvaine or Lugh?"

Damn that elf. He knew we would be safe if he was found. A Fae—their prize.

Footsteps sounded outside the walls—running. Cole was leading them away from us. And without magic or a weapon, he had no chance.

I concentrated on waking my body. One finger, one toe, one movement at a time. Since the Collapse, I had done nothing but sacrifice to keep Lugh alive. My sanity, my pride, my soul. Killing was not an easy thing to accept. No matter the people. Common and Fae both had died at my hand. To sustain us and to protect us. I never questioned it was something I had to do to survive. But it ate away at me until there was but a small sliver of who I used to be.

Until Cole.

The day we met in the tunnel he had shown me that there was another way. His willingness to die…to end it. Just so he wouldn't have to kill us. Because now I knew what he was capable of. He could have ended me anytime he wanted. But he didn't. And now he sacrificed himself again… for us… for me.

How could I not do the same?

Lugh breathed silently beside me, his eyelids and cracked lips trembling due to whatever dream he was having. I took his hand in mine and squeezed it with the little strength that had returned.

If Cole died, Lugh would die. That was for certain. I couldn't do this on my own. Whatever the elf thought, the dirk was not enough to heal my brother, even with the stones. Humans were not meant to use magic. It was too great of risk.

I attempted to rise on my own and fell backward onto the floor again. What if the magic created another Guise? Something worse? *But I had no other options.*

The endowed weapon had to be different if Cole wanted me to use it. It would help me get him back, that way, he could use the stones properly and no more harm would come from another wayward human.

I struggled to grab the dagger from where it rested on my brother's chest, but finally, it was in my hand. "Heal me," I whispered.

Nothing.

"Heal me!" I commanded.

No light.

Look inward. "Help me heal. Help me save Cole and Lugh. Share your light," I sobbed. *"Give me strength."* The thick purple smoke appeared, spreading outward until it encased my entire body. I was afraid I wouldn't be able to breathe, but the light was easier to inhale than air. It was pure and good.

The smoke thinned until it only lingered on my hand and ankle. The throbbing eased, and the pain retreated from my muscles. I rose and unbandaged my hand. The wound was still there, but it was as if it had happened weeks ago instead of yesterday. I tested my ankle with care. It was no longer broken but sprained instead. I could live with that.

I couldn't do anything about my empty stomach, but the pain had been a near constant for the past thirteen years, so it was bearable. The remaining light returned to the dagger, and Lugh and I were cast in darkness.

With only a cursory glance at my brother, I made the climb upstairs, happy that I could. I found the window Cole had used. It was a clear view of the street. No humans were in sight, but navy blue was the color of the sky, and the sun wouldn't be far behind.

The plan formed quickly in my mind. I needed to act before the shadows retreated from the city. I braided my hair, and tied it securely with Cole's gift, concentrating on the next step. With the view, I could see just past the roofs of the buildings across from me, and my heart thudded in anticipation. *We had been so close.*

Limping down the steps, I sheathed the dirk at my side and went to Lugh. "I have to leave, Lugh, but I'll be back. Don't worry, I'll make sure you're safe." With that said, I dragged him across the room and into a closet with empty gun boxes. I made him as comfortable as I could while stacking the boxes on him in case someone found themselves in the shop.

"Keep still, Lugh. Stay silent while I'm gone." I kissed his cold forehead, wishing I would have grabbed one of the blankets from the clothing store for him. The bow and quiver was tucked safely beside him, knowing that I didn't have enough practice with the weapon for it to be useful. It was an art only my brother had mastered.

Once I knew there was nothing more I could do for Lugh, I searched for a way out of the boarded-up shop. A short investigation led me to a hidden opening in the floor inside a secondary closet. The hinges were rusted but manageable. The dagger lit with just enough light for my eyes to adjust in the pitch black below.

The basement was large. Most likely, it had been used for storage when the store was open. Roaming the dust-filled space, I found two empty cots in the corner, the blankets past the point of use due to the moisture. Shelves upon shelves greeted me with nothing but empty boxes of ammo. I grabbed a water cannister, hooking it onto my pant loop. Then I found what I was searching for—the door. The stairs led up and out the back of the building where the shadows would be the darkest. I strode up to the opening and cursed. It was locked, but from the inside.

The dirk was useful for many things, including lock picking. I had mastered the skill when I was thirteen and my five-year-old brother needed shelter in the city. The little satisfying click sounded, and the chains dropped to the floor, right beside a skeleton. I moved the light in its direction and found two people and one shotgun. From the condition of their skulls, it was obvious that they had decided to take fate into their own hands.

I whispered a silent prayer for them as I removed the gun from the grip of the shooter. The chambers were empty, but there was a full ammo box beside them—their last box.

Noise was not preferable, especially as the sun rose, but I couldn't shy away from the weapon. I pocketed the shells and donned the strap, so the now-loaded gun hung over my shoulder. The door squealed as it was forced open, but I was gone before anyone would think to come looking. The Guise hadn't appeared yet, though, I had limited time. I ran, only pausing to check the open spaces I was darting across. The gangs had hidden for the day, reveling in their spoils.

Quickly, I made it to the edge of the city where the dam stood. How I could have forgotten such an important resource was beyond me. I supposed I'd labeled it as impossible, since the last time I had been in this city, the gangs guarded it with their lives. It wasn't worth approaching. Or perhaps I never thought we would make it this far. But there was no one here to stop me now.

Thirst overwhelming, I almost ran up the road and dove off the bridge, but instead, I climbed up the steep grassy bank until I found the water's edge and plunged my head in. It was ice-cold and stung my skin and throat, but it was worth it. By the time I resurfaced, however, I had to vomit half of it due to my weak stomach. Afterward, I filled the canteen for Lugh.

As I was savoring the endless supply of water by scrubbing my arms and neck, a bullet landed beside me. I ducked behind a group of trees and waited. Carefully, I peered in the direction of the familiar sound. There was movement on the rooftop of a fish processing plant. The sky was saffron now, the sun hiding just behind the horizon.

The color reflected on the water, and I couldn't help but stop and appreciate the beauty of the buttery leaves floating on its surface. The water was calm, and seeping over the top of the dam. Angry cracking sounds could be heard beneath the gentle ripples. *I needed to move.*

I ran down the hill to the processing plant, hoping that the shooter would be caught off guard. There were a couple delayed shots in my direction, but they lost sight of me when I darted behind the building. There was a fire escape, and I took the steps greedily. I kept waiting for the shooter to appear overhead and end me, but they didn't. And I couldn't do my job with a sniper stalking us. They had stolen enough time already.

Reaching the roof, I peeked warily over the edge. There was a man pacing the opposite edge of the building. *He didn't know where I was.*

Slowly, I perched myself on the roof and raised the shotgun. "One more move, and you die. Put the weapon down," I ordered.

The man stiffened and turned. He was thin and sickly. Brown, crusted hair hung limply down his back. But despite his weak appearance, there was something in his eyes that told me to keep my guard up. "You," he said with a sneer. He lowered his weapon but didn't put it down.

"So, you are the one who shot at us," I confirmed.

"I wasn't shooting at you. I was aiming for the elf." I looked to his weapon and saw a scope mounted there. "I know I got it. Did you leave it to rot in the sewer? I looked for the body, but there was nothing. It's not often my prey escapes." His voice was rough and lingered on words too long, as if he hadn't spoken in a long time.

"It got away. Thanks to you," I spat. "It was leading me to more of its kind. I'd finally gained its trust, and you scared it off." I smirked. "What are we supposed to do about that?"

The man's eyes widened in delight, realizing he was among kin. "Hunt."

"I've tracked it to the Doms. They put it in the fighting rings, but I don't know where that takes place. Any ideas?" I lowered the shotgun and approached slowly. He did the same.

Cautious, the man said. "There's no getting him back now. The fighting rings involve all the gangs at the center of the city. You wouldn't make it out alive." He paused. "But what is one elf compared to many? Where was it leading you? We could hunt there."

His rotted grin made me want to gag, but I was considerate as I said, "It wouldn't tell me the exact location. Some crap about '*only the magic folk can find it.'"*

"That's too bad." The man clutched his weapon tight, realizing I wasn't going to be of any use.

"But with your help, I can get it back." I took a step toward the sickly man, smiling my cruelest smile.

His eyes lit up, leering.

"You seem like a resourceful guy. Got anything besides that gun? Explosives you were saving for a rainy day?" I knew it was a shot in the dark, but it was the only way out that I could see.

"I might have something. But what's in it for me?" The man's lustful eyes roamed my body. I withheld my vomit.

"Once I get the elf back, you can come with me to find the rest of the Fae. From what it said, there are hundreds north of here. A hunting ground with only two hunters. Wouldn't that be fun?" Without cringing, I touched his soiled forearm, swaying him to my side with the promise of more than just my knowledge.

The challenge thrilled him, and I smiled in triumph.

Before I could tell him my plan, a man's scream erupted from below. We both laid on our stomachs and watched from above, as an Anthros ran down the street. His skin was red and infected from the bones pierced in them. He had no weapon and darted blindly into the light. The sun had seeped over the edge of the horizon and cast rays on the cracked road. Shimmers of gold appeared, followed by lonely moans.

"Looks like dinner got away only to end up in worse hands," the sniper said, chuckling. He rose his weapon and aimed.

I placed my hand on his shoulder and said, "Wait, I want to watch."

The sniper took this as a sign of my character and snickered, overjoyed. But I didn't stop him out of cruelty. I needed to see something I had prolonged for years.

The golden shimmers that were the Guise's bodies came to life and wandered slowly to the screaming Anthros. More and more appeared until the man was cornered by the river. The sun sparkled in the water, beckoning safe haven, but the Guise could follow him there, too. There would be no point.

"Please, stop! Get away!" he yelled, pleading for mercy from monsters that knew nothing of the concept.

The monsters closed in on him and he fell to his knees, crying. He removed the bones from his skin and threw them at the Guise. They passed right through, as if the monsters didn't exist in our world but in a nightmare—a nightmare that had disguised itself as a beautiful fantasy.

The Anthros screamed as his body was encased in their light. He seemed to melt and rise up again in an endless cycle of torture, until finally, he was nothing more than light himself. His eyes opened and revealed golden orbs of sunlight, and it wasn't long before his torturous moans began. The monsters dispersed, their job done, and continued their hunt in the sun.

The numbness didn't return. The only feeling I had was determination as I thought of Lugh and Cole and where they were now. "I have a plan," I said, handling the bank vault keys.

The shadows were vanishing. The seconds ticked by. But I couldn't roam the streets as freely as I could now in the day when the gangs were hiding in their hollows. I ran for Lugh, knowing that I would have to take him with me, despite the danger. Leaving him near the dam would have been easier, but I couldn't risk the sniper seeing me place him; he might use him as leverage later. And the gun shop was no longer an option, my route had changed.

I made it inside the gun shop, through the basement, and up the stairs to the closet. The boxes had been shifted and Lugh spasmed aggressively. I uncapped the water and poured it down his dry throat. "I'm here. I'm here." The leaf was beginning to curl in on itself again, but I couldn't risk sapping my strength right now.

Watered and calmed, I maneuvered Lugh and the weapons onto my back, carrying them outside and into the light. It was going to be a hard run, but there were only shadows under the building's eves now. My ankle pulsed in anger.

Blocks came and went, and I was worried that I'd gotten lost by the time I saw the bank. I darted inside just as the sun moved across the sky and into the windows. My boots crunched over broken glass in my hurry, and the Guise heard. They swarmed the bank, but we were already in the vault with the door shut and locked before they could touch us.

I nearly threw my brother to the ground as I collapsed onto my back and sucked in the air eagerly. I clutched the dagger tight and willed its light to help me heal. Its power seeped into my sore muscles and aching ankle. When the pain was but a dull nuisance, I sat up and watered Lugh again.

"I need Cole to heal you, so I have to go after him." I paused, imagining the horror the elf was going through at that very moment. "To save us." Though I said it was for our survival, I couldn't help but think of Cole's lips on mine, his gentle touch, and his last request. *Live.*

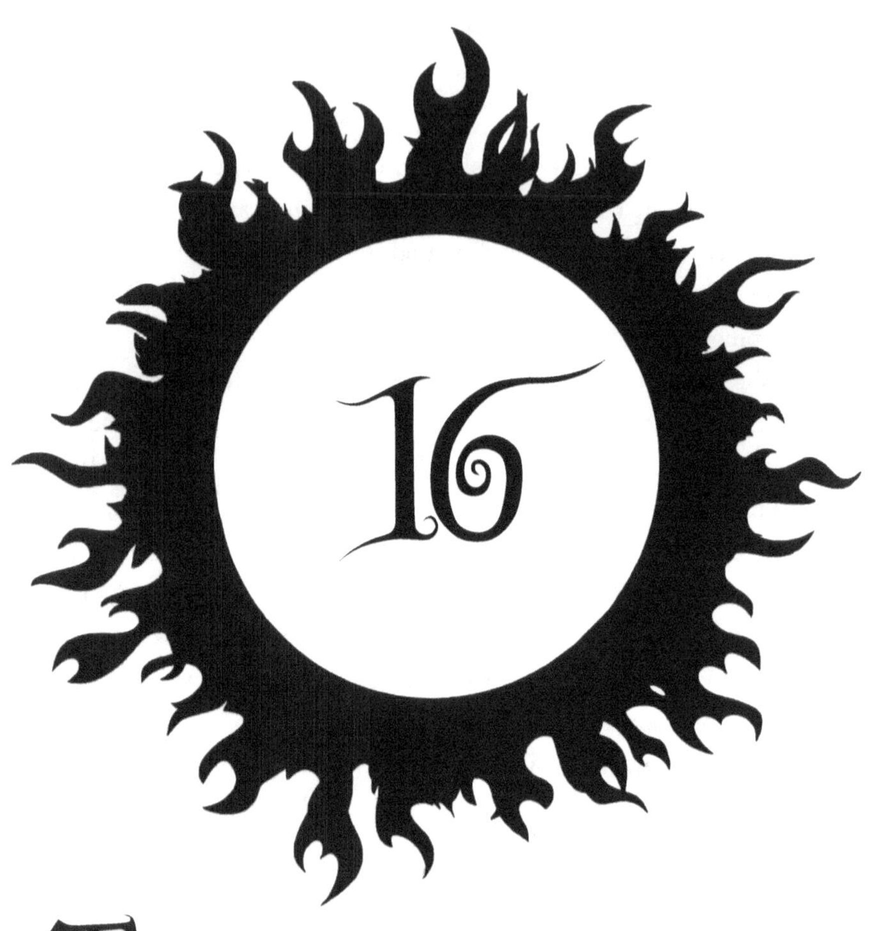

The day crawled by. The dread knotted my stomach so much that I was nauseated. I slept to regain strength and rest my anxious mind, but it would only last so long before I would wake in the dark and scramble to find Lugh, forgetting where I was. I sipped from the water canteen to settle the hunger, but that, too, only lasted a few moments at a time.

I had to guess when it was dark, unlocking the vault and peering out. The sun had just set, the dark-blue sky beckoning me out and into the open. With one last goodbye to Lugh, I locked the vault and hid the keys in my pocket. I left the shotgun and bow behind. I didn't want to attract attention to myself by inviting a fight over the weapons.

What if it didn't matter how much I prepared? What if I died?

Lugh would die slowly, alone in the dark.

I pressed on, concentrating on the directions the sniper had given me. The fighting cage was in the city's old boxing arena. It was large, holding several hundred people at a time. I kept to the alleyways, watching the Doms saunter the same direction. Then the Anthros. Then the Sators. According to the sniper, the Sators were human breeders. They traded their "wares" to the cannibals and slavers.

The adrenaline coursing through me usually brought out the *other woman*, but she was nowhere in sight. And I feared that I wouldn't survive this without her.

There was a man and woman painting each other beside the arena, as well as other things I wished I wasn't seeing. But they were called inside by their peers, abandoning the bucket of paint.

I made my way to the pail and quickly covered myself in red. I hid the dirk in my jacket. I'd been given a small iron-bladed knife from the sniper—a gift—and placed it in the sheathe hanging at my side where everyone could see.

I entered the building with confidence and a condescending sneer. I would have to become one of them, but of course, I was a killer, too.

The ceiling was tall, meant for viewing fights and housed hundreds of seats. Most were filled, but a lot of humans gathered around the cage itself, throwing whatever they could at the fighters. Curses, threats, and taunts came spewing from their mouths. The two men in the ring circled one another slowly. They were both bloodied and bruised, and both stared at the other with anger. *Only one of them would survive.* And they knew it.

There was a woman selling canned food. She wasn't painted or pierced, but instead wore a necklace of tiny skulls—a Sator. I couldn't help but notice her filthy skin was splashed with blood. She yelled out to the crowd, "Come get your food, heathens! Give me what you've got, and it's yours!"

My stomach rumbled painfully. "What do you want for the pears?" I asked, the smirk hid the amount of pain my middle was truly in.

The woman met my challenge by offering a glare. "The knife."

"No."

With a huff, she looked me up and down and finally rested on my braid. "Your hair."

Surprised, I asked, "Why?"

"You want dinner or not?" The Sator was about to turn away and haggle with someone else.

With only a moment of thought, I nodded and said, "Two cans."

"Deal."

With the bargain struck, I removed Cole's gift from my hair and unsheathed the dull blade at my side. It took a couple chops to cut through it, but soon, my waist-length blonde hair was in the saleswoman's dirty hands, and the fruit was in mine.

I quickly tied back my now shoulder-length hair and stabbed the cans with the same blade. The pears didn't taste good, but my stomach stopped screaming, and I could finally concentrate on Cole.

The fight had ended while I was eating, and the next two fighters were sent out. The pears almost came back up when I saw him. I was hoping they'd save him for last, but there he was—tied and covered in blood. I hoped it wasn't *all* his.

I stayed near the back of the crowd. There was no way to get him out of the ring on my own. I'd have to wait until the fight was over and they took him back to his cage. *If he won.* If he didn't…we were all dead.

"Get in, Fae!" Cole's captor ordered. He kicked Cole's leg, and he fell. The entire crowd screamed with laughter and excitement. They threw trash at the elf until he entered the fighting ring. The ring was surrounded by netting made of iron. It made me wonder how many Fae they had forced to fight and die for their entertainment.

Cole didn't bow in pain upon its proximity, and this made his captor turn red. He didn't cut his bonds. "Have fun and remember to put on a good show for us." The man went to kick his prisoner again, but Cole evaded him, causing the man to fall. The crowd laughed just the same.

The mischievous gleam in Cole's eye gave me hope that he had not given up yet. My heart thudded with relief and dread. I was going to have to stand here and watch until it was over.

Cole's opponent was a small, shivering woman. She had just enough clothing to cover her, however, I could see that it had been ripped in multiple places. She was untied and holding a sword much too big for her.

"What is this?" Cole bellowed. "I thought this was supposed to be a fight! Give me a real challenge!" The elf did not want to kill an innocent, frightened woman. He didn't want to kill at all.

The captor laughed from outside the cage. "You didn't have a problem killing that little girl out on the streets."

Cole's face fell, ashamed.

With venom, he said, "Your kind doesn't deserve to live." The man paused. "Cahira, here, had her whole family wiped out by your kind."

"So you force her to fight another?" Cole was disgusted, as was I.

"No. She *wants* to be here."

As the words were said, Cahira leapt for Cole, the sword raised high. He rolled out of the way, and my heart teetered on the edge of an attack. The woman yowled like an animal, her eyes wild with bloodlust. She was no longer sane. She could not be reasoned with.

Cole knew he was going to have to end her, and I suspected that's just what the humans wanted—more proof of the Fae's evil. Proof that they were beneath us. Just monsters like the Guise.

The woman lifted the heavy sword despite her weak body, and swung over and over again, missing every time. They ran around the ring many times, so many, I was starting to wonder what Cole's plan was. But then I knew. The woman was slowing, her breath harsh. The sword didn't raise as high as it had minutes ago.

"Cahira, listen to me. I'm sorry about your family, but I am not the one who killed them." Another swing. "Don't let these monsters kill you."

"Monsters? Monsters?" she cried. "You are the monster! Magic isn't good enough for you. You have to take from us, too!"

"I don't have magic. I never did," Cole said, heartbroken.

This confession didn't make an impact, she simply kept swinging and stabbing, only to miss.

"I'm sorry, Cahira. You don't deserve this." Cole waited until she was close, and the woman thought she was going to make contact. But he was too fast. He kicked the sword from her hands. When she reached to pick it up, he came up from behind and wrapped his bonds around her throat.

She fought to free herself, scratching Cole's arms and face, but in the end she was too weak. I could only hope that she'd reunited with her family in that moment.

The crowd booed and threw waste at Cole again as he exited the ring. He kept his head high, not revealing one ounce of weakness. A tear ran down my cheek, smearing the paint.

Cole had transformed his body into a weapon over the years. The grace and strength of a fighter walked down the ring's steps, despite the guilt in his eyes. And I couldn't help but wonder why he'd needed to. Was it for survival or something more?

I weaved through the crowd, keeping my eyes on Cole. The captor took him down a long hallway, and into what used to be the locker rooms. No one suspected me as I passed by. There were humans fighting, screwing, and using. So, why would they notice a Dom woman strolling past them and hiding behind the locker room door? "As requested, your next opponent will be a challenge, Fae. Now that you've pissed off the entire audience, I'll let them tear you to shreds." The captor spit. "Think on that for the rest of the night. See you at sunrise."

It took all my strength not to stab the captor as he passed by, just inches from me. But I allowed him to return to his domain, knowing he would be gone soon. Along with the rest of them. Through the doorway, there were cages upon cages, each one made of iron. I could hear human moans and cries from the adjacent locker room, so this one must have been specifically for Fae.

I stepped quietly inside. Only a few of the cages were occupied. A dryad: a woman-like Fae that was birthed from a tree. A bannick: a small, ugly creature with sharp teeth and claws, but despite their appearance, their magic was meant for healing. There were more I didn't recognize, and I felt guilty for not knowing.

These Fae were too weak from the iron to notice me, which allowed me to approach Cole's cage without interruption. The elf faced the wall, away from me, his shoulders resigned. "I knew you were a liar, but really? You *never* had magic? What about what you stole from me?"

The elf turned, shock already on his face. "Yvaine?"

"Who else would come after a suicidal elf?" I poured as much sarcasm into my words as possible, but the hurt still trickled out, and Cole could hear it.

"I'm sorry." Our hands met, the iron between us. "I didn't want to, but it was the only way to save you and Lugh." He smiled. "Sacrifice one for the many, right?"

"Of course you listen to me the one time I don't want you to." I looked at our hands and quickly removed mine. "Your hand, Cole."

The iron had left red, angry, diamond-shaped wounds on his hand. "Owe."

"Owe? I thought iron couldn't hurt you?"

"No, I said it was tolerable." He winked, and my heart fluttered.

"Always a way around the truth, isn't there?" I said playfully, but his face faltered. I waited until he met my gaze and said, "I have a plan, but you're going to have to wait a little longer. I can't risk them sending a mob after you yet."

"Yvaine, just go. They'll do worse to you than they will to me if they find out you're trying to help. I couldn't live with that." Cole reached through the cage again but quickly changed his mind.

"None of us are going to live with anything if you don't get out of here. Seriously, Cole, how did you expect me save Lugh without you? We need your magic to perform the banishment spell."

"But the knife— "

"Isn't enough," I interrupted. "I'm only human, there's no way I'm going to risk creating more Guise or something worse. I've used enough already." I looked back at the doorway. "And… I wanted you back. Even if you couldn't banish Lugh's curse."

Something like guilt flashed in his eyes, but it disappeared quickly. "Let's hear your plan, then."

We were going to use Cole's "fight" to lure the gangs into the streets just before sunrise. I'd set him free, and we'd run to Lugh. By then, the sniper would have set the explosives off at the dam, and the city would be flooded in minutes. We only had a short window of time for Cole to work his magic, or rather, the dagger's magic. If not, we would all drown.

The crescent moon moved quickly across the sky. Fights came and went. Bodies were dumped, and live ones replaced them in the ring. I played with the bank keys, unhooking the useless ones, and handling the vault key until I had memorized it by touch. We would run fast enough. We would get to Lugh in time.

The sky brightened from black to sapphire. The hallway was empty this time, but when I entered the room, the captor was there. Cole didn't move his eyes from the man. "Time to die, Fae." He unlocked the cage. My endowed dirk found itself in his back. The man fell forward, dying without knowing who had killed him.

Cole opened the cage and stepped out, pushing the captor aside. "Let's go," he said with sympathy. The other Fae roused long enough to cry out for help, but there wasn't enough time. The dagger in hand, we ran out the back entrance, keeping to the shadows. It didn't take long for the humans to find the captor's body and empty cage. Shouts and curses were flung into the early-morning air.

Beyond the angry voices, there was an explosion in the distance, followed by cracks and moans. "No! He wasn't supposed to do it yet!" Upon my words, a child leapt from the shadows and attacked me. The boy was no older than ten, yet his violence was more intense than most adults. The city was all he knew. For him, there was nothing other than surviving and killing.

I fell, struggling to remove him, but he wouldn't let go. Cole had to rip him from me, hitting his head hard enough to knock him out. I nodded to Cole in thanks and stood, hearing a small clank sound against the pavement. We had lost enough time. So, we left the child and sprinted for the bank.

I exhaled a sigh of relief, but the feelings disappeared when I heard what came for us down the streets. I plunged a hand into my pocket for the key. It wasn't there. I scrambled, panicking, and searching every pocket. Then finally getting on my hands and knees to search the dirty floor.

"Yvaine?"

"It's gone, Cole. The key is gone!" I stood and banged on the vault door. "Lugh! Lugh!" The crashing sounds were getting closer, as were the gang's voices.

Cole steadied me. "The knife, Yvaine, now!"

I unsheathed it and basically threw it at Cole, begging him to take over, because I was obviously incapable of executing a plan.

Cole held my hand as the power burst from the dirk and into the elf. I fell to my knees, weakened, but he didn't let go. He dropped the knife and placed his hand on the vault door. The elf whispered something in a language I didn't understand, and the door exploded, flying back at us. Cole managed to get us out of the way, but when we landed, Cole didn't move.

"Cole?" I forced out. It was the same heavy feeling from the last time he took magic from the blade, but this time, I knew what to expect. The elf didn't answer me. Blood dripped down his forehead. "Damn it!"

I tried to stand, but my legs wouldn't move. I left Cole and pulled myself across the floor to the now open vault. I grabbed the dirk. I looked at Lugh where he lay in the dark, spasming. Then back at Cole where he lay bleeding. The waves were loud now. Buildings were being demolished because of the water's strength. I closed my eyes. *This was all my fault.*

A dream came to me at that strange time, and for once, it was a pleasant one. I was at a lake with my mother. I was young, maybe Lugh's age when our parents had been taken from us. I allowed the memory to envelop me.

"Yvaine," my mother laughed, "come swim with me."

"No, I'm scared," I said, standing on the edge of the dock.

"Why are you scared?" she asked, trying to hide her smile.

"This isn't funny. Someone could get hurt." Tears poured down my sunburnt cheeks. The water was dark. No air. No life for me under there.

The smile disappeared. "I know, honey." She thought a moment. "But if you come in, I'll show you a trick."

"Really?" My tears slowed. Mother's tricks were always amazing.

"Yes, but you have to come all the way out here." Mother motioned to the spot next to her, a mere two feet from the dock, but it was faraway to me. I

dipped my toe in.

Mother nodded, encouraging me to continue.

Slowly, I sank into the water but didn't resurface. I kicked and kicked. I couldn't find the sun. Then there were hands under my arms, lifting me. I gasped for air, the tears fresh.

"Oh, my darling daughter, don't be afraid."

I sobbed. The trick wasn't worth this kind of torture.

"You still want to see the trick?" My mother's golden hair shined in the sunlight, and her voice was soothing.

Hesitantly, I nodded.

"Okay, we're going to go under the water again, but I'll go with you this time. Are you ready?"

I was about to yell, "No!" but she plunged us under, and I kicked and screamed, panicking in the darkness.

Then her voice came to me, as clear as if we were above the frightening water, "Open your eyes, Yvaine. Look at me."

I peeked my eyes open, not knowing they'd been closed. I looked up. "Where's the water?"

"All around you. See? The water doesn't want to hurt you. Just ask, and it will move." Mother said strange words, and the water surrounded her hair but not her face, making the long strands float and expand around her like sunrays.

"Can I do that?" I wondered, wary of trusting the cold darkness.

"Of course. Just try."

"Move!" I demanded.

The water crashed over my head, and I sucked in a lungful of cold. Then we were above the surface, my mother laughing.

"My serious daughter, you have to learn to trust or else more than water will come crashing down on you."

I glared at her, water dripping down my face.

"Are you done for the day?" she asked.

"Yes."

"Let's find your father, and we can have some ice-cream." She lifted me up to the dock and followed close behind, the sun lighting our path.

The memory remained when I returned to reality. I held onto that happy emotion as the waves found us and filled the building. Before the water met my lungs, I said the words my mother had whispered to the water, simply to feel close to her. "Movere cum me."

Then it stopped. The water retreated so it coursed down the road and left the bank alone to stand. But despite its surrender, the building moaned from the pressure and a piece of the ceiling fell beside Cole. *We needed to get out.*

I crawled to Lugh and placed the bow and quiver on my shoulder. I whispered the strange words again, the knife in hand. Its glow was bright and beckoning, almost as if it was communicating with the water. *What kind of power had I held onto all these years?*

The icy water surrounded us, with the allowance of our faces. I whispered again, and it floated us out of the vault to Cole. I grabbed both of them securely and trusted that the knife would guide us to safety. If I didn't, we were going to die.

Entering the tide was shocking. We were all under the waves without air, but we made it the surface in time. We were going against the current. I just kept asking the knife to take us north. Away from the city. Away from these monsters.

The sun was rising, and the water sparkled. Sometimes I would lose concentration and we would go under, hitting debris and bodies that would send us south again. The Guise could appear at any moment, and unlike us, water didn't affect them.

Streets came and went. I worried that Cole and Lugh were drowning, but I couldn't do anything to help until we got to shore, so I pushed us on. There was an Anthros woman trying to escape the water by clinging to a fire escape. She saw us and called out for help. I looked away.

The flood would cleanse this city of gangs. And though there were innocents, at least their suffering would end. The thought made me think of church. I recoiled, remembering how cruel I had accused God to be to wipe out everyone at the time of Noah, but I could see it now. Sometimes the best thing for everyone, was a fresh start. But just like that woman clinging to the building, I would not give up my life easily or the lives of the ones I loved.

The fish processing plant was just ahead; it had taken the most damage. Worried about the sniper, I lowered us under the surface, unable to part it enough to breathe. So I pushed us faster, up the hill and over the crumbling bridge. The forest was barely touched on the other side, due to the incline.

The water deposited us on the moss. After finding my breath, I flung the bow aside and checked Lugh. Water filled his mouth, so I turned him on his side and pounded his back. He couldn't cough, but I considered him safe when I didn't see any more water. The leaf was the same colors as before.

"You actually did it! I don't know how, but you did." The sniper was standing in the trees a few yards away, rifle at his side. He took a step forward.

"Don't come any closer," I warned. I struggled to stand, and he noticed.

"I don't think you should be making demands of anyone, honey." He raised his rifle and aimed. "There's only enough prey for one hunter around here."

I heard a whistle. It was an odd sound for a bullet, but I quickly realized what it was. To my left, Cole had woken and raised his bow. An arrow now rested in the sniper's eye where he'd collapsed against a tree.

The elf coughed up more water, then looked to me. We smiled.

We're alive.

Looking down at the city, I laughed. Disbelief, relief, and fear pulsed through me. The bridge had fallen with the dam, along with the processing plant and first several streets. As far as the eye could see, human structures fell, one by one, into the angry waves. There were shapes floating on the surface, and it took me a moment to realize that they were bodies. The dead washed away, following the river south.

I sank into the soft moss and slept.

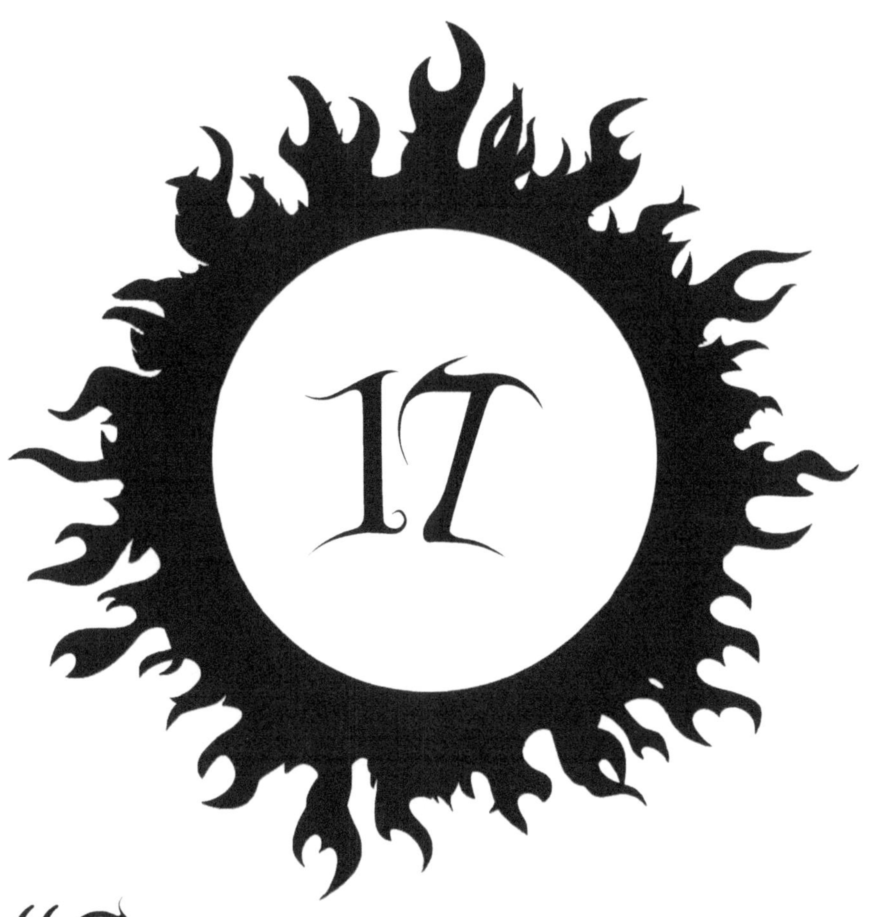

"Stay down," Cole whispered in my ear. I struggled to open my eyes, though my body was already trying to get up and run. For what reason, I didn't know. Perhaps it had become a habit.

"Why?" I asked, finally able to see Cole through the dark. He was staring at something from behind a wall of bramble. There were red and brown leaves tangled in his dark hair, and the desire to brush them away was strong.

"We're hiding."

"So, nothing new," I sighed.

Cole removed his intense focus from whatever we were hiding from, and looked to where I lay beside him. "I'm glad you're awake." The relief and utter adoration in his voice gave me the urge to run again, but I met his gaze bravely and returned the feeling. The elf looked through the brambles and relaxed. "They're gone, for now."

Stiff, I lifted myself into a sitting position. "What happened? Where are we? Where's Lugh?" I searched the darkness for my brother and found nothing.

"Relax, he's well-hidden." Cole motioned to a moss hill just a few feet from us. I could see Lugh's nose poking through the plants. Looking down, I realized I was covered the same way. "We're only a couple miles from the city. I would have taken us farther if I didn't have to stop so much to hide." He unburied a black backpack, revealing treasure.

"Food!"

"Quiet," Cole insisted, placing his hand over my mouth. "We don't know how close they are."

My hand found his, removing it from my mouth, but held it tight in my lap instead. "Who are we hiding from?" It was nighttime, so it couldn't have been the Guise.

"Eat first. You must be starving." Cole handed me a strip of jerky, and I eyed the pack it came from.

"Is this the sniper's?" I asked, skeptical.

"Yes. And no, the meat isn't human," he assured, knowing where my thoughts brought me after being in the city so long.

"How do you know?" I took a bite, deciding that it didn't matter. I peered up at the trees. The color of autumn was disguised by the night, and I feared winter was at our heels.

"Because I know what it tastes like, and that isn't it."

I stiffened, returning my stare to the elf.

"You still can't take a joke, can you? I may have done a lot of terrible things, but cannibalism is not one of them." He grinned. "It's gnome."

I knew we were both thinking of the first meal we shared together. He had been tied up while I forced pieces of gnome down his throat. *Could that have really only been a few weeks ago?*

My stomach calming, I said, "Well, it's much better than pears. I think they were rotten, and not worth what I paid the Sator."

Cole ran his fingers through my shortened hair. "I was wondering what happened."

"I'm going to miss the warrior braid." A sense of grief overcame me, realizing my hair was gone. I had never cut it. When times were hard, I could look at the terrible mess of tangles and remember my mother. It was the same hair she had brushed before I went to bed at night. *It had been the only thing I had left of her.*

"Warriors are warriors, with or without their braid," the elf said, confident.

I stared at the bow secured across Cole's chest and agreed. He had been without a weapon when he sacrificed himself for us. When he was alone in the arena. No weapon or symbol could make a warrior. Just like no lost memento could erase the memory of my mother. The power came from within us, not the other way around.

Several strips of jerky and a mouthful of water later, I asked again, "Who are we hiding from?"

Cole released my hand and stood. "Elves."

"Your kind? Why?"

The elf sent me an incredulous expression.

"Oh, they're the same ones." *The same ones who hated him.*

"There are only a few elf clans, and mine is the largest. They are between us and the stones." He began pacing and said, "I was banished, Yvaine. If they find us, there won't be a happy welcome. They'll kill me and…" He looked to Lugh.

"And us."

The elf nodded.

"Screw them." I stood slowly, my legs weak. "We have the dagger. Use it to get us out of here."

"I can't. Not only are you too weak," I opened my mouth to argue when he said, "but they can scent magic."

"Wouldn't they have found us by now, then?" I asked.

"No. So long as it's not cast." The wonder in his voice was obvious. "How did you do that? The water?" A bird flitted between the tree branches, and I was grateful to hear it.

"The dagger," I panicked. I searched for the dirk for the first time since waking.

Cole removed it from his inside jacket pocket and handed it to me. "I'm sure there's something left, but it needs to rest."

"You still make it sound like it's alive." I ran my finger over the runes on the sleeping blade.

Cole approached and rested his hands on my waist. My breath caught. "How did you get us out, Yvaine?"

I was trying to remember the feeling, the connection I had with the dagger, but all I could focus on was where his hands were and his pine-tree scent. "I don't know. I don't remember most of it." I didn't know why I kept the memory of my mother from him, but it felt private somehow. And something I didn't completely understand yet. "What does *movere cum me*' mean?"

Surprised, he answered, "*Move with me*. Where did you hear that?"

"I didn't. It was spray painted on one of the buildings," I lied smoothly, too tired to feel guilty about it.

"You should rest, Yvaine. We still have a long way to go." He sounded disappointed and tried to step away.

"Wait." He stopped. "Where were you when the Collapse happened? You never told me," I said, desperate for his presence.

"You never asked." His hands tightened, and my skin tingled.

"Well, I'm asking now." I was such a coward. Why couldn't I tell him about my memory? *Didn't I trust him?*

Warmth in his eyes, he started, "I was north of the mountains." The elf looked down.

Eager, I said, "Why were you there?"

"I was looking for something," he answered slowly, as if he didn't know how to say what he wanted.

I nodded, encouraging him to continue.

"Anyway, I didn't find it. The bombing started before I could." Neither of us moved as he told his story, and I felt completely at ease in his arms. "I only got out in time because I was watching the cities evacuate south. I listened to them panic and scream at each other when their cars were blocked during the night." I shivered, and he brought me closer. "I ran as fast as I could away from the cities until I ended up somewhere near Loch Lomond."

"I'm glad you got out in time," I whispered.

Cole gave me a small, sad smile. "I heard the bombs land. And word of the poison spread soon after."

"Yeah, humans have a talent for destroying things, don't they?" I bowed my head in shame.

"It's not your fault, Yvaine."

Ignoring his comment, I asked, "Did you ever find what you were looking for after that?"

Cole loosened his grip. "No, I didn't."

Curious, I pushed, "Are you still looking?"

"I don't want to anymore." His expression was difficult to read. It was the first time that he'd put up a wall. I thought only I did that?

"Then don't," I breathed, wishing he would come back to me.

Cole released me and stepped away.

"I thought that we were all going to die in that horrible place." I dropped the dagger and clutched his shoulders tight, refusing to let him leave. "I didn't know if I was going to make it to you in time. It made me realize…" The words wouldn't come out. I had repressed the feeling since I met him—the sense of belonging.

"Yes?" Cole whispered.

My heart fell to the ground. "That we need to move faster. Winter gets closer every day." Our moment in the gun shop was just that—a moment. He was lonely. And it was the only reason he expressed any interest. There was no point in telling him. What did I expect? Life hadn't exactly been kind, so of course, I couldn't have him either.

I dropped my hands and waited for him to let go. But he didn't. "I thought the *other woman* was frightening, but you, Yvaine, will be the death of me."

It was my turn to step away. "What's that supposed to mean?" I did my best to whisper, but the anger came crashing through my veins, burning away the fatigue.

"You call me a liar every chance you get, and maybe I am, but you are the master of lies. You lie to yourself every day. You lie about what you feel and who you are." Black hair fell into his eyes, hiding whatever emotion that hid there.

"You can't possibly know how I feel! And you certainly don't know who I am." I turned to go check on Lugh.

The elf grabbed my arm. "He's fine, Yvaine. There's nothing you can do for him right now."

I yanked my arm out of his grip. "He's not *fine*! He's dying, and every decision I make keeps him sick that much longer. It's distraction, after disaster, after catastrophe. It never stops!" Tears were falling now.

"And which category do I fall under?" he asked, smirking.

"This isn't a joke, Cole."

The elf responded quickly. "It should be. You use your brother as an excuse to be unhappy."

I turned away, refusing to look him in the eye.

"Lugh doesn't want that for you."

"How would you know? You spent all of a few hours with him before he was cursed, and you were tied up for most of it. You couldn't possibly know what he wants." The night was pitch black; it must have been a new moon.

Cole stepped close to me. I could feel his chest against my back. "Because no one who knows you would ever want you to be unhappy. You are brave, loyal, and selfless to a fault."

My heart pounded painfully. "What did I say about flirting?" The sarcastic comment came out as a sob.

"You said that you love it and wish I did it more often." I could hear the mischievous smirk in his words, and it made me want to attack and embrace him all at once.

"I love you, elf." I didn't turn around.

Cole lowered his head until I could feel his breath against my ear. "I love you, human." His hands returned to my waist, and his lips fell to my neck, kissing the overheated skin.

The rush of relief and pleasure was indescribable.

All I wanted was *him*.

Nothing else mattered.

Leaving Lugh and our weapons by the bramble, Cole led me into an alcove of sweet-smelling trees. Every sense was heightened and focused on Cole. My worries about the elves finding us, the dagger resting somewhere other than at my side, and even my brother lying alone in the dark disappeared. For the first time since the Collapse, I let my guard down.

Clothes fell to the ground. The night was chilled, but the warmth of Cole's skin kept the shivers away. He laid me down on the soft moss, and traced the scars I'd always been ashamed of. I learned to embrace each one simply because he had given them his love. The kisses we shared weren't ones of desperation or loneliness, but of patience and acceptance.

No other Common or Fae was thought of during our time under the leaves. Every sound was music. Every taste was divine. Every touch was love incarnate.

For the first time in my life, I felt happiness.

It was still dark when I woke. Our nest of leaves and moss was warm. My eyes adjusted quickly, and I found Cole's face beside mine. I traced my finger over his cheeks, nose, and lips. No feeling could be greater than the one I felt when I was with him.

Cole's breathing was slow and steady. He was deep in the realm of dreams. I only hoped that he imagined me there with him.

Standing, I dressed and parted the heavy branches that hung in my path. It was only a short distance to my brother, but I found myself running anyway, suddenly very worried about him. Because I realized that I hadn't thought of him since I entered the alcove of trees. The guilt was intense and soured my good mood.

Reaching the bramble, I felt the ground until I found Lugh beside our buried stash of weapons and food. I brushed the moss from his face and placed his head in my lap. "Lugh, I'm sorry I left you alone." It was strangely awkward talking about Cole with Lugh, even though he couldn't hear me. "Cole isn't like other people. He cares." Brushing the long, blonde hair from my brother's face, I said, "He cares about us, and I care about him."

I waited for Lugh to say something or twitch or do anything that would tell me that he was listening. "I wish you were here to make fun of me or tell me that I'm being stupid." I only allowed one tear to fall. "But you will soon enough. We're going to get you to the stones and heal you."

The dirk lit without me having to ask, and I smiled. I lifted it to Lugh's mouth and peeked at the leaf—brown edges. Glancing around to make sure we were alone, I looked inward and asked the dirk to guide me. "Help me heal," I whispered.

The amethyst smoke seeped out of the dirk, slow and weak. But it made its way to Lugh and encased him in its glow. The dead brown on the leaf receded, but it didn't disappear like before. I dropped the dirk, and the smoke hovered, seemingly unsure, before it retreated into the knife. I pulled out a waterskin and let the cold water run over the spell and down my brother's throat. The white scar on his neck was blackened by poisoned veins.

"We will fix this, Lugh. You're not going to die." A breeze hurried past us, bringing the cold of winter with it.

A howl sounded. It reminded me of a wolf, but with a guttural feline whine. A creature I had never heard before.

I hid Lugh under the moss again and stood with the dark blade. Footsteps were fast approaching. I was about to call out for Cole when he appeared out of the trees. "We have to go now," he said. The panic in his voice was alarming.

"Why? What made that noise?" I asked.

"A cù-sìth. It's my kin's version of a dog. It can scent magic miles away." Cole unearthed Lugh and threw the backpack at me, placing the bow over his shoulder. He stopped and looked at my brother. "Did you use magic, Yvaine?"

"Yes," I whispered.

"Can you run?" he asked.

"Yes."

"Good. Because you'll need to run faster than you ever have before if we're going to lose it." Cole went to the bramble and picked a bunch of unfamiliar berries from it, smashing them against me.

"What the hell?" I complained.

"Cù-sìth hate gooseberries. Hopefully, it will mask your scent." He moved to Lugh and did the same. "Run east. We'll have to go around the elf's stronghold." I sheathed the dirk and placed the sniper's iron blade in my pocket. Cole eyed it curiously but didn't say anything.

With Lugh hanging over Cole's back, we ran through the trees. My ankle was not completely healed, but it was well enough that the adrenaline burned the pain away.

A second howl pierced the night.

"Damn it," Cole muttered.

"What does that mean?"

"The second howl means that it's found our trail."

"And the third?" I asked.

Cole didn't answer, but I knew.

"I'm sorry. Lugh needed help," I explained, the words escaping in between breaths.

"I know," he said, understanding. "Just keep running." But no matter how far we ran, the woods wouldn't end. And the sense of dread was still there. Cole felt it, too, because he didn't even stop when we came upon a creek. We leapt across it, ignoring the resource.

Then, the sky brightened, and a horror was reborn. A horn tore through the morning air beyond us. "The howl?" I asked, breathless.

"No, worse. The elves have joined the hunt." We stopped, unsure what direction to run. The dewdrops from the moist leaves above fell down on us. The breeze had turned into wind. Blonde hair stung my eyes, and I finally took a moment to tie it back.

"What do we do?" I grabbed Cole's hand for comfort and guidance. My ankle throbbed again.

Debating, he said, "If we keep running together, we'll be caught. It's only a matter of time. But if you take Lugh, I can lead them away while you head north to the stones."

"No."

"Yvaine, it's the only way to save your brother. And you." He gripped my hand tight.

"You won't be saving anyone by leaving us. Lugh needs you to perform the spell, and I need you to survive. We stay together." I refused to give up my happiness. I wouldn't find it again if he left me.

His beautiful face pinched with frustration. "You don't need me. Just use the dagger, and you'll be fine." His desperate words confused me, but I had made my decision.

"We stay together."

The third howl echoed against the trees.

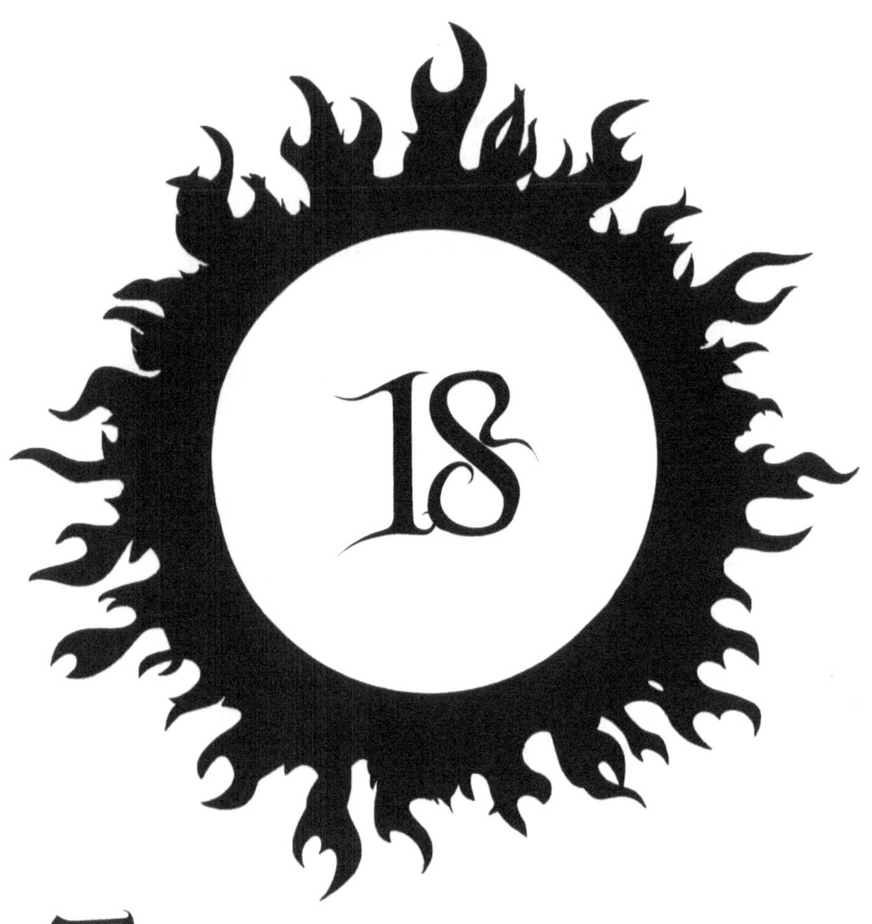

18

The cù-sìth approached on four powerful legs. The fur was long and the color of moss. The ears were large and pointed, hearing every sound the forest made. The eyes were snow white, just like its sharp incisors. The Fae's growl was low and menacing, but it paused, making a sound that could only be compared to a tiger's chuff.

Its claws extended, reaching farther than any tiger's swipe could. It took a step toward us. My heart was pounding, and I was sure that the creature could hear it. It met my eyes, unlike any animal I had come across; the intelligence was undeniable. Though, it didn't speak. It merely crept closer, sniffing the air around us.

"Don't move," Cole said. The elf didn't sound frightened. Just careful. He moved toward the creature, hand outstretched. "Arlen, do you remember me?"

I didn't dare voice the hundreds of questions that popped in my head. I was frozen in place, imagining Arlen leaping toward me and how utterly helpless my dagger would be against it. Yet, the endowed weapon lit anyway, voicing my silent challenge to the Fae. It would not hurt my loved ones without giving something in return. Its stare moved to the dagger at my side. It took another step. I tensed.

"Don't move, Yvaine. Let him assess you."

The creature was two heads taller than me, standing on four legs. His snout was like that of a dog's, but he had long whiskers that tickled my skin when he scented me. As he circled, I noticed his long, curled tail. It gave me the same sense I had when I was a child looking in the window of a pet shop.

Arlen chuffed and sat beside me, licking his already shining fur.

"This is what has been chasing us for hours?" I said to Cole. "Why were we running?"

The elf sighed. "Because he led them right to us." A dozen elves appeared from behind the trees, aiming their glowing bows at the trespassers. All with dark braided hair.

Arlen stayed calm, unsurprised. Too many times in the past weeks had my stomach rolled from stress—it boiled now. I went to grab Cole's hand, but he moved it out of the way before I could touch him.

The elf saw the hurt on my face, but continued to focus on the elves. His expression was confused, mortified even, at the sight of his people. "I'm only passing through. Give me a few hours, and I'll be past the border. You'll never see me again." I couldn't help but notice that he said "me" instead of "us." I clutched the dagger tight, ready to fight.

"You were given that chance already, Coilleach." A male elf stepped forward, lowering his bow. His eyes were dark, and his features were angled much like Cole's, but Cole had a strength in his build that was very much human. Looking at the elves now, I could see that they were built delicately, and the females were even smaller. They moved with a grace I could never hope to achieve. But their skin was darker than Cole's, and it wasn't because of the sun. It was an unnatural color, as if they had painted themselves the color of midnight.

"Darce, it's been a long time. I've never defied the banishment before. But now, I must. If we do not cross, this boy will die." Cole gestured to the human hanging over his shoulder. Lugh spasmed, but I couldn't do anything to help.

"Why would we care about a human? They only bring destruction, as you well know, Coilleach," Darce said. Clearly, we were going to have to fight our way out. I eyed Arlen, and my heart sank. *We weren't leaving alive.*

Cole met my gaze for the first time since the elves arrived. In his eyes was pain and… regret? Was he going to trade us for his freedom? I instantly felt guilty for the thought. Cole would never betray us. He loved us. *He loved me.*

"They have magic," he declared, closing his eyes as he did.

"Liar! Humans can't wield magic. Take the abomination to the chief. Kill the humans." Darce didn't bother to raise his bow again. The rest of the elves moved in, ready to take our lives.

"Why do you think Arlen found us? There's magic here!" Cole bellowed.

Darce didn't stop his advance. "He tracked what little magic you had left from the last theft, Coilleach. And now, you have stolen for the last time."

"Wait!" Cole cried, stepping in front of me. "Listen to me!"

The first of the elves reached Cole and grabbed Lugh. He continued to fight them, screaming at them to listen. A female elf aimed her arrow directly at my heart. The beat stopped when I realized what it meant. The sun was rising. It was only a matter of time before the Guise would appear.

Cole struggled against several of his kind now. He wouldn't let go of Lugh. One of the attackers fell limp to the forest floor. He had taken their magic. A knife was revealed and placed against my brother's throat.

The dirk at my side pulsated with power. I wrapped my hand around it. Magic burst from the weapon, shrouding us in amethyst light. The wave of power forced everyone to the ground. *I would not fail my brother again.*

"I may be human, but I can certainly wield magic. Touch Lugh or Cole again, and you won't survive another sunrise." My bluff was well delivered. They were shocked and disturbed. I helped Cole stand and checked Lugh. The knife hadn't touched him. Arlen circled us, wagging his tail.

Darce looked at me for the first time. "You are not human." The rest of the elves stood and nocked their arrows, but he raised his hand and they relaxed, uncertain of their enemy.

"Of course I am. Didn't you know that humans could use endowed weapons?" I pointed the blade at the elf with purpose, keeping true to my threat.

Darce gave Cole a bewildered expression, but Cole looked away, refusing to acknowledge the silent question. "You have my apologies. All of you are encouraged to see the chief. No one is dying today," the dark elf said.

"We'd rather be on our way. We have no time to waste," I explained. The numbness never returned, even at death's door. It gave me the confidence I needed to face our enemy.

Darce approached Lugh slowly, asking permission with his eyes.
I nodded.
The dark elf peeled the collar of Lugh's shirt back and examined the black veins. "He's been poisoned by a banshee. You are right, there isn't much time left." He opened Lugh's mouth and found the leaf. "Spriggan's

magic is powerful, but you will still not make it to the stones in time."

I masked my surprise. It must have been Lugh's only hope if Darce knew exactly where we were taking him. "I can heal him. It will last long enough to get him there," I said.

"But it's losing its effect, isn't it?" I refused to answer, and he continued. "Each time you perform the healing spell, the curse adapts. Until finally, the spell won't have any influence at all. Why do you think the leaf didn't heal him? Spriggan's magic is powerful, yes, but it is slow. A curse such as this needs to be banished all at once. There cannot be one trace of it left behind." The panic must have been clear on my face because the elf smiled and said, "Do you have the knowledge and skill to make that happen?"

"I don't need to. Cole will perform the spell. The stones will awaken his magic." I sounded unsure now, never having said it aloud. Once the idea was out in the world, it seemed unlikely. Too uncertain to be risking my brother's life on it.

Darce laughed a heartless laugh, his dark eyes betraying the arrogance inside. "Coilleach, you have outdone yourself. But what could one expect from a deformed monstrosity such as you?" The dark elf never removed his gaze from Cole as he said to me, "Even if *Cole* managed to suck every drop of magic from you, he would not be able to banish all of the curse away. He's too weak. Too wrong. The stones would reject him, just as everyone else has."

"You're wrong!" I growled. "You don't know anything about him!"

"It seems that neither do you, *human*." Darce motioned to the dark elves, and they herded us north with threats of arrows in our backs. No one approached Cole again. No one wanted their magic taken.

The sun had fully risen and was beginning to peek through the canopy. Moans could be heard echoing in the woodland. I was about to ask why we weren't running when a dark cloud appeared above us. It was so dark,

I expected thunder and lightning to rain down on us. We were encased in shadow. I looked behind us and saw that two warriors in the back were whispering to themselves. *A darkness spell.*

I couldn't help but chuckle. That was all Lugh and I had wanted when we captured Cole. Now, we had it. Between the light crunch of feet on leaves, I listened to their words. "Sit tenebris vivere. Sit tenebris vivere."

I concentrated on memorizing the strange words rather than what Darce had said about Cole. I *knew* Cole. I trusted him. It took me a long while to get there, but he had proved himself to both me and Lugh. *So why did the dark elf's words bother me so much?*

Dozens of Guise roamed the forest, naturally avoiding the dark cloud. It was strange to walk through the horde. They couldn't touch us, and it felt amazing. It felt powerful. The sun was only inches from me. I stretched my hand out to the rays. A female elf grabbed my arm painfully. "One touch and you become one of them. Stay in the darkness." She motioned forward with her bow. It glowed a dim rose color.

Traveling through the forest, I saw many Fae species poking their heads out of hollows, nooks, and dens. Fear was plastered on all of their unique faces. Whether it was fear of the Guise or the elves, I didn't know.

"I'm sorry, Yvaine," Cole whispered.

Before I could ask what he was apologizing for, I saw a dark wall. It flowed like smoke. *Like magic.* It climbed high and curved, so large that there was no way to see the other side without flying. I stopped at its edge, but the elves pushed me into a small break in the smoke. I clutched Lugh's hand when it lowered behind us.

There was nothing but shadow beyond the wall. The only light that could be seen was the glow of the endowed weapons. Each one had a unique color. The dagger lit on its own, guiding me through the thick shadows.

The clan was large, as Cole had said. There were more elves in this one place than I had seen across the land in the past thirteen years. Though, I could only see their silhouettes, as they had melded with the dark barrier they lived in. Towering trees stood beside us, but they had transformed into something otherworldly. Their trunks were rotted, and their branches had become claws that stretched outward, reaching for any light that passed their way.

"What is this place?" I whispered, shivering in the intense cold.

Darce answered, "The future." With no other explanation than that, I was left with a sense of dread that weighed me down. It was a struggle to stand upright, as if the life was seeping from me and into the cold ground. I looked to Cole to find that he was just as shocked. The strangeness must have happened after he was banished and because of the Guise.

"Take Coilleach to the keep," Darce ordered.

"No!" I threatened, the dirk flaring its light.

"If you want to know how to heal the boy, you will cooperate. Coilleach is ours to do with as we wish." The backpack full of our supplies was ripped from my back by a dark elf.

I unsheathed the dagger.

"Yvaine, stop. I'll be fine. I'll take care of Lugh while you talk to them." He bowed his head in shame and handed the same elf his bow and quiver.

"We stay together." I repeated what I'd said earlier that morning, reminding him how I felt.

"Protect Lugh at any cost," he said. Though I had never said those words to him, they had been my mantra for as long as I could remember. We locked eyes in the darkness for only a moment before he was taken away, Lugh still hanging over his shoulder.

"Come, the chief will want to speak with you." Darce waited for me to move on my own. Slowly, I took a step toward the massive structure before us. I had mistaken it as warped trees before, but now that I was only a few feet from it, I could see the stone structure. The forest was its foundation, while the structure was built around the powerful roots below. It reminded me of the ancient castles, but smaller and much more terrifying. If it was pitch black outside, what would the inside be like?

I was forced up the steps, while Cole took the steps down into a black pit under the Fae castle. The steps were old and crumbling. I tripped over the rubble and Darce caught me, pulling me upright. I ripped my arm away, suddenly very angry.

This journey had been nothing but heartache and peril. It had been since the Collapse, but these past few weeks had been the hardest. Each step Lugh and I took forward sent us hurdling backward ten. Yet, we continued to crawl forward, little by little. We were finally close. So close, I could have allowed myself to feel excited. But these people were in our way. I was so tired of things being in our way.

I needed to clear the path.

My endowed weapon shone like a beacon in the dark, guiding me through the vine-strewn castle halls. Tapestries hung, moth-eaten, from the ceiling. Their once bright colors were now dull and the designs lost to age. The hallway led into a grand room. Many elves dwelled in this space, surrounding each other in whispers. Their eyes flashed in pain upon my light. *How long had they been in the dark?*

Deep in the back of the room, there was a chair made of thorns. In that moment, I realized, though there were plants living here, there was no green. "Chief Dearil, this is Yvaine. She wishes to speak to you on behalf of Coilleach the Banished," Darce introduced.

I didn't bow as he had, but merely shined my light brighter, challenging. "Release Cole. He is the only chance I have to save my brother. We're just passing through. There's no need to keep us here."

Your magic is powerful," the chief said with an old, raspy voice. I still couldn't see him. It was just a figure sitting in a chair.

"Whoever had this dagger before me must have been. It has kept us alive since the Collapse." My heart sped. The darkness was growing, pushing on my skin, sliding into my lungs.

"That is not how magic works, child. Only the magic within can power that weapon. Magic cannot be left behind, and it cannot be given away." The chair cracked and popped as the figure stood. He was tall and thin, with a slithering walk that sent shivers up my spine. "Magic belongs to the caster and the caster alone. That is why Coilleach was banished. He defied these sacred rules. He took what was not his to take." The dagger wavered in its glow, and the chief's shadow danced on the wall behind him. He stopped in front of me, his eyes dark and piercing. The skin was old and withered, and as black as the silhouettes around us. "It is his humanity that does this. Just as his kind unleashed the monsters upon us, he will take what is left and doom us all. That is why he must be put to death."

"You're wrong," I said. "He only takes so he can help. Cole is the strongest person I have ever met. He only gives goodness to this dark world, and you're keeping him from doing it."

Realization lit up the chief's dark face before he said, "Perhaps. Perhaps." Recovering from whatever thought had crossed his mind, he said, "But if he is so good, then why did he lie to you? Certainly, you've figured that out by now." He took a step closer, unconcerned that I was armed.

"I don't know what you're talking about."

"Here, let me help you along. I can see that the human in you has slowed your thoughts." The chief reached out and gripped my head between his hands and said, "Revelare occulta."

A pain shot through my skull, much worse than any migraine had ever done. I could feel invisible fingers pulling at memories, tearing them out and into the open all at once.

I followed my mother down the hallway of our house, keeping quiet. She stopped in front of one of the gilded mirrors and spoke an ancient word to the reflection, "Verum." My mother's blonde hair blackened, her skin glowed, her rounded features sharpened, and her ears became long points jutting through the nighttime waves.

"Mother?" I asked, stepping out from behind the corner.

The strange person disappeared, leaving my mother there smiling at me. "Go find your father, honey. I'll be right there."

Unsure of what I had seen, I ran, all too eager to forget about it.

As I ran, my surroundings transformed until I was standing in the bookstore in Glasgow. People were screaming. Sunlight was streaming in through the windows.

"Hold my hand, Yvaine. Don't let go." Unlike before, when I recalled this memory, she didn't take us to the basement or through tunnels. We were surrounded by a dark cloud. We ran until we found an open car. The cloud followed us all the way home, where my father came barreling out of the house.

"Where's Yvaine? Are you okay?" he questioned.

"We're fine," my mother said. "We need to get inside."

I was about to ask what was happening, when my mother touched my cheek, and I suddenly felt very tired.

More memories flooded my mind, but I found enough strength to pull away. "Stop!"

The chief released his hold on me. "You see, Yvaine? You are much more than a mere human. I am only sorry that you've been lied to for so long. First your mother disguises your memories, then Coilleach betrays you. But now you know the truth. You do not need a banished abomination to save your brother. Unlike him, you have magic of your own." The chief revealed his teeth in what was supposed to be a smile, but instead, it made my skin crawl.

"I'm half elf… That means Lugh is, too." The numbness teetered on the edge of my thoughts, offering sanctuary.

"Indeed." The chief returned to his chair. "We could use someone with your power. Stay and learn. We can teach you what your mother failed to teach. Spells beyond your current comprehension."

"What about Lugh and Cole?" I asked.

"Your brother, if he survives, will be offered the same. So long as he possesses the same…attributes." A small elf child approached the chief with a crystal glass full of dark liquid. He took it and gulped it down before handing it back.

"And if he doesn't?"

"If your brother is without magic, his fate will be the same as Coilleach's." The dark elf wiped his lip clean of the mysterious drink.

I stilled my shaking hands and took a deep breath. "If that's how it must be. Please, teach me the banishment spell, so I may take my brother to the stones and heal him. With any luck, I'll bring you back two magical elves."

"I'm surprised there isn't more protest for Coilleach. I was under the impression that he meant something to you." The chief gave me a knowing smile.

"Cole convinced me that I needed him to heal my brother. Now that I know different, he's no longer necessary. And not my concern." I forced the dagger's light to calm; it was beating in time with my heart.

"Very well. Tonight, under the moon, you will be shown the banishment spell. Until then, rest and tend to your brother as you wish." I turned to leave when he added, "I look forward to seeing what you are capable of, Yvaine."

Dread returned to my stomach while I nearly ran from the throne room, down the long hallway, and outside. Darce followed. "Let me escort you," he offered, leaning toward the descending steps.

The Fae had found their way into their homes for the day. Even living in perpetual darkness, they still felt the need to hide from the light outside their walls. "I'll find my own way. I will meet you here this evening for the banishment spell." I left no room for argument as I plummeted down the dark steps. *I needed to be alone.*

The hallways were long and cold. Shivering in the dark, I concentrated on my light. The dirk had always been there for me. When I needed a weapon or simply company, it was there to banish the darkness.

But I'd been alone all along.

Tears fell down my dirty cheeks. Every speck of dirt, every sore muscle and injury was felt in that moment. The exhaustion from surviving had taken its toll. I crumpled to the stone floor, my back against the damp wall. I squeezed my jacket tight together and listened to my teeth chatter.

Naive. That's what I was. Cole had been right, I did lie to myself. If I had given any extra thought to the topic it would have been easy to figure out—I was half elf. I was just so focused on surviving. On making the next step. There had been no room for anything else. The world wouldn't allow me to rest long enough to think.

Cole. Why had he lied? Several evil theories came to mind, but I forced them away. Last night I had chosen to trust him. To be with him. If he didn't tell me, it had to have been for a good reason. If not…

I stood, remembering that Lugh was probably just as cold down here. He needed my help. I made my way down two more hallways before I saw the cell doors. There were no guards. No one wanted to risk their magic. One touch was all Cole needed to take it.

"Cole," I called. My voice carried down the hall until it morphed into another's and finally disappeared altogether.

"Here," whispered the first cell. Unsheathing the dagger, I raised it high and shined its light.

"Where's Lugh?" My brother was nowhere in sight. "I thought you were going to watch him?"

Confused, he said, "He's in the cell next to me."

Quickly, I went to the neighboring cell. Lugh was lying on the cold stone ground. There was no padding, no blanket, nothing that would keep him warm. "These elves don't care if we die of the cold, do they?" I pushed on the bars and exhaled a sigh of relief when they opened. There was no point in locking the door when the prisoner was unconscious. I took off my jacket and draped it over Lugh, rubbing his limbs before he lost them.

"What did they tell you?" Cole asked quietly.

"They didn't tell me, so much as show me. The chief opened up some old memories in my head." I paused, breathing warmth into Lugh's cold hands. "Our mother was an elf."

"Oh."

"Oh? Is that all you have to say?" I said, waiting for his apology.

"What else did they tell you?"

Slowly, I responded, "You're going to be put to death. Lugh will be to if he doesn't have magic. I need to get both of you out of here. We'll handle it like Inscius. They're going to show me how to do the banishment spell tonight. I'll watch for an opening. Maybe I can bring down the walls. When the time is right, I'll come get you and Lugh. We'll run."

As I breathed another bit of warmth into Lugh's hands, Cole laughed. "You are something else, Yvaine. Even after discovering I lied, you still want to take me with you. It's impressive how desperate you are."

I looked to the man I'd chosen as mine and dropped Lugh's hand when I saw the stranger staring back at me.

"I can't continue this game and keep a straight face anymore. Did you honestly think that I would somehow be able to *awaken* my magic? Of course, it took you this long to realize that you had magic yourself. So, I suppose you did. You'll believe anything if it means you can shirk the responsibilities to your brother." The elf stood and leaned his arms on the cell bars, staring down at me. "You would have rather killed him and your-self instead of accept who you are. That was all I needed to start the game."

"What game?" I stuttered.

"Oh, there's always someone willing to trust others. To share their magic. But this game was going to be the best one yet." He shook his head in disbelief. "The stones were going to awaken *your* magic, Yvaine, and with any luck, Lugh's. It would have felt amazing to absorb all that raw power."

"But, I love you…" I dared to look into his cold green eyes.

"Oh, I know. That part was easy. The trust on the other hand, was a challenge. Though, an enjoyable triumph as of last night." The elf winked.

I flinched. The memory of our touches were now grotesque and wrong. Each kiss was a betrayal. Every word was a lie.

"Why?" I asked, knowing the answer.

"Because I could." The elf allowed the dark hair to fall over his eyes, so all I could see was the arrogant smirk beneath.

With those heartbreaking words, the numbness returned, and I felt nothing but my love for Lugh. I would get him out. I would save him. Like I always did.

I maneuvered Lugh onto my back and turned to Cole before passing his cell. "You were right before."

In a stranger's voice, he said, "About?"

"I *don't* need you." The spell had officially been broken.

The hallways seemed longer than before, but the exertion from carrying my brother kept me warm. Lugh twitched randomly, nearly falling from my back, but I held tight. I climbed the decaying steps and finally stood at the base of the Fae castle. The air was somehow colder. I looked up and saw the faint outline of the sun through the thick dark cloud.

I didn't need anyone.

Without stopping to think, I marched toward the wall. There were many blackened trees and stone homes in my way, but I kept moving. Silhouettes were moving within those homes. I kept my light low, hoping I could just walk out without anyone noticing.

"Yvaine, stop. You are not allowed to leave." Darce appeared out of nowhere, along with three of his fellow warriors. They each held an endowed weapon.

"Step aside, elf." The venom that seeped from my lips was real. I no longer had to act brave or vicious.

"You are one of us. Stay and learn. Save your brother." The dark elf took a slow step toward me, reaching out his hand. His eyelids trembled in the dull light radiating from my blade.

Taking the time to look at the elves and what they had become, I said, "I am nothing like you. You've deformed yourselves and accepted this darkness as life." I gripped Lugh tight and allowed myself to let go of the dormant light. "Let me show you what life looks like."

The light that shined didn't come from my blade, but from me. At my core, I could feel a burn so intense I thought I'd been lit on fire. The magic burst from me in tendrils of smoke and fog. The pale amethyst filled the elf's refuge, pushing against its black walls.

The dark elves scattered, blinded. Screams could be heard from every corner. The Fae were in pain. Darkness had become their shield as it had become mine. But both light and dark needed to exist. One couldn't live without the other.

No words were necessary to release my light. The magic had been hidden inside me all my life and was begging to be freed. I was more than human. I had a right to this weapon.

The burn spread from my core to my limbs, and even to Lugh. I would protect him at any cost. Even if it meant letting go of the one thing that had given me happiness.

It was midday, and the wall had thinned. I approached the edge without challenge. These elves had adapted to darkness and could no longer withstand the sun. I placed my hand in the dark smoke, feeling its power. A clear pathway appeared before me, growing taller and wider every second.

Cole surfaced at the forefront of my mind; his hopeless face as he murdered Nessa and the pain in his voice as he strangled Cahira. I'd called him a killer with a good heart. Even though I was wrong about him, I couldn't help but remember what he'd said in the City of Inscius: *"I don't want to be a killer."*

I stepped past the wall and let it fall into its original place, running north without a second thought about what I had left behind.

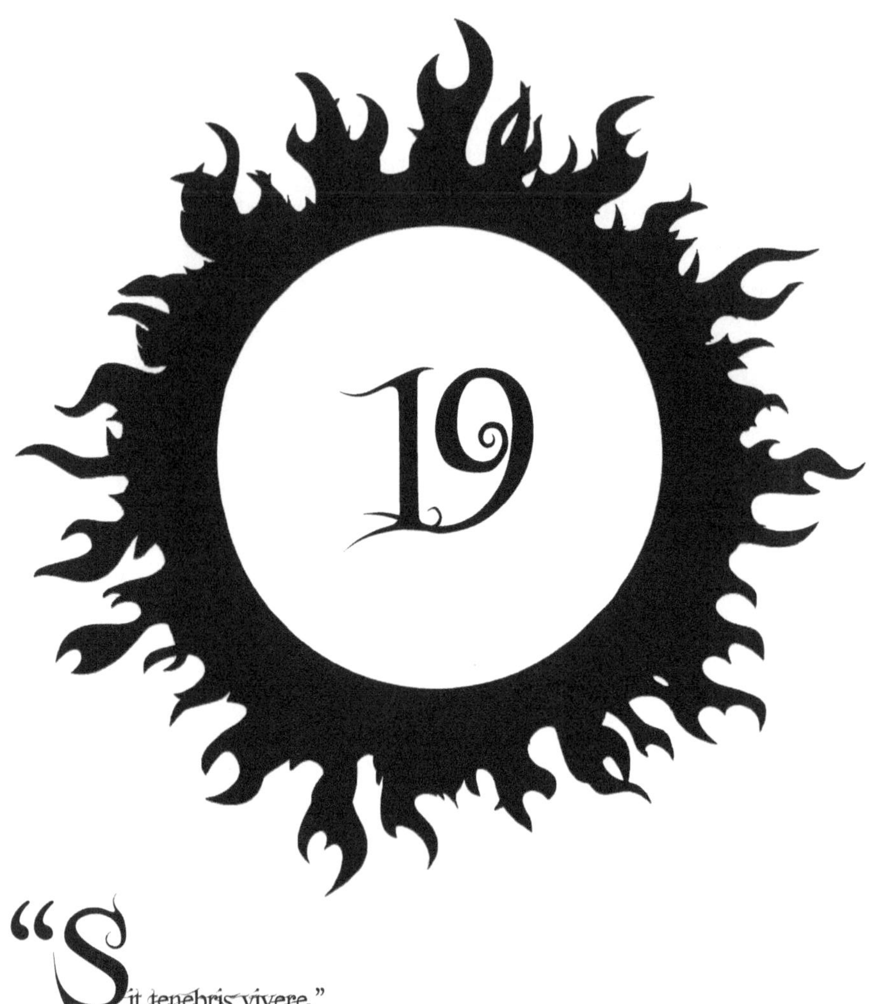

it tenebris vivere."

These words kept us from death. If that's what becoming a Guise was—it certainly looked like it. The dark cloud I created hovered above my brother and me. Concentrating on the spell kept me from dwelling on the intense physical pain I was in. My ankle had developed a sharp pain, my muscles screamed, and I was starving.

I hadn't thought through our escape at all. But I had to leave. There was nothing for us there. Elves were powerful, but those Fae had become something twisted and wrong. Anything they had to share would have corrupted us. And I couldn't risk Lugh's safety. If he didn't have magic…

That's why I refused to rest. We were so close to the stones—only a day's journey. I would break my legs before I stopped. I didn't know if the elves would come after us, but it was a chance I couldn't take. I could sleep after my brother woke up. *Lugh had been suffering long enough.*

The trees thinned, opening into a marsh. The grass and flowers were yellowed and dying from the cold. The day had finally faded, and I let the dark cloud dissipate, leaving me to find my way across in the dark. The north star peered from behind the clouds for only a moment, guiding me to the stones. The dirk at my side begged to light, but I didn't want to risk being seen.

I gasped when my foot sank into the icy water. The moss sucked my boot in until it was full of unwanted cold. The next step wasn't any easier. Neither were the next hundred. One by one, I crossed the marsh. The river was a short distance away. I would need to get us fresh water soon, if not for my sake, for Lugh's. I hadn't dared look at the spriggan's leaf since the cù-sìth's first howl.

It was hard to carry my brother again, but his weight had dropped significantly in the past days, making it manageable. *What would I do when he woke? I didn't have any supplies. No food or shelter…* I banished the racing thoughts away. It wasn't worth thinking of right now. *One step at a time.*

The moon rose, its waxing crescent as white as the coming snow. The shivers wouldn't stop, and I feared that Lugh was going to lose his appendages, but I had no other option than to walk forward. I rubbed his hands between mine. The clouds moved aside for the moon's light, allowing me to see my brother's skin clearly. All the veins in his hands had blackened.

"Stay with me, Lugh. I haven't come this far just so you could die. Keep fighting," I said between shivers. I didn't have the guts to turn and look at his blackened face.

The night came and went before I reached the base of the nearest mountain. To the east was forest. To the west there was more marsh, with a river on the other side. *"Within the Cairngorm Mountains lies a circle of stones,"* the spriggan had said.

Without one idea where to start, I went west in search of water. If the stones were within the mountains, there had to be a way around this one. Did the spriggan mean the stones were in the middle? Between two? Top or bottom? These were things I should have asked when I had the chance, but yet again, I was distracted by the daily trials of surviving.

Fog rolled in, surrounding us in a cold mist. I would have lost sight of the mountain if it wasn't right next to me, and I was grateful for the obvious land mark. Soon, I heard rushing water. The marsh became flat, moss-covered rock. My pants were soaked, but at least the cold had numbed my throbbing ankle.

Beside the river's edge, I set Lugh down for the first time since fleeing the dark elves. No one would be able to see us in this thick fog, which was why I savored the cleansing taste of river water. I propped Lugh on my lap, bringing the water to his mouth with my palm. There was only a speck of green left in the center of the dying leaf. Even his tongue had blackened veins.

"Come on, Lugh. Let's get going." Before I could move, a twig snapped behind me. I turned, the dagger already drawn. It lit, despite my wishes. Eyes reflected in the mist. Predator's eyes. A growl followed. Then a howl.

"Arlen?" I whispered, frightened that he had found us. But what approached wasn't the Fae cù-sìth. It was a Common wolf. Its pelt was grey and rough. Its eyes and teeth were somber yellow. It was not near the size of Arlen, but it was a challenge just the same. Especially when four more sets of eyes shone in the fog.

"Leave! Get!" I yelled, hoping to scare them away. But these wolves were hungry, and day was upon us. Only the dark clouds in the sky kept the sunrays from shining down. Even the Common animals knew about the Guise.

Would there be a day when we could walk in the sun without fear?

It was strange to ask such a question when I wasn't even sure if I'd live through the next minute. But the hope that it would be different someday gave me the motivation I needed to stand.

The nearest wolf lunged. I stepped back, leading it away from Lugh. I sliced its mouth when it lunged again and it whined, blood dripping onto the flat rocks. A larger wolf approached, but it kept a safe distance from my long dagger, waiting for an opening. I looked to Lugh. The other three were surrounding him, nipping at his shoes and jacket. "Get away!" My voice didn't matter to the starving wolves. We were merely meals to them.

Maybe if I ran, they would chase me and leave Lugh alone...

I readied myself for the sprint and inevitable death when I heard a familiar sound. A growl-chuff that could only belong to a Fae creature.

Arlen's towering figure appeared in the fog, his white eyes shining. The wolves' attention was diverted to the cù-sìth for only a moment before they ran down river. Shocked, I darted to Lugh, ready to defend him from the Fae. But he didn't attack.

I stared into the fog, searching for the elves, but Arlen hadn't howled. There was no way for the dark elves to track him without his call. "What are you doing here?" I asked the predator.

Arlen was silent for a moment before turning and walking north, toward the mountain. The dirk pulsed with a sporadic beat. *Follow him.*

The Fae led us up river. The fog was thick, but Arlen never sped ahead; I was always able to find his silhouette in the mist. We climbed the hillside, avoiding loose rocks and slick moss. The trees were dense again, which only created more obstacles.

It was hours before we reached the apex of the valley. From there, it was a steep descent to the bottom. I knew it was madness to follow a Fae into unknown territory, but honestly, I didn't have anywhere else to go. Lugh's life depended on Arlen now.

The fog thinned as the day warmed. I waited to hear the moans of the golden monsters, but they were nowhere near us. The mountains were free from the Guise. I allowed myself a brief moment of rest under the sun. "Do you feel that, Lugh? It's been a while, hasn't it?" I slid part way down the green hillside and caught myself on a branch. "Do you remember Father? How he always wore shorts and sandals? I asked him why one day, and you know what he said? 'What's life without a little sun burn?'" The branch cracked under our weight, and I let go before we tumbled down the valley.

"While Mother took us to bookstores and cafés, Father took us camping, swimming, hiking, anything that involved the outdoors." I took a deep breath. "I guess that's why his face was so tan and his hair so blonde." I nearly choked on the last word, realizing that's the parent we had inherited our hair from. "I've always been too hard on our father. I blamed him for letting the man into our house, but sometimes, to help others, we have to take risks. Make ourselves vulnerable…" Holding back tears, I said, "What I mean is, I forgive him. I forgive both our parents. I forgive myself for my part in it, too." I let the tears fall. "But I wouldn't ever forgive myself if I let you die, Lugh."

The valley curved into a bowl-like shape. I followed it down until I was in its deepest center, where Arlen sat waiting. "Are you taking a break, Arlen?" His white eyes bored into mine, and I shivered.

I searched the valley for any sign of the stones. We'd visited the famous Stone Henge when I was young, and I assumed the Fae's stone circle would resemble it. But there were no boulders or structures anywhere in sight.

"Where is the stone circle, Arlen? Don't tell me that you led me out here for no reason." I laid Lugh on the soft grass, trusting that the cù-sìth wouldn't harm him. I climbed to higher ground, still searching. "Where is it?" I whispered to anything that would listen. More tears threatened to fall, but I wouldn't let them. I hadn't come this far just to fail. "Where is it?" I screamed at the mountains.

The clouds scattered as if they were frightened of the woman below them. The sun could finally shine its full light, and the mountains were ablaze with golden fire. The saffron trees glowed while the yellow grass danced with the breeze. But the beauty was lost to me. Grief pulsed through my tired body. Lugh was going to die because I was in the wrong place. *I was out of time.*

Hopeless, I took a step toward Lugh when a faint glimmer caught my eye. I searched the mountainside for the cause and found writing etched into the stone, markings that could have only been seen in the sunlight. A giant had to have carved the rune for how massive it was. I turned to the mountain beside it. The sun glinted against a carving on that one, too. And the next and the next, until I had come full circle.

The stone circle.

"Lugh, we found it! The mountains *are* the stones!" I rushed to his side and pulled out the dagger. "We made it, Lugh." Arlen still sat beside us, waiting.

Look inward.

I placed the dagger on Lugh's chest and felt for the burning sensation that came before. "Banish the curse." I closed my eyes and concentrated. "Banish the curse." I searched and searched for the burn, but all I could feel was pain.

"I'm trying, Lugh. I'm sorry, I'm sorry." Panic was gripping and pulling me down. My chest was tight. The weight from the journey was collapsing on top of me. It all came down to this moment. I had been relying on Cole to do this for me… I wasn't prepared. I should have stayed with the dark elves and learned how to do the spell properly. But if I had we would have run out of time…

"Curse be banished. Be banished!" Lugh hadn't moved in a long while, not since the riverside. I opened his mouth. The leaf was completely black. The small threads that had been attached to my brother's tongue untethered, and the last bit of hope we had crumbled to pieces, dead. The clouds returned to block the sun, and the mountain's runes disappeared.

"No. Lugh, wake up." I propped his head on my lap and patted his sunken cheeks. "Lugh, brother, you have to wake up." I looked to Arlen for help, but he hadn't moved from his spot in the grass. His white eyes showed no sympathy. "Why did you lead me here just to watch me fail? Your kind did this! Leave!" I threw the blade at the Fae creature, sadly hitting him with the hilt instead.

I clutched Lugh tight in my arms, staring at the boy who would never become a man. Someone who would never find love or even learn about his true heritage. It was strange, but all I could think of was my short time in church and the songs we had sung. Though, I never truly knew what they meant until then. Sobbing, words dripped from my mouth, long and sorrowful, while I rocked my baby brother to sleep once more.

Goin' home. Goin' home. I'm a-goin' home.
Quiet, like some still day, I'm just goin' home.
It's not far, just close by, through an open door.
Work all done, cares laid by, goin' to roam no more;
Mother's there 'xpecting me, father's waiting, too,
Lots of folks gathered there, all the friends I knew.

Morning star lights the way, restless dream all done.
Shadows gone, break of day, real life just begun.
There's no break, there's no end, just a-living on;
Wide awake, with a smile, going on and on.
Going home. Going home, I'm just going home.
It's not far, just close by, through an open door.

I wished with all my heart for Lugh's happiness. But when I looked at the brother I had failed, I could only see the four-year-old boy being cut open by a strange man. I saw the life flow out of him and heard his screams. I traced Lugh's scar with a shaking hand and thought of that bleeding little boy, and how much I wished it was me instead. Tears fell, landing on his cursed skin.

Blood.

If the man from our childhood wanted our blood for a spell, then it must have been special. I raced for the discarded dagger and plucked it from the tall grass, while I remembered what the elf had said to me: "*Powerful spells require the blood to come from the throat. It's been touched by the voice, a spellcaster's most useful tool.*" Cole helped me whether he wanted to or not.

I knelt beside Lugh. "Live or die. We do it together, brother."

The dagger's blade met my throat. Blood poured down my chest and onto the valley floor. Trembling, I coated my hand and placed it over Lugh's old scar and said, "Banish the curse." I ripped his shirt open and smothered the banshee's mark in my blood, as well. "Banish the curse."

Smoke poured, not from the dagger, but from my wound. Amethyst surrounded us in a new kind of fog. I heard Arlen stand and pace. "Banish the curse." Tendrils of magic wrapped around Lugh's body. Still, he didn't move.

"Banish the curse." I used my blood to draw the mountain runes on his chest. Just as the dagger pulsed in my hand, the air did the same, as if the mountains were falling…or growing. The sunlight shone down on us again.

The temperature dropped. My vision was fading. I knew I was dying, but I couldn't find it in myself to care. If this didn't work, I didn't want to live anymore.

Even after all his lies, I wished that Cole was there with me, holding my hand. I wished I wasn't alone. I chose to remember the kind, brave, selfless elf I thought he'd been. Because I didn't love Coilleach. I loved *Cole*. The elf my brother named.

I collapsed beside Lugh, autumn flying up and away from us.

"Banish the curse," I whispered over and over again, as the life drained from my neck. I was numb now. And it wasn't because of the *other woman*. She had already died. This numbness was physical. Too much blood had been lost. Too much warmth had drained from me. Small flecks of cold landed on my body and slept there. The sky darkened.

One last time, I said, "Banish the curse."

Then, someone held my hand.

Lugh

The power and capacity of learning exists in the soul
already; and that just as the eye was unable to turn
from darkness to light without the whole body, so too
the instrument of knowledge can, only by the movement of the whole soul, be turned from the world of
becoming into that of being, and learn by degrees to
endure the sight of being, and of the brightest and
best of being, or in other words, of the good.

—*Plato: The Allegory of the Cave, from The Republic*

20

My favorite toy was a small wooden tree. It was green like the ones in our front yard. I didn't know why it was my favorite. The only thing that mattered was the feeling I got when I held it in my hand. It was comfort. It was home.

My sister often stole it. Usually, while I was sleeping or distracted. She'd hide it and say, "You've got to look hard if you're going to find your tree, or else it might be lost forever."

Panicked, I tore the house apart. Starting with my room, then Yvaine's, then our parent's. Our parents didn't like me doing that and scolded me, but I didn't care because they didn't understand—my toy was lost!

It was during one of these search and rescue missions that a knock sounded at our front door. "Please, help me! The sun is coming up!" a man's voice cried.

Mother had said not to go outside during the day anymore. It was dangerous, even when I wanted to look for my toy out there. I was angry at first because I wouldn't be able to visit the real trees anymore, but Mother had played a funny game with me instead, and I felt better. Holding me in her arms, she told me to look in the hallway mirror and watch.

I'd stared at our reflection and laughed. She'd make silly faces by sticking out her tongue and tickling my neck with her long blonde hair. Then she'd stop and point at me, a child with a goofy grin and a lob of matching hair hanging in his eyes. The child's eyes were blue and shined in the little light that was allowed inside the house.

Then we were gone.

Shocked, I had reached out to the glass. My small fingers found nothing but empty space where our reflection should have been. I'd looked to Mother and began to cry, confused. But she reassured me by taking the same curious hand and plunging it into the shadows beyond the frame.

I'd felt metal and leather. She'd then removed our hands and whispered a few words. Suddenly, there was a small light inside the mysterious frame, and what I saw made me laugh again, content. Though I wasn't quite sure what was in the small space, it glowed with a comforting light and smelled like paper.

But this time, as the man continued to knock on our door, Mother didn't pick me up and carry me to the mirror. Instead, she pushed me behind the couch with Yvaine, and said, "Don't move and stay quiet."

"Open the door! Please, I'm begging you. Have mercy!" the man cried again. Yvaine clutched me tight against her side. I looked up at my sister's face. She was a lot older than me, but she'd always felt like an equal. She was a kid like me, and that was why her frightened face made me cry.

"Shhhh." Yvaine picked me up. "It's okay. Mother and Father will take care of us." I clung to Yvaine, tucking my face into her hair. She smelled like trees, and

I knew that's where she had hidden my toy.

I patted Yvaine and she set me down, distracted by our parent's conversation. Father whispered to Mother, "We have to help."

"We can't risk it. And we don't have enough food to spare anyway. We've already had to sacrifice so much," Mother responded, pain in her voice.

Knowing they were distracted, I made my way to the cat's door at the side entrance. Our black cat hadn't been seen in a while, and I wondered if I would find her outside with my toy.

I hadn't tried to crawl through the opening before. It was a tight fit, but eventually, I was able to wriggle my way out and into the morning air. The sun was just beginning to rise, and it made the sky orange and purple. I smiled, seeing the green trees I loved so much. I ran for the spruce huddled together in our front yard. I inhaled the sap scent and began my search.

There was no cat. And no toy tree.

I nearly started crying again when I heard banging at the front door. "Lugh! Lugh!" Scared, I darted for the cat's door. My hips got caught on my way through, and it hurt so bad that I laid on the ground a moment before standing.

"Lugh!" Father bellowed. The banging continued.

I ran to the front room, hiding behind the couch. My sister entered at the same time, coming from her bedroom. "What's happening? Why is Father taking down the door?" she asked Mother.

Mother was crying and couldn't answer. Father ripped away the last strip of wood that kept our front door from opening. I ran to Yvaine. Mother saw me and screamed, "Don't open it!"

The door was already unlocked and opened. A strange man stood at the entrance, holding something small, dark, and metal. It was aimed at my father's face.

A loud boom screamed through our house, followed by Mother's, then Yvaine's. Father fell to the ground, bleeding from the forehead. "Take Lugh!" Mother ordered my sister.

Yvaine managed to pick me up, but we didn't go far. We huddled in the corner of the room, hiding as well as we could from the man. Mother stared at Father as she said unfamiliar words. The man lunged at Mother but didn't use the same weapon. He pulled out a knife.

Yvaine tucked me under her arm, but I heard everything. Mother fought the intruder. The struggles faltered and Yvaine gasped. Metal clanged against the hardwood floor. The fighting began again.

"Mother!" Yvaine cried.

At this, I peeked out from my sister's arm and met my mother's eyes. She was crying.

The man grabbed the knife from the floor and plunged it into her chest.

There was pain at my throat when I woke. I tried to reach up and clutch it, just to understand what was happening, but I couldn't move my hand. Or my arm. Or my body. All I could do was cry, and that was only because tears fell. I could barely breath, let alone sob. I couldn't open my eyes. Darkness was all there was. Where was Mother? Father? Sister?

Was I alone?

The pain in my throat worsened. What was happening? Then, I remembered the mark on my mother's throat the last time I'd seen her. The man had cut her. Had I been cut, too? More tears fell, unsure what it meant.

I concentrated on my tree. I thought of all the places it could have been hiding. Where would have Yvaine put it? Maybe I would check the hallway again when I got back home. My sister liked to hide it with the knick-knacks that sat on the buffet there. Yes, that would be a good place. I bet it was there.

I could feel liquid dripping down my chest, like when I over-tipped my water cup at night when I was thirsty. It ran down my chest until I was tilted on my side by a pair of large hands. "Father?" I tried to say, but nothing came out.

The pain was intense, but the mystery was worse. Would anyone help me?

"Let my brother go," Yvaine said, her voice rough.

I tried to open my eyes, but my body wouldn't move. I tried to call to her for help, but all that came from me were screams. Maybe, if I kept screaming, she would hear me.

"Why don't you put the gun down, like a good girl, and I'll let you live." A man's voice said. It was the same voice from the front door. The same voice that hurt Father and Mother…

"No," she said. My sister was there with me. That was all that mattered. I wasn't alone. Even in the dark, she was there. She would take care of me.

The man let go of me, and I fell onto my back. I screamed louder, feeling the pain at my throat more than before. Why wasn't she talking to me? What was happening?

Another bang sounded, and all I could hear was the ringing it left behind.

"I don't like the dark," I complained. Yvaine and I were traversing the city's sewers again. And I hated it.

"Why?" Yvaine asked, as she gripped my hand tight. I was eight years old and thought I was past the point of needing to hold my sister's hand, but there I was, clinging to her as I always did.

"Because I can't see the monsters." I thought of all the golden Guise above us and the Fae and the humans. All of them wanted to hurt us. Our steps echoed in the small tunnel. Our only light was the dagger at my sister's side. The light resonated with me, like it was a living thing that wanted to speak to me but *never did. I reached out to it.*

"Yes, but they can't see you either."

I lowered my trembling hand and looked ahead at the darkness. Somehow, my sister's words had made sense and comforted me. The darkness was a place of safety. No monsters could harm me there because they were just as blind.

I let go of her hand and marched down the tunnel on my own.

I kept those words of wisdom close throughout my adolescence. No matter how frightened I was, I would use that dark place as a shield from the world.

Until it turned on me.

"Your sister doesn't like me very much. Have any advice for me?" a male's voice asked.

I tried to open my eyes again but nothing happened. My chest tightened, and my heart sped. My thoughts were a chaotic circle of screams and memories. The panic nearly had me when the voice continued, "Everyone has their demons—I think that's a human expression, correct me if I'm wrong—but she is clinging to hers tight." Concentrating, I was able to feel hands on my legs. My head swam, and I quickly discovered that I was hanging upside down. Someone was carrying me over their shoulder.

They set me down onto what felt like moss; it was wet and soaked through my pants. I tried to tell them, but my lips didn't move. That was when I realized how thirsty I was—my throat was on fire.

"It's all right, Lugh. No need to get worked up. Your sister is cleaning up in the river. I thought she needed a moment to calm down. She's been carrying you all night, you know?"

She had? All I could remember was plunging in and out of darkness. I tried to speak again, but instead, I felt a strange texture on my useless tongue.

"There's no need to worry. I'll check on her in a few minutes." He was silent, and it bothered me. I needed to know what was happening.

"I'm sorry this is happening to you, Lugh. I should have stopped you, but I think Yvaine might be in your place now if you hadn't gone back for her."

I stopped trying to move. The banshee—I remembered.

"Yvaine will save you, and I'll be there to help when I can."

The stranger's voice finally clicked in my mind. It was the elf—Cole. I wanted to cringe. He'd done something to my sister. She was acting strange; bringing a Fae back to our camp to heal him? The way she looked at him was… weird. He must have cast a spell on her.

"Oh sorry, Lugh. I didn't realize I set you in a puddle." The elf shifted me, so I was in a dry patch of grass instead. My skin itched as if it had been burned.

Why was he being kind to me? What did he want?

After a moment of silence, the elf said, "I'll be right back. Something tells me that your sister gets into trouble often." I barely heard the elf's graceful departure; only the slightest swish of clothing sounded as he stood and walked away. I tried to scream for him to stay, but the only thing I managed to do was shed a couple tears.

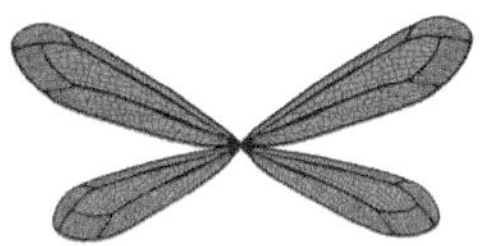

I was laid down on a hard cot. A blanket was thrown over me, and I was grateful. I was so cold. And thirsty… I needed more water.

"Rest well, sister. Don't worry about Lugh. These people will take good care of him," Cole said.

"Okay, you too, bro." Yvaine's voice was tense. I had been sure she wasn't actually going to leave me alone with the humans that had taken us hostage and almost killed me. But she did. Even after losing me to the coblynau—though they were kind—she still allowed me out of her sight. She had always been there to *watch over me. So, why was she choosing to leave? Was it because of Cole?*

I concentrated on my eyelids, willing them to open. But they wouldn't, and the darkness taunted me.

"Lugh, is it? I'm Cara. I'll be taking care of you." A girl's soft voice penetrated the whirling thoughts, and I calmed. "Your sister said not to give you any food or water without her permission, but she didn't say I couldn't clean you up. I bet you're due for a bath." Once it was brought to my attention, I agreed. I could feel the grime on my skin, in my hair, and under my nails. I would have given anything to itch even one part of my body.

"Oh, Cara. Don't bother. He's in a coma. The boy can't hear you," the other nurse said. I sent a mental glare her way, hating her callousness.

"We don't know that. If I were in his position, I'd want someone to talk to me," Cara said with warmth in her voice.

"Suit yourself, girly. I'm going to get more blankets." I heard the curtains rise and fall as the woman departed, leaving me alone with a strange girl who wanted to give me a bath.

I heard a fire crackling across the room and the sound of steps as they navigated the cots. There were moans from the other patients, and I was jealous. I wished I could have let out any noise—just to relieve the pain in my chest. The banshee's scratch pulsed and stung, spreading outward.

Cara approached, and I could smell the sweet-flower aroma wafting from her hair as it tickled my face. She lifted me, taking off my shirt and jacket. It was cold, and I wanted the clothes back, but then a warm rag met my skin. It sent goosebumps across my body, but it felt nice to be clean.

The girl moved from my upper body to my lower, gratefully avoiding my private region. I didn't know how my body would react to touch during this paralysis, but I certainly didn't want to have to worry about that with a stranger.

Cara was kind and soothing as she wiped the grime from me. She spoke of her father and how brave he was to lead their people. If I was able, I would have commented on his kidnapping skills, too, but I couldn't, which made it easy to listen. She missed her mother, who had been lost recently to a selkie. She enjoyed helping people and was training as a nurse. Cara moved to my hair, removing the leaves that had tangled in the knots. She complimented the blonde color, comparing it to sunshine.

Overall, I liked her. She was the first girl, besides my sister, I'd spoken to—if what we were doing could be called a conversation.

The girl dressed and wrapped me in a blanket. "Goodnight, Lugh. I hope you sleep well." The girl's words warmed my heart, but the silence afterward iced it over again.

They'd been running all day. My body hurt from being swung around so much. The pain in my chest was growing. Tingles ran throughout my body, causing sharp stabs in my limbs.

We'd finally stopped, and Yvaine said, "Take Lugh."

"We'll wait here," Cole responded, quiet.

The next thing I heard was my sister screaming. She was only a short distance away. I tried to move again, but I couldn't even scream along with her.

"It's okay, Lugh. Yvaine needs to accept what she's done. It's a hard thing to do." Cole laid a jacket over my cold shoulders.

What had she done? The noise from fighting was fresh in my memory. Screams and the clang of metal nearly shattered my eardrums as we passed it by.

"They weren't going to let us leave. Not with the knowledge we were supposed to have had. And if we told the truth, they would have killed you." The elf paused. "At least the Fae are free. Even if they are dead now."

Strangely, I thought of Cara. Did she survive the chaos? Did she lose her father so soon after her mother? These were questions I couldn't ask, and I was sure they were ones Cole didn't know anyway. Yvaine and Cole had run with *me in tow. Knowing my sister, she wouldn't have looked back. A trait I wished I had.*

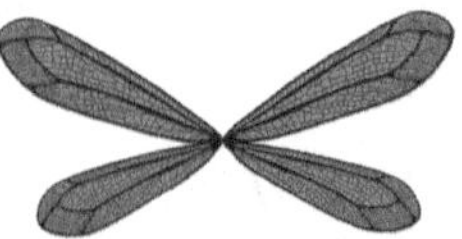

The familiar smell of sewer infiltrated my nostrils. My ears were ringing from the gunshot that had passed overhead. It reminded me of our parents, and I wanted to shudder.

I dropped to the ground with Yvaine beneath me. My hands were limp and landed on the ground painfully, making my previously broken wrists ache. I heard Cole fall beside us. "Cole! Are you all right?" Yvaine left me and rushed to the elf's side, the air suddenly cold.

"It's just a scratch," Cole said.

"Damn it, Cole." Yvaine paused. "It's yours," she whispered. I tried to open my eyes for the millionth time so I could see what was going on, and the pain in my veins spread in retaliation. My throat dried from thirst.

"Good, I'm glad you're safe. Is Lugh?" Cole asked.

I knew Yvaine didn't trust Cole, but he was proving time and time again that he was worthy of it. I just wanted to tell her to stop being so stupid.

Yvaine replied, "He's fine." I heard a cloth rip, and it was followed by, "Keep pressure on it."

"There's no need to get naked, Yvaine. I don't want pity sex. It's just not the same," Cole said, his voice rough.

In all the times of pain and panic, this was the moment I wanted to scream the most. I did not want to listen to any more of their incessant flirting. Cole tried so hard to get a reaction from Yvaine, and Yvaine tried so hard not to show her true feelings.

I wanted to slap them both.

"Can you walk?" Yvaine asked, moving on to more important matters,

though I was sure she was never truly distracted. Yvaine wrapped something under my arms. There was more shuffling, the small noises echoing down the tunnel.

Then she was dragging me. I could feel the slime of the sewer beneath me, and the painful pull of my shoulders being forced upward, but I didn't make a sound. And it wasn't because I was incapable. It was because my sister was struggling and needed my help. A tear escaped my permanently closed eyes, crushed that I couldn't be anything but dead weight.

Yvaine sobbed, "How are we going to get out of here? I can't walk. The dagger is dead. And Lugh doesn't have much longer. Even if we started running for the stones now, we wouldn't make it." Hair fell across my face, making my nose itch.

Cole responded, "Don't say that. You're going to make it, Yvaine. You are the strongest person I know. And I'm not just talking about humans." Someone laid what I assumed was the dirk on my chest. "Lugh is lucky to have you as a sister. He knows you will save him. That's why he has lasted this long. He's fighting, too."

It's true, Yvaine! I'm here, fighting! I tried to tell her. She needed to know. The more I tried to form the words, the greater the thirst became.

"I'm here, Lugh. I'm here." She grabbed my hand. "Keep fighting," she said.

"You are stronger than you know, Yvaine, remember that," Cole told Yvaine. And I was glad someone did. Because I couldn't.

Suddenly, a calm settled over me. The desperation to wake lifted, and I was able to rest for the first time since being attacked by the banshee. My skin tingled with a warm burn. Like the warmth was eating away the poison that ran through my veins.

Yvaine parted my lips to check the leaf that prolonged my life. She wept, but she was happy. I allowed my mind to calm and enjoyed the temporary relief.

There was hope.

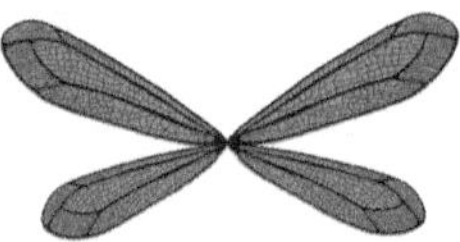

Water filled my mouth and lungs. I couldn't choke or cough or reach for the surface. There was nothing but dark and cold. Every so often, I would feel an arm wrapped under my own, pulling me against the current. I trusted that it was Yvaine guiding us to safety.

I waited for the unknown to end, begging someone to tell me what was happening. Why couldn't I breathe? Why was I freezing to death? Debris hit me in the water, and it was the only time I was grateful to be blind. We reached the surface, and water trickled out of me. I managed to take a small breath when I was empty, but then we plunged into the icy depths again.

There was moment when I thought there was no more fighting, no more hope, when we landed on solid ground. Yvaine's hands were on me, helping me breathe. I couldn't cough, and it was becoming harder and harder to take a breath.

"You actually did it! I don't know how, but you did," a man's voice said. I assumed it was the sniper and wished I could stand to defend Yvaine.

"Don't come any closer," she warned.

"I don't think you should be making demands of anyone, honey. There's only enough prey for one hunter around here."

I heard Yvaine's sharp intake of breath, and I tensed, waiting for the worst.

There was a whoosh sound and a thump. Someone coughed up water.

No one said anything for what felt like eons until Cole reported, "We're all right, Lugh. Rest now."

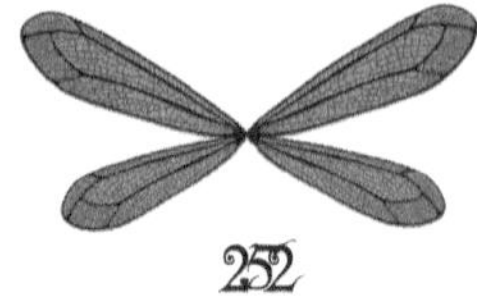

The howl ripped through the forest. It was the third one. The last one.

Yvaine had shared the dagger's magic with me just hours ago, yet my body didn't feel as it did. It didn't wash a sense a calm over me. There was no peace. The burn only touched the curse before the cold returned in full force. I could feel the poison now, creeping outward from the wound on my chest, and through my veins. There was no stopping it anymore. If Yvaine didn't get me to the stones in time…

Panic overwhelmed me. Thoughts raced, one across the other, painfully. I couldn't focus on reality anymore. What I saw was blackness. What I heard was nothing. I could barely taste the bitter leaf on my tongue. Touch and smell were all I had, and they were fading. It was becoming more difficult to distinguish between Yvaine and Cole's hands. The smell of the forest was dull and lifeless. The trees no longer smelled sweet and comforting. They were lost to the cold chill of winter.

I hadn't heard them say it had snowed, but it felt like I was laying in ice, my veins slowly freezing.

Suddenly, there was a burst of magic. But it was gone as fast as it came, and I was alone.

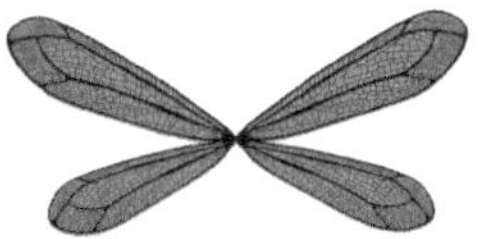

The cold was different in the place they had brought me. It was dead. Empty. Gratefully, my hearing had returned, though it was difficult to concentrate.

"I'm going to have to hurt Yvaine," Cole whispered.

Why would Cole want to do that? He loved her. That much was obvious from our journey. Annoyingly so. But I was glad that Yvaine had a protector. She deserved one. And I didn't have much time left.

"I'm sorry that I lied to her, and to you, Lugh. I know you're in there. I can see you fighting." Cole didn't sound like himself. He was always the voice of positivity, but his words were now dark, resigned.

What do you mean, Cole?

"It took me a while to figure it out, but once I did, I couldn't tell her. She's been so fragile. I didn't want to risk breaking her. She needed to concentrate on you. And honestly," he paused, "I didn't want to lose her."

I ached to open my eyes just one last time. The questions swarmed my tired mind. *What did he mean?*

"If Yvaine knew she had magic, that she could heal you herself, she wouldn't need me anymore." Cole shuffled, and the sounds carried.

Where were we at? I wanted to shiver.

He laughed, bleak. "And now, I need her to leave me. If she somehow forgives my lies, I'm going to have to stay, Lugh. My kind will follow me, and you need all the time you can get."

I tried to reach for the surface. It felt like I was drowning all over again, suffocating under my own weight. *We had magic? It wasn't the dagger? What did that mean? Were we not human?*

"Even if we never see each other again, I'm happy to have met you both. I love your sister. And I wish that you had a chance to call me brother, because that's what I consider you, Lugh." Cole was pacing, I could hear his soft steps whispering across the stone floor.

"Cole," Yvaine called.

"Here," Cole said, the break in his voice disguised.

"Where's Lugh? I thought you were going to watch him?" she questioned, worried.

"He's in the cell next to me."

From the moment Cole began his tale of lies, I couldn't focus. I fought and fought to resurface from my paralysis. Yvaine needed to know it wasn't true. She needed to take Cole with us. But as hard as I tried, I could not defeat the poison coursing through my veins. I could not defeat the darkness. I could not defeat time.

My senses were nonexistent. I had lost. I couldn't fight long enough for Yvaine. The last thing I'd heard was a wolf's growl. It had been close—too close for me to survive. I only hoped Yvaine had and made her way back to Cole.

I wondered what was beyond the darkness. Was it the afterlife? Was there a heaven as Yvaine described? Was there light? Or just more shadows that teased at the chance of reality?

Nothing was for certain as I finally fell backward into that pool of black. It beckoned me to give up. To end the pain. I floated on its surface, debating the choice.

A burn ripped through me. It rippled in the water. I hadn't realized until then how cold the black water was, and I cringed away from it, standing in the shallows.

The burn started at my chest and worked its way outward. The black that had overtaken me receded, my blood expelling the curse. My pallid skin shone in the blackness now. I turned my hand over and traced the lines on my palm with my other hand.

I could move.

I laughed and took a step. A leap. Then ran. I ran forward, not knowing where I was going. Anything would be better than that dark, cold place. The black ground inclined until I was running uphill. There was a small glowing orb at its peak. I ran faster, climbing higher than I ever thought I could.

I found the light.

I had only to stretch up and touch the golden sky that peered into this lonely place.

Without hesitation, I reached my hand through the opening and grasped the only anchor I had.

My crusted eyes peeled open to reveal snow-covered trees. I smiled at the swaying branches.

Gradually, I reconnected with my body. Each limb was slow to respond but it did. They ached from fatigue and bruising, there was a thick layer of grime, and my throat was parched. But I was alive. I inhaled a grateful breath.

Soon, I realized how cold it was, and my body shivered in response. All except my hand. In it, I clutched something tight. Shifting my head, I found what I clung to so desperately.

There, covered in snow, Yvaine laid with her throat cut open, our hands intertwined with blood.

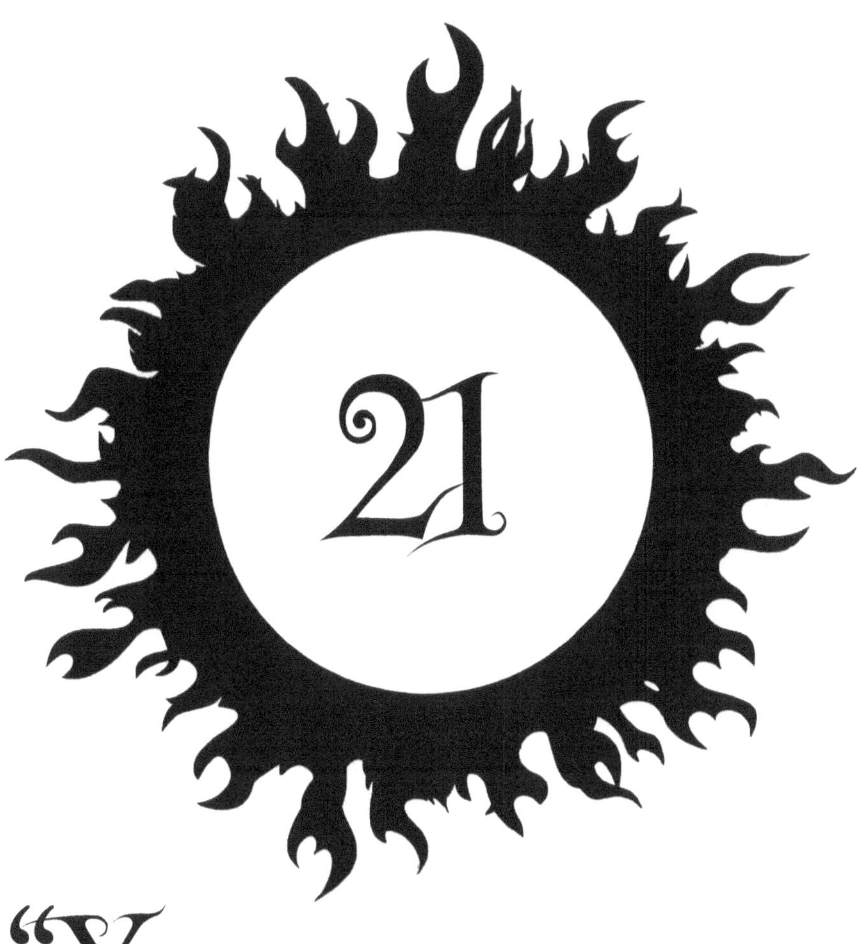

"Yvaine?" I whispered, my voice no louder than the falling snow. I tried to wake my sister by shaking her hand, but her fingers slipped out of mine, slick with red. I willed my body to crawl closer. I gently tapped her face. "Yvaine, wake up," I begged.

What had happened? The sound of growling wolves echoed in my memory, then there was darkness.

Pushing Yvaine onto her back, I was able to see the cut better. It was deep. Still, I pressed my fingers under her jaw and felt a heartbeat. She wasn't gone yet. I brought my hand back and examined my fingers. They were as thin as a skeleton's—I knew because I'd seen many over the years.

The same could be said for the rest of me. I was malnourished, dehydrated, my sister was bleeding to death, and we were in the middle of nowhere.

The clouds parted just enough to shine light down, and I flinched, waiting for the Guise to appear. I waited and waited, not making a sound. But none showed, and I allowed myself to calm and examine our surroundings.

We were at the bottom of a slope surrounded by autumn trees, though the snow was quickly burying the colors. The mountains circled us. As I peered closer, I was able to make out strange shapes etched into their sides. It reminded me of the writing on Yvaine's dagger. Searching, I found the dirk resting in her hand, the amethyst light nowhere to be seen.

Yvaine had done it.

She'd reached the stones in time and performed the banishment spell with her own blood.

I maneuvered my weak legs under me and tried to stand. The muscles didn't even scream or burn. There was no feeling at all. I collapsed, hopeless.

There was movement in the corner of my eye. I whipped my head to the trees nearest to us, instantly regretting the quick action when my neck cramped. When the black spots faded from my vision, I saw a monster.

It was bigger than a horse and had long green fur. Its eyes were pure white and gazed at me with such patience I thought it might speak. I waited for the Fae animal to voice its thoughts, as I slipped the dagger from my sister's hand into mine.

Instead, it howled, though its voice wasn't loud enough to leave the mountainside. That was when I remembered. "Are you Arlen?" I asked, my speech clearer.

The Fae took a step toward me, watching the trembling weapon in my palm. Taking in its long, deadly claws, I decided to let the dagger drop into the snow. If Arlen wanted to kill us, there was nothing I could have done to stop it.

Arlen relaxed and lowered its head into the tall grass. When it returned, it was holding a dead rabbit in its teeth. The animal's fur was white except for the bloody wound through its gut—Arlen's fang.

The Fae approached and dropped the rabbit in front of me. I didn't think before I moved. Instinct took over, and I ripped the fur from the small animal until I could sink my teeth into the raw flesh. I ate for the first time in weeks, relishing the feeling of food hitting the base of my stomach. I cupped handfuls of blood and snow and drank it as it melted in my mouth.

I had only ever eaten raw meat once, right after the Collapse. We'd been hiding in a shed and managed to trap a crow inside with us. We'd been terrified of light even more than we were now and didn't dare make a fire. But we'd still needed to eat.

My stomach had rolled for days afterward. I knew my crying made Yvaine feel that much worse. I regretted every moment I'd made it difficult for her to raise me. It wasn't her job. And it was my fault she had to.

I broke the small rabbit bones and sucked the marrow from them, too. I needed to become stronger. There was no way Yvaine would survive if I couldn't stand. We needed more food, shelter, and warmth. We needed protection.

I turned my back on Arlen, and my spine shivered, knowing it was watching. The dagger in hand, I tried to summon the magic. Yvaine had been the only one to use the dagger's light before, but I had to try.

The longer I was awake, the clearer the memories of the past few weeks became. *Cole said we had magic.* And it was obvious that he'd been trying to tell Yvaine that all along.

"You are so stupid sometimes, sis." I hovered over her body, debating on how to attempt the spell. "Heal my sister," I asked. Cole had told my sister to ask it nicely before. Did that ever work for her? Or did she find another way?

Gathering all my strength, I looked inward, searching for that light. Instead, I groped around in the dark. It was eerily similar to the blackness that had almost taken me. I pushed through the midnight waters, eager to pass it, but there was only more of it. And all the fear I felt these past few weeks came rushing back.

My chest tightened and my stomach simmered. Coherent thoughts fled, and in their place there was only fear, swirling and attacking. *You're not going to survive…Yvaine is going to die trying to save you… Even if you are saved, it isn't worth it…This life is too painful… Too hard… Pointless… Lonely… You will never be happy.*

I dropped the knife and clutched my head, begging the screaming voice to stop. The sun was too bright. The wind was too loud. Breathing became difficult.

Fur tickled my forehead. I looked up and found white eyes inches from my face, hovering over my sister. "Get away from us!" I demanded, shoving the Fae's head away. Arlen chuffed and laid beside Yvaine but didn't leave. "What do you want?"

Arlen tilted its head in my sister's direction.

Distracted from the void, I was able discern what the animal was offering. "Get it together. We've survived our whole lives without magic. We don't need it now," I said to myself.

Melting snow in my palm, I poured it over Yvaine's cut to clean it. I ripped grass up and covered the opening. I used the knife to cut cloth from my shirt, struggling to tie the bandage with shaking hands.

Careful of her head and vulnerable throat, I rolled her onto Arlen's back and followed myself. I was aching by the time the Fae stood and began climbing out of the valley. The sun disappeared behind the clouds, and the mountain's symbols vanished.

Yvaine was limp against my chest as I fisted Arlen's fur tight, willing us to stay upright. For the second time, we were trusting a Fae to save us.

Blood was already seeping through the cloth by the time Arlen found us shelter. The cave was nestled into the side of the mountain beside the river. He'd stopped so I could drink my fill. I had tried to give some to Yvaine, but she'd coughed it up, and I worried that she would injure her throat more if I tried to force it.

The cave was dark and damp, but it was better than being under the approaching storm. Winter had come quickly, and it raged from the thick clouds. Though, I was grateful when night fell and there was no risk of the Guise making an appearance.

After unloading us onto the cave floor, the Fae had gone back out into the storm and returned with a pile of dry twigs. Arlen looked like an animal, so it was disturbing when it showed intelligence beyond any of them. "Thank you, Arlen." Slowly, I reached for the wood and arranged it into a small tower. Crawling to the edge of the cave, I plucked two rocks and settled myself in by the wood again. "Get comfortable. I've never been good at this." I smacked the stones together, hoping for a spark.

I gave up once my fingers went numb. "Sorry, Arlen. If Yvaine was awake, she would have been able to use magic to give us fire." I dropped the stones, defeated. Body heat was going to have to save us tonight. I pressed my side against Yvaine's, and hoped her wound was clotting. *What if you woke up and she was dead? It would be your fault. Blood loss or hypothermia, either way, it would be because of you.*

Flames filled the space and shadows twisted on the walls around us. Eyes darting to the wood, I discovered Arlen sitting there with smoke seeping from his nostrils. "You're Fae. I forgot you had magic." I paused. "Guess, I'm just a dud like Cole. Maybe male half-breeds don't inherit the gene."

Arlen chuffed.

"Agree? You must be a female." I scratched my very dirty scalp and hoped there wasn't any tiny living creatures crawling around on it.

Arlen walked to the entrance and lifted his leg, marking the territory.

"Sorry, my mistake. Though I bet you can't tell the difference between us just by looking either, pal." I shifted on the hard ground, my bones rubbing painfully against my skin.

Arlen huffed out a small flame toward the storm, his cat-like whiskers twitching with discomfort.

"See anyone out there?"

The Fae sat but never took his eyes off the darkness outside.

Feeling useless, I practiced flexing my fingers and toes until they moved without effort. With weak hands, I massaged the muscles in my thighs and calves, hoping to revive the limbs. I pulled my pant leg up and scrutinized my skin. It was just as white as it had always been, but now I had bulging veins. The veins were mostly blue, but some were too dark, nearly black.

"I guess the curse left a mark." Looking farther, I found that most of my veins were now visible. "I wonder if they'll ever disappear, or if I'll have to wear them like scars." I clutched my throat and looked to Yvaine. *We share a scar now.*

Yvaine fought hard to get me to the stones. She nearly died so many times. And all I could do was listen as it happened.

"The leaf is dying. I gave him water, but it didn't budge. It seems the magic is being fickle as the spriggan warned. It doesn't know what to do with Lugh," Cole said, the smell of smoke heavy.

"We have to move faster. There can't be any more interruptions," Yvaine said, and I could tell she was fighting back tears.

"Do you think I planned those interruptions? My goodness, Yvaine, you can't control everything."

"Obviously," Yvaine replied bluntly.

I could hear someone moving from one spot to the next. "We'll make it in time," Cole assured.

"Stop pitying me. I hate it," Yvaine spat. I wanted to tell her that he wasn't. That he was trying to help her.

"It's not pity, Yvaine, it's worry. Don't you know the difference?"

She said, "No. I haven't had anyone worry about me before."

My heart stopped, the comment sent a stabbing pain through my chest. I hadn't realized until then how selfish I had been. Yvaine was strong. She was always there to help me. But she was a kid just like me when the Collapse came.

"I'm sure Lugh worries about you all the time. You're a handful," Cole commented, knowing that I could hear them.

"It's not the same. I've raised him since he was four. I'm basically his mother. It's not his job to worry about me." A tear fell from my paralyzed eye. "But that's okay. It's the least I can do for taking away his real mother."

"What do you mean?" he asked.

"We were there when our parents were killed. I kept Lugh from seeing, but I watched it happen. Father was shot before the man stepped through the door. Mother went to him and had her throat cut. The psycho pinned her down. And then, she was miraculously winning. She was strong. She was fighting for us." Yvaine sobbed. "I called out to her because I was scared. That was all it took, and he plunged this knife into her heart." Another tear fell from me without anyone noticing. "Because of me, Lugh doesn't have a mother. And you know the worst part?"

"What's the worst part?" Cole asked. My side was warm, and I finally realized there was fire right next to me.

She whispered, "I didn't do anything. I didn't try to run or hide Lugh. I just sat there and let the monster take us. And I've done nothing but fail my brother since."

"That's not true."

"Yes it is," she argued.

"Yvaine—"

"You wanted to know how the man died? The one who tried to rape me and failed?" she said.

Quietly, Cole said, "Yes."

"Lugh killed him. He saved me. A ten-year-old boy had to save me because I trusted the wrong person. I couldn't even save my baby brother's childhood. It was taken away the same way mine was."

The tears fell from my closed eyes. Guilt clawed at my insides. Yvaine blamed herself for our parent's deaths—for our lost childhoods. But it wasn't her fault. It was mine. And I'd never had the courage to tell her. I didn't know if I ever would.

The next thing I heard was Yvaine asking, "Lugh? Can you hear us?"

I couldn't tell her yes, but I wouldn't have even if I could.

I was a terrible brother.

Flipping onto my stomach, I forced my arms and legs to obey. They lifted my body upward until I was standing. It was disorienting to be vertical. It hadn't happened in a while.

The memories from the curse were strange. There was no visual to remember. No colors or shapes. Just voices and touch. Somehow, it made them even more real.

I closed my eyes, battling the darkness under the lids. I took a step toward the fire, light and shadows dancing beyond the walls I kept secured. Another step had me shaking. Another brought down a knee. I nearly fell forward when my hand caught warm fur.

Opening my eyes, I said to the Fae, "Cole sent you, didn't he?"

Arlen held my gaze, and I wondered if he would accidentally exhale more flames and burn me.

"Thanks, but I can take it from here." Arlen allowed me to stand alone. And that's what I did for the rest of the night. I stood vigil over my sister by the fire, refusing to close my eyes again.

Yvaine's fever raged and calmed depending on the hour. The snow only grew deeper outside. If it hadn't been for Arlen hunting for me, Yvaine would have woken to her brother's corpse. But the Fae kept me fed, and the snow kept me hydrated. Every day, I practiced sitting and standing until I was strong enough to walk again. Around and around the cave I went, studying every crevice and shade of the grey stones. Sight was a blessing I would never take for granted again.

Arlen dragged a wolf into the cave one night. I recalled the predator's growls from before and didn't feel any remorse as I skinned it with the endowed weapon. Its pelt kept Yvaine warm, warding off the fever.

I picked grass from the cave's entrance, digging until I found it under the snow. I changed her bandage often. Once, I even asked Arlen if he could heal her, but he'd just chuffed and laid down on the cold floor. Apparently he didn't possess that kind of magic.

The cut had clotted, but it was red and angry around the edges. *If Yvaine's wound was infected…* I didn't finish the thought. She would survive. She had to. She had to know the truth.

"I wish you would wake up, sis. I have something important to tell you, and you can't leave me without hearing it." I chuckled, recalling her famous words to me.

"Lies are for the Fae. We're human. We can at least be honest about our stupidity." She'd said that to me when I was learning how to shoot my bow. I'd told her that I could do it myself and to leave me alone. I'd returned to her and bragged that I had hit all my targets, when in reality I hadn't hit any. But she knew I was lying. Now, I wondered if she'd been watching me all along.

"Cole was lying to you before." I struggled to recall where we had been when he said the words. "But it's not what you think. He was helping us the whole time. He never wanted to take from us. The only reason Cole didn't tell you about our magic was because he didn't want to hurt you…he didn't want to lose you either." I grabbed Yvaine's hand and held it tight. "You can be a hard person to please, sis. No wonder he felt like he had to lie." I laughed. "That poor guy didn't know what hit him when he met you. Talking to you is like a punch in the face. You don't know how hard it's going to land until it happens. You literally scared him to death."

Arlen huffed behind us at the entrance.

"Sorry, Arlen. I'm sure he's still alive. Though, honestly, I can't quite remember where we left him. I don't know if I can find him on my own." *Useless, as always.*

My sister's fingers tightened around mine. "Yvaine?" My heart leapt with hope and fear. *What should you expect from her? It was a long, hard journey. Could it have broken her?*

Rough with sleep, she said, "Maybe if I actually punch you, you'll realize how pleasant I am."

Of course it hadn't.

My sister opened her eyes, revealing the same blue color that shown from my own. "Where are we? Where's Cole?" she asked, twisting her head. "Owe!"

"Don't move. You've got a nasty cut, and it might be infected." I felt her forehead, registering the intense heat before she swatted my hand away.

Yvaine felt along her bandaged neck and gasped, remembering. "Oh! Lugh, you're alive!"

"Thanks for noticing."

Despite the pain, she lurched upward and enveloped me in hug, sobbing. "I can't believe it worked! I'm so sorry, Lugh. I should have stopped that banshee. I should have been faster. I should have—"

"It doesn't matter now. You saved me. You made it in time, Yvaine." I returned the hug, squeezing her as hard as I could, which wasn't very hard.

My sister let go only to examine me. "Are you okay? Is the black gone?"

I showed her my arms where the veins were the worst. "I think so, but my veins took a beating."

Yvaine felt the raised skin and sobbed again. "It has to be all gone or else it will come back. I didn't know what I was doing. I might have missed some of the poison. Lugh… I don't…"

Moving the sleeve back into place, I said, "You got it all. I feel much better. Here, look." Slowly, I stood and took a few painful steps. I overestimated myself and walked too quickly, but Arlen was there to catch me.

"Arlen? You're still here?" Yvaine said to the Fae. My sister ripped the hairband from her hair, letting the waves fall loose.

"Without him, neither of us would have made it. He got us here and fed me. Speaking of…" I reached to the fire and tore some meat from the wolf's hide and handed it to her. She dug into it but slowed when her throat caused her grief. My sister was in more pain than she let on, but she didn't voice it. Though, I could see the burning question in her eye. *She'd heard me.*

"Cole," she started. Yvaine let the meat fall to her lap.

"Cole loves you, and you left him behind," I accused.

Instantly angry, she said, "He said that he was going to steal our magic! Why would he lie about that?"

"Isn't it obvious?"

She gave me a confused look, and I sighed. "I didn't hear everything, so I was hoping that it was obvious to you. All I remember was him saying that he needed to lie so you would leave him behind. Why you needed to do that, I don't know, but it sounded like it was really hard for him to do."

She thought silently for a moment before saying, "The elves would have hunted us in force if he had been with us." A tear escaped the corner of her eye. "But he lied about us. About our heritage." Yvaine was angry and clenched her fists together stubbornly.

"He lied to keep you sane, and some more insecure shit that you should ask him about. So, where did we leave him?" I sat, unable to withstand the soreness in my legs anymore.

Yvaine was about to answer, but she paused, staring at me. "You were awake? The whole time?" My sister was nearly hyperventilating by the time she finished the question.

A wall went up as it always did when she asked painful questions. Our parents, our childhood, and now this. "Only the last bit. The rest was just… nothing."

My sister waited for me to continue, but when I didn't, she relaxed and said, "We left Cole with his kind—our kind, I suppose. But they've changed. They live in total darkness now, so much that their bodies are like shadows."

"Our kind… You mean that we're part elf?" This was news to me. I had heard that we had magic, but elves? The most powerful of the Fae? The ones who sent shivers up my spine.

"Yes, and Cole is half human, too."

I pulled my knees up to my chest, clutching them protectively.

"There's a lot I need to tell you, but now isn't the time. We need to go back for Cole."

"You think?" I remarked, contemplating our existence.

"Don't be a jackass."

"Oh, I'm sorry. We're just supposed to travel how far? And fight who? While we were both just on death's doorstep? How do you expect to pull that off?" I rocked back and forth, comforting myself. Now that my big sister was awake, I guessed it was okay to fall apart. *You are so weak. Worthless.*

"Where's the dagger?" she asked, already forming a plan.

"Next to you." I pointed to her side, where the dirk was sheathed in its proper place.

Surprised, she gripped the handle, and the amethyst light returned, outshining the fire. Smoke poured out of it, and I gasped. "Heal," was all my sister said, as the smoke surrounded her in a swirling cloud, tendrils breaking from the smoke and tending to her throat and ankle.

I had forgotten she'd hurt her ankle. I hadn't checked it at all, and I cursed myself for it. Lost in my self-loathing, I didn't realize the light had spread to me until it had encased my whole body. I laid back, allowing the peace to settle over me. Every inch was cared for. The hunger and thirst lessened. The ache disappeared. I could move my limbs without the joints screaming. "How did you do that?" I asked, entranced by the retreating magic.

"We're half Fae on our mother's side," she explained, distracted.

Instead of asking more about our parent, I said, "Teach me."

"Lugh, it took me a while to even accomplish this one spell. Don't be surprised if it doesn't happen right away." Despite her reservation, she handed me the dagger and said, "Look inward. Find your core—I suppose it's the soul. Your motivation. Your purpose."

I gripped the dagger with stronger hands. I stood with ease and went to the entrance. Gazing at the trees, I said, "Heal." No light shone in the cave besides the fire. "Heal." I looked inward.

Find your soul. How was I supposed to do that when I didn't believe the soul existed?

Find your motivation. Nothing motivated me.

Find your purpose. The universe was a mess of random chaos and evil. There wasn't purpose in anything. Especially me.

Still, I heeded my sister's advice and dove in, scrambling through the darkness again. My thoughts returned to our mother. Questions arose, and I squashed them, refusing to ask. I didn't deserve to ask. My bones ached again.

I threw the knife at the cave wall. "It doesn't work!"

Yvaine laughed. "We are definitely related."

Furious, I said, "What's that supposed to mean?"

"Nothing. We can work on our magic later, Lugh. Right now, I need to leave. Cole is supposed to be executed, and I don't know how much time he has." She instinctually looked around for supplies but found none.

"Executed for what?" I demanded.

"Being magicless. It's taboo to the elves." Yvaine stood without issue and picked up the dagger from the stone floor.

"They sound fun."

"Definitely." She looked outside. "Arlen got us here?" My sister grabbed the remaining meat from the fire and fed it to the Fae, but not before handing me a large chunk of hide.

I nodded and Arlen finished his meal, already knowing what she wanted. She picked up the wolf's fur, appreciating it for only a moment before handing it to me. "Stay warm and safe. I'll be back with Cole."

I just stared at her, refusing to take the pelt.

"What?" she said.

"You can pull that crap on your boyfriend all you want, but I'm your brother. You're not leaving me behind." *I refused to be left alone again.*

"Lugh, they kill magicless elves. We don't know if you have it or not. I'm not going to risk losing you, too." She looked down, hiding the tears forming in her eyes.

"Either you take me with you, or you leave me behind and I go after you alone. In the cold, without protection. Which will it be?" I climbed onto Arlen without waiting for a response. I tried to hide the fact that the healing magic she'd cast over me had somehow reverted; my body rejected it. I thought I had until she wrapped the wolf's pelt around me like a babe and said, "Fine. It's easier if I keep an eye on you anyway."

Letting out an angry, adolescent breath, I submitted to the over-protective sister behind me while Arlen began trudging through the snow.

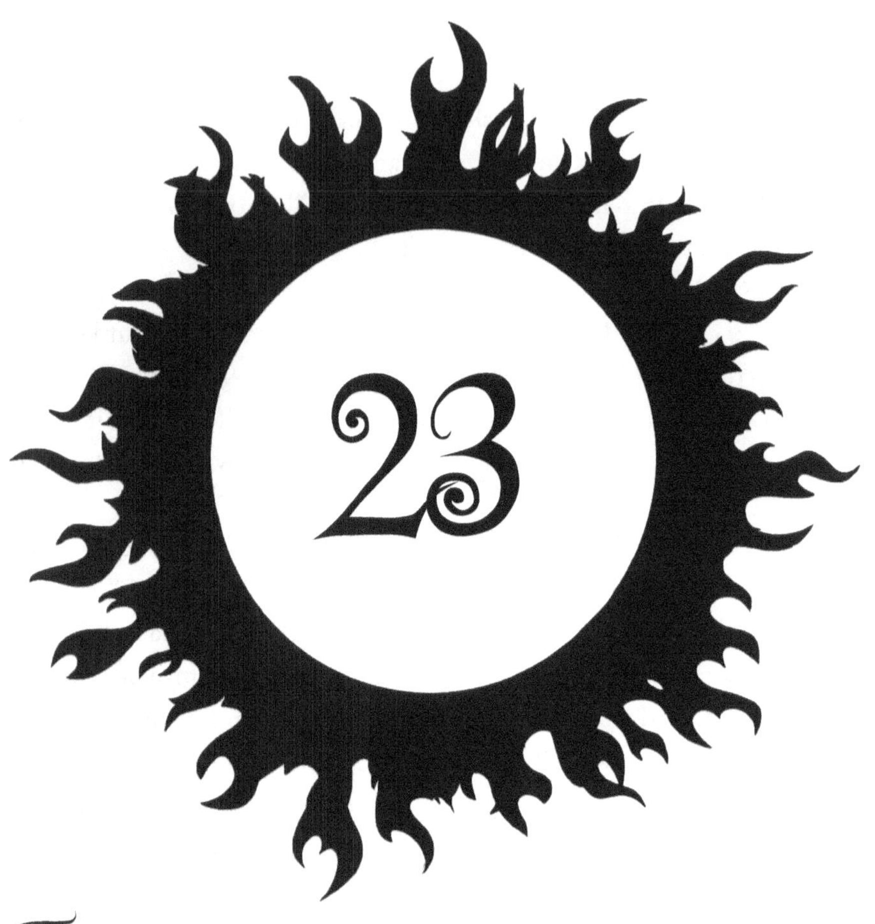

It was less than a day's journey to the elves with Arlen carrying us through the snow. Yvaine told me every detail of the journey, thinking that I didn't know. Some details were new, and I wasn't sure how to feel about them. She told me about the chief unlocking her memories—our mother was more than she had led us to believe.

My sister said that she didn't know much about our magic yet. But she explained what she had been able to accomplish so far. We shared a laugh when the dark cloud appeared above us, protecting us from the Guise. For years, we wished for that kind of magic and protection only to find out that we had it all along.

Then there was Cole.

The combination of admiration and frustration in her voice told me just how much she had changed in the few weeks she'd been with the elf. It was hard not to be happy for her, but it left me with a sense of loneliness. It had always been just the two of us. Now, things would be different whether we were able to save Cole or not. And it wasn't just her. I had changed, and it certainly wasn't for the better.

No matter how weak I was, I would fight for Yvaine's happiness. And honestly, Cole had grown on me. He was a kind person. It made me wonder how he'd lived so long.

Yvaine's voice faded with the sun. The night was cold and windy. We shared the wolf's pelt, and it was enough to ward off the chill, but something about the darkness made my heart race. *How were you going to survive in this dark world now? How were you supposed to see it as a shield when it had swallowed you whole and tortured you for weeks?*

"We're close," Yvaine whispered.

The only sound was Arlen's padded footsteps on the snow.

Crunch… Crunch… Crunch.

"Are you sure?" I asked, the trees sprinkling snowflakes onto our hair.

"Yes, look for endowed lights. It's night, so the elves will be out harassing innocent people like us." Yvaine was focused, alert—frightening.

"Why?" I said.

"I never asked, but I'm starting to think that they steal magic. That's why they use the cù-sìth, like Arlen here, to track for them." My sister fidgeted with a band around her wrist; it was braided, and I wondered if it was what Cole had given her. It was frustrating to piece things together with sight now that I had it back. It made me realize how little people actually said to one another.

"Why would elves with so much magic need more? Also, I thought you said that they didn't believe in stealing magic? That's the whole reason they're going to execute Cole?" *Something wasn't right.*

"They're more like humans than they would ever admit. Just as big of hypocrites, and just as fearful. Bottom line, Cole threatens them." Yvaine was stiff behind me, her tone cold.

I concentrated on Arlen's breathing as I thought on what I knew of the dark elves. "Then why wouldn't they use Cole to their advantage? It would be a waste to kill him."

Quickly, she answered, "Maybe they can't control him."

"With all their knowledge and power? I'd think that they could make him do whatever they wanted." I could feel Yvaine's glare boring into the back of my skull. "Just thinking like an elf," I explained.

"Well, you are one, I suppose."

I nearly flinched at the comment. Was this how Cole felt? Like there was a piece of himself missing? Had that feeling always been there? Fae were magic. They had a right to it. And I found myself craving that light. I *needed* it.

"I hope you're right," she whispered.

"You *hope* they are using him?" I asked, confused.

"Yes, because that would mean he's alive." Yvaine kept her tone in check, refusing to let her fear show, but it was there in the trembling of her hands.

Understanding, I quieted and concentrated on searching the forest.

Arlen stopped and crouched, shaking us from his fur. Surprised and dumped onto the snow, Yvaine said, "What the hell, Arlen?"

The Fae huffed and disappeared into the dark trees.

"Guess, he considers his job done," I laughed.

"Can't trust anyone," Yvaine muttered, as she stood and brushed herself off.

Honestly, I'd been surprised to get any help at all from Arlen, and we couldn't ask him to fight against his own masters. Yvaine reached out her hand. I took it automatically but cringed when I leaned on her more than I should have. *Your big sister can't help you forever.*

"Look there," she whispered in my ear. There was a blue light moving among the forest trees. We followed behind it silently, and it was a struggle to keep my breathing under control. The light stopped beside a dark wall. A sliver of the shadow lifted so the elf could enter. No light could be seen beyond it.

"Even at night, the wall is up. This is going to be tricky. I barely made it out last time, and I had to make a spectacle of myself. I don't want to risk that." Yvaine looked to me. She was worried I wasn't strong enough to fight.

"We do what we have to, sis. Cole is in there." I stared at the dark wall for answers, but none came. I was not going to watch Yvaine suffer from grief because we didn't do everything we could. *Not again.*

Yvaine placed something in my hand. "This is an iron blade. Use it if you have to. Stay here until I return." She stepped forward, and I grabbed her arm.

"No way." I took a deep breath and summoned my courage. "I'll find Cole. You distract the elves." Yvaine debated, conflict raging across her face. I clutched her hand with my bony fingers. "I can do it. Trust me."

Resigned, she said, "They were keeping him under the castle. Get him and get out fast, or I'm coming after you." She readjusted the wolf's pelt, so it was secured to my shoulders.

"Threat received." I smiled to reassure her, and she couldn't help but return it.

We crept our way across the snow, our boots shattering the frozen crystals and leaving behind evidence of our visit. Reaching the wall, I stared into its swirling, smoke-like tendrils. It was like Yvaine's healing magic but pitch black. Though, where the amethyst light of my sister had felt alive and peaceful, this one felt alone, empty.

Blade in hand, I nodded to Yvaine, and her magic weapon lit, slicing the darkness open. I ran as fast as I could to the largest shadow within the wall. Flashes of light guided my path. Footsteps ran past me, their weapons lighting in retaliation. No one had noticed me slink along the misshapen trees or the stone walls of the village. Each step brought me closer to Cole, as well as exhaustion. I hadn't had enough time to heal. Even with Arlen and Yvaine's help, I was weak.

I felt naked without my bow, and I pondered what had happened to it. The small dagger I held nearly slipped from my hand several times. Not from sweat, because I was far too dehydrated to do such a thing. It was the cold. My hands were numbing from the intense chill. The dark barrier was not only a wall but a roof. It was a dark dome that kept the warmth and light from entering. Why would anyone want to live like this?

I stopped and hid behind a statue. The dark elf that had been running toward me paused and sniffed the air. There was so much that we didn't know about our own race. Could they smell the fear wafting from my skin? It took a step toward the statue when another one of Yvaine's magic waves sent tremors through the air. I was able to get a good look at the Fae when the light reached us, and it sent shivers up my spine.

Tall, lean, and angled features like that of an elf were there, but its skin had unnaturally blackened as well as its eyes. The texture wasn't smooth like skin, but rough and deformed. As if frostbite had taken over. *A walking corpse.*

The dark elf leapt in the direction of Yvaine, abandoning me. With shaking legs, I ran to the castle only a short distance away. There were stairs going up and into the structure. And there were stairs going down and into the bowels. I took a step toward the bowels when a light caught my eye from a second-story window. Lifting my head as high as it would go, I searched for that light. It was stationary, so I changed direction and went upward.

I didn't know why I decided to follow the light like a child follow-ing wisps into the forest. I didn't know why I chose to leave Cole in the darkness that much longer. Or why I risked my sister's life so that I could satisfy my curiosity. But something called to me. And instinct was all I had left of my past self.

I struggled to find the stairs inside the dark castle. It was an effort not to hyperventilate every time I lost the silhouettes of the statues and tapestries. But Yvaine's light penetrated the darkness, even here. Flashes through the windows allowed me to climb the stairs and look down a long grand hallway filled with glowing weapons.

Hanging on the walls were swords, daggers, axes, hatchets, sickles, katars, scythes, maces, and bows with their respective quivers. I walked down the hall, amazed by the collection. I questioned how they managed to glow without their wielders. Then, I came across one particular bow. I recognized it instantly from the city tunnels—from when we stabbed an elf and captured him, extorting him into giving us magic. I'd been en-tranced by the bow Cole possessed, hating mine in comparison.

Cole's bow was the only one not glowing. *Did that mean he was dead?*

"The half-breed has returned as you predicted, Chief Dearil. Would you like her weapon brought here to join the other's?" a male's voice said, its low timbre carrying down the hall. I barely had time to dart behind a book shelf before they turned the corner.

"Yes. And the brother?" the Chief asked.

I clutched the iron blade tight.

"There's no sign of him. He probably died at the stones. A novice like her would be more likely to kill her subject rather than save them with that kind of power surrounding her."

"Agreed. A shame though. If he was the same as Coilleach, we could have used him." The chief stopped in front of Cole's weapon. I stiffened, not daring to breathe.

"It will work. The spell you created will save our people. The solar eclipse is only months away, and Coilleach's deformity will finally be of use." The dark elf beside the chief sounded confident about his leader's plan.

The chief took his time answering, "But will it be enough? Have we gathered enough souls? Enough magic? This has never been done before. Can he contain that much power if there is? Who's to say that the magic won't turn on us?"

The warmth in the elf's voice was clear when he said, "We have worshiped magic for eons. It has never failed us before. And it won't now. I have complete faith in you, Chief Dearil."

"Your faith is a great comfort, Darce." He paused. "At least my daughter will finally be at peace once it's done." From behind the shelf, I could see a hand reach out and stroke Cole's bow delicately. No more words were spoken between them as they stared at the dark weapon. My breathing hitched, and I slowly lifted a hand to cover my mouth. My legs were tired from standing. I didn't know how much longer I could do it. My chest tightened with fear, knowing my fate if they found me.

"Chief, the half-breed has escaped into the forest!" a voice called from down the corridor.

"Find her before the sun rises," the chief ordered. I listened to the elves' light footfalls depart. I waited a few moments more before letting out a breath. Stepping from behind the shelf, I reached for a glowing weapon, needing to know if I was the same as Cole.

My skin tingled from the touch of the stranger's light, but it didn't leave the sword it lived in. No magic absorbed upon my touch. Instead, I found that the books on the shelf were illuminated by the weapon's light. The writing glowed, begging to be read, though I couldn't have if I tried. I picked out the brightest binding and placed the glowing weapon back on the wall. I plucked Cole's bow and quiver from its placement and slung it over my shoulder.

Book and weapon in hand, I ran for the castle's bowels. Yvaine was fighting for her life. I needed to move faster. I didn't see any endowed weapons in the night, or my sister for that matter. They were hunting her past the wall, and she was relying on me to get Cole out.

I felt along the walls, using the brief glimpses of the castle I had beforehand as a guide. The deeper I went, the colder it became. My eyes were so wide that they hurt. There was no light below the castle. I called out, feeling dangerously exposed as I did so. "Cole? It's Lugh. Are you down here?" My voice carried, giving me an idea of how long the dungeons were, and I grimaced.

Footsteps shuffled along the stone floor. I stopped and wished I had brought one of the glowing weapons with me. But Yvaine had taught me early on that carrying a light was like painting a target on your back.

"Lugh?" a small voice breathed.

"Is that you, Cole? Where are you?" My fingers stuck to the icy walls, and I winced when the skin ripped from my fingertips.

"Th..th..the last one on yo..yo..your right."

"Are you hurt?" I asked, continuing my journey down the cold tunnel.

"Free..freezing."

"I'm coming." I pulled out the iron knife.

"Yv..Yvaine?" he asked, worried.

"She's distracting them, so we'll have to hurry. Can you walk?" I reached the cell and felt for the lock. The metal bit my skin as I maneuvered the blade's tip into the opening. *You're not as fast as Yvaine. She would have freed him by now.*

"Ye..Yes." His silhouette shook in front of me.

"Damn it!" I couldn't feel my hands anymore. I blew hot air into my trembling palms. The darkness was overwhelming. It wasn't safe. It wasn't a shield. It was a gaping hole.

"De..de..deep breath," Cole said through the bars.

Steadying my panic, I returned to the lock. A few painful clicks later had the door swinging open. I removed the wolf's pelt and draped it over Cole. "Yvaine led them into the forest, but I'm sure she's circling back by now."

"Le..let's go." Despite the intense cold and impending death, I swore that I could hear a smile in Cole's shaking words.

We made it to the top of the grueling steps when my heart stopped. Two elves had come back to guard the prisoner. "It's the brother! He's freed Coilleach!"

I lunged for the closest one, knife in hand. He evaded me and pushed me into the ground. An endowed spear hovered above my face. I tried to push it aside, but I was still too frail. My bone-thin limbs were no comparison to these powerful Fae.

The sunset-orange light of the spear illuminated the elf's frostbitten skin. Its face was twisted as if it was in pain and wished for me to feel the same. *You are one of them.*

The dark elf spat foreign words, and my hands pinned themselves to the ground. I screamed when a sharp pain pierced my palms. It felt as if stakes were being shoved through my skin, but when I looked, nothing was there. Then, there were invisible stakes thrust through my feet.

I'd dropped the bow and quiver when I fell, and it lay on the frozen ground beside me. Cole struggled with the other dark elf, and I was sure he would fail as I had. He was weak from hypothermia.

An amethyst light flashed in the distance.

Cole's opponent screamed, "Monster!" I watched its weapon dim, flickering like a dying flame. He gripped the dark elf's arm tight, taking in its magic. He released the stolen magic, shooting fire into its eyes. Cole dove for his bow. The elf above me was downed by an arrow in the next instant. The stakes disappeared, as well as the pain. The burned elf chased after Cole. I stretched out my leg and kicked the dark elf's knee as it passed. Cole had another arrow nocked and flying by the time the elf stood up again.

"Lugh! Cole!" Yvaine screamed. My sister came hurtling through the shadows, dirk in hand. She was obviously exhausted, but the determination in her eyes was unmistakable. She wouldn't stop until the battle was done.

Cole's forlorn face warmed when he saw Yvaine. He took a step toward her, but she continued running past him until she reached me. The pain in his eyes was something I didn't want to see. *Poor guy.*

"Are you hurt?" she asked, examining me.

Slapping her hands away, I said, "I'm fine. We need to leave." The book was tucked away in my pocket, whispering strange words and beckoning me to open it.

My sister nodded and helped me stand. I staggered a few steps before she wrapped my arm over her shoulder. Cole took my other side without another glance at Yvaine, the bow and quiver strapped to his back. Both refused to look in the other's direction, and I sighed.

Cole was warmer than before, but I was the one freezing now. Yvaine was simmering with magic, and I leaned into her for warmth.

We reached the edge of the dome and Yvaine said, "Get out of my way." The wall split, allowing us through. The air was instantly warmer on the other side, despite the falling snow.

I laughed. "What the hell was that?" My legs were failing, but I didn't want them to carry me. I had enough of that for a lifetime.

"Spells are nice, but *will* overpowers any prewritten word. Especially for those who have raw, untrained magic like your sister," Cole explained, his speech finally under control.

"He..hear that, sis? Your magic is ju..just as stubborn as you are." I smiled through the pain.

Yvaine huffed and ignored us.

The trees trembled as we passed. The wind was pushing against us, so hopefully it would be strong enough to hide our trail. The sky had brightened to navy blue, and the heaviness lifted from my shoulders ever so slightly.

"Wh..where are the elves?" I wondered.

"Retreating behind their walls. I gave my boots to a brownie, so they probably followed that trail for a while before they realized it wasn't me." Yvaine hadn't calmed yet. Her eyes darted around the forest, locking on to anything that moved.

I looked down to find she was indeed barefoot. "Yvaine, you idiot. You're go..going to lose your toes." I imagined the three-foot tall, naked creature with large red eyes running around in the snow with my sister's boots. I also imagined the dark elves finding that brownie. I wanted to laugh with absurdity and sorrow. *You're a cruel person, Lugh.*

"Better than losing a brother…and elf." She cringed against the cold ground now that the immediate threat had passed. Cole tensed beside me, but we kept moving.

Knowing it was no use to argue with her, I said, "The chief said that they were waiting for a solar eclipse. There were these glowing weapons on the walls, and Cole is supposed absorb them?" I concentrated on remembering the conversation instead of feeling the cold.

"The chief? Why were you anywhere near him?" Yvaine fumed.

"I'm fine. Listen to me! There's something going on. Cole?" He had to have answers.

Cole nodded, tired. "They're going to rid the planet of Guise."

We all stopped.

"How?" Yvaine asked, looking at the elf for the first time.

"The endowed weapons you saw, Lugh, were from dead elves. When our kind dies, it's traditional to keep a piece of them with the living, as a reminder of their time on Earth." Cole released me. "They're going to have me absorb all of it and perform a spell for them during the eclipse in three months."

"What kind of spell?" I asked.

"They want to stop the proper rotations of the stars. They want a permanent solar eclipse. That way, no light can ever shine down again. Hence, ending the age of Guise." The elf bowed his head.

"Isn't that a good thing?" Yvaine commented, irritated.

Keeping his head bowed, he said, "You've seen how they live. In darkness and cold. They've completely deformed their bodies to do so. They're prepared for that kind of world. The rest of us aren't."

Understanding, I said, "You mean…"

"Yes, everyone would perish in the new frozen world." Cole lifted his head and stared at Yvaine, trying to meet her gaze, but she continued to scrutinize the ground.

"Would you survive?" she asked.

"That much magic would be impossible for anyone to hold for long, if at all. And even if I did, I would just freeze with the rest of you once it was done." He took a step toward Yvaine. She released me and stepped back.

"Are they capable of doing it without you?" I questioned.

"No, there's no one else who can absorb magic like I can." Cole met my curious gaze with his own. *Was he truly the only one?*

"Then why did the chief tell me that you were going to be executed?" Yvaine demanded.

"Something or someone changed his mind, and made him realize that he had the perfect tool for the spell," Cole answered, indifferent.

Yvaine's eyes widened, but she quickly hid her terror. "Let's get moving. Looks like we're not done running." She turned south, the dagger dangling in its sheathe at her side.

Cole turned to me. "Can you walk?"

I nodded, despite my reservations.

Quicker than I could comprehend, Cole lifted Yvaine into his arms. "You aren't running anywhere without shoes."

"Put me down, elf!"

"Not a chance." Upon his words, she met his gaze, and I was forced to look away. This was their reunion despite Yvaine's efforts to fight it. She couldn't stay mad at him forever, just like I couldn't rely on her forever.

I led the way, refusing to stare at their ogling eyes the entire journey. A feeling of loss overcame me as I trudged through the snow, imagining the new lightless world the dark elves wanted.

The world was going to end if you didn't walk faster.

Yvaine took the warm pelt from Cole's shoulders and hung it over mine.

The sun shone down on the water. It was quiet and still. The snow had ceased falling for the time being, and I was grateful. My face was windburned and stung. If we didn't find warmth soon, I was going to blacken like my mother's kin.

"We should rest for a while. We need to get warm," Cole told Yvaine, the snow sinking beneath our feet.

My sister hadn't lasted long in his arms. Barefoot and pissed, she strode down the snowy hillside that led to Perth. The bruising on her ankle had spread to the rest of her foot, purple and angry. Still, the dark cloud hovering above us didn't waver in the slightest. "We have to use the daylight to our advantage. The elves won't want to travel in the sun."

Cole and I shared a knowing look. "We have to rest, sis. Or else we're not going to make it very far."

Yvaine turned, her lips poised with an argument, but something about my appearance changed her mind. "Fine." She looked out at the flooded city. "The houses on the outskirts of the city should have survived. Maybe we can find some warm clothes." Satisfied with her compromise, we followed her lead, staying well under the dark cover she provided.

The Guise flickered in and out of existence, disappearing when a dark snow-cloud obscured the sun. But when the wind stole the vapor away, the monsters would appear again. They circled us, waiting for our own cloud to be blown away. It was the closest I had ever been to them. Staring into their golden eyes was trance-like, glittering with unknown promises. Their skin was smooth and bare. There was no hint of what they had been before.

When Yvaine had told me that Guise didn't kill, but spread, transforming any living thing they could into monsters, I was terrified. Death seemed to be the kinder option. They wandered and cried out painful moans. Each time I heard one of their calls, tears gathered in the corners of my eyes. Now I knew, whether they were aware or not, that the Guise were begging for help. And there was no one who could save them.

"Cole," I started.

"Yes?" he responded, surprised to be addressed after such a long silence.

"You said that the dark elves would make you absorb the magic and then cast the spell." I paused and he waited patiently for me to continue. "*How* would they make you? Magic?"

Cole nodded, staring at the same Guise I did, and most likely suspecting the same thing. "There are several types of magic. Each Fae species has their…specialty. But the elves have mastered all of them—or most. That includes manipulation."

"You mean mind control?" I clarified.

"I suppose you could call it that." He nodded to the Guise at our side. It never took its eyes away from us. It just floated beside our darkness, like a cloud of gold fog drifting with the breeze. "But manipulation can be many things. I suspect that it was part of the spell that created *them*. The humans manipulated both their body and mind, maybe even their souls."

"The chief mentioned something about souls. Do they steal them, too?" I tightened the pelt around my thin shoulders, remembering we were close to warmth.

"Yes and no. The elves consider magic and soul to be one and the same. That is why they covet it so much. It's why they find something like me so…threatening. Would you feel safe knowing someone could take your soul?" Cole looked to Yvaine, watching her part the water before us while whispering a familiar phrase I couldn't place.

"Considering that humans don't have souls, I'm not that worried," I dismissed. The water crashed down and splashed us, but Yvaine righted herself again, moving faster than before. The water froze to my clothes instantly, and the chill deepened.

"Why do you say that?" Cole asked, amused.

"I assume none of the Common species have them because they don't have magic," I explained. *Wasn't it obvious?* It would explain the emptiness I felt all the time. Maybe Common people were broken. Missing something.

Considering, Cole said, "Maybe, but I don't think that's true. I've been around Common and Fae alike. They both have good and bad. Some more than others. But there's something about the Common that I couldn't quite name until I met the two of you."

"What's that?" I asked.

"Love."

"Love?" I repeated, confused.

"It's the one emotion I've never seen among the Fae. They care for each other, sure, but it's more out of obligation than anything. An instinct to protect their own." We finally found a road that wasn't flooded and Yvaine was able to release the water. The houses had been abused by the waves but not overcome. I shivered, thinking of the fire to come.

She veered to the left where a small tan house sat among fallen trees. "This house is as good as any," Yvaine said quietly, finally allowing her limp to show. The windows were shattered, and the door hung halfway off its hinges, but the structure itself looked trustworthy enough.

As we stepped through the doorway, I asked Cole another question, "What does that mean for us half-breeds?"

Cole's tired face lifted into a smile. "We're lucky enough to get a version of both, I suppose."

Yvaine marched into another room. I heard the springs of a mattress squeak. She wasn't moving anytime soon. Cole entered and began rummaging through the cupboards.

I chose to follow Yvaine's lead and fell onto the couch, hating every muscle and tendon in my body. As my eyes closed and darkness fell upon me once again, I thought to myself, *Magic and love. You're the one half-breed who inherited nothing.*

"Lugh, wake up," Cole said calmly.

I struggled to react. My body wanted to stay still—paralyzed.

"Lugh," he said again.

I sat up, instinctually reaching for the weapon in my pocket. The iron blade kissed my finger but didn't break the skin. "What's wrong?" I mumbled.

"You were having a nightmare. Are you okay?" he asked. Flames were burning in the small fireplace, a kettle hanging above it. The door and windows had been boarded, so at least no one could wander in unnoticed.

"Yeah, I'm fine."

Cole looked at me a moment more before nodding, clearly not fooled by my words. He returned to the kettle.

With his attention elsewhere, I took the time to banish the memories of being locked in a bank vault. Yvaine had left me in there alone. There was no noise in that place. No way to know if my sister would come back again. The smell of iron and the unforgiving touch of the hard floor was all I had. After she'd left to save Cole from the gang, I'd feared the worst. That feeling stayed with me even now. Even knowing we were safe—safe enough—I couldn't shake it. Slowly rotting away without the power to save myself… There were no words strong enough to describe the emotion.

"Here, drink." Cole handed me a chipped coffee mug with steaming water. "Sorry, all the food has been taken, but I remembered that trick your sister taught me about the wells."

"Why not take from the river?" I asked, my brain full of fog.

Reluctantly, he said, "There were too many bodies to risk it. The well water smelled safe, though."

Realizing what the dark shapes in the water had been, I gulped the hot liquid, relishing the warmth. I had Cole bring me four more cups before my stomach protested. "Thanks, I needed that." I peered down the hall to Yvaine's room. "My sister get any?"

Cole's face soured. "No, she refused to open the door."

"Figures." I ran a hand through my knotted hair and sighed. "How much water do we have?"

"Help yourself to a bath if you'd like. I sure did." Cole walked over to the fireplace and took a dry towel from the mantle. "The tub is in the room next to Yvaine."

"That's okay. I'm too tired for the full shebang." Standing with care, I made my way to the kettle and poured a generous amount over the towel, washing my face and neck. The warmth seeped into my pores, and I nearly moaned with relief.

"You sure? It's not often that we get the chance to clean up properly," Cole asked, concern in his voice.

"I said that I'm fine," I spat. I dropped the towel and tried to hide my shaking hands. The very thought of being submerged in water, no matter how warm it was, set me on edge. I didn't trust my body anymore. I couldn't rely on it to follow my commands. Nearly drowning while I was in that state… I knew Yvaine did all that she could to save me, but normal things weren't ever going to be normal again.

"Okay, don't worry about it. At least pour some water through your hair though. I think I saw something move," he suggested, his smile tight.

I laughed. "Yeah, I think I feel it, too." Taking his advice, I leaned over and poured the hot water over my head, letting it fall to the floor. My hair had grown long during the few missing weeks. Taking the small blade, I cut the strands and enjoyed watching the grimy, twisted locks fall to the wet ground.

Cole handed me the dropped towel. "Not a fan of long hair?"

"Not really." After drying my shortened hair, I realized how disgusting my clothes were. Mud and blood clung to the fabric, as well as a sickening odor. I eyed the pile of clothing on the table.

"Take your pick. That's all I could find, though." Cole sipped from his own cup of water, pretending not to watch me.

Turning my back on the Fae, I nodded and skimmed through the options, finding pants long enough and a shirt and jacket warm enough. "There was one winter, Yvaine couldn't find us any warm clothes in time. So, she gave me her extra layers. I remember watching her shiver while we hid in the sewer tunnels at night. We were still too scared to light a fire back then." I threw the clothes back down, disgusted with myself. "I'll never be able to repay her. I'm not strong enough anymore, if I ever was."

A primal instinct took over. Sensing danger, I turned just as Cole was about to hit me with the end of his bow. I reached out and grabbed it tight, twisting it so he had to release the weapon and ripped it from him.

Cole smiled. "You're a fighter, Lugh. I saw it when you were cursed, and I see it now." I handed him his bow back, my fingers cramping from the abrupt use. "Did you and Yvaine ever train with anyone? To fight, I mean."

"No. There wasn't anyone we trusted enough to learn from. Any *skill* we have is self-taught." I laughed, though I didn't know why. At the absurdity of it? How were Yvaine and I still alive? We were children who had no protection, food, shelter, or guidance. Realistically, we should have died long ago.

"I've trained with the salamander people. They are the most talented fighters I've ever seen. I could show you what they taught me if you'd like?" Cole propped his bow against the wall, waiting for my answer.

Strangely invigorated, I said, "Sure." I peeled off my dirty jacket and stepped into a defensive pose.

"Your instincts are right. Keep your hands up if you need to block a blow quickly. Keep balanced." Cole threw a punch. I dodged it barely and hit him in gut. My blow was unimpressive; his abs almost broke my thin fingers. I'd always been thin. I was built lean and tall, and we didn't have much food. Though, in the past couple years, I'd been able to put on some muscle, and I was finally starting to feel strong—I was starting to feel like a man instead of a boy. But it only took a few weeks to undo years of work.

"You're quick. That's good. Use your momentum to strengthen the hit," Cole advised.

I advanced, throwing myself forward. But it was too much, and I lost my footing. Cole hit me in the back of the neck with a hard slap.

"Remember to stay balanced. If you have an opponent stronger than you, use their own weight against them. Make them come to you."

I circled Cole, fainting in and out of his reach. I was out of breath. Still, no sweat formed. Cole lunged forward, purposefully leaving himself open. I took the bait and dodged his hook, kicking his thigh. He tripped but caught himself before he fell.

"That was good."

"You left yourself open," I argued.

Somber, he replied, "Until you get your strength back, you're going to have to be creative when you fight. Practicing will help get you there."

Strangely, I found myself smiling. Was there really a chance I would be strong again?

"What's going on?" Yvaine stood outside her doorway with her arms crossed.

Excited, I explained, "Cole has trained with the salamander people. He's showing me how to fight like them." I looked to the elf and asked, "What are they, anyway?"

Never taking his eyes from Yvaine, he responded, "They're lizard-like creatures that wield fire magic. Very aggressive, but honorable. They live to fight."

"We've never come across them before, have we Yvaine?" I said, still catching my breath.

My sister's eyes were as sharp as dagger's as she said, "No, we haven't. And I'm glad. They sound dangerous. You should be resting, Lugh. Not tiring yourself out learning about a deadly Fae people." Though she was responding to me, she directed her spite at Cole.

"C'mon, sis, you know how much I like to learn about Fae culture. This is something that we can all use." I paused. "Especially, while we're being hunted." My voice quieted to a whisper, and the dread returned, my gut clenching. *You don't have enough time to learn even if you tried. They're going to find you, and you won't be ready.*

Yvaine finally looked at me, her eyes softening. "You almost died, Lugh. Rest will save you now." The scab across her neck was red with anger.

I nodded, defeated. There was no point in arguing with Yvaine. I reached for the clean clothes I'd dropped.

"We *all* almost died. That doesn't mean we can stop moving. Both of you need to learn to fight. And Yvaine, you need to hone your magic," Cole said. The book I stole from the dark elves pulsed in the pocket of my old jacket. Though it was still on the floor, it called to me. I opened my mouth to offer it to Yvaine, but no words came out. For a reason I didn't know, I wanted to keep it a secret.

"We've survived for thirteen years without magic or special lizard-fighting! My brother needs to heal. You're lucky that we even had the strength to free you from the elves. So, why don't you do everyone a favor and leave! We don't *need* you." My sister's outburst caught me off-guard. Her hands were balled into shaking fists at her sides. The dark circles beneath her eyes were severe. She hadn't bathed or changed her clothes. She was a mess, and I hadn't even noticed.

"Yvaine…" I started.

"I'm trying to help." Cole took a step back, but kept his gaze locked on Yvaine's.

"Help? You lied to us. You lied to *me*. If you would have just told me that I had magic, we could have avoided so many obstacles. Lugh was on the brink of death. I barely made it in time…" Yvaine was fighting back tears, and I had to fight back my own because of it.

Without thinking, I said, "He tried to tell you, but you weren't listening. He told you to use the dagger. He told you to ask it for help. Only *Fae* can use magic, sis." I gave her a dumbfounded expression, knowing how far her tunnel-vision went.

Startled, she said, "How do you know what he said?"

Cole was quick, recognizing my panic. "I told him when we got here."

Yvaine huffed and went silent.

I moved toward the front door and pulled on the top board, my arms screaming, while Cole continued, "I didn't know that you were Fae for sure until you healed me from the gunshot wound in the city. You cast a spell on me while we slept. At that time, you didn't trust me. You were losing your mind, Yvaine. You were in survival mode. I didn't know what a revelation like that would have done to you." The elf's voice was full of regret. "I couldn't use your magic either. You weakened every time I took from you. I had to choose my moments carefully."

No one noticed as the second and third board came loose, and I moved on to the fourth.

"Liar! You wanted my magic for yourself! That's why you wanted to go with us to the stones." Yvaine threw her arms into the air, furious. "Sorry, your plan didn't work, but I'm not going to let you make another. You need to leave!"

I rolled my eyes and begged the nails in the final board to release their hold.

Cole moved forward quickly and grabbed Yvaine by the arms. "I'm not lying! I never wanted your magic! I just didn't want to be left behind!"

Surprised, Yvaine said, "What do you mean?"

"If you were aware of your magic, you wouldn't need me to perform the spell at the stones anymore. I knew there was a chance it wasn't going to work if I was the one who did it, and I was going to tell you about your heritage if it didn't. But…you were right not to trust me. Though, I was worried about you, it was also for selfish reasons that I only left you hints. I wanted you to realize it on your own, so I could have that much more time with you." Cole dropped his hands. "You would have left me if you had known the truth."

The final board flew from the doorway and landed on the hardwood floor. Yvaine and Cole looked at me, alarmed. "Where are you going?" Yvaine demanded.

Motioning to the sky, I said, "The sun is nearly down. I have a weapon. And you two need some privacy." I grabbed the clean clothes and filthy jacket from the ground and stepped back, cringing when my knee wobbled.

"Nighttime is just as dangerous, Lugh. You're weak right now." Yvaine stepped toward the door.

"I'm going to rest under a dark tree by the house. Just *stay with Cole.*" I met my sister's stare, and I could see that she understood what I meant.

Reluctantly, she nodded, and I stepped outside to breathe in the fresh air. As I slowly made my way to the fallen trees by the roadside, I heard private words whispered between two lovers. "I don't want you to leave," Yvaine admitted.

With a smile in his voice, Cole said, "I thought that you didn't need me? That you could survive on your own?"

"I can survive without you, but I can't *live* without you."

The prickly branches of the pine trees were welcoming as I lowered myself beneath their fallen canopy.

The snow started to fall about an hour after the sun went down. But the cold didn't reach me in my place beneath the heavy tree branches. The grass wasn't yet buried, and the smell of pine was calming. I'd quickly changed into the clean clothes Cole had found, and I ditched the old rags outside the small shelter. Afterward, I'd clung to the book through the old jacket, refusing to take it out.

Whispers seeped through the fabric, taunting me. What they said, I didn't know. Different languages swirled together, creating beautiful, chaotic spells.

Slowly, the small book slipped from the pocket and into my hands.

The cover was leather, and I wondered why the elves' herbivore nature didn't hold true for their spell books. The dark binding had a rough texture with intricate designs along its borders; they swirled outward from the four corners. The markings reminded me of the ancient gravestones that rested near our childhood church in Hamilton.

I flipped to the first page, and I stopped breathing. Something clutched the air tight and refused to let go. I banged on my chest, hoping to shock my lungs out of their paralysis, but they didn't move. The book wouldn't close. I threw it aside and crawled out of the trees. I tried to scream for Yvaine, but nothing came out. There was nothing I could do but lay in the snow and suffocate.

Just as my vision was fading, flames flew above me. What looked like a grasping arm caught fire, though there was no arm there before the flames appeared. The grip on my lungs released. I sucked in the smoky air, smelling burnt skin. Then, there were white eyes hovering above me. Long green fur teased my face. The cù-sìth's breath was hot, and smoke leaked from his dog-like nose.

"Arlen?" I choked. His whiskers twitched with what looked like amusement, and I laughed, sitting up. The spell book was beside me, the snow dented as if the text had been dragged, though I distinctly remembered leaving it in the trees.

Arlen chuffed and rubbed his head against mine.

"That must have been some creepy booby trap from the elves, huh?" I commented, rubbing my chest.

Arlen confirmed my thought by breathing out another flame, though this one was significantly smaller.

"Thank you for saving me. Again." I ran my hand through Arlen's soft fur, and he purred. "What are you doing here?"

The cù-sìth laid beside me in response and pressed his warm side against my leg.

Looking at the small house that Yvaine and Cole were in, I suddenly felt very grateful for the Fae animal. "You can stay with me as long as you want." I placed the spell book back on my lap, its binding still folded open at the first page. The ink swirled in ways I'd never been able to comprehend, despite Yvaine's attempts to teach me to read. But I didn't think she would know any more about these markings than I did. The passages were inked in heavy handwriting. The farther I went into the book, the darker the ink was—the most recent additions.

The calmer I became, the clearer the whispered words were. I concentrated on Arlen's breathing, so I wouldn't ruin the feeling. Words like heal, endowed, curse, shadow, and sun were uttered in my mother tongue. Unable to put together complete sentences, I told the Fae, "Maybe Cole will know more about this." I stood and pointed a finger at the beast. "But don't tell them what happened. I don't need Yvaine freaking out again." I went to bury my old clothes under the snow, as to not attract visitors, but they were gone. Little footprints the size of my fingernail surrounded the area. "Damn, fairies."

Arlen followed me to the house where I knocked on the front entrance. A freshly bathed Yvaine opened the door. She had found warmer clothes, too. Cole appeared behind her, his hair wet. I turned to Arlen, and was grateful I had been outside for their reunion. "We have a visitor," I announced, rubbing the Fae's snow-covered fur.

Cole bowed to the Fae and said, "Welcome, my friend." My sister nodded her greeting to Arlen and stepped aside, allowing us to enter. The cù-sìth's massive body barely fit through the doorway, but when he did, he found Cole and nuzzled him. "Thank you for helping them," the elf said.

"*You* sent him?" Yvaine asked.

Cole released his hold on Arlen and took Yvaine's hand. "Just in case." The elf winked, and my sister laughed, pulling Cole in for a kiss.

I reached for the spell book and stopped. Instead, I examined the small house and plucked a moldy paperback from its shelf. Opening the novel to the last page, I said, "Remember when you tried to teach me to read, sis?" I scanned the scribbles on the page, lost.

Yvaine swiped the book from my hands and sighed. "Yeah, I'm not much of a teacher, am I?"

I laughed. "There were more important things to worry about. It's not like we had magic to protect us. We had to do it the hard way."

Yvaine's face brightened. "But we can do it the easy way this time." She grabbed Cole's arm and continued, "The language spell. Teach me how to do it."

I listened to the elf and Yvaine's conversation while hanging limp over a shoulder. "I tried to teach him to read after the Collapse, but surviving takes up a lot of time, and its especially hard when you're hiding in the dark," Yvaine said sadly.

"Maybe when he's healed you can find someone to cast a language spell on him," Cole suggested.

"A language spell?"

"Yes, each Fae is given the spell when they're born. There's no need to learn to read and write. It's put in their mind already. Every language on Earth, both Common and Fae."

"I always wondered how the Fae could understand me. Now I know, they cheated in school," Yvaine said with a smile in her voice.

The memory was clear despite being blind during the exchange. I put on a surprised, but hopeful face. Cole glanced to me curiously. "Of course," he said, unable to refuse my sister her excitement. "I didn't learn a lot of spells from the elves, but I do remember this one." Following Cole's lead, we all sat on the warm floor with Arlen. The elf took the book from my sister and laid it between the two of us. "Now, join hands. Yvaine, look inward, and repeat after me."

Yvaine nodded eagerly, and I withheld a chuckle. Her mood had drastically changed from that morning. I took Yvaine's hands and waited for her to calm. A few long minutes passed, and I opened my mouth to say something when purple smoke came tumbling from my sister's body, as though her pores excreted magic rather than sweat. Cole whispered the spell in her ear:

Scientia praeteritum et praesens loqui ad me

Loqui cum tua lingua retorta

Scribere cum eleganti manu

Replete mentem, cum omnia verba unquam edidit in arboribus

Dux manu cum omnibus symbola semper signátum sub caelo

Coniungere me cum meis Terrena rex

Yvaine repeated the strange words, her magic surrounding me in a peaceful mist. The paperback's pages flipped as if a breeze had infiltrated the small house. I gripped my sister's hands tight. *If you had magic, it would be seen in this moment.* I looked inward and searched for that supposed light inside. But there was only darkness. Defeated, I concentrated on the book before us and laughed. The first page read: "*I decided not to question the mysterious happiness inside me. I let it envelop me until it spread electrical currents throughout my body, starting at my core and working its way outward.*"

Then the words from the language spell became clear:

Knowledge of the past and present speak to me

Speak with your twisted tongue

Write with your graceful hand

Fill the mind with all the words ever uttered in the trees

Guide the hand with all the symbols ever etched under the sky

Connect me with my Earthly kin

"I can read!" I exclaimed. The spell book in my pocket seemed to yell rather than whisper now, twisting words in many different languages. Yet, they all flowed together now because I knew what every word meant. I looked to my sister and the elf to see if they could hear it, too, but they only had eyes for each other. Pride in Cole's and gratitude in Yvaine's.

I grabbed the paperback and scanned the writing, astonished at the new skill. I could imagine everything in my mind's eye. Every detail the author gave me contributed to the new world. *Amazing.*

Cole spoke to Yvaine while I continued to fawn over the paperback. "Your will is strong, and you can create spells on a whim. But casting a spell that's been used by several of your kin has its own kind of power. Each time a spell is cast, a piece of the caster stays with it. It gains more power the more it's used. It grows and learns."

"Like it's alive," Yvaine said, beaming.

"Yes, because you give it life."

The spell book was screaming in my ear, begging to be opened. *Shadow, shadow, shadow!* I knew I should have given it to Yvaine. She could learn so much from it, but…

"What spell did the elves use to become…what they are?" I asked, unsure what to call the alterations.

Cole's face fell. "The spell is not as simple as a few words or the will behind it. It requires sacrifice."

"What kind of sacrifice? More souls?" I said, putting the old paperback back on the shelf.

The elf shook his head, his stare dead. "I'm sure they made use of them, but no. The caster must drink the blood of their sacrifice under a new moon." Cole stood and ran his hand across Arlen's back. The beast whined, feeling his friend's distress.

"Who do they sacrifice? Humans?" Yvaine asked. My sister's light had gone dark, and so had its peaceful presence.

"Anything with magic in its blood. Thirteen moon cycles, and the transformation is complete. Though, most don't make it that far." The elf bowed his head.

"What do you mean?" Yvaine stood and grabbed Cole's hand.

The elf's voice was tight as he said, "My mother didn't live past the second cycle. Her body couldn't handle the change." A tear trickled down his cheek, and he quickly wiped it away.

"I'm so sorry, Cole." Yvaine held him tight. Cole glanced over his shoulder at me, but I said nothing. There were no words to express how one felt when a loved one was lost. Though, he nodded once to me in recognition. We both knew the same pain.

"How are we supposed to fight them?" I pondered aloud.

Yvaine released Cole and sternly said, "We are *not* fighting them. We are running."

"We can't run forever, sis. Cole is all they need for the doom spell. They're not going to give up." I straightened my back, and it screamed in protest. "We need to get stronger."

"Cole can teach us more magic. We can hide, can't we?" she said to the elf, her dagger pulsing in time with her rapid heart.

"Honestly, I don't know as many spells as you think. I don't have my own magic, and I hate taking from others. So, I didn't bother, other than the basics for survival." The elf's black hair fell into his eyes, and he pushed it back, irritated. Yvaine mimicked the motion with her own hair unknowingly.

The two debated visiting a spriggan or finding the salamander people for assistance. But the dark elves had earned a reputation as Fae hunters, so it would be unlikely that anyone would be willing to hide us. "Mother was an elf. Maybe she could help," I suggested.

Yvaine left Cole and put a hand against my forehead. "You do know that she's dead, right?"

I slapped her hand away. "Yes, I know that. But we should return home. We never did after…" Yvaine cringed, but I continued, "She might have left something behind. Something that could tell us who we are. If we know more about our heritage, maybe we could defend ourselves better."

The play of emotions on my sister's face brought painful memories to the forefront of my mind, but I wouldn't allow them to overtake me. *Not in front of Yvaine.*

Cole chimed in. "I think it's a good idea. There's nowhere else that's safe, Yvaine."

"If it was safe, then we wouldn't be two orphans on the run, would we?" The venom in my sister's voice was like acid, sizzling in the silent air that came afterward. Guilt flooded in, and I nearly told her that I'd changed my mind when she said, "Fine."

"Fine?" I repeated.

"We had to go back someday." Yvaine went to the front door and looked up at the clearing sky. "Let's go while there's darkness left."

"What happened to traveling during the day?" I sputtered.

"I can't hold that darkness spell all day. Who do you think I am?" She reached for her new boots, though they looked too big for her.

"A crazy, barefoot heathen who bosses everyone around," I responded, angry at her fluctuating decisions.

"I'm not barefoot anymore," she muttered.

"So just a crazy heathen, then?" Cole laughed.

"Stop ganging up on me and grab your weapons." My sister stomped outside and into the snow. Arlen trailed after her.

I went to the fireplace and absorbed one last burst of heat. Cole patted my shoulder before following Yvaine with his bow and quiver. "We're going to be okay, Lugh."

I clung to those words as we walked down the snow-covered streets, past the demolished buildings, and outside of the city where we followed alongside the river's new path. The snow had passed on for the moment, causing the cold to seep into our bones. The stars that guided us south were bright, but for once, I didn't fear the Guise appearing. We had protection. We had magic and will to protect us.

I looked back at the once gang-ridden city. Though it had been full of pain and suffering, it had been full of life. The will of one person had taken that away. The will of a few humans had caused the Collapse. The elves wanted to make the darkness permanent.

What was my will compared to all of theirs?

25

The river had filled the ravine. The bridge that rested miles from the city hadn't survived the impact of the flood. Looking at Yvaine's face, I guessed that this had been the bridge with the humming trows. I reached for her hand because I could see the tears gathering in her eyes, but Cole beat me to it, grabbing her left hand. "Trows are very good swimmers. There's a chance they survived."

From Yvaine's right side, I met Cole's gaze. There was sorrow there. I looked away, realizing just how often Cole lied to Yvaine. Though his intentions were good, it didn't sit well with me.

Her brother falling behind, Yvaine decided that we should stop at the road's junction to rest. Cole offered, "I'll hunt. Maybe the river has attracted some life." The elf adjusted his bow, so it rested across his shoulders.

"The sun rises soon. Hurry back," Yvaine said. I could tell she didn't want him to leave on his own, but the worry she had for me made the decision for her. Cole kissed her forehead and darted into the tree line with Arlen. Yvaine fell to the ground, exhausted.

I joined her and commented, "Are you going to do anything about your ankle, or are you happy hopping around on one leg for the rest of your life?"

My sister chuckled. "Who needs to walk when you can just carry me?"

Scoffing, I said, "Oh yes, you would handle that well. Having no control over your own body. Having no say in where you go. Please, you wouldn't last five minutes without wanting to rip my head off."

Yvaine sat up and grabbed my hand. "I suppose you're right about that." Pausing, she asked, "Are you okay?"

"I'm wonderful. I'm being chased by evil elves while I'm half-starved. Why would you think any different?" I squeezed her hand but let go so that I could lean back; my arm shook from the added weight.

"I'm sorry."

"For?" I asked.

Yvaine took off her boot and examined the swollen ankle before she said, "I didn't get to you in time. It's my fault you were poisoned. It's my fault you're half-starved." She placed her foot in the river's icy water and growled with distaste.

My chest tightened with guilt. It wasn't my sister's fault that I was cursed. And it wasn't her fault that we were orphans. "I'm sorry that I left our prisoner alone just so I could prove to you that I could handle myself. I mean, you know how much more fun we could have had making Cole think we were going to eat him? Such a waste of an opportunity." A buzzing sounded in my ear, and I swatted whatever it was away.

Yvaine laughed hysterically, and I joined her after a moment. The sun was rising, and we didn't care. Noise would attract the Guise, but we had magic to protect us now. *She* had magic. "Oh, Lugh. I'm tired of running. There's always something to run from." Her laugh died down to a whisper. "I wish there was a way for everyone to be safe."

My sister's comment surprised me. It wasn't like Yvaine to care about anyone but the two of us. Cole changed that about her. *Would that change get us killed?* "Don't worry about me, sis. I can take care of myself."

Before Yvaine could open her mouth to argue, a stranger spoke from the tree line. "Well, well, well. It's blondie back from the dead. I was sure that if the pears didn't kill you, the flood would have." A tall woman with greasy black hair sauntered out of the brush. There was a string of tiny bones hanging around her neck.

Yvaine shot to her feet and unsheathed her blade. I did the same, but slower.

"Don't be like that. I just want to trade." The woman revealed a long dirty braid of blonde hair. "You can have this back if you give me those boots," the woman taunted.

"Not interested." Yvaine didn't dare reach down to put her boot back on. Not when two men joined the woman, both of them holding hatchets. Their pierced skin was infected and grotesque. They were bottom feeders that had their territory washed away.

"That's okay. I wasn't going to give it back anyway." She stroked the braid tenderly. "It's too lucky to trade away, like a rabbit's foot. It saved me from the flood."

"Glad you got some use out of it. Now leave, or I'll wrap it around your throat," Yvaine threatened.

The strange woman chuckled. "But we're hungry, and I would love to add more to my charm." She turned her sights on me. "Your hair is too short. Maybe we'll keep you around until it grows out." I nearly gagged thinking of her creepy fingers running along my scalp.

The men moved as one, aiming for Yvaine. They didn't consider the skeleton beside her a threat. "Movere cum me," she said. *Move with me.*

The river rose and fell down on the man closest to me. She held onto the water, forcing him down to the river floor. I lunged for the second attacker. Hitting him was like hitting a brick wall. We both dropped our weapons, and he threw me aside like I was nothing. *Because you were nothing.*

Just as she released her hold on the river, the second man found her and ripped the blade from her hand. She moved to knee him in the gut, but her ankle gave out before she could, and she fell. The man gripped her neck and squeezed. My sister didn't bother trying to remove his grip, instead, she lunged for his eyes, scratching and clawing at his face. He screamed but didn't release his hold on her neck. The endowed dagger fell to the ground when he tried to restrain her arms.

The iron blade found its way into my hand again. I tried to stand, but my legs wouldn't follow commands—they were paralyzed. I threw the blade with all my strength, desperate to help my sister.

The former gang member let go of Yvaine, falling to the ground with the knife resting halfway into the back of his skull. My sister looked at me with awe, rubbing her throat. I looked away in shame—I couldn't stand up.

The snow sounded with footsteps. The woman was running. "You're not getting away that easy. Stay here, Lugh." Yvaine didn't bother taking the dirk with her.

Without another option, I watched as Yvaine chased the grimy woman. I couldn't see what happened, but I heard it. There was a short struggle in the trees, though I wasn't worried.

My sister came limping out of the tree line holding a blonde braid. "What are you going to do with that? It's not like you can put it back on your head," I said, baffled.

"All I know is that she can't have it." Yvaine wrapped the braid around her wrist like a trophy and returned to icing her ankle, as if she was never interrupted to begin with. "I know you can handle yourself, Lugh. You always have."

The feeling in my legs returned incrementally, and I was able to crawl my way to the riverside. My sister's slit throat from the stones had re-opened and bled slightly. I didn't respond because it wasn't really about proving to Yvaine that I could handle myself. It was about proving to myself that I could protect her like she's protected me.

Cole came crashing through the brush and stopped when he saw us lazing by the water. "I heard screams…" He saw one body with a dagger in its head by the shoreline and the other rising from the depths and floating down the current. "Never mind, then. I guess that I'll return to what I was doing."

"Wait," I said to Cole. With shaky legs, I stood and motioned for the bow. "It's been a long while. Can I?"

Unsure, the elf handed over his endowed bow and quiver to the malnourished teenager and watched him walk into the forest alone.

"I can you hear you, Arlen." The Fae shifted in the tree's shadows, his snow-covered green fur disguising him perfectly. "Are you the reason I can't find any food? You're probably scaring them off." Once the cù-sìth was close, he dropped a small doe to the ground. The red blood dripping from his jaw was a brutal contrast against his pure white eyes.

"Oh." I patted Arlen's forehead. "Thank you, but I wanted to do this on my own. I was the one who fed us before…" I forced away the dread. "Take your kill to Yvaine and Cole. I'll follow soon."

Arlen grunted with displeasure but did as I asked. The snow had returned and fell silently to the frozen ground. The clouds would give me more time, but sunrise was moments away, and it wouldn't be long before Yvaine would start her own hunt.

I forced my feet to traverse the uneven ground while following a set of rabbit prints. There were two good things about winter: tracks were clear, and the nights were longer.

The clouds were tinted orange by the time I found the small animal digging up roots near a log. I nocked Cole's arrow and drew it back. Before I could aim, the muscles in my arm spasmed, and the arrow shot into the darkness, well away from the target. The Common animal quickly disappeared into the snowy brush.

I roared in frustration, scaring away any chance at breakfast. I retrieved the errant arrow. My wrist ached when I pulled it out of the tree. They never healed right after they were broken, but I'd been able to feed us anyway. The bow introduced us to fresh meat. After years of expired canned food, it was a welcome change.

Too bad you can't feed her anymore. Cole's with her now anyway.
Who needs you?

"Lugh?" Yvaine's soft footfalls were the only sounds in the forest.

"Here," I said.

"I was worried when you didn't come back with Arlen." She found me staring at the magic bow, and I wondered what my face looked like.

"I caught a trail, but there's nothing here. Let's go back." I returned to the path I made, intent on following it, when Yvaine pointed the dirk at my chest. I raised my eyebrows in question.

"You've always been a bow hog. It's my turn to learn." She raised the bow up and over my shoulders and placed it on hers along with the quiver.

Confused, I didn't put up a fight. "Here, you can have this instead."

The dirk was placed in my numb palm. Yvaine even wrapped my fingers around it when I didn't move them myself. "What?" I said.

"I don't want it anymore, and that blade I gave you wasn't much to boast about. It chipped when I ripped it out of that guy's skull."

"You've never let this thing out of your sight, and you're just *giving* it to me?" The times I held the dirk in my hand were rare. I recalled a moment when I was six years old: Yvaine was asleep, and it was dark in the basement we hid in. I barely touched it with my fingertips when the amethyst light appeared. When I removed my hand the light went out. It made me question if Yvaine was awake and teasing me.

"Well, I don't plan on letting *you* out of my sight. So, nothing is really changing, is it?" My sister smiled and wrapped her arm around my waist, leading me out of the forest.

The dagger was heavier than I remembered. It took a few tries before I could unsheathe it smoothly. Yvaine had willingly handed over her leather sheathe, too, but I could hear a small twinge of sorrow in her voice when she said, "Don't lose it, brother."

It was the sorrow she had for giving up her precious, life-saving weapon that had me determined to prove to her that I was worthy of it. Standing in the shallows of the river, I plunged that long dagger into the water dozens of times before I finally pierced a scaled backside.

The dark spell hovering above us, Yvaine and I made our way to the temporary shelter. Cole had discovered a rotting cabin hidden in the tree line down the road. The fire inside warmed the damp shelter and set everyone's face aglow with sunset light. The doe and fish were prepped and set on the grating above the flames. Though, most of the raw doe was already being devoured by Arlen in the corner.

I cleaned the endowed blade with an old rag and river water while Cole showed Yvaine how to properly hold a bow. She had no problem nocking an arrow and pulling back the string, but her patience was nonexistent as she argued with the experienced bow user about technique.

"Dinner time," I said, saving Cole from being shot by Yvaine. He gave me a grateful nod, and led Yvaine to the bedding beside the fire. Her limp was worse. "Are you going to take care of your ankle, sis?"

Still irritated from the bow lesson, she said, "I already did, but all my spell does is relieve the pain for a bit. It's just going to have to heal the old-fashioned way."

"Don't you know a better spell, Cole? You healed from a gunshot wound, right?" I asked, cutting the fish and doe into three sections with the tip of the blade.

"Yes, but that wasn't my spell. It was Yvaine's." He looked pointedly at her as I handed him his meal. The meat wafted upward, and my mouth watered. I basically threw the meat at Yvaine before digging into my own portion.

"I thought it was the *spriggan's spell*?" Yvaine teased around a bite of fish.

The elf's mouth full, he said, "Don't even start with me, woman."

"If it was the *other woman* starting it, you would be more apologetic about your lies." They shared a glare, but once the food hit their bellies they were both full of love.

I interrupted before they could start fighting again. "So, Yvaine is capable of casting a powerful healing spell?"

"Yes, but she was in survival mode when she did. Similar to an adrenaline rush that saves you during a fight. It's not something you can repeat without practice. Hell, she didn't even say an incantation. It was all raw power. And she was asleep." Cole wiped empty hands on his pants and said, "It's how she was able to save you at the stones. Most experienced elves can't accomplish what she did."

"Another thing you should have mentioned," Yvaine growled, tossing her meal's bones aside.

"I didn't know it would take that much until the elves told me." Arlen stood and sat beside Cole, pressing his side against the elf's. "I told you before, they only shared things that would hurt me. And making me think that you might make it in time only to fail from inexperience certainly did the trick." Cole ran his hand through Arlen's fur. "That's why I asked Arlen for help. He came to see me in that dark cell soon after you left with Lugh."

The cù-sìth purred, and I smiled. "You all went through so much to save me. Thank you."

My sister's irritated expression disappeared, and she grabbed my hand. "You know that I would die for you, Lugh."

Guilt crawled its way up my throat. "Why don't you try living for me instead, Yvaine?"

"As long as you do the same."

Strangely, for a moment, I couldn't tell her yes. So, I nodded and squeezed her hand.

Satisfied, she said, "I'll take the first watch. You guys get some sleep."

Yvaine reached for the bow at Cole's side, but he swiped first. "No, I'll take the first watch." The command in his voice left no room for argument, even for Yvaine.

"Fine." She fell back onto the cabin's old, soggy bedding and was snoring within moments. Arlen found his way by the fire again.

"Does he need to power-up his fire magic or something?" I asked, noticing how little tendrils of black smoke leaked from the Fae's nose.

Cole smirked. "No, he just likes to be warm."

Restless, I picked up the rag and began cleaning the dagger again. It shined in the firelight. The runes were subtle against the metal. The pearl handle was smooth and slid out of my grip easily. It felt wrong to keep it when it had potential for so much more than a magicless half-breed like me.

Cole interrupted my spinning thoughts. "I was thinking that we should take the road instead of the forest tonight. We'll be less likely to run into the elves there, and Yvaine says it's the quicker route to Hamilton."

"Probably a good idea, but we're also more likely to run into humans." The blade shone bright, yet I couldn't stop polishing the metal.

The elf wrung his hands together, distracted. "Well, from what I've seen, you guys can handle a few humans."

"I suppose." I cringed thinking of that morning. *You're no use in a fight. You couldn't even stand.*

"Plus, you have Arlen and me now. You two aren't alone anymore," Cole said, his voice small.

I looked up at Cole's sincere face, and I couldn't help but feel angry. "Why do you lie to Yvaine? She can handle more than you think."

Taken aback, he said, "I don't lie… I withhold the truth to protect her."

"If you keep doing that, you'll lose her. She's not a fan of trust. So, if she's giving it to you, don't spit on it." I rubbed the blade harder and harder, trying to control the rage boiling in my stomach.

"If you think that, why are you hiding the fact that you were aware during the curse?" Cole accused, his hands free and dangling over his knees.

My hand slipped off the flat of the blade and over the edge. "Shit!" Blood gathered in the palm of my hand. My eyes shot to Yvaine, but she was still sleeping soundly. "I'm her brother. Knowing that would kill her."

"'She can handle more than you think.'" Cole repeated my words back to me, but it wasn't out of spite. "I think you should tell her. I think it would help both of you move on if you did."

I laughed without humor. "How is someone supposed to move on from that? 'Hey sis, I remember being lugged around like a backpack. I remember being left alone in the dark without knowing if you were going to come back for me. I remember breathing in water without the power to even cough it up on my own.'" I started rubbing the blade again, but the cut on my hand wouldn't stop bleeding. "'I remember dying and clawing my way back to life only to find you bleeding out beside me. I remember...'" *our parent's murder. I remember that it was my fault they were dead.*

Cole grabbed my wrists and held them apart. "Breathe, Lugh. Breathe." Black dots spotted my vision. My thoughts were loud and unforgiving. Flashes of our parent's dead bodies flooded my mind. The memory of Yvaine's face after she killed their murderer was the worst. Because she wasn't just my sister anymore. Saving me had made her into a killer.

Coming back to reality, I saw that the dirk was covered in my blood. The pearl handle was smeared with red. "It's my fault," I whispered.

"What's your fault, Lugh?" Cole asked, concerned.

"I can't." I looked at Yvaine where she still slept by the fire.

Cole followed my gaze and said in a strangely regretful tone, "Yvaine will understand whatever you're holding on to. Don't torture yourself by keeping it a secret."

I stared at my sister's calm face—sleeping was the only time it wasn't pinched with worry or set with a menacing glare. "I kil…" An amethyst light appeared, outshining the warm fire. Cole released me. The runes on the endowed blade were lit ablaze with magic. Yvaine was still sleeping. "How?" I whispered.

Cole returned to his bedding and said, "Well, it looks like gender doesn't matter with half-breeds. It's simply who gets lucky."

"But this is Yvaine's magic?" The amethyst light dimmed and lightened with the rhythm of my sporadic heart.

"It's normal for families to share the same color of magic, but it is very much your own, Lugh. Congratulations." Cole was trying to be happy for me, but he couldn't hide the disappointment on his face.

"I'm sorry," I said, the dagger going dark.

"Don't be. I have something much better, remember?" He turned to Yvaine, his smile tight.

"Please, don't tell her what I said," I whispered. Wrapping the rag around my cut, I used the outside to clean the blood from the blade.

"Don't worry. That's for you to decide." Cole turned away from me and covered himself with his jacket.

"Thank you for talking to me while I was…asleep. It made a difference." And I meant it. If Cole hadn't taken the time to tell me what was happening when I was paralyzed, I would have lost my mind much sooner.

Instead of acknowledging my gratitude, he asked, "Are you going to be up for a while? I'd like to get some sleep."

"Yeah, go ahead."

After a few moments, I heard Cole's breath deepen and sync with Yvaine's. I took the spell book out of my pocket, and Arlen peeked his eye open. I raised a finger to my lips to silence him. He chuffed but fell back asleep anyway.

I opened the book with new eyes. Every strange scribble now had meaning. Flipping through the pages, I stopped when I saw a spell titled: Healing Fire.

Fires of the sun gather
Warm that which has faded
Kindle your power and consume the pain
Burn the dead away
Ignite the healing flame

Amethyst flames consumed the blade. But they didn't burn my hand. I hadn't uttered a word of the spell, yet it had come to life in front of me. I could feel energy being drawn from the fireplace. Smoke and flame entered the dagger and exited as magic.

I directed the cool flames at Yvaine, whispering the spell under my breath. Her blackened ankle twitched, and I was afraid that she was going to wake, but the swelling disappeared, and she breathed out a content sigh. The bruising was gone in the next instant. The lingering cut on her neck closed next, sealing with a scar that matched mine. I allowed the purple flames to encase her body, searching for other injuries. The magic lingered on her chest and stomach, causing me to worry.

The flames roamed over Arlen and Cole. Arlen rejected the magic immediately by rolling over and grumbling. Cole took longer than Yvaine had, the magic lingering over his limbs. It seemed that he'd been hiding how badly he was hurt. *Could the elves have tortured him?*

Finally, I allowed the magic to settle over me. But once it reached my skin, the flames died and the smoke vanished into the air. I repeated the spell a second time only for it to reignite and die again. I placed the dirk back in its sheathe.

You didn't deserve to heal anyway.

I moved closer to the fire, suddenly very cold. I listened to the forest outside and waited for another attack, but all I heard was the wind passing through the leafless trees.

A deep howl hit the cabin's outer walls. Arlen leapt up from his place beside the fire and crashed through the door. From the small window, I watched him speed upriver and disappear into the trees.

Cole and Yvaine had woken from sleep and were still confused when I said, "We need to leave!" I'd been appreciating the sunset from a small stool by window's ledge. It was the only thing that had calmed my mind after a sleepless day of toying with the spell book. I must have cast Healing Fire a hundred times, but it wouldn't fix me—body or mind.

"Did Arlen howl?" Yvaine asked drowsily. She stretched as if she had the whole morning to laze. For once, she wasn't a crazed lunatic hell-bent on running. I hated to ruin the moment.

"That wasn't Arlen," Cole said. The elf strapped his bow on and held out a hand to Yvaine. She quickly slipped her feet into the boots and accepted the outstretched hand. "Arlen is going to buy us some time. We need to run," Cole explained, his expression hard.

I stood and walked to the doorway, trying to get my blood flowing. It stung and my muscles pinched and ached, but I would do what I needed to survive. "Let's go then," I said, assuring them that I was capable.

I led the way down the old highway. The closest town was Stirling, and it was at least a day's journey from where we were. There was nowhere to hide. All we could do was run.

A second howl sounded.

"Lugh, we need to move faster," Yvaine said, finally awake.

"I know," I breathed. My mind was fast and ordered the body to move faster, but the connection wasn't there. The body wasn't a part of me anymore. It had its own desires, and its main one was to lay down and not get up.

Snarls rumbled down the tunnel of trees that surrounded us. The road left us bare for the world to see but it was the quicker than maneuvering trees, especially with me in tow. Sweat formed at my brow, and I couldn't help but laugh—it was the only water I'd managed to drink, and I was wasting it.

An arrow landed in front of us, sticking in a pavement crack. I was so slow to react that I would have tripped over it if Yvaine hadn't pulled me in her direction. I didn't dare look back. All I could do was concentrate on moving my feet forward. "Cole, what are you doing?" Yvaine demanded. Her voice was behind me now. She'd stopped. Another arrow passed by my head. Runes were etched into its sides like Cole's, but these arrows were pitch black, blending with the coming night.

"Just go! I'll slow them down!" I could hear the strain in his voice as

Cole pulled his bow string back and fired. The cù-sìth's growls and whines intensified in the trees. Arlen was outnumbered. A tear managed to slide down my cheek. *You're going to lose him. You're going to lose all of them because you're too slow.*

"No! You're coming with us! Run!" There was a desperation in her voice that Cole couldn't ignore. She wasn't going to leave him behind again, and we all knew it.

I heard Cole's approaching steps between my rapid breaths. "Lugh, I have to carry you. They're getting closer." Cole's voice was as hard as his expression. He was scared, too.

"No way."

"Lugh, it's okay," Yvaine reassured. Dozens of arrows fell down on us. I finally stopped, preparing for the worst. But none hit their target. Magic burst from Yvaine, causing the arrows to fall aside. We started running again while Yvaine continued to send her magic outward as a defense.

"Lugh, she can't do this all night. There are too many of them. Let me carry you." The elf grabbed my arm, and I forced it away.

"Don't touch me!" The panic and darkness was like reliving the past few weeks all over again. I refused to be helpless. I couldn't let the world decide if I was going to live or die simply because I couldn't move.

Cole tried to grab me again. He was done being patient. I pushed the elf back, and he fell. The cù-sìth's snarls were so loud that I had to cover my ears. "Just stop! Stop!" I screamed.

I felt my sister's gentle hand on my shoulder. I turned around and saw the handle of the endowed blade descend on my face.

I got what I asked for. Everything stopped.

"Where did he get this anyway?" Yvaine asked.

My head was hanging upside down. The familiar curve of Cole's shoulder dug into my gut. My legs had gone numb.

"Probably when he went looking for me at the elves' stronghold." Cole's deep voice was familiar. Listening to them speak when I couldn't utter a sound was the only thing that comforted me. The silence was something to fear.

"I wouldn't call it a stronghold. As difficult as it was to get you out, it should have been much harder." I could hear the pages of the spell book flip back and forth with Yvaine's impatient touch.

"I suppose. They lost a lot of their clan to the transformation spell. There's not enough to defend it anymore." In spite of all that his people had done to him, he still mourned their hardships.

Careful with her tone, my sister responded, "Well, there's enough to hunt us." The book slammed closed.

"I think he's waking up," Cole said. He stopped walking and laid me down on cold grass. It was interesting to know that I could identify things based on touch alone now. There was no need for sight.

I opened my eyes, relieved that I could, and immediately felt pain. "Owe." The hand followed my command and reached up to touch my swollen temple.

"Sorry." There was no remorse in my sister's voice, only anger.

I saw the book in her tight fist next. "You searched me?" I accused.

"It fell out when Cole picked you up," she spat.

I huffed. "You mean after you knocked me out?"

With a death glare, she said, "You left me no choice, Lugh. You were hysterical."

"*I* was hysterical. That could be your middle name. I've never knocked *you* out!" I rose slowly. My mouth was dry, and the bulging veins under my skin ached.

"Why were you hiding this?" she demanded, holding the evidence in front of my face. The leather's smell was strong and drew me in. I reached for it. Yvaine pulled the spell book away, and my stomach sank. "You're not getting this back until you tell me."

"I don't have a reason! We've been busy trying to survive. There was no time to show you," I said, my head pounding.

"That's a load of shit!"

In disbelief, I said, "Between running from the elves and you spending the night with one, I couldn't get a word in. I've been trying to find a way out of this for us, and that book has the answer." I reached for it again, but this time, she didn't stop me.

"Is that what this is about? Cole? Grow up, Lugh. You're not a child anymore, and I'm not your mother."

The words hurt worse than the pain in my temple. I knew she wasn't my mother. I was glad that she'd found someone to make her happy. I just never realized how unhappy she'd been with me. *You were a burden long before the curse.*

"The town isn't too far away. I'm going to check it out," Cole said quietly.

Neither of us said anything as the elf melded into the trees.

"How did we get away? Where are we?" I asked. We weren't on the road anymore. There was less snow here, and the nighttime sky was clear.

"Cole is very good at avoiding his people. He's been doing it a long time." She paused to glance behind her, waiting for the elf to return. "We're about a mile out of Stirling. We're going to see if there's still people living there. If not, we're going to search for abandoned supplies." Yvaine refused to look me in the eye.

Confused, I said, "How did we get here so fast?" There was no way we reached the town within the night, even while running.

Yvaine chuckled. "You've been asleep for a day and a half."

"What?" I didn't remember anything. Not even dreams. *A blessing.* "Where's Arlen?" I asked, worried for my friend.

Numb, my sister said, "We haven't seen him since the elves attacked. He's the reason we had time to escape."

"Maybe he's lost. Do some magic so he can track us," I suggested, assured that he'd merely lost our trail.

"If I do that then the other cù-sìth can track us, too. Magic is only to be used in an emergency now." Strangely, my sister smiled. "So, you have magic."

Alarmed, I blurted. "What did he tell you?"

"Just that your magic awakened." She tapped the book in my hands. "You healed us, didn't you?"

I nodded, worried that Cole had told her more than he should have.

Yvaine unzipped her jacket and lifted her shirt, so her stomach showed. "Finley's scars are gone, Lugh." I was instantly furious, hearing that man's name. *My first human kill.* My wrists ached with the memory of the struggle. My sister's screams echoed in my ears. The more I thought on the experience, the more I wondered how I had truly escaped from the handcuffs. I didn't even remember sliding out of them. One moment, I'd been trapped. And the next, I was free. Could it have been magic? Or sheer will? *Maybe they were one and the same.*

Stunned, I stared at the scarless skin. "Healing Fire." I held out the book to Yvaine. "That's the spell I used. Here, take it." Curiously, I glanced to her exposed neck. The wound from the banishment spell was healed, but a faded scar remained—a near replica of mine.

The book's whisperings from the night returned to me: *Healing magic is unable to completely heal wounds of self-sacrifice and not at all for those who do not wish to be healed.*

She shook her head. "No, I want you to keep it. Study as much as you can, so when we're safe, you can cast all the spells you want. After all, you just learned to read. How can I take your first book away?" Yvaine was excited for me, but all I felt was dread. Then she asked the last question I wanted to answer. "Why didn't you heal yourself while you were at it?"

"It didn't work on me."

"Why?" she asked.

"I don't know. Maybe the spell doesn't work on the caster." My arm brushed against something cold. I looked down to find that the dagger had been returned to my sheathe.

"When we've put some distance between us and the elves, I'll cast it on you," she promised. Yvaine's hair whipped back and forth with the wind. I noticed that she hadn't used Cole's gift to tie her hair back since the mountains.

"The healing spell took a long while on Cole."

"What do you mean?" she asked, instantly concerned.

"I think that you should ask him what happened when he was locked up." *Please, stop worrying about me.*

Before Yvaine could answer, Cole hollered through the trees. "Yvaine? Lugh? There's some people you should meet."

Grateful for the interruption, I shrugged and followed the elf's voice to the roadside with Yvaine trailing close behind.

Stirling had been the first town converted into a military base after the Collapse. It was a refuge for the fleeing humans. All the buildings had been blacked out by spray paint, curtains, tarps, and anything else that barred the sun from entering. We'd heard that Stirling was a place for humans to rebuild, but by the time we made our way here after our parents were killed, it had collapsed from within. The humans had turned on each other.

We approached the town gates. The entire placed was surrounded by iron-wire fencing. The smell was strong and burned my nose, but it was nothing compared to how the residents felt—bannicks. They were small, peculiar creatures. Even though they offered us sanctuary, my instinct was to hunt them.

They were healers by nature. They weren't gentle like the coblynau, but they had enough patience to barter. That was exactly what they did here. They'd taken over the town and offered their healing services to travelers passing through.

Maybe there was hope for me.

It took four male bannicks to open the gate. Their hands reddened from the contact, but once we were inside the barrier they whispered incantations to themselves, and their burns were healed instantly. I cringed, finally realizing why iron had always bothered me. And nearly slapped myself for not questioning it before.

There was one building that wasn't crumbling under its own weight—a tower. There were no windows, but there was a ledge that circled the top. A heavy tarp was tied above it, so whoever stood at the peak would be protected from the sun. A spell was painted on the door at its base. *Banish the light.*

Tanks and patrol cars were rusting away on the roads. I remembered peering out the window at my parent's house during the Collapse and watching them roll down the streets. They were terrifying. The humans had been dressed in camouflage, holding metal weapons. Now I knew that they weren't trying to defend us from the Guise—that was a lost cause—they were trying to keep order. *Didn't do much good, did it?*

I often wondered what humanity had been like during a Guise-free world. Was there ever truly order? Were people kind? The thought was from a boy who still believed in fairy tales. That boy died with the curse.

"What's wrong with you?" the bannick beside me asked angrily.

I stopped and stared at the small creature. His ears were unkindly large and pointed. His skin was grey and lumpy. The bannick's teeth protruded from his mouth, and his claws were long and stained brown from the earth. "What's wrong with *you*?" I said, returning the rude question.

The bannick hissed and lunged at me. "We welcomed you inside our shelter. Show your respect."

"Not if you're not going to show any in return!" I managed to miss the bannick's swipe. I didn't want to be on the other end of those sharp claws.

I may have been able to avoid our host's outrage, but not my sister's. She hit my arm hard. "What's the matter with you? These people offered to help us. Don't be impolite." She turned to the enraged creature. "I'm so sorry for my brother. He's very tired and hungry from our journey. He meant no disrespect. Thank you for letting us inside." She held out her hand, presenting a human greeting custom. "I'm Yvaine. This is Cole. And the rude man here is Lugh."

The bannick took her vulnerable hand in his small but tight grip, familiar with the custom. "I'm Alasdair."

"A strong name," Yvaine commented, releasing his hand.

"A human raised me in this place before his kind fell. Now, it is a place for my kind. We will not fall." Alasdair eyed me, and I rolled my eyes.

"We are on a journey to our own homeland. We'd hoped to find supplies here. Is there any chance you have food or water to spare?" Yvaine asked kindly. Cole was smiling at my sister proudly. I was trying to figure out if it was my sister.

"A deal can be made. Join us by the fires. It's cold." The bannick gestured to the bonfires built around the tower. The Fae were already surrounding them for warmth, whispering amongst themselves. The smoke hovered above us like clouds.

"But the sun is rising. Shouldn't we go indoors?" I asked.

"The Guise will be dealt with," he spat.

I was about to protest when Yvaine said, "We would be glad to join you."

With those words, Alasdair turned away, expecting us to follow.

Then, I asked the most important question. "Who are you, Yvaine?"

"She's your sister," Cole said, grabbing her hand. "Strong *and* kind."

Appalled, I said, "Since when?"

"Since I thought you were going to die, Lugh. I couldn't kill my way to the finish line. I had to ask for help." She looked up at her lover with sparkling eyes.

As I walked away from the couple, I said under my breath, "It looks like we both changed then."

They continued to ignore me as we joined the bannicks by the fire. The flames transformed from orange to blue to black and back again. The smoke swirled around us, smelling of black pepper. It irritated my nose. I had to constantly squeeze my nostrils to keep from sneezing all over the easily-offended Fae beings. The bannicks were feeding the fires black wood. The wood burned faster than I'd ever seen before. The smoke became overwhelming, and I choked. I moved to leave when one of the Fae grabbed my arm and said, "Wait, it will clear soon." The female's voice was rough, as if she inhaled the strange smoke every day of her life.

I looked up at the rising sun, then to the Guise appearing outside the iron gates. My eyes were watering. I wished to close them, but I refused to take my gaze away from the lifelong threat. Yvaine needed to cast the darkness spell, but magic would attract the elves. We would trade one death for another. Which one was kinder?

I stared into the golden eyes of the monsters until the smoke had completely overtaken my sight. Darkness surrounded me. I couldn't breathe. I groped the air, hoping to find my sister in the chaos. But I was alone.

I fell to my knees, unable to escape.

A small hand gripped my shoulder. "Open your eyes, human."

I coughed and wiped away the water seeping from my eyes. The Guise were still outside the gates, but the sun had disappeared. I looked up and found the peppered smoke hovering above the base—a thick black cloud. I met the bannick's eyes across from me. "The smoke protects you," I said.

"So long as the fires continue to feed the sky." The female gripped my chin, her hand as hot as flames, and met my stare. "There is a darkness that festers in you."

"No, my sister banished the banshee's poison. It's gone." I refused to believe otherwise. All Yvaine's sacrifices had not been in vain.

"It is not a banshee's curse," she said slowly, allowing me to comprehend her gruff words.

"Who poisoned me? How can I banish it?" I grabbed the bannick's small arm, begging for her wisdom.

"Only the one who cursed you can banish it." The bannick smiled, revealing sharp teeth. I withheld a flinch.

"Who did this to me?" I needed to know why I was so weak. I needed to know why I couldn't heal.

The smoke drifted down to us and back up again. I held my breath until she gave an answer. "One who is both elf and human."

My heart stopped, and I released the Fae's arm. I looked to where Yvaine and Cole spoke by the black fire, their hands intertwined.

There is a darkness that festers in you.

The weakness wasn't my fault after all.

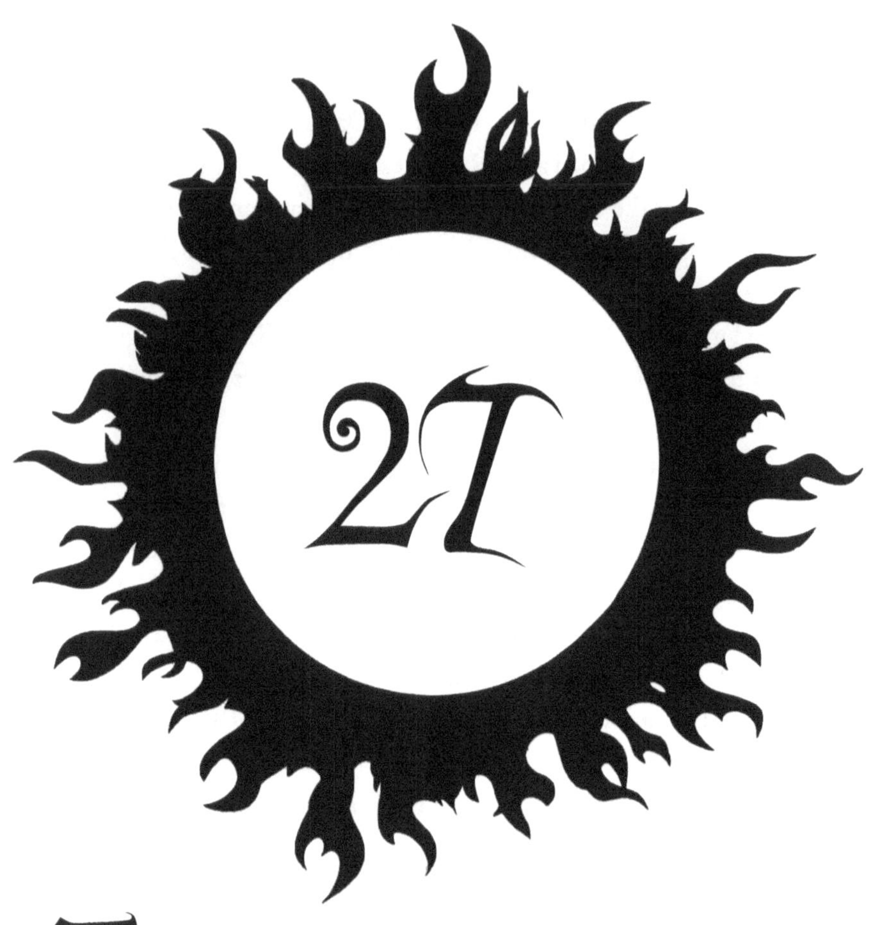

The day was filled with dancing and strange Fae foods. My hunger was satiated for the first time in years. The fires warmed my chilled skin. I drank gallons of water, but still, I felt thirsty. By the time the sun had set and the smoke cleared, my suspicions about the bannicks had settled. And left room for new ones to grow.

Yvaine and Cole had enjoyed themselves, as well. They laughed and danced together—they'd been happy. Yvaine rarely looked in my direction, and when she did, her face was full of guilt. My mouth opened and closed several times as I debated asking what had been done to me. Had there been a price to banishing the banshee's curse? Was it an accident? Was this darkness living inside me caused by Cole? Did my sister know? If she did, why did she let it happen?

The thoughts swirled together until I couldn't formulate a single one. The spell book in my pocket whispered spells, histories, and knowledge to me as I fell into my own pool of despair.

Banshees excrete poison from their claws, entering through the bloodstream and immobilizing their prey, allowing them to feed more easily.

Memory removal is a skill mastered by the elves. Their ability to cast many spells at once allows them to enter one's mind and pluck and pull at the thoughts available.

A caster's magic is stored, not only inward, but outward as well. Magic can be found in a lost tooth, so long as they possessed magic at the time.

Nature created iron to keep balance. No one thing, including the Conscius, can have more advantage than another.

Trance magic is used by healers to calm those in need.

Sacrifice can be used to enhance a caster's magic by absorbing the light of the deceased, though this method can ultimately damage the caster's mind, causing unforeseen side effects.

Despite the rare exception, magics are inherited and passed down through bloodlines.

I focused on the endless words, committing them to memory, knowing I would need to use them one day when the use of magic was permitted by my sister.

You still need your sister's permission?

Why do you let her control you?

Is she the only one allowed to use magic?

No. She's not.

The bannicks used magic constantly. This was the perfect place to cast spells. The cù-sìth wouldn't be able to distinguish the type of magic used, could they?

Listening to the whispers crawling up from my pocket and into my ear, I decided that it was worth the risk. I reached for the spell book.

"Give me that dagger, and I'll heal your mind," a brusque voice said beside me.

I turned to find Alasdair glaring up at me, shadows from the fire cast upon his ugly face. "I was told that it can only be healed by the one who cursed me."

The bannick's glare turned deadly. "You were told wrong. Only those with powerful healing magic can help you, human." He took a small step forward and reached for the endowed dirk.

I retreated, clutching the precious weapon. "I don't need your help."

Alasdair lowered his arm. "We only offer sanctuary to those who need our healing magic. You've accepted our offer by entering our gates, eating our food, and sheltering under our smoke."

Carefully, I responded, "We are grateful for your help, but it's time for us to leave. We have a long journey ahead." I turned toward Yvaine and Cole where they swayed by the fire. The Fae music had continued to play into the night, and for the first time, I wondered where it was coming from. I searched the base and tower, expecting to find the creatures playing strange instruments, but the music wasn't coming from any specific direction. I watched the Fae sway beside my sister, and the answer came to me.

Trance magic.

The music grew louder. Yvaine and Cole laid down on the bedding beside the warm fire and fell asleep. I took a step toward them and fell, exhausted. "Yvaine," I called. But she didn't move. Her breathing was long and deep. Cole's eyes twitched as if he was going to wake, but it didn't take long for the music to soothe him into a deep slumber.

"What are you doing?" I asked Alasdair, as he ripped the dagger from my sheathe.

"Helping you. We can see you are suffering. We, as healers, will put an end to it." More bannicks surrounded me. But all I could do was lay helpless on the ground. *So tired.*

Small hands dragged me to the fire's edge. Alasdair raised the blade above my heart. And it wasn't the imminent pain or even the thought of death that had me worried. It was the fact that I wasn't worried. There was just…*nothing.*

I closed my eyes.

Gunshots sounded, and it wasn't long before all I could hear was the ringing they had left behind. The music was gone, and Alasdair was bleeding on the ground beside me. I plucked the knife from his clawed hand and crawled my way over to Yvaine, keeping low.

The bullets flew past me and into the fire. The wood splintered and flew upward, cascading down on us. I shook my sister until she roused. The panic on her face told me that she knew exactly what the sound was that passed us by. She gripped Cole's shoulder, but he had already woken. "Head for the tower," he said, the bow still strapped across his shoulders.

We crawled across the dirt and ash until we reached the metal doorway. On creaky hinges, it opened enough to let us in. The iron was heavy as we slid the barricade lock into place. Fortunately, the bullets couldn't penetrate the walls. "We're trapped," I said, my breath uneven.

"Let's head to the top," my sister suggested.

"They'll see us," I said, grabbing her arm.

"It's dark, and we need to figure out who we're dealing with." Yvaine placed her hand over mine, loosening my tight grip. "We're going to be okay, Lugh."

"Like we were two minutes ago when Alasdair had the blade to my chest?" I accused. The blade lit and pulsed with my angry heartbeat. Our faces were revealed in the dark tower, all painted with fear. *My sister's newfound kindness had allowed this to happen.*

"It's my fault. I should have watched longer before approaching them for help." Cole reached out to me, and I stepped back. "This new world has even made the healers into monsters," he said.

"Or brought out what was already there," I responded. I marched up the steps, cringing against my sore legs and hips. The staircase spiraled upward four stories. The door was locked just like the first one, so we carefully lifted the iron and stepped into the night. The metal burned my fingers.

The tarp above us provided the perfect cover. So long as I kept the dagger's light under control, they would never know that we were lurking at the tower's peak. We waited until the gun fire had died down before peering over the edge.

Humans.

They swarmed the base, ending any wounded bannick they found with swords and hatchets. Their mission was simple: kill all Fae.

What did that mean for the three half-breeds?

"Are there any survivors?" a woman asked, her voice gentle yet firm.

There was enough firelight left that I could see the man who answered; he was well into his forties with dark hair and a harsh expression. "No, they've been dead for days."

"That can't be. I saw others here," the woman argued, her voice familiar.

"Their bodies were being kept in a shed. You can see for yourself if you like." The man wasn't cruel, but he didn't soften his words either.

"No, I believe you." The woman stepped into view, and I realized it wasn't a woman but a girl. She couldn't have been older than I was, yet she held herself with such authority—confidence.

"Shit," Yvaine spat under her breath. She yanked me down, so I sat on the cold tower floor.

"Agreed," Cole commented.

"What?" I whispered.

Yvaine shook her head to silence me and turned to Cole. "We need to wait them out. There's no way this will go well if she sees us."

"They're going to want to check the tower," Cole argued. Just then, there was faint clanging coming from below. They were trying to get in.

"Who are they?" I demanded.

"We're going to have to use magic, Cole. She *can't* find us." Yvaine whipped to me. "Give me the spell book."

"Who are they?" I repeated.

My sister reached for my pocket, impatient.

I slapped her hand away. "Tell me!"

"Lugh, stay quiet," Yvaine demanded. She placed her hand over my mouth and clutched me tight, similar to what she'd done when I was young and naive to the dangers around us.

The dagger ignited with a fierce flame, making the tower into a beacon of light.

Neither of them said anything when the light faded. Yvaine released me and gripped my hand instead, frightened. "Who's up there?" the man said from below. I could feel every gun aimed at the peak of the tower, waiting for someone's head to rise.

The girl spoke when no one answered, "Reveal yourself or we shoot. Your choice."

We all looked at each other, knowing that even if the bullets managed to miss us, they would ricochet against the metal walls and kill us anyway. There was no time to figure out the right spell to counter something like that.

"If she sees us, she's going to shoot, Lugh." Yvaine gripped my hand tighter. I thought on who would want to kill Yvaine. Then I remembered.

"Is that you, Cara?" I said to the girl below.

"Yes. Who's asking?" I heard the shifting of feet on the ground as the humans surrounded the tower.

"You took care of me while I was poisoned. My name is Lugh." I slowly rose to my knees. "And you saved me just now. The bannick was about to kill me, though I don't know why."

"They've been taking wandering humans and sacrificing them to gain more magic. We lost a few of our own to them." She paused before asking, "Where's your brother and sister?"

Both Cole and Yvaine shook their head.

Pausing for only a moment, I said, "Dead."

"I'm sorry for your loss. Though, maybe it's for the best. If they were here, we'd have to kill them ourselves." Cara's voice shook as if she was fighting back angry tears.

I handed Yvaine the spell book and continued, "I remember what they did. I was aware the entire time. Did you lose your father during the attack?"

"Yes. We lost many good people that day." I could feel the hate drifting upward from every human lurking below.

"I'm sorry. Just know that my siblings never wanted to hurt anyone. They were only trying to survive, like we all are." I took a chance and peeked my head over the edge. "Thank you for helping me."

"Which time?" she said, a smirk in her voice.

"Both, I guess." I stood. "So, have you decided whether or not you're going to kill me?" I saw the female bannick's body lying near Cara; the only bannick I suspected that didn't agree with her kin's tactics.

Cara raised and aimed her rifle. Yvaine flipped through the book quickly, searching for the spell that would save us. Cole watched me carefully, ready to pull me back from the edge.

Cara stared at the darkness of the tower. She would only be able to see my silhouette, if anything, when she fired. She lowered her weapon, and the rest followed her example. "Not today."

"I'll meet you at the bottom then," I replied, keeping my voice as even as possible.

I handed Cole the dagger and sheathe while Yvaine whispered an incantation. They melded into the shadows, becoming darkness itself. I shuddered and made my way down the long staircase. Alone, it was more difficult to unlock the door, but I felt faint hands over mine as I lifted. Firelight welcomed me on the other side.

Humans entered the tower, searching for the lies I had told. With a wave from one of the soldiers at the top of the tower, Cara approached me and held out her hand. "It's nice to officially meet you, Lugh. I'm Cara."

Cara wasn't the same girl I remembered. It surprised me how much I had discerned from her voice while I was paralyzed. She wasn't as young nor as warm as before, but I could still see the kindness there behind the wall she'd built upon her father's death. Her brown-gold hair was darkened by the fire's shadows, but those same shadows accentuated the beautiful angles of her face. She'd set aside her weapon while we watched the bannick cook on the rotisserie.

I watched the humans gather supplies from the buildings. Blankets, clothes, water, canned food, and anything else the bannicks had stolen from travelers. I also watched the humans carry out the dead and bury them in the forest. The smell of the deceased drifted to us, and I immediately lost my appetite. Cara didn't seem to notice, and I pondered if the elf part of me had given me extra strong senses. The way her ears missed sounds in the distance, unlike mine, supported the theory. Though, I hadn't noticed it until recently. Maybe I had been just as blind as Yvaine.

"How did they die?" Cara asked, distracting me from my curious thoughts.

"They drowned in the flood at Perth," I lied smoothly.

"I heard about the flood. Some of the city dwellers spilled over into the forest. Nasty people." Cara sat cross-legged and twisted the laces on her boots.

"Yeah, they are."

"Did you live there?" she asked, cautious.

"No, we were just passing through," I assured.

A long silence passed us by before she said, "The treatment your siblings were trying must have worked. I mean, you're alive."

I met her curious gaze. "It kept me alive long enough to get help." I didn't want her thinking that the herbs my *siblings* used could cure banshee poison. There was no reason to give her false hope. "They ended up making a deal with an elf. It healed me with its magic."

"What did they trade for the spell?" she asked, unconvinced.

"I don't know. I didn't have a chance to ask before…"

"Understood." She stood and tore some meat from the bannick's hide. She offered me a piece, but I politely declined, nauseated. "What were you doing here? Did the Fae trick you into coming inside their camp?"

I laughed. "No, I entered willingly."

"That was stupid. You can't trust anyone." She returned to my side, sitting closer than before.

For some reason, I smiled. "I trusted you not to shoot me. I was right about *that*."

She smiled back. "Well, I'm still mulling it over, so don't get too excited."

The man that spoke to Cara before approached. "You need your rest, Cara." His eyes darted to me, his expression full of hate.

"Go ahead and get some rest, Logan. Someone has to watch Lugh, here. He's a slippery one." Cara winked at me, and Logan's glare intensified.

"I can watch him. You haven't rested in days." Logan was clearly concerned about Cara spending time with me, and I wondered what it was that labeled me as a threat: a weak, weaponless teenager who was supposedly alone.

"Don't worry about me, Cara. Get some rest," I encouraged, though I didn't actually want to be alone.

Before she could respond, Logan asked, "What was that light in the tower? It looked like magic."

Knowing that he was the only one who'd seen, I said, "What light?"

Logan growled and took a step forward.

"Put two men in the tower. I'll lay down in a bit. Thanks Logan," Cara dismissed. Logan met my challenging stare once more before disappearing into the tower himself.

"So, you took over your father's position?" I said.

"Is that so hard to believe?" she asked, insulted by the surprise in my voice.

Looking into her calculating eyes, I said, "No, it's not. I'm sure he would be very proud of you." Her eyes softened, and I couldn't help but appreciate how beautiful she was. I'd rarely had any contact with humans, let alone a girl my own age. It left a strange, pleasant feeling in my gut.

Cara pushed her hair aside, placing it behind her ear. "Where are you headed, Lugh? Hopefully not into more traps."

"My parent's house. I thought I could find something there to help me."

"Help you with what?" she asked.

"Survive. Move on, maybe?" It was strange to admit it aloud, but it was the truth. I needed a way to continue on. This world was all I had ever known. And yet, when I woke up from the paralysis, everything had changed.

The shadows that the fire cast behind me flickered, and it wasn't because of the flames.

"That's what I'm doing, too. Trying to survive, I mean." She looked out at her people. "It's my job to take care of them. It's a lot to handle sometimes."

"You must be doing something right. They respect you enough to follow you into battle." I rested my thin arms on raised knees and bowed my head, the skin hot from the fire.

Embarrassed, she said, "I wouldn't call today a battle. Bannicks aren't very strong opponents, just tricky ones."

"Every day is a battle while the Guise exist." Until they were gone, every species and peoples would continue to fight each other. For survival, yes, but also because of fear.

Cara examined my face carefully. "I suppose you're right." She grabbed my hand and said, "But we don't have to fight alone."

I offered a tight smile and said, "Your people called their city Inscius, right?"

She nodded, confused about the topic change.

"You should rethink the name," I said, eager to distract her.

"Why?" she asked.

Thanks to the language spell, I now knew what Cole had been laughing about when I was cursed, so I suggested, "For new beginnings. New people and place. So, you need a new name."

The girl smiled back. "Good idea."

The rest of the night disappeared quickly. Talking with Cara was an experience I'd never had before. A new, strange form of comradery. By early morning, I was grinning. But of course, the sun began to rise, bringing with it the fear that had been cast aside for the few hours we'd been together.

The fires were only smoldering coals on the ground now. There would be no black smoke to protect us today. "I need to go," I said while holding Cara's hand. We hadn't let go of each other since she placed her hand in mine hours ago.

Cara frowned at the amethyst sky. "You can stay with us, with me, if you want. You would be safe here."

I unlocked my stiff fingers. "It's not safe anywhere, Cara." I stood on wobbly legs and caught the concern in her eyes. In the clear light of day, she could see how weak I truly was. I looked away, ashamed. The shadows were retreating, as well as my own. Cole and Yvaine didn't have much longer.

"At least take some supplies and a weapon." Cara ran for the stockpile that her people had collected. I followed as quickly as I could. When I entered the tent, she was filling a backpack full of traveling supplies. I glanced to the weapons in the corner. She followed my gaze. "Have a preference?"

Astounded, I picked up a familiar bow, the arrows I'd carved were sitting within the quiver, unused. "I'll take this one if you don't mind."

Cara nodded and asked, "How are you going to avoid the sun? It's a clear day."

I peered out the doorway and examined the sky. "There's dark clouds in the distance. A storm is coming. I'll manage until then."

Though she was baffled by my reasoning, she finished filling the backpack and handed it to me. "I'll walk you out. I don't want them to shoot you by accident."

"Appreciated." I laughed, though, she probably had the right idea. The guards at the gate scowled at me when we approached, and Cara directed them to open it. The iron reeked and burned my nose. The shadows following my steps were tense, their space becoming smaller. "Thank you again, for saving me."

"No problem. I hope you find what you're looking for. If you ever need a safe place to stay, you'll always find one here." Cara fidgeted with the rifle strap clinging to her shoulder.

"You plan on staying?" I wondered, looking out at the old crumbling town.

"It's time to rebuild. To move on." I met her kind gaze, wishing I could stay longer. The girl stepped forward and inclined her head, so she was looking up at me. She fisted the front of my shirt and pulled me down, so we were eye to eye. Then, she gently placed her lips against mine. Our eyes remained open during the embrace, both of us shocked by the experience. "Stay alive, Lugh. I want to see you again one day."

I answered by kissing her once more.

Outside the gates of Stirling, my mind cleared. The air was ice cold. My limbs were just as sore as before. The darkness still festered beneath my skin. But the happy feeling in my gut didn't leave. Even when Stirling was but a speck on the road behind me, and Cole and Yvaine had returned to their true forms, the feeling stayed with me.

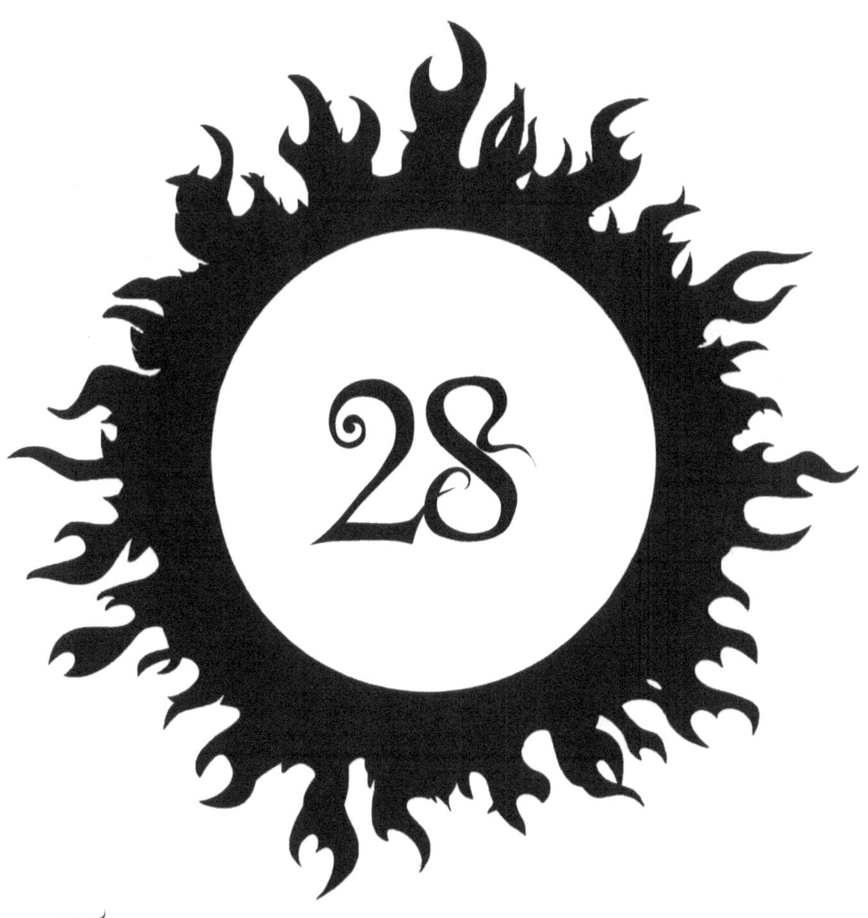

It was a day's journey to Hamilton, so long as there were no interruptions. I looked up and down the long, empty highway and sighed. *There were always interruptions.*

Though, I was glad that we didn't have to pass through Glasgow on our journey home—the place the banshee had poisoned me. The city had been destroyed and remained abandoned. That was why we had chosen the place to begin with. But I wasn't ready to revisit that memory yet.

The road forked. There were signs that had an arrow alongside the word *Hamilton* printed on metal paper. I'd inwardly smiled when I read the directions, for the first time, capable of doing so.

Yvaine had been quiet since we left Stirling that morning, with only a snide remark about taking too long to leave. She had to hold the shadow spell for hours, which had made her tired and cranky. But for once, I didn't care. I was glad that I'd stayed as long as I did. Cara may have been the only brief glimpse of joy I'd have in the near future. With the Guise swarming our dark cloud and the elves hunting us, there wasn't much to look forward to but running and hiding.

Cole slowed his walk so he was beside me, Yvaine leading us down the cracked pavement. "How are you feeling?" he asked me.

I eyed him curiously and was surprised to find a smirk lifting the corners of his mouth. "I feel fine," I replied, glancing at Yvaine.

"Your walk has improved. Do you feel better?" Cole coughed and tucked his face into his elbow, hiding laughter.

"Yes, I feel better, Cole." I rolled my eyes.

Releasing a snicker, he said, "I bet you do."

My smile from last night returned, and blood warmed my face. I punched the devious elf in the arm. "Mind your own business."

"How could I when I was trapped in your shadow all night? I never realized what a smooth-talker you were. Females like a guy who knows how to make them laugh."

Yvaine huffed but didn't turn.

"Females also love a guy who pisses them off. They love a challenge. Don't let them tell you any different." Cole winked, and Yvaine finally turned around.

"Don't fill his head your fairy tales. *Women* want a guy who is sweet and listens to them when they speak." She brushed her hair aside with an angry flick and continued down the road.

"Ah, but you're not just a woman are you?" Cole challenged, his stride confident as she turned and smacked his arm.

Yvaine's temper was volatile. If I was being honest, she scared the crap out of me sometimes. The look on Cara's face when she spoke of her lost father only fed that fear. My sister was capable of terrible things. I just hadn't realized it until recently.

Interrupting the couple's flirtatious argument, I asked, "Was it really necessary to kill all those humans? Cara's father?"

We all stopped walking. I swore I could hear the natural dark clouds from the north flying in our direction. Cole looked to Yvaine while she met my questioning stare. "Those humans weren't going to let us leave. They needed more people for their 'city' and wanted the treatment we were giving you."

"Did you ever ask? Surely, they would have released you if you'd tried?" I gripped the backpack that Cara had filled. Yvaine had tried to take it from me after we left, but I'd wanted the extra weight. I'd wanted to keep the gift that had been given to me.

Confused, Yvaine explained, "You know how humans are, Lugh. I tried to part ways with them peacefully when they murdered that nest of coblynau. They took our weapons. They took you. If I had tried to argue with them they would have killed us or worse."

The words that came tumbling out of my mouth had a will of their own—fueled by guilt and anger. There was no way to stop them as I said, "Cara isn't like that. Maybe you should have tried harder before murdering innocent people."

Yvaine's hand met my cheek before I could think to defend myself. The stung it left behind pulsed in time with my heartbeat. The dark cloud my sister created dissipated, leaving us exposed to any Guise who wanted to attack. Fortunately, this part of the highway was empty.

"Anyone who stops me from saving your life is not innocent, Lugh. Hate me all you want, but that will never change. I will sacrifice the whole world before I let you die." Yvaine eyed my bow and quiver. "I'm glad you got your weapon back," she whispered before turning away.

Cole cleared his throat and faced the north. "The storm is almost here. We need to find shelter."

Irritated, I argued, "But Hamilton is only a few hours away."

Cole met my stare. Though there was no hate in his eyes for what I had said, there was something worse—sadness. "We're not faster than nature, Lugh."

"I know a place," Yvaine said, her back straight as she left the highway and disappeared into the trees. Cole and I followed quickly when snow began falling from the sky.

The entrance to the underground cave Yvaine led us to was concealed behind a group of pine trees. We had hidden there on our way to Stirling when we were young, running from a few men who'd seen us on the road. I laughed, remembering the incident, only because of how frantic Yvaine had been when she found that I'd fallen into a hole in the ground. I dared a glance at my sister, and she frowned, most likely remembering the same thing I was.

"I've traveled this forest dozens of times and have never found this place." Cole allowed himself to free fall into the dark hole, trusting Yvaine's directions. "There is still so much to discover about our own lands."

I followed close behind. Finding that the cave's floor was stable beneath my feet, I stepped forward and summoned the dirk's light. Amethyst crystals made up the walls that surrounded us. They glittered, reflecting light back at one another.

"Put out the light until we know we're alone," Yvaine scolded.

"How are we supposed to know unless we can see?" I argued. *You have lived in darkness long enough.*

"You're not supposed to be using magic anyway, remember?" Shadows danced across Yvaine's angered face as the dagger dimmed and rebelliously lit, refusing to die.

Instantly furious, I said, "What? You've been using magic *all* day! Hypocrite."

"That was necessary! Don't argue with me about things you haven't taken the time to think about." My sister lunged for the darkness ahead, and the endowed blade dimmed.

I refused to take another step until my rage subsided, though I wasn't sure how long that would take. Each time I tried to calm myself, I remembered all the *necessary* things Yvaine had done to save me while I was cursed. And the families who had lost their loved ones because she wanted to heal me.

Cole placed his hand on my shoulder and gripped hard when I tried to move away. "Yvaine broke the magic trail at the roadside. She's not trying to stop your magic use. She's being smart." He paused and looked down the cave to where Yvaine lurked in the dark. "But with that said, the blizzard coming, and the seclusion of this cave, I'd say it's safe to use it." The elf removed his hand. "*Wisely.*"

Cole loyally trailed after my sister. I looked back at the entrance where it was quickly filling with snow. I unsheathed the dim dagger and pulled the bow over my head. I stared down at the two weapons in my hands and nearly threw myself onto both of them. My bow had been taken by Cara's people. So had the dagger. Though the bow had saved us when we were starving, Yvaine had deemed her weapon more important. *Worth something.* She'd killed to get it back.

I cut the bow string and snapped the weapon in half. The overused line hung limp from the splintered wood frame. The initials I'd carved into it had faded beyond recognition. The leather handle was torn. This weapon wasn't worth saving.

I climbed up the amethyst wall to the cold surface and tossed the bow and quiver outside where it would be buried and forgotten. Placing the dagger back in its sheathe, I traversed the cave in pitch black.

Yvaine and Cole had stopped a few minutes into the cave. It was long and curved and forked from what I remembered. We'd never explored the other end, afraid that we would find something that would consider us trespassers. "We can make a fire here," Yvaine suggested.

"Won't that just make us targets?" I remarked, my voice dead. Our silhouettes were the only things visible in the dark space.

My sister met my eye, asking a silent question, but I gave no answer. "Yes, but our priorities have changed. We need warmth if we're going to survive." She approached and grabbed my cold hand. "I'm not going to let you freeze."

I didn't even bother slapping her hand away as I began gathering what little twigs and moss had been tracked in by other animals. Once we had a decent pile, I opened my backpack and pulled out a matchbox. "Why don't you use magic for this one, Lugh? It would be good practice in case you ever need it," Cole said, trying to act disinterested.

Reluctant, Yvaine agreed, "Yes, it would be a good thing to learn. For both of us." She took out the spell book, revealing where she'd kept it hidden in her pocket. The voices reached for my ears once again, but I wasn't interested in hearing them.

I handed her the dagger. "Go ahead. I'll watch." Rubbing my hands together for warmth, I stared at the pile of forest scraps and thought of Arlen. *We would already have a fire if he was here.* But there was a chance he would never find us. There was an even bigger chance that he died trying to protect us.

The dagger lit, and flipping through the book aggressively, Yvaine muttered, "Fine."

"It shouldn't be too hard. I have a feeling that fire magic agrees with you." Cole smiled while he mocked my sister. The snide remarks I wanted to add rose to my tongue and fell just as quickly into the pit of my stomach.

"Don't test me, elf. I'll direct the flames at you," she threatened.

I glanced over my shoulder, toward the entrance we'd come through. It was utter black, and I wondered if we would even sense the elves approaching.

"Here, I think I found something. Inner Fire." She recited the new spell, and amethyst smoke poured from the dagger, filling the cave with magic that made my heart race.

Inner Fire

Rise up and meet me

Reveal your passion

Accept your nature

For I am you

And you are fire

Flames burst from the dark smoke. First purple, then blue, then orange. The colors cast rays of energizing light across the underground cave, the crystals dancing with joy. The fire was hot despite its small size. Warmer than even the bonfires in Stirling.

"Your turn." Yvaine offered the book, but I shook my head.

"You already made us a worthy fire. You don't need me messing it up." I allowed a playful tone to coat the words, but she wasn't falling for the facade.

"I bet you'll feel like practicing after you're healed." She flipped through the book again, the whispers growing louder. It didn't seem like that either one of them could hear the book, and I started to panic.

"That's okay. I'm healing on my own just fine. We can't use magic for everything." I clenched my fists, forcing the voices to calm and the shadows at my back to retreat.

"Don't be stupid. It's long past due. You said that you couldn't make the spell work for you, so maybe I can." Finding the page, she scooted closer to me. "Lay down."

"Why?"

"Just do it," she ordered.

Reluctantly, I laid back and stared at the crystal ceiling. Each rock was an amethyst, but each one was colored a different shade from the one beside it. Yvaine laid the dagger on my chest and repeated the spell that I'd said over and over the night I discovered my magic.

Fires of the sun gather
Warm that which has faded
Kindle your power and consume the pain
Burn the dead away
Ignite the healing flame

The smoke became cool healing flames, and Yvaine's magic surrounded my weak body, poking and prodding at the skin, searching for a way inside. The sensation was familiar, like it had been when she healed me while I was cursed, but this time, the peaceful sense didn't wash over me like gentle rainwater. This time, it felt wrong. Unwelcome. Unwanted.

A barrier that I wasn't aware I was capable of rose up from my skin—a shield of dark violet appeared, smothering her flames. It wasn't anything I'd seen before. It wasn't calming smoke or determined flames. The physical form my light had taken was hard and unmoving, and as heavy as it looked.

"What's happening?" Yvaine said, panicked. "What did I do wrong?"

"He's blocking you," Cole explained.

"Why are you blocking me, Lugh?" Yvaine reached for my hand, and pierced the shield. Apparently it could only stop magic from entering.

"I'm not," I blurted.

"Why are you lying? Why are you keeping things from me?" She stood, and I followed, dazed by the magic I was wielding.

"I'm not keeping things from you!" The shield thickened.

"You lied to me! You told me that you didn't remember anything from the curse." My sister let a tear fall, and I cringed when she aggressively wiped it away. She slammed the book shut.

I'd known this conversation was coming. She'd heard everything I said to Cara. I'd known things Yvaine hadn't told me. I'd recognized the sound of the *inscius* girl's voice. "What good would it have done? Yes, I remember. And it was awful! It was…" There wasn't a word strong enough to describe the horror I felt, and Yvaine could see that.

"I could have helped you. Talked to you. Explained things that you heard and felt. Ask me anything you want! I can still help you, Lugh. I'm so sorry that you had to go through that. I can only imagine what that must have been like…" She dropped the dagger, and it clattered against the crystal ground.

"You can't."

"What do you mean?" she asked. Cole moved to Yvaine's side, picking up the dagger.

"You *can't* imagine. You can't help. No one can. Something happened to me. Something is wrong," I attempted to explain.

"The curse? Is it still in you? Did I fail?" my sister cried, her hands trembling.

"This isn't the banshee's curse! It was put there by a half-breed. The bannick told me as much." Thin hands ripped through my hair, and I was suddenly very warm. I unzipped my jacket and tossed it aside.

Looking to one another, Cole answered for Yvaine, "Lugh, we rid you of poison. If something else is wrong, it's not our doing."

With shaky hands, Yvaine handed me the spell book. "Try the Healing Fire again. But this time, let it in. Accept the magic. *Your* magic."

"Yvaine, you don't understand…" My magic shield dropped.

"Just try," she whispered, offering a small encouraging smile.

Without the proper words to explain why it was a bad idea, I took the leather book from my sister and opened it to the page I needed. The book spoke to me before I laid eyes on the words. Its whispers grew loud and chaotic. I tried to concentrate on the healing letters, forcing them to obey, but they swirled and deformed so much that I thought I was going to hurl.

"Lugh, that's not the spell! Stop! What are you doing?" Yvaine said, grabbing her brother's arms—the same ones that clutched the leather binding with desperation.

Words formed and twisted on my tongue. Hundreds of languages melded together to create wonderful and awful spells. The book's voice had trapped me in a trance much like the bannicks had done to those human travelers. I couldn't stop the sounds tumbling out of my mouth. The dagger's light filled the cavern and shuddered with the magic that refused to be released from my own body. I felt it crawling under my skin, waiting.

I forced the dagger out of Cole's hand.

Then its crawl became a sprint.

The darkness that had been hibernating inside me since the curse had been banished. Maybe even longer.

As I gripped the dagger tight, thick purple ink poured me, as if I was bleeding. It moved past my eyes, nose, ears, and mouth. It dripped down my body and pooled onto the amethyst ground. The magic ran down the cave, toward the fire. The flames sizzled, but they weren't smothered.

"What's happening?" I managed to choke. The book had stopped speaking, but the results of the spells I had brought to life were torturing me. Instead of healing the malnourished, sore muscles, they were being devoured. Instead of quelling my hunger, I became ravenous. Instead of peace, I felt chaos.

Small crystals fell from above and landed in Yvaine's loose hair. A large piece hit Cole on the shoulder, and he winced. The cavern rumbled in anger, and I feared that we would be buried under the rubble for the remainder of time.

"Lugh, calm down. Breathe!" Cole said, his voice firm.

I sucked in a lungful of cold air and coughed, inhaling the magic ink pouring from my lips.

The elf wrapped his long fingers around my thin arms. A sensation worse than the one I was experiencing happened upon his touch. Exhaustion and heaviness overwhelmed me. I fell to my knees, the book falling from my hands. Yvaine immediately snatched it from the liquid coating the ground.

"Let it go, Lugh," Cole encouraged, his brow dripping sweat. I could see the same ink that excreted from me was now falling from his eyes, like bloody tears.

Yvaine took the dagger from my hand and placed it with the book on the other side of the fire. She fell to my side and held me tight. "I'm here, brother. You're not alone."

Those words were enough comfort that I allowed my body to relax, and let Cole absorb whatever magic I had released. There was nothing I could do but wait for the tremors and aching to stop as my sister laid my head down on top of my discarded coat. She stroked the shortened hair hanging from my forehead and sang a nursery rhyme quietly.

When we were barely surviving, in the dark and cold winter of our youth, she would sing to me. It was the only thing that kept the nightmares away—the only thing that kept the fear away. Because I wasn't alone when she was with me.

It was within her sweet voice that I realized Yvaine nor Cole had cursed me with darkness.

It was me.

It was all me.

After a long while, my breathing evened out. Yvaine covered me with her warm jacket and kissed my forehead, leaving me alone by the flames.

A few moments later, I heard Yvaine's quiet sobs on the other side of the fire. And the reason for her tears was a simple, terrible truth: her brother was broken, and he didn't think he was worth mending.

I woke to find Cole and Yvaine huddled by the smoldering flames, blanketed in the elf's winter coat. I rose and placed both Yvaine's and my coat over them, refusing to look at my sister's still-wet cheeks. The dagger and book were tucked tightly against her chest.

Paranoid about the dark cave, I hugged the sharp wall until I reached the entrance. I climbed to the top and peered at the nighttime sky. The blizzard had passed. The stars glittered as bright as the fallen snow. Daring to stick my head out of the near-buried entrance, I gazed at the white light in the sky. The moon was waxing and beautiful, and I was grateful that the dark elves weren't drinking blood tonight. But Fae died at their hands every night anyway. Could the path they chose be considered life? Existing in the darkness and cold forever?

A moan sounded in the trees, and I ducked behind the embankment. A Guise drifted across the snow's surface. No footprints were left in its wake. Alone and forgotten, this bastardized creature roamed the forest in the moonlight. Its usual gold glimmer was nowhere to be seen. Instead, it was nearly translucent, invisible, or maybe not quite alive in this kind of light.

The sound it whimpered was of grief. Of sorrow.

This being was truly alone.

Perhaps the dark elves had the right idea after all.

Quietly, I climbed back into the hole and disappeared down the crystal cavern. The fire had gone out, but I followed the smell of smoke until I reached our camp. I sat beside the coals and whispered to my Inner Fire.

A small purple flame appeared in the palm of my hand. I allowed it to flow down my fingers and across the ground like water until it met its brethren in the ash. Together, they created warmth and light.

With my sight returned, I could see the inky residue from the failed spell staining Cole's face and hands. Whatever had been living inside me now lived in him. I only hoped that he was able to manage it better than me.

I found myself meeting my sister's wakened eyes, and she smiled. "Go back to sleep. I'll keep watch," I whispered. For once, my sister didn't argue. She closed her eyes and moved closer to Cole, asleep within moments.

I stared at the flames for the remainder of the night, content with my small victory.

# 29

Cole had woken in the early morning, allowing me a few hours of rest before our departure. It was his voice that I heard while I slowly roused, hungry and begging for water. But I didn't move, not wanting to disturb the story he was telling Yvaine.

"There are many different versions of the Separation. It depends on what people you are speaking to. The elves, fairies, giants, all of the Fae prefer their own words."

"Giants?" Yvaine questioned. My thoughts mirrored hers: if there were giants, we would have seen them by now.

"The giants aren't native to this land. They live in the southern hemisphere, near the equator. They like the heat," Cole explained with a dull voice, and I wondered where his cool optimism had disappeared to.

"I forget that there are other lands sometimes," Yvaine whispered. "Our home is overwhelming enough that I rarely think of leaving."

"Maybe we will, someday. When things are different," the elf said.

"That would be nice." The longing in my sister's tone was bleak, as if she didn't really expect it to happen.

Cole shifted. "Now, are you going to let me finish my tale without interruptions?"

I heard the slight movement of my sister's hair as she assumingly nodded her head.

Cole continued, "As I was saying, every Fae people have their own story. I am going to tell you mine. I've heard many, and I think I have a pretty good idea of what actually happened," he said with deserved pride. I couldn't imagine the stories he'd been told and the cultures he'd studied in his time away from the elves. Though he was alone in his travels, the elf's experiences made me jealous. What had I done with my time on Earth? Since the Collapse, I'd done nothing but see everything as threat, afraid of dying by some unknown consequence. The curiosity that grew over the years had been squashed by the fear of the unknown.

"The Separation of the Fae and Common. Though at the time, which was thousands of years ago, they were known as not two but one people—the *Conscius*. Even though the world was kin to magic, there was still fighting amongst the species. Some wanted more power. Some wanted the histories of magic kept all to themselves. Some wanted to rule. But others wanted something else entirely. They wanted to end the use of magic."

From the pause that ensued, I could only imagine the look of confusion on my sister's face.

"These species saw how the pursuit of magic harmed each people. There was war, famine, magic abuse, and deformity. There were species that had taken to inbreeding to purify their bloodlines in hopes to strengthen the magical gifts that had been honed over generations." Sighing, he continued, "It was an ugly time to have lived in, and that's saying something, considering the state of the world right now."

"What changed it?" Yvaine asked quietly.

"Humans."

"Humans?" she questioned.

"Humans were one of the species that supported the abolishment of magic. They rallied what others would join them and performed one last spell." Cole shifted, and I could hear the small crystals shatter beneath his body.

Yvaine asked, "What was the spell?" It was difficult not sit up and ask the same.

"No one knows."

"Well, that was anticlimactic." Yvaine slapped his arm, and he chuckled darkly.

"Whatever spell they performed cleansed their bloodlines of magic completely. And those I speak of became the *Caecus* or the Common. The *Conscius* had no reason to fight the *Caecus* anymore because there was no power or knowledge to be gained, and no one wanted to rule over magicless peoples—they were useless in their eyes. The Common had burned everything they'd written down and banished the knowledge from their minds with that final spell. Everything was gone in hopes that peace would follow."

"Did it work?" my sister asked.

"I suppose it did in a way. Eventually, the Fae were forgotten along with the magic. There were so few of them left that they melded into the shadows, doing what they could with the magic that was left." Did Cole think of the dark elves in that moment? Did he pity the dwindling clan?

Yvaine argued, "But there was still war, famine, and horrific things that happened. Then the Collapse… Humans tried to use magic again, and it backfired. Do you think that was part of the original spell? To stop the Common from ever using it again?" Yvaine was pissed, and I couldn't help but laugh.

"What do you think, Lugh?" Cole asked, realizing I was awake.

"Sounds like us." I sat up and stretched, rolling out the sore muscles and bruises from sleeping on unforgiving rocks. "Looks like there's a loop-hole, though."

"What do you mean?" Yvaine asked, her hair tangled in the crystals behind her.

"Half-breeds." All of us stared at the ground, trying to comprehend the strangeness of our existence.

Snow fell at the entrance, followed by the sound of crunching rocks. Peering down the tunnel, I could only see blackness. I grabbed my jacket and backpack. Yvaine put out the fire and handed me the dagger without question. Though, I noticed she tucked the spell book into her own pocket.

Yvaine took my hand and Cole's, leading us in the opposite direction of the entrance, but I didn't dare argue. Something was tracking us. And I couldn't help but acknowledge that this might be where we died—in the dark.

The tunnel forked and we went right. There was a breeze, and I won-dered if Yvaine had taken notice of it or if it had been random chance that she'd chosen the tunnel that she did. The cave narrowed. I could feel the crystals scraping along my sides and the top of my head soon after. Cole and I had to let go of Yvaine so we could begin crawling. The space became smaller and smaller. So much that Cole had to remove his bow and drag it along the ground as he crawled.

I heard footsteps behind us.

"Yvaine," I warned.

"I know," she breathed.

Our pace quickened, but abruptly ended with Cole saying, "There's nowhere else to go."

"There has to be," Yvaine urged. We felt along the walls, the dirt scraping against our knees.

I paused and concentrated, smelling the fresh air that drifted past my nose. I rose up and placed my hand on the ceiling, afraid that if I pushed too hard, the cave would fall down on us. The footsteps grew louder, and my worries became unimportant. I plunged my hand through the earth that connected the amethysts. Beyond that was cold snow.

"We need to dig our way out." I found Yvaine's hand and placed it on the earth ceiling.

"That's a bad idea." Despite her words, she felt along the soil for more weaknesses.

Knowing the answer, I asked, "Do you know any spells that could do it for us?"

"No, but maybe I can make one," she suggested, unsure.

The footsteps drew closer with each moment. They were calm and sure. They knew we were cornered and had no way to escape. "There's no time," Cole said as he plunged his own hand upward, pulling the earth down.

The dirt, snow, and crystals were quickly filling the small space. As Cole and I pulled it down, Yvaine shoveled it down the tunnel, toward the tracker. We would be trapped completely if we couldn't dig our way out. I had never been particularly claustrophobic, unlike my sister, but the more I clawed my way upward, the more desperate I became for fresh air and open space.

Finally, my hand reached skyward and grabbed nothing. I pulled myself through the small hole and reached down for Yvaine. She clawed at the soil and nearly pulled me back into the cave, but soon, we were working together to unbury Cole.

After dragging the elf to the surface and onto the snow, we collapsed and gulped down air. Yvaine rose first and began filling the hole with snow, hoping to keep whatever was down there trapped. Then, the snow began to melt.

"Cole," Yvaine called.

Seeing the retreating snow, he said, "Run!"

We had emerged in the middle of a clearing. We ran for the tree line where there would be cover. The sun had risen, and its rays fell down on us, revealing us to the world. There weren't many Guise in this area, but the few that haunted the place had heard the noise and drifted in our direction.

"Use the darkness spell!" I told Yvaine.

"I can't! What if it's the elves after us? They can track it!"

"We don't have a choice, sis." Our pace was slowing. The snow was deep and cold. The sun was the only thing warming us. The Guise were drifting closer. Whatever had tracked us in the underground tunnels had dug their way out of the ground and barreled through the snow behind us.

I waited for my sister to cast the spell, but she was breathing hard, panicking. Gathering my strength, I said the words that we'd needed our whole lives, and the ones that I most hated. "Sit tenebris vivere." *Let darkness live.*

The dagger lit and out of it poured smoke so dark, it was nearly black. It rose and hovered above us while we ran, nearing the forest. The Guise had found the forest's edge, waiting for us to fall into their touch, but we were safe—from them at least.

Refusing to look back, the three of us darted into the trees, staying well under my dark cloud of protection. We didn't know what hunted us, but if we stopped running it could mean our deaths. And we hadn't come this far just to die.

Hot breath exhaled down my neck. A claw scraped against my spine and pulled me back by the hood of my jacket. I was forced onto the ground, and pushed deep into the snow. The cloud disappeared with my concentration. A heavy paw pushed against my chest. Flames landed beside my head in warning. A familiar bow was dropped on my chest.

"Arlen," I breathed, handling the discarded piece of weapon.

The Fae bent down and peered into my eyes, communicating his frustration.

"I'm sorry we ran. But why didn't you howl?" I asked, my blood rushing through swollen veins.

"Our friend didn't want to lead the elves to us," Cole explained. Him and my sister now stood above me. Arlen removed his heavy paw and rubbed against Cole, whimpering.

Yvaine helped me stand and laughed, "Good thing it was a friend, or you would have been puppy chow." She stroked Arlen's fur gently, and he chuffed in response.

"Puppy chow?" I questioned. My sister said the oddest things sometimes. She eyed the splintered bow that I tossed aside.

"Never mind." She shrugged. "Sit tenebris vivere." Without aid from the dagger, the cloud formed above us again, and we took the moment to realize what Arlen's appearance meant.

"If Arlen found us, that means the elves can't be far behind," Cole said, his tone dark.

"We better start moving," I said, rubbing Arlen's forest-green fur. He was free of injuries from what I could see. Maybe he had his own kind of Healing Fire. "Thank you for saving us. Hopefully, you won't have to do it again," I told the beast. His white eyes pierced me with an emotion I was unfamiliar with.

After the panic subsided and we were well on our way south, Yvaine asked me, "Why do you think the humans turned away from magic? I know it was to stop the fighting, but to be left helpless…"

Pondering, I answered, "Maybe they weren't turning away from magic, but rather turning toward something else."

Considerate, Yvaine quieted and watched Cole's bowed head as he trudged through the snow.

Hamilton was home to old structures from centuries past. How many centuries, I didn't know, but now that I could read, I planned on learning as much as I could. Finally aware of the magic boiling inside me, I could feel it in the air, the ground, and even in the ancient ruins that the town had treasured.

"Do you feel that, Yvaine?" I asked, my sister walking dutifully by my side while Cole led us forward. Arlen was guarding our backs, and I felt safer with him being there.

"Yes," she whispered, looking around as if she was seeing our home for the very first time. We nibbled on crackers from the supplies Cara had given me, but my stomach growled for a hot meal.

Cole threw a glare over his shoulder, and I said, "Do you know where we're going, Cole?" I hadn't heard Yvaine give him directions to our house. Night had fallen, and the moon was hidden behind angry clouds. We hadn't returned to this place since our parents were killed, and I questioned whether Yvaine would be able to remember the way.

"I'm sure you'll correct me when I make a wrong turn. Maybe you should learn a manipulation spell, so it will be easier to direct me." Cole's voice was tight—angry.

"What's up with you?" I asked, confused.

Yvaine reached for the elf's hand, but he ripped it away from her and said, "Just tired."

My sister and I shared a concerned expression. It was unlike Cole to be angry. I'd seen him freezing to death with a smile plastered on his face. I'd helped him by casting the healing spell, but was there something else that he wasn't telling us? Worried, I asked, "Did you get hurt in the cave? We can use fire magic—"

"I said, I'm fine. No need to waste your precious magic on me." Arlen trotted forward and rubbed against his side. The elf flinched away but raised his hand and scratched under the cù-sìth's chin, as to not hurt his feelings.

Yvaine shook her head at me, mouthing, "I'll talk to him later."

Ignoring the strangeness of Cole, I concentrated on the path ahead of us, searching for any sign that humans still dwelled in the small town. The pavement had cracked and crumbled, allowing the earth to rise up. Trees and shrubs had formed over the abandoned cars. The buildings were rotting from the inside out.

"Do you think there will be anything left to find?" I asked Yvaine.

Taking my hand, she said, "Even if there's not, we need to do this. We need to move on, Lugh."

I squeezed Yvaine's hand, acknowledging that Cole hadn't been the only one listening to me while I spoke to Cara. My sister had heard me, too. *But she didn't know everything there was to know, did she?*

I slipped out of her grip and reached for the dagger. I stared at the runes etched into its blade, and realized that I couldn't read it. I opened my mouth to ask Cole why, but he had marched farther ahead and out of hearing distance.

The snow glowed bright, even in the darkness. The crunch beneath our feet was loud in the quiet nighttime air, and it made me worry that someone would hear us passing through. I looked back at our tracks and paused, forgetting that Yvaine had found a spell to cover our movements in the town. There was no way that the dark elves would be able to follow us by tracking alone. There was no evidence that the four of us walked this path. We had to use magic, but with the magic emanating from the ruins here, it would be hard to find us.

"We're getting close," Yvaine said under her breath, her exhale creating a cloud that drifted higher and higher until it dispersed into thin air.

"You remember?"

"Of course I do," she said.

"I just thought…"

"That I was too young?" Yvaine guessed. I nodded and she sighed. "I was older than you think I was. I remember what it was like before the Collapse. Before they were gone." *Our parents.*

"What were they like?" I asked.

Yvaine focused her eyes on me. "You've never asked that before."

Guilty, I tried to explain, "Well, I thought it was time…"

My sister waited for me to continue, but when I didn't, she said, "They were writers, so they were a bit strange. Though, now I know why they kept to themselves more often than not. I'm sure it had to do with Mother's heritage." Yvaine paused and carefully wiped a tear from her eye. "They liked to travel for research purposes. When you were two years old, they took us to Hadrian's Wall—the Romans built it to control movement on the land, but Father always said it was because the Romans were frightened of the Picts and wanted a barrier between them." She smiled. "To this day, I don't know if the facts I know about history are true or just Father's theories."

"I don't remember that," I said truthfully.

"You were young. And honestly, you didn't miss anything. The wall isn't much of a wall anymore, so much as a few bricks laying in the grass." My sister looked ahead at Cole and rubbed her temples, irritated. Arlen trotted ahead after the elf.

"What did they write?" I asked.

"Fiction." When I gave her a confused expression, she clarified,

"Made-up stories. Fake. Fantasy."

Recalling the word from my new arsenal, I nodded and asked, "Then why did they need to research?" I asked.

Forming a confused expression of her own, she answered, "I don't know."

"Did we always live here?" I asked, desperate to know more.

Slowly, she said, "I can't remember." The skin between her brows pinched in frustration.

"Well, it's a good thing that I never asked about them before. I wouldn't have learned anything anyway," I laughed.

Yvaine punched my arm and said, "It's been a while, okay?" My sister's blow didn't land as hard as it used to.

Cole and Arlen stopped at the four-way ahead. The cù-sìth turned and watched our approach while Cole stared at a tree that penetrated the nearest house's roof. "This way," Yvaine said, refusing to stop. We turned right and followed the street until it ended with a familiar green house. The spruce trees in the yard were taller and thicker than they had been thirteen years before. The front door was open, the hinges still strong.

We walked around the property, assessing if it was safe to go inside. I glanced to the cat's door that was cut into the side entrance. The flap had been pulled off by wild animals. The claw marks in the wood proved as much. I squatted and peered inside, finding nothing but darkness.

On my knees, I stared into that hole in the wall. I expected my body to react poorly as it always did, but instead, it did nothing. There was no shake in my hands, no tremble in my lip, no panic seeped into my lungs. My heart seemed to stop completely.

I rose on two feet and followed my sister around the rest of the house, feeling nothing but the dread that pooled in my gut. At the front door, with Cole and Arlen standing beside us, she said, "Welcome home, Lugh."

30

W*elcome Home.*

That's what the picture said when we entered. It was right above us, the mudroom tiny yet comforting. The walls were a light green color that complimented the dark forest-green exterior. The furniture was made from cherry wood, though most of it had been destroyed by squatters. The paintings that hung in the living room were of the forest: trees, waterfalls, and Common animals. The couch was rotting, but it was the same one that I remembered; a blood red that stood out drastically against the calm forest colors.

All these details kept me sane, as I looked down at the body lying at the living room's entrance. After years of seeing the deceased, I'd been able to deduce who they'd been before becoming nothing but bone.

A male human who had died in his early forties. His skeleton revealed that he'd broken his right leg once before, and I wondered what he'd been doing that caused such an injury. Being so close to the open front door, his corpse was sprinkled with snowflakes. I tried to examine his face, but there was an obstacle in my way, a live woman's head had bent over the corpse, her tears dripping onto the stained bones.

Yvaine, I'm so sorry.

She reached out to our father, but retreated, unsure what to do.

"Let's keep going," Cole suggested quietly. I was grateful he was here because no words of comfort would come from my lips. If I spoke, my sister would learn the truth.

Nodding, Yvaine stood and approached the next corpse. This one was smaller with a fragile build. A female elf that had never broken a single bone—or had healed them so completely that it hadn't even left a scar. My sister couldn't bring herself to kneel over this one. The two of us stood by Mother's resting place, staring at the black locks of hair that sprouted from her skull.

Cole kneeled for us and whispered over her body with what I assumed was an elvish prayer. Unable to watch, I lowered my backpack to the ground and walked down the long hallway that led to our bedrooms.

Our parents buffet still rested against the long wall. A decade's worth of dust coated the statuettes, frames, and silly knick-knacks living there. Instinctually, I searched for the one I wanted, as if no time had passed, and I was still that four-year-old boy looking for his favorite toy. Disappointed, my head fell backward until I stared at the ceiling. There were stains from water damage, and the pea-green paint was cracked from the foundation shifting.

"It's underneath," Yvaine said.

Slowly, I lowered my head and raised my brows in question.

Smiling, my sister reached under the buffet and felt along the drawer's seams. A moment later, she revealed a small carved tree. The emerald paint looked brand new, being protected the past decade. She placed it in my open hand. I laughed upon its touch, suddenly overjoyed. And lighter than I had been in years. I realized that I hadn't been happy since I last held the toy in my hand. "Thank you." I pulled my sister in close and hugged her—something else I hadn't done in a long time. My tears soaked her loose hair that was so much like Mother's.

"If you want to remember them, I can unlock your memories. I know the spell," Yvaine offered, her voice cracking.

Panicked, I said, "No. I don't want to remember what I've lost." I pulled away from her. "But someday."

Fighting back tears, Yvaine stared down the hallway, and recognition flashed in her eyes. "A mirror is still here."

"Really?" I asked, disbelieving.

"Yes, here." She sprinted the short distance to the family artifact, and I followed quickly. The mirror was untouched, gleaming, pristine. How had this not been stolen?

Thinking the same thing, Yvaine reached up and tried to remove it from the wall, but it didn't budge. "Do you remember what was in it?" I asked.

"In it?" she questioned.

"I remember something being behind the mirror." I stroked the cold glass, only to focus on my own reflection. A young man with uneven blonde hair and a virtuous face covered in dirt. The first signs of frostbite, nipping at the lobes of his ears. Beside him stood a woman with a delicate face framed by tangled waves of golden hair. She too, was covered in dirt. Both of them had curious eyes but a hopeless expression.

"Verum," Yvaine whispered. Her breath clouded the glass. When she lifted her hand to wipe it clean, her fingers plunged into darkness. We watched as the fog dissipated and revealed a dark hole residing behind the mirror's frame. The dagger at my side lit automatically, and I placed it near the hole's entrance.

The smell of old paper and metal met my nose, as if the hidden treasures had released a long-held breath. Yvaine reached inside and pulled out book after book—all of them bound in leather. She stacked them in my free arm and pulled out two shining weapons. Swords etched with runes. The weapons were much longer and heavier than the dagger. But they, too, were forged with iron. The handles were detailed with silver and gold. The designs were Celtic in nature, but had a Fae touch that only endowed weapons possessed.

"Do you think…?" I whispered.

Without saying a word, Yvaine awakened the amethyst light inside the twin swords. Familiar smoke tumbled out of the weapons, shrouding us in tranquility. I set down the books and held out my hand. My sister placed the blade from her left hand into my right. The light flickered, but I managed to keep it alive with some effort.

"What else were our parents keeping from us?" Yvaine asked, placing her hand on the flat of the blade. Apparently, iron didn't bother my sister.

Looking down to the books, I said, "I think we'll find our answer in there." The magic weapons dimmed slowly until blackness surrounded us once again.

"While you guys have been playing with your new toys, I've found a clue." Cole's voice was neutral behind us. We turned to find him leaning against the wall, holding up a badge dangling from a lanyard.

Refusing to set aside her new weapon, Yvaine grabbed the badge and read loudly, "Dr. Harris Anderson. PhD in Mythology, Occultism, and Linguistics." She paused and stared at the picture beside the strange title. "That's him," she confirmed.

I took the badge from her trembling fingers and asked, "What is this?" I pointed to a shape on the back of the badge. It almost looked like a…

"Edinburgh Castle," she answered. Once she said it, the black shape became clear: a castle, like the ones we'd spent our days in over the years. If it hadn't been for the structures crumbling under their own weight, we might have made one a permanent residence.

"Why would a doctor go out of his way to attack our family?" Yvaine asked.

"He had an endowed weapon and tried to drain you of blood with it," Cole stated. "Dr. Harris Anderson was going to perform a spell."

"Wasn't he human, though? He couldn't do it even if he tried. I mean, wasn't the Collapse proof enough of that?" I asked, wondering what could have been so important that it was worth tearing apart my family.

Taking back the badge, Yvaine asked Cole, "Where did you find this?"

"It was in your mother's hand."

Swallowing the bile that rose up both of our throats, Yvaine stalked farther down the hallway and opened her bedroom door. "There's only one way to know if that bastard was Fae or not."

All three of us stepped inside the young girl's bedroom, our eyes meeting the remains of the murderer who trespassed in our house thirteen years before. Squatters had shoved the remains aside, so they were crumpled in the corner. The bed's blankets had been stripped and stolen. No one had been interested in the toys, though. The dolls and stuffed animals littered the shelves and floor. There were patches of rotted wood in the floorboards from the leaks in the ceiling, as well as the decayed remains.

I had never seen such disgust on another person's face as I did right then, looking at Yvaine. The immense hatred she had for the man in front of her saturated the air, the bullet hole in his skull prominent. She took the new sword and moved the skeleton into a better viewing position.

The man was just that—a man. If he was Fae his bones would have been thinner, more delicate. The angle of his cheekbones would have been sharp instead of round, and his fingers and toes would have been longer—claw-like. It made me wonder what our skeletons would look like to curious eyes. Would they see a human or an elf?

"He's human," Yvaine confirmed. "So why did he bother? Why did he need *our* blood?" she spat. She ripped open his pockets, and found a damp piece of paper. She spread it open on the floor for us to read only to find that we couldn't—runes. "More mystery. Just what we needed."

I grabbed the scrap of paper before Yvaine could rip it apart. Loosening my sister's grip on the badge she still clutched, I said, "Maybe we'll find answers there." I traced the castle's shape, hoping for something more than a picture.

"We were supposed to find answers here," Yvaine growled.

"We came here so that we could move on." I grabbed my sister's hand when Cole didn't. "Let's bury them and do just that."

Cole interrupted, his tone bitter, "You found weapons and books. All you have to do is look, and you'll find something." The elf left us alone with the dead doctor, and I gaped in his direction.

"Something is wrong with him," I said, suspicion setting in.

"We'll deal with him after we bury Mother and Father." Yvaine squeezed my hand and led me out of her old bedroom. I closed the door behind us.

The bath was hot and burned my sensitive skin. Yvaine had explained that it was customary to bathe and dress nicely for a funeral. I'd never been to a formal human funeral before, but I found the occasion depressing. Wasn't it hard enough to stand up when one was grieving? But society expected flowers, caskets, nice clothes, and clean skin, too? Sometimes I pondered if human society before the Collapse was worth living in at all.

Despite the oddness, I'd wanted to do this for my parents. I forced myself to haul bucket after bucket of snow into the bathtub down the hall. Arlen had heated the container until the snow melted and steam clouded the air. The Fae had done the same for Yvaine's own bathtub—the one that connected to my parent's bedroom. Cole had said he'd stand watch while we cleaned up with no prospect of cleaning himself or joining Yvaine for that matter. Though I was glad that particular activity wasn't happening next door, it left me worried for the elf.

My backpack was bulging with my parent's books, the sword standing beside the bathroom doorway with the bag. Though, I couldn't part with the dagger. It was in the tub with me, soaking in the scalding water. I traced the blade along my arm, around the thickest of my veins. They bulged with anger. The banshee's poison had traveled through every part of my body, marking my skin as its own. The angriest of the wounds was on my chest where the curse had entered; it was now a pink scar. The Fae's claw had raked across me, yet when it happened, I hadn't felt a thing. I'd simply fallen asleep. And woken paralyzed.

I plunged my head under the water, wishing to wash away the memories. I forced myself to stay under longer, fighting against the instinct to flee. *You are alive. You survived. You are alive.* Each time the words were uttered, the memories dulled to lost dreams: being drowned in the flood, laying trapped and alone in the dark, hearing the sounds of my sister crying for help.

I didn't rise above the water until they were quiet, and all I could hear was the sound of the dagger scraping against the inner tub. I gulped down mildew-filled air, concentrating on what I was going to tell Yvaine. *If you tell her the truth, she'll never forgive you. You'll be alone.*

Doubt crept in as it always did. I wished Yvaine had given me the spell book, only so I could concentrate on its voices instead of mine.

I climbed out of the tub before the water was cold and dried off with a child's shirt—my old shirt. It was orange with illustrated trucks on the front. With cleaner hands, I pulled out one of the books we'd found and prepared myself for the worst as I opened it.

But nothing happened.

It wasn't a spell book at all. There were maps and histories drawn and written. Page after page of Fae species were detailed. Hadrian's Wall was one of the places marked on the map. Had our parents been to all these locations? There were markings across the whole world. Each one was noted and described. The first page listed the title and the authors.

Our parents hadn't written fiction.

I placed the book back in its place and dressed for the funeral. We'd found some of our parent's clothes tucked away in drawers that had managed to escape looting. My father supplied me with dark jeans and boots with a black coat and gloves. There had been no shirt, so I was stuck with the one I had been wearing, but I'd washed it, letting it partially dry before putting it back on.

Peering in the mirror, I ran a hand through my hair, away from my drawn face. The dark circles beneath my eyes had always been there, but they were nearly black now, as if I'd been punched. I stared at the tips of my ears, noticing the slight angle for the first time. They wouldn't alarm a human if they examined me, but I knew where the deformity came from now.

I wondered what Cara had seen when we'd spoken beside the fire.

A knock sounded against the door. "Are you ready, Lugh?" Yvaine asked, her voice tight.

"Yeah." Picking up the backpack and sword, I opened the door to find my sister. She was clean and dressed in black jeans and a purple shirt. Her original boots and jacket had been wiped clean, and her hair hung long and damp behind her. "You look good, sis."

Surprised, she said, "You too. Our parents would be proud to see how well you've grown up."

I huffed out a laugh. "I grew up but not out. I'm just waving in the wind now. There's no roots to keep me from falling over."

With a raise of her brow, she argued, "You're not done growing yet, brother."

And I supposed that was true. But would I have a chance to finish growing? "Where's Cole?" I asked.

Yvaine's smile disappeared. "He's making sure the path to the church is clear before we carry the bodies there."

"Should he be out there alone?" I asked.

"No, but he insisted." She sighed. "I'm just not in the mood to fight him." Yvaine reached into her own backpack and pulled out a silver stick. "I'm hoping that this will help whatever he's going through."

"It's nice." I nodded. "What is it?"

With a chuckle, she answered, "It's a flute. He told me once that it's his favorite. I found it in the mirror." She stashed the instrument beside more of our parent's books and pulled out a belt. "This should hold your sword for the time being."

Looking to her own belt, I saw that the sword rested on her hip. "Thanks." I secured the new weapon to my waist and took a quick glance in the mirror. A dagger and sword glittered at my side. I was a glowing beacon to any thief we came across. Hopefully, I would learn how to use the sword soon.

"Admiring your new playthings?" Cole appeared from the shadows of the hallway, making me flinch.

"How was the church?" Yvaine asked, her tone simmering with rage.

"Abandoned. The sun is rising soon, though, so let's make this quick."

The elf turned, expecting us to follow. Yvaine's face turned red with fury. It was very unlike Cole to be so dismissive and callous toward anyone, especially Yvaine.

"Were you able to find some sheets?" I whispered.

Calming, she nodded and led me to Mother and Father's bodies, already wrapped tightly by the front door. "I thought you could be the one to lower them into their final resting place," she said, dividing the load. And honestly, I was grateful for this role. I didn't know if I was capable of even touching their corpses unless there was a barrier between us.

Allowing Cole to take our packs, we each took a parent; Yvaine carried Mother and I carried Father. Arlen was our guide to the church, having followed Cole beforehand. I breathed in the fresh air and realized just how much our childhood home had smelled of decay. Our parents didn't deserve that kind of resting place. They didn't deserve that kind of death.

The Church of Perpetual Light rested three streets down from our house. As we approached the graveyard, I recalled our Sunday visits. And I finally figured out where Yvaine learned all her songs. The stained-glass windows were mostly broken, but I could still see where the remnants of a sunrise rising over a vast field of fireweed used to be. The tower was still tall and strong.

We passed the iron gates and my skin itched, but I suspected that it was the sword at my side. Endowed weapons with iron blades. The Fae or *Conscius* had created deadly weapons to kill each other with. That fact saddened me. Even in a magic-filled world, fairy tales did not exist.

The tombstones were tall and gaudy mostly. Some had angels sitting upon the tops, some had children, and some only had small plaques in the ground that had been overgrown with grass. What did we have to offer our parents other than our thoughts?

We reached the edge of the cemetery and placed our parents on the wild, snow-covered grass. Cole and Arlen sat beside them as guards, while

Yvaine and I went to the empty plots to dig. Searching the grounds, I asked, "Where do we find shovels?"

"You forget so quickly, brother, that we have magic," my sister said, her forehead creased with worry despite her offer.

"But the dark elves…?"

"I think it's worth the risk. What do you say?" And my sister meant it. She was letting me decide.

"Yes. What do I do?"

Anticipating my answer, she said, "I thought it would be fitting if we used one of Mother's spells. Movere cum me."

"Isn't that for water?" I asked.

"It can be used for anything, really. You just have to concentrate. Look inward." Yvaine looked to Cole when she said the last two words, expecting a reaction, but Cole continued to stare at nothing, ignoring us completely.

I stood across from my sister, with enough space for us to work in between. Taking a moment to gather the strength we needed to continue, we said as one, "Movere cum me. Movere cum me. Movere cum me." The earth before us rose, parting from its home for the time being. We instructed the soil to rest beside us, all the while, chanting the phrase our mother had taught Yvaine.

The graves were deep and dark, causing doubtful thoughts to arise. Yvaine put a stop to them. "Our parents loved this church. Though, I don't think they were truly religious, I think they loved to be together in a place meant for peace," Yvaine explained. She looked into the same dark grave that I did with a very different expression—relief. This was something that had haunted her for years. She'd always hated that we left our parents behind; there had been no way to know if more people were going to come and try to take us. Even though it was something she had to do to save me—to save both of us—it's one of her greatest regrets.

"You're giving them a proper place to rest together. They're going to be forever grateful that you came back for them, Yvaine." My sister collapsed to her knees, no longer able to hold her emotions inside. She sobbed openly, allowing her grief to flow down and into the grave.

Leaving Yvaine, I went to our parents. Arlen bowed when I approached, showing his respect. Cole didn't look up at me from where he hung his head, though, I could have sworn I saw a black tear escape his cheek. I picked up Father and carried him to the grave. Carefully, I climbed down and placed him on the left side. When I went to climb back up, Cole was there with my mother in his arms. The elf lowered her into my grip, but I couldn't see his face underneath the long black hair. I placed Mother beside Father, unsure what to do next.

Yvaine joined me in the grave and revealed a blonde braid—the one she'd sold and then taken back from the city woman. She tucked it into Father's sheet. Slowly, I removed the wooden tree from my pocket. Palming it for a few moments, I kissed the old toy and placed it within Mother's wrappings.

I helped Yvaine climb out of the grave and followed after. Arlen and Cole were now looking over the edge with us. The cù-sìth's pure white eyes glowed in the light of the rising sun. Neither of us could say anything other than the spell as we lowered the earth over our parents. Afterward, there was only silence. The town had truly been abandoned—a grave that held our childhood within its borders.

"Crescere et florebit," Yvaine whispered. Blooms of white snowdrops appeared on our parent's grave, the disturbed earth serving as fresh soil for the new flowers.

"Where did you learn that?" I asked, amazed.

"I created it for them." Yvaine tried to smile but it faltered. "I wish I could do more."

I opened my mouth to speak the truth: My sister wasn't to blame for their death. She did everything that she could. It was *my* fault they were gone.

"What more do you need? You've buried and put them to rest. All with *magic*." Cole's voice was full of venom, causing the veins under my skin to crawl.

"I just want them to be happy, Cole. Don't you understand?" Yvaine pleaded.

"Oh, I understand perfectly. I lost my mother, too. Though, I'm sure you've forgotten. It's always been about you two. Ever since I met you, I've sacrificed everything to make *you* happy." Cole was as still as one of the gravestone statues, unnervingly so.

Yvaine reached for his hand and said, "We know you lost your mother, too. This isn't just for us. It's for you, too. We all need to move on from our grief."

The elf didn't give her a chance to touch him. Tossing aside his bow and quiver, he said, "How am I supposed to move on? My mother was raped by my father, forced to raise a deformed, magicless child, and then killed by a spell that her people forced down her throat. I never had a chance to bury her or mourn her. I haven't even seen her in twenty years because she banished me!" Cole's hands ripped through his dark hair, ink pouring from the strands. "I was alone for decades. My only purpose was to find my father. Maybe if I found him and brought him back to her, she would forgive me. Maybe if I slit his throat in front of her, she would love me! But now... Don't *you* understand?"

Yvaine gasped, and my stomach sank. The ink continued to pour from Cole, the ground pooling around him, slowly soaking in the darkness that had been festering—the same darkness that he'd absorbed from me—the spell that had gone horribly wrong. "Cole, you need to calm down. You need to let go of the darkness. You took too much from me," I said.

"You think that this is all yours!" The elf finally looked up and met my gaze. His emerald eyes were wide and furious. "I've been absorbing magic for years and storing it. I've been training with the deadliest Fae, so some-day, when I found my father, I would be able to trap him and take him back home." Breathing hard, he added, "I save a little bit from every Fae that I take from. You only added to the stockpile."

"Cole," Yvaine started. The elf whipped his eyes to hers, unflinching. He was falling apart. Even Arlen stepped back from him, afraid. "You need to let it go. Whatever you took from Lugh has changed you. You saved him. You saved me. Let us save *you*." Yvaine was hurt, that much was obvious, but Cole needed our help.

"As usual, you didn't listen to what I said. I don't want to let it go. It's mine. It's the only magic I'll ever have. I'm not like you two. I don't have magic of my own. No soul. I'm not good." He stepped away from us when we moved toward him. There was a gravestone at his back, a child offering flowers. "I can't go home. I'll never see my mother again. But I can finish what I started before I met you. I'll find my father, and I will kill him with this magic. He will know what he did to her and regret it."

Tears were falling down Yvaine's cheeks, but her voice was strong when she said, "I always listen to you. It's not my fault what you say is wrong. You're just a helpless boy who never grew up. You hoarded the mag-ic instead of using it to save us. You took advantage of me when Lugh was hurt. You flirted and harassed me until you got what you wanted." Taking a deep breath, she added, "You're just like your father."

"Yvaine!" I said, appalled.

My sister gave me a hand signal that I learned when I was eight years old—a twirl of her pointer finger below her waist. We were on the offen-sive, and she wanted me to trap the opposition while she distracted.

Understanding, I inched toward Arlen where he stood behind Cole. I begged that the beast understood what we had to do. I stared into his eyes and spoke as clearly as I could without words. The Fae backed away, allowing me to do my work.

The dark ink poured from Cole's eyes and mouth, disrupting his speech. "I am nothing like him!"

"Yes, you're exactly like him. You take what you want, and you leave. You don't care about us. You're just along for the ride because you don't want to be alone," Yvaine spat.

Cole shot out a spell that caused the gravestone beside him to explode. Yvaine blocked the shards with her own light. The elf continued, "I gave everything to you! I sacrificed myself so you could heal your brother! I stayed with the elves, and they tortured me because of it. Every day, they tormented me with manipulation magic, tearing apart my body and putting it back together again. They filled my head with memories of my mother dying!" The ink took on a smoky form and rose from the ground, surrounding him in a cocoon. "Over and over they broke my bones and reshaped my body, telling me it was only a matter of time before you and Lugh died." He was crying now, and the smoke became volatile, angry. Lightening shot from the dark cloud, nearly hitting Yvaine. Cole had forgotten about me.

Choking on her words, she said, "You deserved it. Every minute of torture you endured was nothing compared to being with you."

Thunder sounded, though the sky was clear. The sun was peeking over the mountain tops. Soon, Guise would appear. The smoke cleared enough that I could see Cole struggling to stand. The magic was too much for him. All the power he'd saved over the years was rolling out of him in waves. My deformed spell had been too much for him to take. Yvaine was forcing him to use it.

"Everyone hates me. They always have. Of course you would, too." The elf fell to his knees. The lightening continued to shoot out of the smoky cloud. A strike landed just beside my foot, and my stomach fell to the ground in panic.

Yvaine didn't say anything more. Her work was done.

I lunged for Cole and pinned him to the ground. Yvaine joined, as well as Arlen. I immediately felt weak upon his touch. The elf was draining us, so I was eager to see what Yvaine had planned.

"Arlen, give us your fire," my sister commanded.

The Fae exhaled open flames and Yvaine began the spell for Healing Fire. I joined her soon after. Cole screamed in protest, refusing to let anymore of the darkness out, but he could only hold so much magic and what he was absorbing now was nothing but light and goodness. As the darkness poured out of him—the ink I created—I knew that if the dark elves ever managed to capture and use him for the eclipse spell, Cole was going to die. He would not survive that much magic filling his body.

"Let it go, Cole," Yvaine whispered in the elf's ear. She pressed her lips against his head, and he closed his eyes. The thunder and lightning vanished, and the black smoke drifted away, leaving a sleeping elf who'd suffered for far too long.

The three of us released Cole and caught our breath. "How did you know that was going to work?" I asked Yvaine.

"I didn't," she said, her tears dry.

With waning judgment, I commented, "Your kindness phase didn't last very long."

"You're such a jackass."

The moans of Guise sounded in the clearing. They weaved around gravestones and drifted through tall grass. With one last goodbye to our parents, Yvaine and I lifted Cole and cast the darkness spell, the cloud hovering above the four of us.

The ink stopped dripping from Cole by the time we reached the roadside. Deciding against a day's sleep, we headed east to Edinburgh, knowing that, with the magic that was cast in the graveyard, the dark elves wouldn't be far behind.

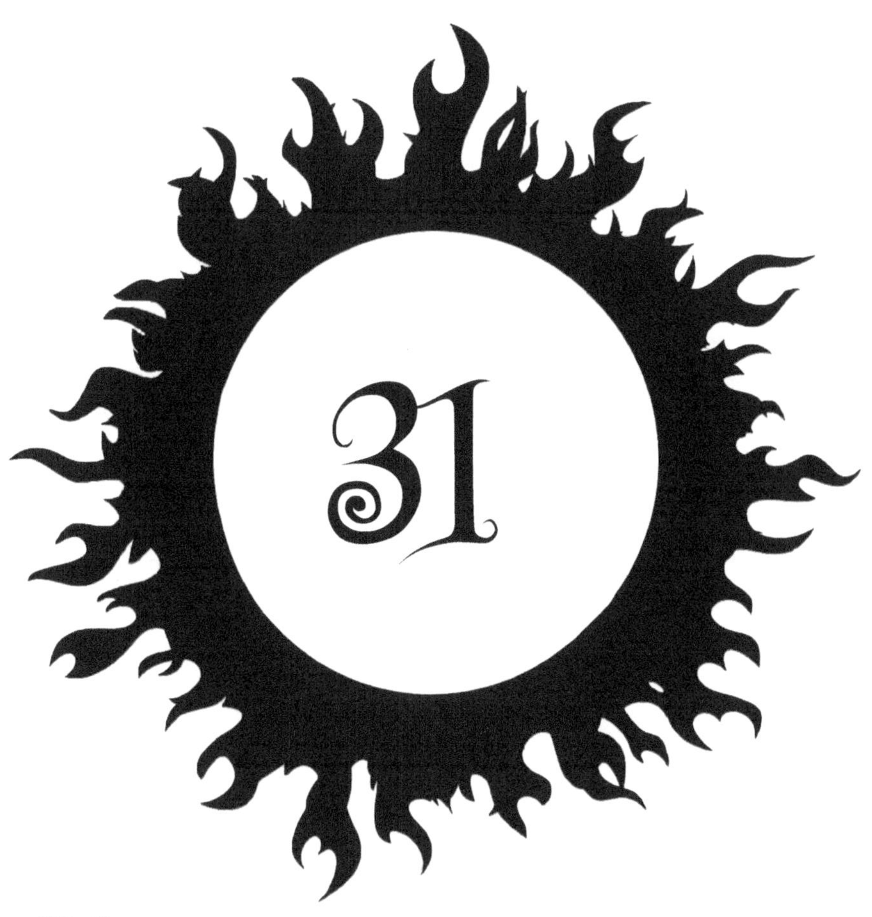

31

Once we were well down the east highway, we situated Cole so that he was laying across Arlen's back. But Yvaine refused to let go of his hand. "I'm sorry, Yvaine," I said.

"For?" she asked, distracted. She looked to the elf, worried, but the Healing Fire would do its work soon enough.

"It's my fault that Cole broke. The magic he absorbed from me… It wasn't good." I took a breath, trying to organize my thoughts. "When I tried to perform the healing spell on myself in the cave, it was as if every bad thought and memory joined together and attacked my body. I couldn't think straight."

"I don't think those things he said were just from the spell, Lugh."

"No, but my darkness was the reason it spilled over." I adjusted the weapons I carried; the sword and dagger hanging at my side, Cole's bow and quiver over my back, along with the backpack full of books and food. It was slow, but I was regaining some strength in my muscles. Walking was easier. So was breathing. And I had Cole to thank for that. "I never thanked him for taking it from me."

"You'll have your chance. I'm sure he'll wake up soon." My sister stared straight ahead. She was worried about what she had said to Cole.

"And you'll have your chance to apologize," I commented.

Instantly angry, she said, "For what?"

I gave her a dumbfounded expression.

"I only said those things so he'd be angry enough to expel some mag-ic. He knows that." Her grip tightened around the elf's hand.

"Never hurts to reassure someone." I nudged my sister into Arlen's side, and the Fae huffed.

"Well, he has to apologize for lying. Again." Yvaine sped her walk, pissed.

"Well, he did tell you," I remarked.

"When?"

"At the graveyard. It may have taken him a while, but the truth came out." I met her pace and smiled encouragingly.

Yvaine rolled her eyes and checked on the dark cloud hovering above us. The road had narrowed into two lanes, the abandoned cars thinning the farther we drifted from Hamilton. The trees thinned, as well, and I heard running water somewhere in the distance. I picked up the fresh fallen snow and stuffed it in my mouth. It melted and trickled down my throat, icing my stomach.

"Have we taken this road before?" I wondered aloud.

"No, we've kept to the west mostly." Yvaine ripped her hair out of her backpack's grip and tried to detangle the curls. She eyed the hairband on her wrist, but decided against using it.

"We're not ones for adventuring are we?"

My sister huffed. "Well, we've gotten plenty of excitement in the past couple months. I'd be glad to plant my butt somewhere for a while. Somewhere warm and free of people."

My sister's wish sounded unreal. All I wanted to do was go back to Stirling and help Cara establish her new city. I smiled, surprising myself by the desire. *Maybe someday.*

A familiar howl sounded behind us.

"Shit," Yvaine spat. "They've caught our scent." She dropped the darkness spell, and the sun shone down on us.

"How did Cole lose them last time?" I asked.

"Cole is an expert on cù-sìth. He knows exactly how they track, and how much they can smell." Yvaine ran for the forest's edge, and Arlen and I followed quickly after. "We need to disguise our scent."

"With what?" The Guise's moans were, thankfully, keeping their distance.

"Look for gooseberries," she ordered.

"I don't know what those are!" Panicking, I looked around for geese with berries in their mouths.

Frustrated, Yvaine said, "I don't see them, anyway. It's probably past their season."

The second howl echoed down the highway, hitting the tree line.

Arlen's ears lay flat, and his long, saber-like teeth were revealed.

"Just run!" she said. Yvaine tightened her pack as she ran, so she wouldn't make noise. But the weight we carried was slowing us down. And that included Arlen. He couldn't fight if he was carrying Cole. They were going to catch us this time.

"Go to the water," I said.

Without argument, my sister changed her route and followed the sound of falling water. By the time we reached the falls, we were out of breath and desperate for a break. Avoiding Guise had been the most difficult, but we couldn't risk using strong magic at the moment.

"Get in the water." I moved to step into the stream, toward the darkness of the falls.

"Wait." Yvaine pulled me back by the collar. "Why is the water red?"

For the first time, I examined the stream coursing over the sharp edge and cursed. The water was the color of blood, from the edge of the cliff to the bottom of the pond. We scrutinized the depths for predators—both Common and Fae. No movement could be seen in the murkiness below. I reached down and plunged my hand into the strange liquid and lifted it to my nose. "I don't know, but it smells fine." I looked back at the direction we had come from. "It's our only chance. We're not fast enough, and Cole can't help right now."

Yvaine nodded, and together, we waded into the pond. I held the packs full of our parent's books above my head as we treaded the shallow shoreline. Yvaine kept Cole's head above the surface while Arlen began to swim. The cù-sìth hated water, and his eyes narrowed in distaste.

Unable to wade any longer, I held the packs with one arm above the surface and swam with the other. My muscles were burning, but I refused to destroy what our parents had created. They held answers that we needed, and honestly, it was the only thing we had left of them.

Yvaine and Arlen passed under the falls, disappearing into the alcove behind it. I followed quickly, nearly throwing myself past the wall of water. There, I was able to place the packs on a boulder, and hold onto it myself, breathing hard.

The small alcove was dark, protecting us from the Guise.

Neither one of us knew if it would protect us from the elves, though. Our scent ended at the water's edge. Yvaine had covered our tracks with the cloaking spell, and although it wasn't wise to use magic, hiding our footprints was the priority. Would they know to check behind the falls?

I helped Arlen stay afloat while Yvaine kept Cole breathing. It was impossible to see beyond the wall of scarlet water. All of us quieted our breaths as the sound of footfalls reached our ears.

Familiar padding paced the water's edge. *More cù-sìth.* They huffed and growled, clearly displeased. "Where have they gone?" The chief's second hand was the one hunting us—Darce.

"They crossed the water." The female's feral voice was unfamiliar, and I imagined it belonged to someone who would slice me in half for simply looking in her direction.

"Even Coilleach isn't foolish enough to do that. The spirits aren't worth angering," Darce argued. Arlen's kin continued to pace the pond's edge, their growls growing louder by the moment. I kept my hands near his face, just in case an instinctual sound decided to slip out.

"Yes, but a desperate elf does not reason with fear. He merely bows to it," the female elf said.

Darce thought on her words a moment before he said, "Perhaps. We'll go around and hope that the red water hasn't killed the abomination. The eclipse is only a short time away. We need him."

"If so, it is possible that the boy survived," the female said.

"Two abominations." Darce sighed. "Their existence will at least serve a great purpose."

"As you say," the female agreed. I could feel the presence of many elves, but they remained silent, allowing their leader to decide the course.

Once their steps had faded, Yvaine and I met each other's stare. "We need to get out," she said, frightened. Quickly, we made our way the shoreline, refusing to cross to the other side. If what the elves said was true about spirits…

Arlen slid the elf off his back. Yvaine patted Cole's face where he lay on the mossy ground. "Please, wake up. We need you right now."

I turned to a very wet Arlen, who was attempting to lick his fur dry. "Do you know what's wrong with the water?"

The Fae simply ignored me and continued tending to his forest-green locks. The beast coughed, expelling red water.

I smoothed Arlen's forehead fur back. "Thanks for the help, buddy." Yvaine had her fingers to the elf's throat, checking his pulse. "He just isn't ready yet, Yvaine. Let the poor guy sleep," I said, irritated.

A glare pierced the back of my head when I turned away to figure out which direction the elves had taken. Elves were difficult to track. I'd tried a few years ago when we were especially desperate for a darkness spell. They were light on their feet and melded into the forest with ease, even in the winter. Cù-sìth on the other hand, didn't particularly care what they disturbed. Who could blame them? If I was a massive-sized predator with unrivaled senses, I wouldn't care where I left my shit either.

"If they don't want to cross the water, they're going to have to go back to the road. The stream changed direction there," I explained, staring at the embankment across the pond.

"We'll go the opposite direction, and go around, too."

"The water could go on for miles. They'll be in front of us by then. We need to cross here if we have any chance of getting ahead." I stood at the shoreline, staring into its depths. And hoping that I didn't find any spirits looking back.

A cold ball of snow hit the back of my head, and I nearly fell in.

"What the hell?" I complained, brushing away the ice chunks.

My sister laughed.

"Are you insane? We're in a life and death situation here."

"We're always in a life and death situation. I'm beginning to numb to it," she said, her voice tired.

"You mean that the *other woman* is coming out?" I teased.

"You little shit. You heard way more than you were supposed to when you were sleeping, brother." She threw another snowball, but this one missed and landed on the other side of the pond.

Laughing, I said, "I think you just crossed the water."

My sister sighed. "Then we better hurry before the spirits catch us."

Finding a narrow point in the stream, the four of us crossed over the red water. And it wasn't long before the angry spirits found us.

A shadow loomed above me. The sound of sad, soft music was in the air. My feet were cold.

"You doing okay, Lugh?" The voice I heard was deep and fading, as if they were falling down a well.

"What?" I asked, my voice slurring. I looked down at bare feet. "Where are my shoes?" The snow crunched beneath my soles, and I shivered.

"You two can't go one day without me, can you?" The music started again, and I followed it toward the large shadow until it became clear. A castle stood high above me. Its bricks were grey and large. Moss grew within its cracks. We stood at its entrance, a strange metal box sticking out of the front door.

Someone tumbled into me, and I flew forward, hitting the box. "What the hell?" I complained.

"Get out of my way. I'll get us in." A blonde woman drew her sword and began swinging it, striking the box over and over again. Her shoes were missing, too. "Why won't it open?" she growled.

The music quieted, and a slender hand reached out and took the sword from the woman's hands. "You'll ruin your sword, my fierce warrior."

Confused, the woman said, "Who do you think you are? You can't tell me what to do!" She reached for the sword, but an elf held it high above his head.

I peered into the box and recognized the symbol etched into its face. I pulled out a badge with the same symbol and placed it in the slim slot that was offered. "Welcome, Dr. Harris Anderson," the box's monotone voice said. The door it was protruding from opened, and the smell of fear came tumbling out of it.

The bickering beside me stopped. I turned to find that Yvaine had tackled Cole to the ground, struggling to get her weapon back. Immediately, I felt my side and found the dagger and twin sword still hanging there. Two backpacks were sitting beside the open door.

"How did we get here? What happened?" I asked. Twigs fell from my hair, and my hands were scratched and bloody.

With a growl, Cole said, "Fine! Here!" He threw the sword into the deadened grass beside us, and Yvaine released him to go after it. Finally upright, he explained, "You tell me. I woke up hanging from Arlen's back and found you two wandering the forest, calling out for the elves to come fight you!"

"Why would we do that?" I asked, mostly to myself.

Yvaine answered from her place in the grass; she was swinging the sword at phantom opponents. "We got tired of trying to hide from them."

Cole and I looked to one another. "Where are our shoes, Yvaine?" I asked.

"Gave them to some fairies." My sister continued to circle, her eyes darting from one shadow to another. I looked up to find that the sun was setting and was casting its last warm rays over the castle.

"Why?" we both said.

"To throw the elves off our trail. You know, like the brownie did at their fortress." The Guise in the distance drew closer, yet I didn't seem to care.

Cole snickered. "Fairies can't wear shoes, Yvaine."

"Whatever." Yvaine suddenly leapt into the air, kicking with all her might and fell to the ground. "Damn."

Choosing to ignore my insane sister, Cole asked me, "What do you remember?"

After a moment, I recalled, "Red water. The elves had tracked us to the red water. They left, and we crossed." My head ached, struggling to clear the fog. "Then nothing."

The elf burst with laughter. I was instantly afraid that the Guise would begin to swarm, but there was still only one. And it was slowly inching toward us. "You two drank the red water without me?" Cole was appalled, insulted even.

"We never drank it. We swam in it to hide." I circled, searching for our fourth member. "Where's Arlen?"

"Well, that explains why it lasted so long. It soaked into your skin." The elf gave me a mischievous grin. "The red water causes hallucinations. Fairies use that place to wash away their excess magic. Fun right?"

"Fun?" I choked. "I don't remember anything!"

"Oh, well, it affects everyone differently." Cole looked to where Yvaine now sat, stroking her sword with a menacing eye. "And Arlen is fine. He's checking the perimeter. The red water doesn't affect cù-sìth the same. It probably just gave him a headache." Cole ran a hand along his scalp, pushing his long hair back. The flute rested in his other hand.

"I see that you found your gift. Yvaine thought it would help." I smiled and tasted dirt. Sand shifted in between my teeth, and I cringed, imagining what I'd done while hallucinating.

Cole smiled back. "Yes, it did. You both followed its sound."

Though he'd misunderstood what I meant, I was glad that Cole had found a way to herd us. I pulled the I.D. badge out of the entry key slot. The door was still open. I took a step toward it and collapsed, exhausted.

Helping me to my feet, Cole explained, "You've both been wandering for a couple days. It's amazing that the elves never found you. Or something worse for that matter." He went to Yvaine and helped her up, as well, leading her to the door. "But perhaps Yvaine scared them off." Arlen rounded the corner and loped toward us, a Guise drifting after him.

I laughed without humor and dragged the packs inside the dark castle.

The inside of the castle was pristine, untouched. Other than the occasional piece of overturned furniture, it was as if the Collapse had never happened. Automatic lights flickered on above us. I stared at the illumination, rarely having seen electricity. "How?" I asked.

Cole reached toward the light, though it was much too high for him to touch. "Humanity may have abandoned magic, but it opened up their minds. Creativity. Science." He smiled, awed.

"That doesn't explain how it's working now," I said.

"Generators," my sister muttered under her breath, her eyes dialing in and out of reality, as if she was fighting against the red water. It had not agreed with either of us. I blacked out, and Yvaine became even more paranoid and neurotic than she usually was.

"Do you smell that?" I asked Cole. The scent of fear had perfumed me when we entered, but now I was drenched. What had happened here?

Raising his nose, he said, "No. What is it?"

Apparently, only I had the refined senses. And it made sense then why that was. After weeks of being blind, the only way I could survive was to listen, smell, taste, and feel. Being paralyzed had altered me. "Something bad happened here."

We stalked down a few more halls. They were grand, ancient. If it wasn't for the cameras spying on us from the ceiling, I would have thought we were in the dark elves' fortress. Yvaine saw them, too, and gave them a vulgar gesture. I laughed, and Cole restrained my sister's hands, hoping to distract her.

There were no signs to direct us like most of the office buildings I'd seen. Though, of course, this was no office. What was so important that they needed a castle to protect it? What was Dr. Anderson doing here?

The questions began to circle and peck at my psyche, especially when we reached a bolted entrance. Nodding to Cole, we both pulled aside the strong metal latch and opened the wooden doors. There were stairs leading down. *Just like the bowels of the elves' castle.*

Cole had the same thought and shivered, obviously remembering the terrible things that happened to him. "I can go alone. Just watch Yvaine," I said, taking a step forward.

"No!" Yvaine's cry echoed down the halls and into the dungeons below. If anyone was here, they knew about us now. Arlen's fur ruffled from fright.

Cole placed a hand over her mouth. "We'll go together," he assured her. She nodded, and he released his tight hold.

I sighed and took the first steps down into the pit below. The descent wasn't steep, but it was long. I was sweating by the time we reached the bottom, yet the fact that I could assured me that I was staying hydrated. More lights turned on automatically and revealed the strangest sight I'd yet seen.

"What is this place?" Cole asked, his green eyes wide.

"A lab." My sister strode forward and grabbed the glassware sitting on the table. I vaguely recalled the name of the equipment beside it—microscopes. My sister had shown me one before while we were squatting in a school classroom. "But Dr. Anderson wasn't a doctor of science."

"How are you feeling, Yvaine?" I asked, worried.

"Pissed." She stalked to a door with another metal box. She held out her hand. I gave her the I.D. card, and she inserted it into the slot. But this box didn't welcome us after it opened. Dust flew up when the door swung aside. Computers and several screens rested on a long table. The screens were dark but when Yvaine reached over and flipped the wall's switch on the face's lit up with blue, then white, then images. I recognized one of the images as the front lobby.

My sister was still jittery from the red water, but being in this place must have given her a rush of adrenaline, so she was able to focus. She sat in front of the middle computer and began typing. My head still ached as I stared at the screens, but I couldn't take my eyes away from them. Especially when we somehow appeared on them. The past repeating.

"How did you do that?" Cole asked Yvaine.

She smirked. "I had an A+ in my computer class. I guess the skill stuck with me." Her fingers flew across the lettered keyboard, changing the images on the screen rapidly. She read just as quickly, as if the past thirteen years had never happened. As if she was just another human in the Old World.

"Show off," I muttered, jealous of the things she'd been able to do that I had not, simply because I'd been too young.

After typing in random dates, she stopped when we saw dozens of people roaming the castle halls. The sun was shining through the stained-glass windows. They were smiling, content with their work.

"There he is," Yvaine growled. The man from the I.D. strolled down the hallway with the same badge swinging from his neck. He held two books at his side. Dr. Anderson stopped to chat with a woman for a moment before continuing on his path. Yvaine followed his course with the different cameras until we saw him walk into another room. She sped the video until he left in a panic several hours later. "Room 99. Second floor."

Yvaine rose to follow the lead, but I held out my hand. "Find the date of the Collapse," I requested.

Without question, my sister did as I asked, quickly typing in the date; the day after the doctor left his office in a panic. The workers acted the same for the morning, greeting each other with smiles and exchanging papers as they passed by. Had society really been this peaceful? Had people enjoyed each other's company rather than feared it? My question was answered when the clock hit 12:00 P.M.

Those same friendly faces twisted into fear and confusion. Humans were screaming at each other, yet there were no Guise in sight. "What are they saying?" I asked, frustrated.

A few clicks later, we were able to hear their voices. Cole squeezed Yvaine's shoulder, and I was relieved to see it. I didn't get to enjoy the emotion for long before a woman's frantic voice penetrated the screen, though she was nowhere in sight. "The test on Orkney Islands has failed." Her voice echoed down the halls, though people didn't stop to listen. "Until we have more information, return to your homes. Keep your family indoors." A sob. "God bless you." The voice disappeared, allowing the voices of the rest to seep through the speakers. A man was on the phone, telling his wife to get the kids from school and meet him at the house. A woman was carrying a box full of her belongings and tripped, scattering them across the floor. She abandoned them and ran.

Yvaine exited out of the video and typed in something else. *Orkney Islands.* One result.

The document explained as such:

Project: New World
Location: Kirkwall Facility

Objective: Return sight to the blind

Head of research: Dr. Harris Anderson
Consultants: Dr. Edward Rice
Dr. Mary Armstrong
Professor Ronald McCollum
Raymond Reynolds
Lynne Reynolds

"There's a video link attached to the file," Yvaine whispered, her voice cracking. One click led us to more surveillance footage. The upper right-hand corner said: *Orkney Islands.* The footage dated back several years before the Collapse. We were staring at a vast room with a skylight above it. The ground was bare. The earth never covered with concrete. There were computers along the walls, lit up with information I didn't understand. There were humans in long white coats holding papers and several more dressed in black, holding guns.

Yvaine typed in the date of the Collapse, and the video adjusted.

A man now stood in the center of the room. He held a paper and a small knife in his shaking hands. The rest stood aside, now dressed in rubber suits that covered them from top to bottom. The sunlight shined down directly on the man. A voice sounded from the speakers. "Whenever you're ready Ronald."

Ronald nodded his head and began reading from the paper. He sliced his arm open vertically, allowing the blood to fall to the soil below. The man was sweating, overheated in the sunlight. His speech wavered when the building around him began to shake, but the voice from the speakers encouraged him to continue.

Ronald fell to his knees, weakened from blood loss, but he continued to say the words. His skin was turning red from sunburn, though it seemed impossible for it to happen so quickly. The ground cracked beneath him, angered. The humans screamed. The camera dropped from its place on the wall but still watched the catastrophe before it. Ronald wasn't conscious when he fell into the earth. The voice spoke over the speakers again, calling the man's name.

The quakes stopped. Everyone stilled, waiting to hear Ronald call out for help. When he didn't, a few stepped forward and peered into the crevice. And screamed.

A Guise rose from the earth, bathing in the sunlight above.

The first one of many.

It grabbed the nearest victim, and soon, that human had transformed into a golden beast. The rest ran, naive to the only defense they had. None ran for the dark, only the light as they disappeared from the camera.

Yvaine paused the footage.

"We've known that it was the humans' fault all along, but to see it…" she whispered.

I unzipped one of the packs and opened to the first page of the first book I grabbed. I lifted it up and compared the words to the ones written on the computer. They were the same. "And our parents helped."

With dread pooling in our stomachs, we stared at the familiar names on the screen. The same ones that had authored the books we'd carried across miles.

Consultants:
Raymond Reynolds
Lynne Reynolds

Below, lies the blood of those who turned

Waiting for the return of awareness in the land of sorrow

But only when the voice of old is given life beneath rays of gold

And the bonds of peace have been bled

Will light shine from the inward soul again

I read the spell over and over again, wondering what had gone wrong. The doctor's handwriting had irritated me so much that I wrote it down myself on a separate paper, though it wasn't much better.

The spell site, according to all of Dr. Anderson's research as well as my parent's, was the correct spot. I'd combed through all of their books, and every piece of history had led them to Kirkwall—where the original spell had taken place. I thought on how terrible the world must have been for several species to willingly erase the magic from their bloodlines. All that power and knowledge—gone.

The Common animals had lost more than magic. They'd lost their intelligence. Their free will. Was that the future of humanity? Would we someday evolve into mindless creatures, surviving on nothing but instinct? I peered out the castle window and watched the Guise wander the court-yard.

We were already there.

It had been several weeks since finding the lab. Since then, we'd watched the surveillance footage of the backfired spell hundreds of times. I'd found Dr. Anderson's journal in his office. He'd been researching magic and Fae culture his entire life. Until one day, on an archaeological dig in Kirkwall, he found a scroll with the answer.

Covered in runes—a language even magic could not translate—an ancient spell was found. It had taken him three decades to translate it, bringing in consultant after consultant. The last ones had been my parents; the people that gave him the final piece of the puzzle. Before they disap-peared.

And his goal became clear: return magic to humanity. He had the right words, the location, the sun, and the blood. Yet, magic had not greet-ed us. Guise were born instead.

I read over his journal entries again, morbidly curious to discover what kind of person had been capable of murdering two people and bleed-ing out their children.

Arlen shifted below me, expelling smoke from his nostrils.

I chuckled, appreciating the comfort my friend provided.
I returned to the journal, and the feeling disappeared.

My most recent consultants have proven useful. For decades, I've searched for the key to unlock magic. Ever since I saw that fairy in my backyard wielding plant magic, when I was but a child, I'd needed to know. I'd needed to know what secrets the world had yet to tell.

Legends upon myths piled up, but eventually I found Fae who would tell me their histories. Of a time when all of Earth's peoples were one with magic. I can't say that I understand the ancient ones' decision to abolish the gift, but according to their reversal spell, I believe it is the time to bring it back.

"When the bonds of peace have been bled" These words encourage my beliefs. Humanity is in a time of peace. They have bled to make it happen. If not now, then when?

This spell is the answer. I know it is. But these foreign words have evaded me. Until now.

Raymond and Lynne had been doing their own research and had found a similar document in their travels. They managed to decipher the ancient language, something that I have regrettably failed to do. Those above me had grown impatient, due to my continued incompetence. No matter where it came from, though, it will benefit humanity. I am grateful for the contribution and the knowledge they have shared. Soon, magic will be a part of us again.

With hope,
-H.A.

Closing the faded journal, I left the office to do a perimeter check. Arlen had been sleeping peacefully at my feet, but he stood and followed.

The dark elves had yet to find us. Combining both Yvaine and my magic together, we were able to perform a cloaking spell over a shield incantation—something even cù-sìth could not sniff out. The power that had rushed through me… There was nothing like it. I agreed with the doctor in this one thing: magic was a gift.

But Yvaine disagreed. She'd forbade me to perform magic other than reinforcing the castle's barrier. She kept the spell book with her as a precaution, untrusting as usual.

My fist met the brick wall.

Cole had been training with me to strengthen my body, as well as relieve the anger inside. But the physical fighting wasn't enough. I needed something stronger.

Arlen whimpered and licked the bleeding wound. I sighed. "Sorry, Arlen." I began my trek down the hall again. "But we can't hide in here forever. We need to get stronger."

I reached the first doorway and stepped outside. The barrier was invisible to the eye, but I could feel it there. It was my magic. My kin's magic. I raised my hands in concentration, feeling the wall that protected us from intrusion and the cloak that hid it from the world. The walls were connected to us, so the original incantation didn't need to be said. A simple offering of myself kept the walls strong. It took what it needed, and I sagged against the door after it closed, exhausted. *One entrance done.*

After making my rounds, I found Yvaine and Cole in the lab. Cole was just as quick with the computer as my sister now. His fingers danced across the keyboard while Yvaine stood behind him. She turned and found me standing in the doorway with Arlen looking over my shoulder.

My sister's eyes were bloodshot from staring at the screen for weeks. I swore she'd seen all of time on that thing, searching for our parents, but she wasn't one to give up. "Any luck?" I asked.

She shook her head. "They never came in the building. The doctor left the castle a lot, though." She paused to gather her thoughts. "Memories have been slowly coming back to me ever since the elvish chief cast the revealing spell. Though, I didn't understand what was happening at the time, I remember our family traveling a lot. Meeting with strangers. Maybe even *him*." *Their killer.*

"Yeah, apparently our parents had their own way of reading runes. The journal said that they'd deciphered the language before they even met him." I rubbed what little hair had grown on my cheeks.

"What were they doing?" she whispered.

"The same thing as the doctor. Bringing magic back," Cole answered, spinning toward us in his chair. "I'm curious as to why they disappeared before the spell was performed."

"Maybe they knew it would fail?" I suggested.

"Then why wouldn't they try to stop it?" Yvaine argued.

"Whatever they did or didn't do doesn't matter anymore." I stroked Arlen's fur, and he purred. "The Guise exist, and the elves want to darken the world because of it." I paused, preparing for the fight. "We need to become stronger if we're going to defeat them."

"We're not going anywhere near them, Lugh." Yvaine was firm in her belief that we could hide forever.

Regurgitating an old argument, I said, "We can't stay in here much longer. The supplies are running out."

Yvaine straightened her back, peeved. "The eclipse is only days away. We can wait them out."

"There's no shortage of eclipses. They'll just use the next one. They will find us and take Cole unless we practice magic and learn to defend ourselves." Arlen backed away and left the room. Cole stared at Yvaine, and I wondered if he was going to side with me for once.

"If we use magic, they'll find us for sure," she argued, crossing her arms.

"That's a risk we're going to have to take. I mean, we're already using a shield incantation. How long before one of them passes by and notices it? Or that someone is living here? We're going mess up at some point." I ripped my hands through my shaggy hair, pulling out strands.

"That's what the cloaking spell is for! Enough Lugh! We're not exposing ourselves so you can satisfy your curiosity." She whipped her blonde hair aside in anger.

"It's not about *curiosity*. It's about survival." My head ached. I hadn't been eating enough because Yvaine failed to let us outside for anything other than to gather snow for water. My body still refused to heal. I was tired of limping around on twig legs.

"I'm doing what's necessary, Lugh. I wish you would trust me." Water met her eyes, and she blinked the tears away.

"Like you trust me? You haven't let me anywhere near the spell book," I growled.

"Lugh—"

"I promise not to use magic. Just let me study it, so someday, when you *deem it necessary*, I'll already know the spells." I held out my hand, anticipating another rejection.

To my surprise, the book was gently placed in my palm.

"Don't abuse my trust." Those were the only words she said before she marched out of the room and up the stairs. I stared at the book, nearly drooling with excitement.

"You know that she's keeping us alive, right?" Cole said, his eyes on me. The computer screens were shut down with a swift peck of his finger.

I nodded.

"I know why you want to use magic. It's powerful. Addicting." He stood and met my gaze, our eyes an even match. I'd grown in the past weeks despite my hunger. "Fear is powerful. Don't let it consume you."

The elf passed by me, but before he reached the stairs, I said, "Like you?"

Without missing one heartbeat, he responded, "Yes. Like me."

"I never thanked you for absorbing the darkness from me." I paused, refusing to turn. "I don't know what would have happened if you didn't. Thank you." I gripped the spell book hard, remembering the ink that had oozed from my skin. *The fear that had taken form.*

Cole snorted. "Don't thank me. That was the best thing that's ever happened to me. Other than your sister, of course."

I turned. "How so?"

The elf smiled and strode up the stairs.

Arlen was sitting in the corner of the lab, sniffing a glass tube.

"Deranged Fae. All of you."

I couldn't stand the stuffy castle air any longer. And since I wasn't allowed to leave through the front doors, I went to the roof. The spell book and journal were stacked in front of me. I'd been carrying books all over the castle in the past weeks simply to strengthen my muscles.

The air was crisp and unforgiving high above the ancient stones. And I had made an exciting discovery during my explorations, one that I'd neglected to share with the others. There was a landing pad built into the back side of the castle with a helicopter sitting within the painted marks, waiting to fly away.

I peered over the side, as I always did when I visited, and stared at the corpse splattered on the ground. The snow refused to cover the gruesome sight. They had chosen to jump rather than escape. If I had been standing on this edge a few months ago, I might have joined them at the bottom.

With the sun hovering over me, I felt better when I slid the helicopter's door open and made my way to the pilot's seat where it rested in shadow. There, I took inventory of the controls, as if it had changed since the last time I'd been there. The owner's manual had been an interesting read, and I was confident that if I tried, I could fly it. Though, the machine required fuel, which we did not have in supply.

Transfer magic can give dead things life, so long as the caster is willing to share their light.

The book's whispers came alive, startling me after being away from them so long.

Endowed weapons absorb their master's magic over time, so if the wielder is ever in need, they will always find a way to survive.

The skill needed to create endowed weapons was lost at the time of the Separation. None have been born since.

I pulled out the dagger and scrutinized it carefully. The runes seemed to twist and taunt me. That must have been the reason we couldn't read or speak runic. If the markings were as old as the weapons, maybe the language was lost with the rest of the knowledge. *My parents must have been very good at their job.*

I flipped through the spell book, reading over spells I thought would be useful. But not being able to practice what I studied quickly became infuriating.

I traded the spell book for the doctor's journal. I flipped through the pages, having already read everything. I scanned past several blank pages until I hit the back cover. There was another entry I never noticed before, being alone in the back of the book. The writing had been scribbled in haste, barely legible.

I was wrong. So very wrong.

I know that my superiors will never listen to me, but I can try to fix what is about to happen. The blood…blood. It was always about the blood. I'd always found it odd that Raymond and Lynne disappeared after gifting me with such vital knowledge. Lynne's heritage had been such a magnificent resource that I'd wanted to respect their wishes. But I was so wrong. They knew. They knew my interpretation of the spell wouldn't work. They kept a piece of the translation to themselves. A piece that I realized too late, because I trusted the wrong people.

For humanity to regain magic, it would take these ingredients:

> Land of sorrow—Kirkwall
>
> Rays of gold—perform the spell directly under the sun
>
> Voice of old given life—the translated reversal spell
>
> The bonds of peace that have been bled…

I never thought. I never imagined that it would mean something much different…

I should have known that they had the answer all along. If they knew the outcome, would they have translated the spell? I don't think so. But I will find them. And I will fix my mistake before the world collapses on us all.

I will find the children of peace and bleed them dry.

> God forgive me,
> H.A.

What followed was another copy of the spell with a new, vital addition to the text.

Below, lies the blood of those who turned
Waiting for the return of awareness in the land of sorrow
But only when the voice of old is given life beneath rays of gold
And the bonds of peace have been born and bled
Will light shine from the inward soul again

I closed the journal, my hands trembling.
"And the bonds of peace have been *born* and bled."
We were the children of peace. And we ended the world.

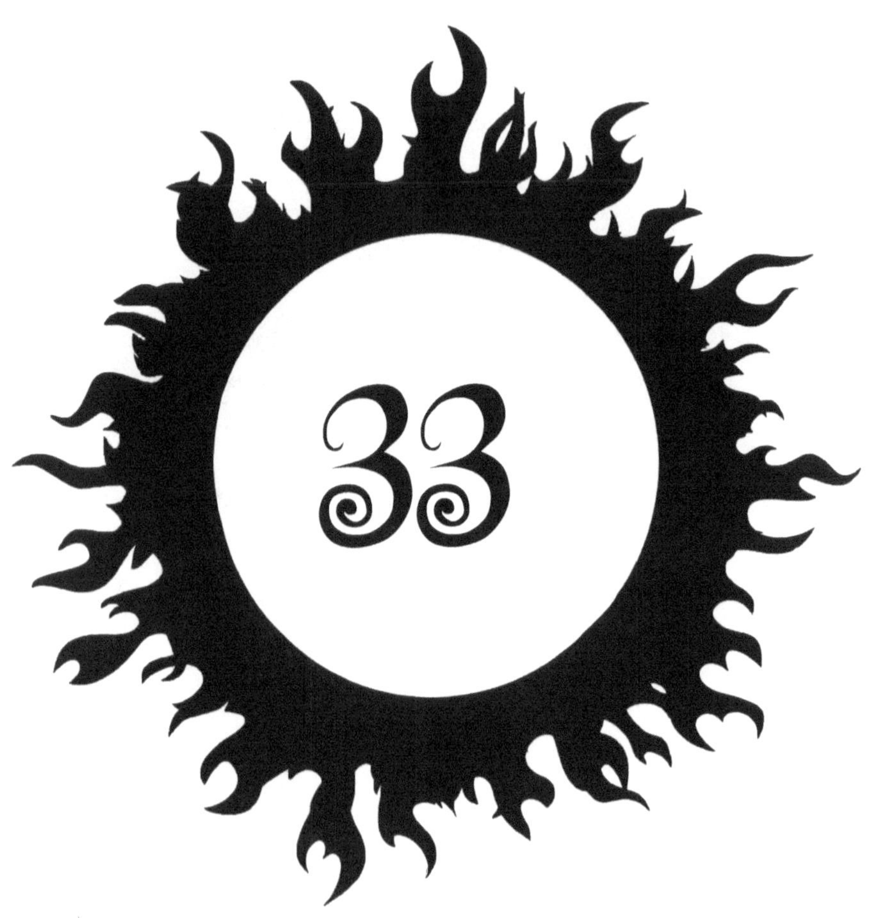

I stayed in the helicopter for the rest of the day, debating the choice. But honestly, it was never a choice. The problem was accepting the answer.

We didn't have to run anymore.

I added the additional words to my own scribbled version of the ancient spell. Stepping out and under the clear nighttime sky, I took a deep breath. The stars were bright. There was just enough light from the waning moon to allow Guise to exist and wander the courtyard. I held the journal in one hand and the spell book in the other. The whispers were quiet, as if they knew I needed the silence to think.

Was it really possible?

I strode into the castle. My heart was racing from excitement. I hadn't felt this way before—like there was something other than misery looming on the horizon. I allowed hope to fill my damaged veins and fuel my steps.

The castle was vast, so finding Yvaine and Cole wasn't easy. They weren't in the office or lab. I searched the lower floors and found Arlen sleeping by the front entrance. I itched behind his massive ears as I passed by, grateful for the guardian. I was about to start yelling for them when I heard voices coming from the east wing—the part of the castle that had been reserved for tourists. There were maps and pictures of clan leaders hanging on the walls in the corridor. I stopped before I turned the corner, hearing my name.

"Lugh has a point. There will always be another eclipse," Cole said, his voice gentle.

"You think I don't know that?" my sister growled.

"I think you're a wild animal that's been cornered. You want to fight." A chair's feet screamed as it slid across the floor.

"Of course I do. This place is creepy, and I want fresh meat," she acknowledged. "But this is the safest place to be. It's a fortress."

"So, we're going to stay here the rest of our lives?" Cole asked, amused.

Yvaine waited a moment before answering, "It's better than dying."

A heavy head pushed me from behind, and I fell forward and into my sister's line of sight. "Hey, guys," I said, as if I'd just arrived. Arlen chuffed and sauntered ahead of me. The room was large, filled with relics—items that had been cared for by the museum staff. They each had a description below them, describing what era they'd come from. I'd already studied each one, and found that I wasn't interested in anything that wouldn't help us leave this place. The tapestry on the wall fluttered when Arlen sat down beside it.

I rubbed the spell book for comfort before I started. "I think…" I took a breath. "I think I've found a way for us to leave."

Cole lifted a brow, and Yvaine sighed. "I've read all the spells in that book, Lugh. None of them can give us a permanent solution." Her forehead was pinched with stress.

"It's not from the spell book, and it is permanent." I smiled, excited.

"What did you find?" Cole asked. Yvaine turned to him, annoyed, but he dismissed her.

I opened to the last page in the journal and read the doctor's words aloud to them. "What do you think?"

"I think that I'm glad I killed the bastard." Yvaine ground her teeth so hard, I could hear it across the room.

"Cole?" I asked, begging him to see what I did.

The elf looked long and hard at the both of us before answering. "It's certainly an option."

"What is?" Yvaine said, confused.

I spoke before Cole had a chance. "We can fix it. All of it. We can cast the spell again, but right this time." I took the scribbled spell out of my pocket and handed it to her. "Imagine it, sis. A world without Guise. A world with magic."

Yvaine stared at the ancient spell, reading the new translation through. "You want to sacrifice yourself for this? Lugh, the world is going to be shit even without Guise. And magic… There's a reason our ancestors renounced it. People are always going to fight for power." She handed the paper back. "And most importantly, you would die. So, no, it's not an option."

"We don't know that it would kill us," I said, forcing myself to calm.

She gave me a dumbfounded expression, as if *I* was insane.

"Are you kidding me? The elves are literally going kill everyone on the planet when they find Cole. No one can survive a dark, frozen world. This spell and our blood are the only things that will stop that from happening. If the Guise are gone, the elves won't have a reason to hunt us.

We'll be free."

"We'll be dead."

"I don't care. Anything would be better than this darkness." I paused only because of the utter agony that shaped my sister's face. "Just let me do this. You don't have to be a part of it."

"You're still weak, Lugh. What you need is rest, not to be drained of blood. And honestly, considering that the good doctor translated it wrong the first time, we don't know if the new one is even right. He could be wrong again." Yvaine was stubborn, painfully so, but even she had to see that this was the only way. *The only way to stop surviving and finally live.*

"He's not wrong! Our parents kept the information from him before. This is right. I know it is, Yvaine. Why can't you see that?" I growled, slamming the journal on the floor. The thud boomed against the castle walls and carried down the halls. Arlen whined.

"I didn't risk everything to save you, just so you could die anyway!" Yvaine looked like she was going to hit me, but Cole placed his hand on her arm.

"Why did you save me just to bring me back to a dead world?" Whether or not the elves found us, I was going to die. Slowly. Alone. In the dark. "It's not just about us anymore. This affects everyone."

"I don't care about everyone," Yvaine spat.

"Even when they take Cole? Because you know they eventually will." There was no way she would let him die.

Yvaine's only answer was a glare.

I turned to Cole, desperate for his support. When I found none, I said, "I hope you see now that Yvaine isn't capable of kindness."

With sadness in his eyes, he said, "Don't say that about your sister."

Refusing to meet her gaze, I said, "Sister or not, she's no longer my family."

I left the room and ran for the roof, silent tears falling to the ancient castle floor, along with any hope that I'd had for a better life.

Checking that I wasn't followed first, I burst through the door and threw myself into the night. I screamed, letting out the anger boiling inside. The stars flickered in protest, as if I was disturbing their rest. "You're stars! Literal balls of light! You have no right to complain! You never have to worry about the dark because you are so much brighter and stronger than it." A sob broke loose from my chest. "You never have to worry about being alone. There's so many of you." The sobs turned into wails. I'd rarely cried in my life, and it seemed my body was making up for it now. I felt the pool of black still festering inside me. Every tear that bled from my eyes emptied the pool a little bit more, but I knew it would always be there. Cole hadn't taken it all from me. It filled with more black every time I had to run or hide. Every time Yvaine was hurt protecting me.

And it wasn't ever going to end.

I walked over to the roof's edge and stared down at the skeleton for the hundredth time, still clinging to the spell book. *You could end it.*

Frightened, I fell backward and landed on my side. The rough roof scraped my skin, and I bled onto the grey stone. Whimpering, I opened the book, flipped to a random page, and spoke the words without hesitation.

Raging light
Reveal your glow
Steal and flow
Pierce the night

The familiar burn of magic warmed my chest until it turned into pain. The familial light shone from every pore in my body. I was on fire, unable to scream or beg for Yvaine to help me. Similar to a lighthouse I'd seen on the coast, I was a beacon. A target.

The castle's shield shifted, cracking without the support of its wielder. My magic was being drained by the raging light. Yvaine would feel it breaking. She would reinforce it and find me.

I was blind again. The light forced my eyes closed. My flesh smelled like our dinner while it cooked over the fire. I rolled on the ground, hoping to smother the light, but it kept blazing—piercing the darkness. Any longer, and I would be burned alive.

With the only option being to help myself, I imagined that pool of black spilling over and dousing my light. It was the only thing I had left to give. The inky blackness moved slowly, running over every inch of my skin. The light dimmed as the darkness worked. My screams faded to shallow breaths.

I opened my eyes and closed the book.

Standing carefully, I examined my surroundings and found that the castle wall and roof had been singed, blackened by the intense burn. My skin was red and irritated and covered in ink, but it had survived.

I looked out to the forest, and my heart stopped. In that moment, I wondered how much more my heart would take before it gave out. Because in the distance, where the moonlight met the woodland's edge, shadows were rushing toward the castle.

The dark elves had found us.

In my shock, I tried to recall the name of the spell they'd planned to use for Cole during the eclipse, but none came to mind. That was because it wasn't meant to exist. No one had done it before. And for good reason. A spell like that could only be called Death.

"Yvaine!" I screamed. Adrenaline kept my feet moving and terror had me tripping over them. The cracks in the shield weren't healing. Each moment, the fissures spread. "Yvaine!"

"Lugh?" Cole called. The elf rounded the corner and nearly slammed into me. He immediately scrutinized the ink stains on my skin.

"Where's my sister?" I implored. "The shield is coming down!" My heart was pounding so hard that it hurt.

"We know. She's at the front entrance trying to salvage it. What happened?" he asked, as we ran in Yvaine's direction.

"I'm sorry! It's my fault! I was angry, and I used magic. I'm sorry!"

"Lugh, calm down. We can fix the shield." Cole didn't know. He didn't know how badly I'd screwed up.

"They're here, Cole. The elves saw me," I said.

The elf stumbled, but he kept moving. "Okay." And the way he said it made my gut drop. This wasn't like before. It wasn't just a couple of humans, or even the elves chasing us through the forest. We were trapped. There was no option other than to fight. And we weren't ready. I wasn't ready.

Transfer magic can give dead things life, so long as the caster is willing to share their light.

The book's voice snapped me out of my terror. Why was it repeating this? It hadn't repeated anything before. What could I do with this piece of knowledge?

We reached the front and found Arlen guarding Yvaine. She had her hands against the closed door, repeating the incantation over and over again, spitting it at the entry in frustration. She fell to her knees.

"What's wrong?" Cole kneeled beside my sister and helped her stay upright.

"I can't hold it by myself," she breathed.

"They're here," I said, afraid of her response.

Quickly, she turned to me. "I know. The elves are trying to get in through the weak spots. I can't hold it much longer, Lugh. Help me."

A tear ran down my cheek at the request. Instead of begging for her forgiveness, like I wanted to, I knelt beside her and looked inward. I said the spell over and over, but the magic wasn't there, or it was too small. It was barely a glimmer inside me. The black pool had doused the flames, and the light hadn't had a chance to heal yet. "I can't. I used too much magic."

Yvaine wept, forcing every ounce of magic out of her body and into that shield, giving every bit of her soul to the cause.

"Stop!" There was another way. That was what the book had been trying to tell me all along.

"They'll get in, Lugh!" she choked.

Cole's face was pure agony, unable to help the one he loved.

"There's another way out of here. I need you save the rest of your magic for it. Stop!" I covered her mouth with a trembling hand so that she would stop whispering the shield incantation. "Follow me!" I paused. "But Mother and Father's work…" I stepped in the direction of the lab where the books were kept.

Yvaine grabbed my arm. "Leave them." She managed a small, sad smile. "We've both read everything. Their life's work is with us now." She pressed her hand against my heart, leaning against Cole for support. Arlen growled at the door.

I nodded, unable to express the grief. It was as if we were losing them all over again. But there was no time. If we wanted a future, we'd have to leave the past behind. I clutched the dagger at my side and felt the weight of our parent's sword hanging beside it. "This way."

When we stepped onto the roof the shield shattered completely. "Get in!" I handed Yvaine the spell book and said, "There's a spell for transfer magic somewhere in here. Share your light with the helicopter, and it should come to life." I took the pilot's seat and nearly threw up, knowing what I was about to do.

"Where?" she said, panicked. She placed the book on her lap inside the flying machine. The pages opened on their own and flipped to the middle. Yvaine was startled, but decided that it wasn't the time to question the living thing in her hands. Cole settled in beside her and Arlen after him. The helicopter sank when the massive beast climbed on.

"Here it is, Soul Sharing."

To the slumbering, I say wake
To the dead, I offer life
For I have much
And you have none
For a time, you need not lay alone
For a time, I beseech you to share

The helicopter roared to life. The buttons on the panel lit with purple light. I laughed, hysterical, until I saw shadows climbing up the side of the castle. Concentrating, I flipped the switches and pushed the buttons that the manual had instructed me to use. The blades that rested for thirteen years were slow to move, but after a moment, and Yvaine's continued chanting, the strange wings circled. It sounded like a giant wasp boring down on us. I grabbed the stick and placed my feet on the petals, realizing just how out of my depth I was.

I moved one controller slightly, and the machine groaned in protest. "Any day now, Lugh!" Yvaine called over the sound of the engine.

Cole placed his hand on my shoulder and said, "Remember to

breathe. You've studied the manual. You can do this."

I peered over my shoulder at him, shocked. His bow scraped against the roof of the machine.

The elf breathed out a laugh, just as nervous as the rest of us. "We knew where you were the whole time, Lugh. It's our job to protect you."

Our job. Not just Yvaine's.

I couldn't allow the dark elves to take Cole. He'd become part of our family. And we fought to the end for our family. The shadows drew closer. I gripped the controls and managed to get the craft off the castle roof. It wavered as I experimented with the movements. I was sure that I'd managed to figure it out, but the machine was sinking toward the courtyard. "Why isn't it working?" I growled.

The shadows abandoned the stronghold and slithered toward us. A pack of cù-sìth were below us, nipping at the machine's feet. Arlen growled and lunged at them through the window. The helicopter tipped sideways, and Yvaine and Cole had to cling to the seats so they wouldn't fall into him. I pulled and turned the controls to balance us, but Arlen was too heavy. "The machine can't take this much weight," I said, my voice dead.

No. We couldn't leave him behind again. Arlen…

"They'll kill him if he's caught. Cù-sìth are bonded with the elves and serve only them. He's broken a sacred agreement," Cole explained.

"We're elves! He hasn't broken anything!" I shouted, grieving.

"No, he hasn't. But they won't see it that way." I turned and met Cole's gaze. It was utterly peaceful. Determined. "They'll stop hunting you if they get what they want."

"Don't you dare!" Yvaine threatened. She was weakening. Her magic was feeding this beast of a machine. How much could she give?

"I'm not going to let one of my family members go into battle alone. I already failed him once because I was selfish and wanted to stay with you." He held Yvaine's face in his hands. "This way, everyone has a chance to survive."

Yvaine stared at the elf with piercing eyes. "But I want to live."

"We will." The elf placed his forehead against Yvaine's, and she let out a sob. "Go to Kirkwall. Perform the spell. We will find each other after. Arlen and I will stall them as long as we can." Cole pressed his lips against Yvaine's, knowing what he said might not be true—that we might never see him again. "You give me a reason to live," he said.

The elves had reached us. Arrows clattered against the metal machine, useless. But then one freezing arrow pierced the wall. Ice spread from the arrowhead. The metal around it froze over. More followed, weakening the metal. We'd sunk so low that the cù-sìth were able to pound against the weak spots. The screeching metal rang in my ears despite the engine's roar.

Cole slid the door open. Yvaine sent out a flare of magic to block the oncoming arrows, and the machine lowered farther. I steered the helicopter away from the attack as well as I could. Arlen had been concentrated on defending us the whole time, growling at his own kin, but now he looked back at me with a farewell in his white eyes.

"Thank you," I whispered, assured that he'd heard me.

"Don't!" Yvaine said, and lunged for Cole as he jumped out after Arlen.

Without the extreme weight of the cù-sìth, the adjustments I'd made before had us flying fast and hard to the opposite side and right into the horde of elves. The blade cut the snow, and one could only hope that one of the Fae had been hit, too.

I corrected before we crashed and looked back at a sobbing Yvaine. "Land! We need to help them!" She prepared to jump. I reached back and grabbed her arm, forcing her back inside. Controlling the machine one-handed was difficult, but my sister continued to fight me. "Let me go!" she demanded.

"If you go after them, we'll all die! Yvaine, I need you here." *For more reasons than one.* I needed her to feed the machine, yes, but there was no way I could perform the ancient spell without her. The fate of the world was a heavy burden to bear, and I could only do it if she was by my side.

"No! It's my fault they're after him! I was the one who told the chief to use Cole!" I pulled Yvaine back again. "I was trying to save his life. I didn't know the elves would… I didn't know." She struggled to remove my hand, pulling with all her strength. In that moment, I realized how much stronger I was than her.

"It's too late, Yvaine. All we can do is listen to Cole." She met my gaze, tears spilling over. "I need you to share your light. Please, sis. Let it go." My sister fell back into her seat and whispered the incantation, but she continued to stare out the open door.

Confident that she wasn't going to jump, I adjusted the controls, and we rose high in the air. Over the courtyard. Above the trees. Above the castle. We soared north, following the stars. Before the town below disappeared from our view, we saw Arlen running with Cole on his back. The elf was firing arrow after arrow from his bow at the Fae hunting him, the arrowheads alive with Arlen's flames.

The elf and cù-sìth vanished into the tree line, leaving us with no way to know how far they were able to run before the Fae trapped them.

he sun rose above the horizon, painting the sky with fire. Other than the machine's growls, there was no sound. We hadn't spoken. There were no words sad or great enough to express how we felt about our family's sacrifice.

The controls were mastered, and I flew us through the air with ease. We passed over forests and towns. We'd flown over Stirling before I realized we were off course. Yvaine hadn't reprimanded me for the mistake. She simply kept whispering the Soul Sharing incantation under her breath and stared out the window, as if she was waiting for Cole and Arlen to miraculously appear.

I sighed, exhausted. I hadn't slept in two days, but of course, sleep didn't come easy for us. Even when we found the time, both of us had nightmares. Lost in thought, I pondered if this kind of life had aged us. Yvaine had told me once that it was a well-known fact in the Old World that stress harmed people's bodies. What were we now? In our fifties? It certainly felt like it.

The sky was clear, but I could see dark clouds looming in the distance. Worried, I thought on the spell. It needed direct sunlight. Would the weather end up dooming the world?

An alarm sounded in the cockpit, and the helicopter veered to the left due to my surprise. A rapid light shone from the panel. "What's that mean?" Yvaine asked, her voice thick.

Staring at the light, I recalled, "It's the Geiger Counter. It senses radiation."

"Oh no." Yvaine rushed to the window. "Where are we?"

"I think somewhere over Aberdeen," I answered. "Why?"

"The humans sent nuclear bombs to the north, trying to kill the Guise. We need to fly away from the radiation. Let the alarm guide you," she instructed. Though it was another dire situation, I was glad to see that Yvaine had woken from her grief.

"What will happen if we don't?" I moved the machine to the right until the alarm stopped screaming. We were hovering over water now. The waves were calm, thankfully, but the panic still gripped my gut tight.

"What do you think? This whole planet wants us dead. Even the thing that was supposed to save us." Boiling in her anger, she added, "And why are we so off course? We're never going to reach Kirkwall in time at this pace."

"Sorry, it's not like I have a map in front of me. I'm going off memory from the ones I saw in Mother and Father's books." I veered left again, wanting to be over land, but the alarm sounded again, and I had to retreat.

"The mountains were the farthest we'd ever been north. What if Kirkwall was bombed? What if we can't go near it?"

Yvaine shrugged. "Then we can't. We'll have to find another way to survive." With the way she spoke, I suspected that my sister hoped this was the case. Even if Cole and the rest of the world died. "Cole is very good at escaping. He'll find a way to hide from the elves until we can find them again," she said.

"Yvaine…"

"What?" she snapped.

"Cole had magic stored inside his body before," I reminded her.

"And?"

"When he was shot, and even when he was being tortured, he didn't use it to heal or escape. And now he doesn't have any." The alarm notified us of radiation, even over the water. I veered left and found a clear area.

"What are you saying?" My sister's voice cracked.

"I'm saying that we should do everything we can to perform this spell."

My sister didn't speak to me again until we'd passed over the North Sea and hovered over Orkney Islands. Fortunately, the radiation had ended at the shoreline before we crossed the water.

Both of us peered out of the windows and down onto the crumbling human towns. Each one had swarming Guise. No sign of life, Common or Fae, was seen. This place was the outbreak's origin. The chances of anyone surviving were slim, especially after so long.

Approaching Kirkwall, I saw the docks. There were many boats still tied to the walkways. We'd never used a boat before. And I found it strange that Yvaine wouldn't have tried to take us somewhere else; safety could have been just beyond the sea. But understanding my sister answered the question for me: it's better to fight the evil you know than the one you don't.

I thought the government facility would be hard to find, but luck was on our side for the moment. "Land there," my sister said. Below us dwelled a large fortified building surrounded by a metal fence. But what stood out was the massive opening in the top of the east end. We hovered over the building and peered into the hole, seeing the familiar cracked earth.

"There are Guise everywhere." The sun was near its highest point, and the rays cast down on the landing pad outside the fence.

"Just land. I have enough to cast a darkness spell." Yvaine was sweating. She was near her limit and we both knew it. I felt for the magic within and found it cowering beneath the black pool, as if it was afraid to expose itself again.

"We'll make it quick then," I said.

As we neared the ground, Yvaine cast the dark cloud. The Guise kept their distance as I rushed to land for the first time. It wasn't smooth by any means, but we didn't crash. And Yvaine was able to release the transfer spell and concentrate on the keeping us in the dark. The blades slowed to a stop, and I climbed into the back with Yvaine.

I slid open the door, allowing the cold winter air to bathe us in ice. Already shivering, we ran for the building's front door. To both of our relief, it wasn't locked. Slamming the door closed, we felt our way down the dark hallways. The building was almost as cold as the dark elves' castle.

"Do you think we're lucky enough to find a generator here?" I shivered beneath my thin jacket.

"Probably, I don't think the people here had time to take anything when it happened." Yvaine tucked her hair into her jacket for extra warmth.

Following the maze-like hallways together, I said, "I'm sorry for what I said before."

"Don't be. It's all right."

"No, it's not." I took Yvaine's hand and squeezed it tight. She looked to me with surprise, and I realized that I hadn't reached for her hand in years. She was always the one reaching out to me.

My sister gave me a small smile. "You're forgiven if you find us some warmth."

I laughed. "Deal." We opened door after door, searching for anything that could do just that. "If Arlen were here, we could just stand near him. He's always so warm."

Yvaine didn't say anything. She just kept searching for heat. For food. For water. She was trying to survive. If the spell worked, would things like that become unimportant? Would the world finally be at peace? We wouldn't know until we tried.

"Here," I said. There was a room with a breaker and a generator already attached. I flipped on the main lights, and the building lit up with florescent bulbs.

"Wait!" Yvaine warned.

But it was too late.

Guise awoke with vengeance. People that had slumbered in the dark since the Collapse came to life. Their sunlight skin and golden eyes were frightening. The moans of anguish filled the facility with torment. Three of them manifested directly in front of me, blocking my path to the breaker. I drew the iron sword while Yvaine hurried to create the dark cloud. It formed and dispersed several times before she said, "Run!"

We flew down the hallway only to find more Guise. There were dozens. And all I could think of was the surveillance footage of the failed reversal spell. All the scientists and soldiers. They stood in front of me now.

The monsters had cornered us. We both struggled to move past them and find a way outside, but there would only be more to find. With no other choice, we swung our swords and cut through their ghostly bodies. The Guise vanished like tendrils of smoke, but their agonizing voices stayed with me.

"There are too many!" I said, frightened. All it would take was one touch, and we would become what we most feared.

"We don't have a choice, Lugh! I'm out of magic." For once, she allowed fear to seep into her voice. This was our worst nightmare come to life. Throughout my upbringing, we'd always been able to run or hide. But this was…war. We were soldiers just like the ones who had turned and currently advanced on us. I felt for the small piece of light inside me, drowning in inky black. It was swimming to the surface, but it wasn't going to save us in time.

"Together, then." We worked to clear the facility. Fighting back-to-back, we moved slowly down the halls, not allowing one golden finger to touch us.

Eventually, we found ourselves at the spell's site, the roof nonexistent. The sun had moved on, so the rays didn't directly hit the exposed soil. We had missed our chance to perform the spell today.

The solar eclipse was tomorrow.

Yvaine and I swung our swords one last time. The final two Guise vanished from existence, and we collapsed.

Breathing hard, I asked, "What will happen to the Guise when we perform the reversal spell?"

Leaning on her sword, she said, "They'll die, I think."

"You don't think they'll come back? Be who they once were?" I asked.

Yvaine met my concerned stare. "We didn't have a choice, Lugh. Don't feel guilty about what we just did. Even if the Guise do revert back to who they were, we sacrificed a few to save them all."

I nodded in agreement, but I questioned how that made us different from Dr. Anderson.

After a long rest, we continued our search for supplies. The generator had allowed us to heat the building. Things like food, water, propane, and fuel were all in full supply. Yvaine had been right, no one had a chance to escape when the Guise were born, so of course, everything was stocked.

We kept the lights off just in case we missed one or two, even after night fell. I searched the office's anyway, finding things like family photos, knick-knacks, and clothing. I gathered as many as I could carry and brought them to the spell's site. Against the opposing wall, where I saw the first person transformed, I organized the items and placed a candle in front, lighting it with an old match. "I'm sorry," I whispered to the shrine.

It was our fault that they'd turned at all. If our parents had given us over, we could have brought magic to the world and prevented its destruction. And years later, we came back and killed them—ruining any chance they had at a life again. There hadn't been one corpse in the whole facility. No one had died here until we came.

"It's not your fault, brother." Yvaine kneeled beside me. "It was the only way to survive."

"I know."

Considering, she said, "Then why are you taking responsibility for it?"

"Don't you?" I asked.

"Yes, but that's my job. I'm the eldest." Yvaine took my hand and shoved my coat's sleeve up. She pointed at the bulging, darkened veins. "Today was my fault, just like this was."

I pulled the sleeve back down. "Not everything is your fault."

"Yes it—"

"No," I interrupted. "It's not." I sighed, unable to hold the truth in any longer. "Our parents…"

Yvaine sucked in a breath. "I know, Lugh. If I wouldn't have distracted Mother—"

"It's my fault."

"What?" she asked, confused.

"When the doctor came to the door… I'd lost my toy, and Mother wouldn't help me look, so I decided to do it myself." I exhaled a shaky breath. "I couldn't find it in the house, and I wanted to check outside. I escaped out the cat's door… I'm not sure how long I was gone… It only felt like a moment, but before I knew it, Father was screaming my name. I heard loud pounding at the front door."

Yvaine let go of my hand and clutched her mouth, fighting to keep the emotions inside.

"By the time I got back inside, Father had taken down the barricade and opened the door. Mother tried to stop him, but it was too late. The doctor was standing there, and he…" A sob escaped. "See? It isn't your fault, sis. It's mine. They opened that door because they were looking for me. I'd broken the rules and went outside. They're dead because of a stupid toy tree. I killed them." I wanted to reach out to her, but I couldn't find the courage. "I'm sorry that I never told you before. I was ashamed."

Yvaine lunged and held me tight. "Don't you dare think that. You did not kill them. It was an accident. Everyone could have done something to change the outcome." She clutched me tighter. "I was supposed to be watching you. I was the one who hid your toy. You were *four*. This is *not* your fault." Her tears dripped down the back of my neck, but I didn't care.

"It's not yours, either, sis."

Weeping, she finally acknowledged, "I know."

Even if their death wasn't our fault, the birth of the Guise was. "They saved us, and it caused…this…" I stammered. "It's about time we fixed it."

"Fixed it? Lugh, this isn't our burden to bear. It's not our fault that the ancient humans took away magic. And it's certainly not our fault that the humans wanted to bring it back. They should have never touched it." Yvaine stood, staring at the shrine. "And we might make it worse."

"There's no way it could be worse."

"That's just it. It could be." She began to pace. "The spell book has the transformation spell the dark elves used. It's a new moon tonight. We could protect ourselves."

"What are you saying? Become like them? Drink Fae blood? Even if we did, it takes thirteen moon cycles." I couldn't believe what I was hearing…but actually, I did. Of course Yvaine would try to find another way out of this. "What about Cole? He's not going to survive the spell. All that magic will kill him! And Arlen… He's waiting for us to save him."

"The chances of saving them are so slim, Lugh." Her tears had dried, and someone I hadn't seen in a long while appeared. "It's about survival now. The reversal spell will kill us. You. At least with the transformation, we stand a chance."

I stood, my legs steady for once. "Don't do this to me."

Baffled, she said, "Save your life?"

The opening above us had displayed the stars earlier, but now, the clouds hid them from view. If they didn't clear by tomorrow… "Don't make me exist in the dark anymore. I can't do it," I begged.

The black pool boiled inside me, festering, reminding me of all the darkest times in my life. I remembered laying in that poison. At the end, when Yvaine was fighting to save my life, hiking through the mountains with me on her back. When I heard her crying over my dead body. *I had been dead.* But something pulled me back. There was light. I thought I had lost feeling a long while before, but it was there, the sunlight on my skin. I felt it warm me. The Guise made me fear it all my life, but I had wanted it so badly that I chose to rise from the black poison and run to it…sunlight…hope.

With dead eyes, Yvaine said the worst words ever spoken. "There's no other way, Lugh."

Losing faith, I said, "Don't do this. I can't perform it without you."

"I know."

With those words, I left my sister under the falling snow. It's icy flakes were unforgivably cold. But there was no use complaining because by tomorrow the whole world would feel the same.

I'd found a dark corner and curled up in it. It was pitch black. There was no sound.

This was our future. Complete and utter nothingness.

I couldn't do it.

I'd perform the spell without my sister. The spell didn't specify how many needed to be born and bled. For a spell of this magnitude, it would need a lot of blood, though. So, I'd thought if there was two of us… It didn't matter.

Yvaine had left to hunt a Fae. The blood we'd drink from it would begin the transformation so long as we did so under a new moon. There was no moon to be seen outside. I unsheathed the dagger, unable to see the intricate runes etched into its shining blade. I felt along its edge and cut my finger.

Who was I kidding? I wasn't enough. I might as well wither away with the rest of them. It was what I deserved. I allowed the dagger to light one last time. Though, this light wasn't from me or Yvaine. It lit on its own, like it had its own amethyst soul.

"Lugh?"

I opened my mouth to respond but nothing came out. So, I let the dagger glow until my sister found me, then it dimmed, and the magic disappeared. I didn't plan on lighting it again. "You have the blood? What was it? Gnome? Elf?" I asked.

Yvaine flinched but sat beside me. "No. I couldn't do it."

"Oh? I guess we're just going to freeze to death then. Well, at least we won't feel anything after a while." I sheathed the dagger and bowed my head, tired.

"Mother spoke to me."

I turned to my sister, though I couldn't make out her face expression. "Great, you lost your mind. We'll just add it to the list of awful things that have happened."

"Shut up and listen," she said, frustrated. "Here, it's easier if I show you."

"Where did you see her? Out in the wilderness? Maybe it was just a wisp playing with your mind," I suggested.

Yvaine growled and grabbed my head between her hands. "Share the past with that of my bloodline."

Before I could pull away, a memory flooded my thoughts.

"Yvaine, my lovely daughter, I care for you and your brother so much."

"I love you, too, Mother," I said, though it wasn't my voice, it was Yvaine's.

"I need to tell you something. Just in case anything happens to your father and me." Mother sat beside me, or rather my sister, on the couch.

"What's wrong? Are you sick?" I asked, panicked.

"No, Yvaine. Listen carefully." Once Mother was sure I was going to listen, she continued, "You haven't met any of your extended family, and I'm sorry for that." She took my hand. "But they wanted me to keep something from humans. It was my job to hide the truth from them."

"What truth?" I asked.

"Magic," she explained. "They wanted me to keep magic from them. But then I met your father, and I decided that hiding it was wrong. Humans deserved it. They are kind, brilliant, creative, and full of love."

"Where's the magic? Is it here?" I looked around the house, expecting something new to appear.

"Yes and no." Mother put her hand over my heart. "It's in here. Only you can bring it out."

"Does that mean everyone has it now?" I was excited to use magic. All the fairy tales had magic, and all of them had happy endings.

"No. I tried to give it to humans. I did. But the cost was too great." A tear slid down her cheek.

"Why are you crying?" Tears welled up in my own eyes, though I didn't know what was wrong.

"Because you and Lugh are worth more to me than all the magic in the world. Remember that, will you?"

"Yes." Mother was beginning to worry me, and I leaned in to hug her. "It's going to be okay."

She laughed. "Yes, everything will be okay. But I need you to do something for me now. Can you do that?"

"What do you need?" I heard Lugh run into the living room, his little feet slapping against the hardwood floor.

"I need you to let it go, Yvaine. This memory, just for now. Let it go." Her hands were gentle as they brushed out the tangles in my hair. I was so relaxed. Tired.

Lugh jumped into my lap and laughed. Startled, I asked, "Should I get Lugh something to eat?"

Mother smiled. "Yes, that would be lovely." She squeezed Lugh's cheek. "You have such a good sister."

The four-year-old boy asked, "Am I a good brother?"

"Yes you are," I said, confident in my answer.

Yvaine released me, and I snapped back to reality, my head aching. "What the hell?"

"You were right. We are the last ingredient for the spell. Mother said as much." I heard her sniff, trying hide her tears. There had been so much crying lately, I was dehydrated again.

"And? I already knew that." What was her point? It didn't change anything.

"*I* didn't. I needed proof if we were going to risk our lives for it." She sighed. "And I needed to realize that you are a good brother."

"Gee, thanks."

"I mean, if you really think that this is the right path, I trust you to make the choice for us." She shifted, and her sword scraped against the floor, the metal slicing into the cement.

Trust you to make the choice… With a smile, I asked, "So, we don't have to drain any Fae blood tonight?"

My sister took my hand. "The only blood being drained is ours, tomorrow, under the sun."

35

The clouds dispersed by early morning. We risked going outside, simply so we could watch the sun rise. Neither of us cast the dark cloud because we needed to save our magic for the reversal spell, and we also wanted to enjoy the sun. It could have been our last chance.

"Where do you think Cole and Arlen are right now?" Yvaine asked, her voice calm.

In the dark stronghold. Trapped. Tortured. "I think Arlen was too fast and Cole too clever to ever be caught by those idiots. They're probably at the red water getting high, laying back while we do all the work."

Yvaine laughed. "But Arlen can't get high."

"Then he's probably taking a nice swim. All that fire in him probably warmed the water. So, they're enjoying the hot springs." Glancing around, I watched for approaching Guise. Luckily, they were distracted by the birds that had come to visit.

"Yeah, Arlen hunted and Cole gathered. They're feasting on meat and berries right now, while we have to eat stale chips." Yvaine smiled, and her eyes warmed. The sun cast comforting heat on us, and I was content despite the chill. "That bastard," she whispered. "Cole never said that he loved me before jumping out of the helicopter."

"I think the jump implied it," I commented.

Yvaine wrapped her hand around my waist, and I placed my arm over her shoulder. The hill we stood on looked out over the water, where the ferries and smaller boats floated. The dark water glimmered, reflecting the rays. "When this is all over, we should explore more. Take a boat and go somewhere new."

"It's about time," I said.

Neither one of us wanted to leave the sunny hill, but the birds had left, and the Guise turned their attention on us. Their moans still gave me chills, but for the first time, I questioned if they were meant to warn us.

We made it to the front door just in time, and locked it behind us for good measure. We walked down the hallways slowly, acknowledging that the steps we took might be our last. The main room was larger and more intimidating than it was the night before. The sky was daunting, the openness of it. The firepit we made last night was ready to be lit. I double checked that the sword was hanging at my side. The iron blade shone with a personality all its own.

I went to unsheathe the dagger and my gut dropped.

"Where—"

"Calm down. It's right here." Yvaine waved the dagger from her place at the center of the room. I'd been so distracted, I hadn't felt her take it, but she was a natural thief. "I just wanted to hold it for a bit. Sentimentality and all that." My sister cast Inner Fire and flames flowed from the dagger into the pit. The smoke was calming, reminding me of all the fires we had shared together.

"You don't have to give it back if you don't want to."

"Nah. It's yours now. Do what you will with it." Yvaine stroked the blade's edge lovingly. It had kept us alive for so many years. The endowed dirk had become part of our family, too. I joined her in the center, and we both sat down on the earth near the crevice. I'd avoided looking down at it, but Yvaine couldn't help herself. "Deep," she commented.

"It'll probably get deeper and wider during the spell. How are we supposed to avoid falling in?" The thought of being buried alive made my heart race, and I clutched my sword's handle.

"Run, I suppose. So, don't pass out like the first guy," she said, her voice even.

"Great."

She shrugged. "We've survived this long. What's another disaster compared to our luck?"

"You're being awfully positive today." As much as Yvaine could be positive that is.

"What else do I have to lose? Might as well try it." My sister took a long time doing her hair. She tied the end of her intricate braid with the hairband from her wrist.

"Have someone to impress?" I asked.

"Just me."

The first rays of sun shone over the facility's walls. A few minutes more had them warming the earth beneath us. Yvaine was breathing hard, afraid. I was, too. Acknowledging all the sacrifices she'd made for me, I said, "Live or die. We do it together, sister."

We joined our left hands, and she nodded. "Together." Yvaine placed the dagger in my hand, motioning for me to start. "Horizontal not vertical," she reminded me. The first Guise had drained his blood too quickly, despite having the wrong heritage anyway. But honestly, it reminded me of the bonds that tied us. The ancient ones did like their metaphors. *At least it was better than what the desperate doctor had in mind.*

My hand shook as it sliced into Yvaine's wrist, but she didn't make a sound. I looked up to find her smiling, encouraging me.

"What? You afraid of a little cut?" she teased, as her blood poured onto the ground and soaked into the soil.

"Show off," I muttered, cutting my own wrist. "Shit!" I spit. But I held onto my sister and the blade.

The sunlight dimmed, and I was worried that the clouds had returned, but it was much worse.

"The eclipse is starting," Yvaine warned. "Say the words."

I nodded, refusing to look up at the shadow.

Below, lies the blood of those who turned
Waiting for the return of awareness in the land of sorrow
But only when the voice of old is given life beneath rays of gold
And the bonds of peace have been born and bled
Will light shine from the inward soul again

Yvaine's voice joined with mine. Immediately, the ground began to shake. The crevice rumbled but didn't spread. We both watched it, ready to leap out of the way if necessary. But as the blood drained from my body, I didn't know if I would be able to move fast enough. Our blood mixed and soaked into the earth. Dark blood rose up, creating a pool of its own. It was the ancient ones returning to the land of sorrow.

As Yvaine continued to chant the spell, I cast Healing Fire on both of us, the fire from the pit feeding the incantation. Yvaine's voice strength-ened, but her cut did not close, for it was a wound of self-sacrifice. Amethyst smoke cocooned us in healing magic, but my body still wouldn't accept it. If I didn't want to heal, I wasn't going to.

I nodded to Yvaine to reassure her. Her face was pinched with worry, but she didn't dare stop saying the spell. We couldn't risk it going unsaid during any of this. One of us had to be chanting at all times.

It felt as if the mountains were crashing down, and I was worried that the sea would retaliate. It wasn't long before I had to lay down. Yvaine came with me, clutching my hand tight. The walls around us were cracking. The motion from the shaking earth made me nauseous. Equipment crashed to the ground, breaking apart after thirteen long years of stillness.

The ancient ones' blood had risen high enough to soak into my clothing. How many had died to banish magic? Would two of us be enough to bring it back? Yvaine was resting beside me, her blonde hair now dipped in red. I fed her the healing incantation again, keeping her strong. Again, I tried to heal myself. And again, the flames were smothered.

The walls fell and sunlight poured in.

The cries of Guise were heard even over the crumbling chaos. The sunlight bathed me in warmth, yet I could no longer feel it—I had lost too much blood. *You're not going to survive this.*

Still chanting, Yvaine reached her free hand out to me and held my cheek. Her blue eyes that were so much like mine said everything. "We are going to live."

Kissing our joined hands, she let go and stood, unsteady on her feet. She drew her sword and faced the approaching Guise, still, she never stopped chanting.

I couldn't stand. I couldn't move. The dagger was cold in my limp hand. The spell formed on my lips, but the sound was small, and I hoped that the ancient ones didn't mind. Yvaine took her first swing, and the Guise vanished with a scream. Their gold forms blended with the sun shining behind them, so much so, it looked as if Yvaine was fighting nothing—lies whispered in the wind, frightening those who crossed their path.

All I could do was bleed and chant. Bleed and chant.

Our ancestors words flowed through me and into the air, giving them life after centuries of silence. Maybe it would be enough. Maybe it was enough to die trying. It was better than doing nothing.

Just then, the sunlight that Yvaine swung her sword at became visible. A shadow was cast across the ground, over my eyes. A human stood there. She was small and frightened, shielding herself from the swinging sword. Yvaine looked back at me and smiled.

The Guise were turning back.

A rush of emotion coursed through me—something I'd never felt before.

Desperate to heal, I looked inward and into that pool of black. It wasn't as full as it had been, but there was enough to stop me from moving on.

Then suddenly, I realized… I *wanted* to move on.

I'd said as much to Cara, but I hadn't truly meant it. I was wandering through my life, waiting for something good to happen. I'd been harboring all the bad, clinging to it for survival because that had been all I'd known. *Survival.*

It was time to let it go.

Instead of expelling the ink like before, I cast Healing Fire one last time. The pool didn't empty or move. It burned. The black boiled and burned away. Its smoke mixed with the familial light and vanished into the brilliance that was our magic.

My mind was finally clear. And it told me that I'd lost too much blood. I still couldn't move, and it had taken the rest of my magic to burn away the darkness. I no longer felt that glimmer of light.

There were more humans and animals and Fae when I looked up at

Yvaine again. The remaining Guise had stopped their attack and twisted and writhed on the ground. My sister dropped her sword and collapsed, crawling to me. She took my hand. I looked to the fire burning in the pit, but she shook her head. *She'd used all her magic, too.*

Though the Guise had reverted, the ancient ones continued to take our blood. It was no longer a willing offering. Our blood drained faster and faster from our wrists, and was forced to join the red pool we bathed in. There was no stopping it now.

We lay there, staring at each other. There was nothing else we could do but bleed. Yvaine had paled and her eyes closed. Her lips stopped moving. *Yvaine…*

My eyes darted around the pool of blood, hoping that one of the reverted Guise would help us, but they were still weak from the transformation. We were alone. And we were going to die.

As my eyes searched for help, the sunlight glinted against the dagger's blade. The amethyst smoke had dissipated, but the dirk continued to glow. And I remembered the spell book's words: *Endowed weapons absorb their master's magic over time, so if the wielder is ever in need, they will always find a way to survive.*

I clutched the dagger's pearl handle with a weak hand, the precious weapon that had kept us alive for years. Raising my other hand, I gripped the blade and made a choice. "We are going to live." Using strength that I didn't think I had, I broke the dagger in half.

My body had given its last drop of blood, yet my eyes were wide open. The light that was released outshone the golden sun. It bathed us in peace.

As the magic settled over me, and the sun disappeared behind the moon, I accepted that, no matter what happened to me, the emotion I felt was worth every moment of hardship and pain I endured to get there. Because I had changed the world for the better. I'd found my purpose.

I'd found happiness.

My kin didn't need to tie me up or hold me down. Their manipulation spell was enough to keep me contained. I stood at the roof of their stronghold, the chief beside me. *At least Arlen had escaped.*

Once I knew there was nowhere left to hide, I told my friend to run and find the siblings. This was the only way he would leave me. And honestly, I wanted them to be together. To protect each other. I had faith that

Yvaine and Lugh would survive this. Yvaine was too stubborn to let them die. I could feel the cold metal of the flute she'd gifted me pressing against my back. My kin hadn't touched me, for fear of having their light taken, so this item remained with me.

I thought of her lovely face as I looked up at the sky. The shadow shield had yet to come down, but the star's light peered through anyway, unable to be smothered. Only when the sun was completely masked by the moon would the chief allow their protection to fall. It wouldn't be long now. The edge of the sun was already in shadow.

I wished to feel magic coursing through my veins. I'd had it locked inside me for so long that it was unnerving to be without it—empty. The Healing Fire had done its job; healing my body and burning away the darkness inside. I smiled, thinking of Lugh. He'd changed my life. The magic I'd stolen over the years had weighed me down. My father's sins had weighed me down. I'd held onto that burden rather than use it to save myself or the ones I cared about.

I regretted not using it to escape the last time I'd been the elves' prisoner. When I'd discovered that my mother had died, my reason for living had died with her. I hadn't known that Yvaine would come back for me—I thought she would leave the banished lying bastard behind. But she came back, and still, I didn't use it to save us. It was all her.

Letting go of the stolen magic was the best thing I could have ever done for myself.

"Are you smiling because you're moments away from saving your people? It would be a good reason." The chief took a step, now facing me.

"I'm smiling because I'm happy—enlightened even." I smirked, unable to resist.

"Oh, how so?" The chief was curious. He'd always been a strange elf, but he'd never been cruel. I doubted that he knew the others had tortured me during my time under the castle.

"You banished me because you were afraid of my nature. And now your survival depends on it. Just interesting is all." I tried to shift into a more comfortable position, but my body was like a statue, the incantation working its magic.

"We didn't know how important you would become. We did what we could to ensure our survival at the time. Just as we are now. It was never because of hate, Coilleach." The chief's blackened skin was swollen and tight.

Liar. "At least, I'll never look like you. I'll die handsome." Smiling, I returned my gaze to the sky, enjoying the sun as much as I could. The freezing cold of the shield made me want to shiver, but I wouldn't give Chief Dearil the satisfaction.

All the dead elves' weapons were laid out on the roof around me. There were orbs full of light in between—the stolen Fae magic. They'd killed so many to obtain this power. I only hoped that when I absorbed the magic it would be too much for my body to take, and there wouldn't be enough time to cast the spell. I hoped that I died fast enough to protect them.

The chief stepped away and traversed his spoils. "You joke, but I am sorry for your pain, Coilleach. I'm sorry this had to happen. I'm also sorry for your mother's death."

I tensed. "Don't talk about her." I didn't want to be reminded of her hate.

"As a parting gift, I grant you this knowledge, and hope it gives you peace." The chief was behind me now. "I remember the look on your face when your mother told you to leave. You were hurt. Betrayed. Oh, how you screamed and fought as the defenders dragged you away… But know this: it was your mother's words that convinced me to banish you."

"Stop," I growled. "I already know that she hated me."

"But that's where you're wrong. She saw how frightened our people were of you. You didn't have a friend in the whole clan. Not one. It was only a matter of time before you were attacked." I took a deep breath, having forgotten to do so in the past minutes. "Your mother told me to banish you, not out of hate, but compassion. She did it to protect you."

I laughed.

"You think I'm lying?" he said, unsurprised.

"Not at all. I think that I wasted a lot of years, and it's only fitting that I'm going to die just as I learned how to be happy." I looked around at all the glowing weapons. They were brighter now that the sun had vanished.

"It's time." The chief's voice was sympathetic. Still, he raised his hands and called out the words that would lower the shield. The elves below shouted in excitement. This would be the only time in my life that they accepted me. And despite the wrongness, it felt good.

The dark sky greeted me, and the world-ending words met my ears. "Cast the spell, Coilleach. Save your people." The chief stood at the edge of the roof, away from the magic bomb.

Free to walk, I began touching each weapon and orb, absorbing their magic. The power was intoxicating, and I thought about using it against them, but the manipulation spell was still in effect. They'd been very careful with their wording when they cast it. *I was helpless.*

Each addition left a dark weapon behind. Smoke of every color poured from my skin. The smoke itself was light and goodness. How could something that beautiful and pure be used to make darkness? Shadows danced below the castle, celebrating their soon-to-be freedom. No more Guise. No more fear.

The light grew the more I absorbed, and it was bright enough that the golden beings appeared. Once their moans were heard, the dancing stopped. The elves aimed their weapons, waiting for the Guise to advance. But they didn't move. They just stared at me. Then they fell. Their gold bodies transformed into fur and claws, skin and hands, feathers and wings.

As the spell commanded, I continued absorbing the light. It had become painful. The only thing that distracted me was the miracle happening before me. Where a Guise had stood, a wildcat now growled, exhaling ice. It ran away, frightened by the darkened elves, as well as its newfound magic.

"Daughter?" The chief was at the very edge of the roof, peering down at a female elf that lingered at the border. This elf hadn't been transformed into shadow before she was taken by the Guise. Her skin was as pale as the moon, and her eyes were a deep crimson.

I gritted, spitting the words out through the pain. "If you force me to cast the spell, your daughter will die."

The chief couldn't take his eyes off his child.

"Dearil! She will die! Tell me to stop!" I touched another weapon, and more light shone from my skin. My heart hurt. My lungs. My soul. It hurt so bad that I had to crawl to the next weapon. I screamed. The piercing agony of my voice woke the chief from his stupor, and he finally met my gaze. "It's over! There's no reason to continue!" Forcing a smug smile, I said, "My family has brought magic back and rid the world of Guise. I want to live in that world. Don't ruin all their hard work by casting a shadow over it." I reached for the last weapon.

The chief ran to me, and stole the bow before I could touch it. "No more, Coilleach. Release!"

The magic burst from my body. Released from their control, I was able to cast a final spell. One of my own making.

Kin of mine
Lost to time
Heal and warm
Feel and flourish
Accept and love
Become one with the sun

The magic spread outward, enveloping the dark elves in light. They flinched away from it. Some even ran. But there was no running from the truth. *Light shines from the inward soul again.*

The moon continued on its natural course, and the sun shone down on the elf clan. Their frostbitten, deformed skin had healed. Their eyes were no longer black but green, blue, orange, purple, and red again. The only darkness that had stayed was their hair. But our kind's hair had always been the color of raven feathers. It was how we knew we were kin.

The last of the magic abandoned me, and I was left alone again.

Chief Dearil offered his pale hand. "Rise, Coilleach. You are an elf through and through. And you have no reason to fear us anymore." He helped me traverse the castle's corridors until we were outside. I nodded my thanks, and he rushed to his daughter, who stood shocked at the border.

Nervous of their reactions, I walked slowly through the elf clan. They parted as I moved past them, just as it was before I was banished. No one had wanted to touch me, afraid of losing their magic. Despite their fear, I kept my head high and continued on my path. *I needed to find Yvaine and Lugh.*

Then there was a hand on my back.

I turned and found a child. She was peering up at me with big blue eyes, and my heart ached for Yvaine. "Thank you." Her sweet voice was what made the tears fall. I quickly wiped them away before anyone could see. But then another hand gripped my shoulder. This time, it was a male. He nodded in acknowledgment. Another approached and pressed my beloved bow and quiver into my palms.

I continued walking away from the clan, toward the forest. As I passed, every elf made contact with me, proving that they no longer feared what I was. They had accepted me as one of their own.

I was tired as I passed the border, but I kept my footing, refusing to fall at a time when I felt so tall. The forest had been my home since I was ten. I'd explored nearly every inch of this land, and ate with all the Fae peoples. And two humans.

Leaving my kin behind to heal on their own, I looked north where my family was waiting.

A chuff sounded from behind. I turned to find Arlen studying me with those open eyes of his. "I thought I told you to help the siblings?" I scolded with a smile.

Arlen approached and rubbed against my side, nearly knocking me down.

"I see. You're a good friend, Arlen." I motioned to his back. "You mind? I'm a bit drained."

Arlen knelt and allowed me to climb on.

"Let's head north," I said.

Arlen huffed in disagreement.

Then I remembered a very important detail. "The north is poisoned. There's no way to get to them on foot," I growled. "What are we supposed to do?"

Arlen faced south.

"The city. Maybe there's a boat there." In agreement, the two of us set our path for the flooded human city of Perth.

Due to Arlen's speed, we reached Perth by nightfall. It had been bizarre just to concentrate on the path ahead rather than where the sunlight cast its rays. The Guise were gone. I saw the occasional lost Common or Fae wandering the woods in confusion, but I couldn't stop to help. Someone needed me more.

The water was calm. Still, it would be a battle upriver until we reached the sea. Looking out over the fallen city, I knew that we weren't going to find a boat, at least one that hadn't been destroyed during the flood. I climbed down from Arlen's back and sat on the snow-covered hill overlooking the river. Arlen lay beside me as we debated.

"If they survived, they'll either be taking the helicopter or a boat back. If they think the elves still have me, they'll come through here. They know the north is poisoned." I pushed my dark hair back and away from my eyes.

Arlen laid his heavy head on my leg.

Sighing, I said, "You're right. We should wait here."

The thought that they were wounded, or worse, dead and rotting away had me itching to move. I stood and took a step. But even if we went from city to city, searching for a boat and fought our way upriver into the sea. It would be days, weeks, before we reached them. Arlen's massive form hovered at my right. *And Arlen wouldn't be able to come.* It would take a ship to carry him, and I was not as skilled as I would claim to be.

"The siblings are alive. Yvaine is coming back for me." I sat down again. "First lesson of survival, right? If you're lost, stay in one place. Someone will find you eventually."

Three days.

It had been three days since we'd decided to wait. What a stupid idea. I'd wasted precious time getting to them. What if my hesitance had cost them their lives?

Arlen and I huddled by the fire. He was kind enough to let me lean against his body, so I burrowed into his soft fur. We'd set up camp on top of the hill and out in the open. If they flew overhead or flowed down the river, they would see it. *See me.*

My friend kept the fire burning at all times. I was grateful for the warmth. After being trapped in the shadow shield and thrown into winter, my bones were frozen. The magic had strained my body, but after I cast the healing spell over the elves, a sense of peace settled over me, as well. Maybe the magic had cast itself on me in the end.

I peered down the river for the millionth time. My neck had started to cramp, I'd done it so much. But I couldn't stop. I listened for the helicopter's growl and heard nothing but silence in the night.

The reversal spell had wanted half-breeds. I could have gone with them and helped. Maybe they would have survived if there was more blood to give... The bonds of peace have been born and bled. My parent's union wasn't a bond of peace. Had it resulted in my lack of magic?

I hung my head, tired. There was no way to know, but either way, I couldn't risk adding my questionable blood to the mix. I'd kept my kin away from the important half-breeds. That was my role.

I wrung my hands together, trusting that they would get each other out.

But... Yvaine had nearly killed herself twice when she thought Lugh was dead. Once at the beginning of our journey: she had chosen to die with a poisoned Lugh and become a Guise. The second time was slicing her throat open for the spell at the mountains.

If Lugh hadn't survived this spell... Would she have chosen to die with her brother instead of coming back for me?

I didn't like the answer.

Arlen chuffed in frustration.

"Sorry, I know I'm worrying over nothing. I don't mean to bother you." I forced my muscles to relax and my mind to clear.

Arlen stood, and I fell backward onto the snow.

"What the hell?" I whined. There was a splash in the water below. And I was suddenly nervous to turn around and look. What would I find?

"Hey, elf! You mind getting off your ass and helping me?"

Smiling, I stood and answered, "I believe you're as much as an elf as I am. Should I start calling you as such?"

"Nah. I'm human through and through." Lugh's choice of words had me chuckling.

I slid down the hillside and met the young man as he docked the small boat. Looking at the engine, I realized just how distraught with worry I'd been to neglect hearing its rumble. "Yvaine?" Lugh threw out a couple bags of supplies, as well as their swords. The spell book peeked out of one of the pack's pockets.

Uncovering the unconscious body of his sister, he explained, "Sis took a bad hit when it happened." He peeled back a bandage on her stomach. "The dagger exploded, and a piece is still inside her."

I pulled the boat up and onto the shore. Surprised, Lugh nearly fell into the water, but I didn't care. Yvaine needed me. I rushed to her side, and the first thing I noticed was the defender's braid tied with the hairband I made her. She hadn't worn it since Lugh was asleep. It took the world ending for her to finally forgive me for lying. "Yvaine, I love you. I didn't tell you that before I left. I'm sorry."

"She forgives you. Now help me get her out."

Together, we carefully laid her by the fire. I placed a hand on her forehead. "She has a fever," I said. I noticed a new scar on her wrist and found that Lugh had the same one.

Lugh nodded. "I keep waiting for it to break like it did last time." Lugh took a deep breath. "I thought the spriggan could do something. He helped me, so maybe…"

"You did the right thing, Lugh. The spriggan will help. His magic is powerful." I straightened Yvaine's clothes and brushed the loose strands of hair from her eyes just as I'd watched her do for Lugh over and over again. "Do you need to rest?" I met the human's eyes and found something new there.

"No way. Yvaine didn't stop when I needed help." He looked to his sister with gratitude. "It's my turn to be strong for her." I noticed the damaged veins that once bulged from his skin were gone. *He'd allowed himself to heal.* Yet, the white scar on his neck remained. I supposed that some scars would always be with us, no matter how much we wanted to forget.

As I clutched my loved one's hand, I smiled at her brother and said, "Good answer."

We kept to the road. Hundreds of Common and Fae wandered the land, confused. But as the night became day again, the expression on the those faces changed—they were happy. Old friends and family reunited. Some went from person to person, asking if they'd seen their father or cousin or even their lost dog.

As we passed them by, we were asked if we needed help. They looked at the bleeding woman in our arms with concern and wished us well when we politely declined their assistance. It was a strange new world these siblings had created.

It was amazing to watch Common humans and animals discover their new magic. Smoke full of rainbow light filled the sky as they let it shine. I looked to Lugh. Though he didn't break a step while he carried Yvaine down the road, his face was grim. "It's not your fault, Lugh. If you hadn't broken the dagger, the spell would have killed you."

"It seems cruel for the ancient ones to kill the bonds of peace, don't you think? We're the ones who offered our blood to them. The least they could have done was leave us a little."

"I don't think the ancient ones were in the right state of mind when they made the spell to begin with. It was a harsh time. They were desperate." I paused. "Just like you were at the end. That dagger was all you two had left of your light, and it saved you once the spell was complete. So, what I mean is, don't regret what you did."

Lugh snickered. "I don't. Being magicless is better than being dead."

We both looked at Yvaine and walked a little faster.

It only took a few days before we reached the spriggan's woods, and we had no interruptions, especially with Arlen guarding us. No threat wanted to challenge his sharp, saber-like teeth. The spriggan's roots were planted near the same tunnel we'd camped in—the same tunnel Lugh had been poisoned.

Lugh set Yvaine down against the tree beside the tunnel's entrance, her sword laid beside her. I frowned, remembering Yvaine's face the last time we'd been there. Now, she was the one slowly dying in the sunlight. The blood that coated her hair glowed brighter than it should have.

"I'll be back," I told Lugh. Arlen stayed to protect the siblings as I set off into the woods to search for the healer.

The forest was cold. The snow crunched beneath my feet, and I made sure I was loud enough to announce my arrival. "You have returned, my young friend." The spriggan's voice was deep and as rough as his bark.

"Alon, I'm afraid it's not under pleasant circumstances. Yvaine, the human, needs your help." I turned toward the shifting tree branches.

"The human, is it?" The spriggan chuckled, and a full-grown owl flew from his mouth.

Suspicious, I said, "You knew, didn't you? That she was like me."

"Wasn't it obvious?" Alon's feet unwrapped from his roots and stepped onto the snow. His branches groaned in protest, but he didn't complain.

Irritated, I said, "Not to everyone."

"She was lost. I am happy to hear that you have guided her to her true self." The spriggan plucked a leaf from his brow. "I have lived a long time, so I can tell you that most aren't as lucky."

"I will have guided her to her grave if you don't heal her." I reached out to the spriggan, helpless.

"Then we mustn't keep our savior waiting."

Lugh was startled when Alon crossed the tree line after me, but he adjusted his face and stood. "Thank you for helping me. I owe you my life."

"You owe me nothing, youngling. You have brought magic back to the world. Your debt has been paid a hundred times over." Alon pinched his face in what looked like a smile, and the bark peeled slightly.

"In that case, I'm calling in the debt. Heal my sister, would you?" Lugh moved out of the spriggan's path, and Alon stepped forward slowly.

"It would be my honor." A branch peeled back the blood-soaked bandage. From that branch grew more until they were smaller than any child's finger, and as long as the endowed dagger had been. The delicate roots entered Yvaine's wound, yet she didn't make a sound. *She's almost gone.*

Carefully, the spriggan pulled the dagger shard from her skin and placed the leaf from his brow into the opening. Alon didn't speak an incantation, instead, he merely let his green light shine down on her.

Lugh, Arlen, and I stood motionless, afraid that one distraction would mean the end of Yvaine's life. But sooner than we thought, Alon stepped away from the dying woman.

"Is it done?" Lugh questioned. He ran to Yvaine and took her hand.

"The rest is up to her. I have done all that I can." The spriggan didn't move to leave, and I noticed that he kept the dagger's shard for himself, absorbing it into his trunk.

I knelt beside Yvaine, her brother shedding tears on the opposite side.

I recalled the first time I saw Yvaine. She had just stabbed me, and then a light lit up in her hand, illuminating a lovely, yet angered face. I had told her to finish what she'd started because I hadn't had the will to end her life. Something about her made me want to stop, even if it meant dying.

When the banshees attacked, she had chosen to fight alone, so her brother would be safe. Lugh had led me outside only to untie his prisoner. He'd refused to say a word to me, too desperate to go back and help his sister. At that moment, I knew there was something special about her.

It was the first time I ever felt needed.

"It's time to wake up, Yvaine. You've been sleeping long enough." I took her other hand. I glanced back and saw Arlen sit beside the spriggan, where he slowly rooted to the ground. I shuddered, barely holding in the frantic emotions. All I wanted to do was shake the woman until she opened her eyes. "You would die for any one of us. And we've proven that we would die for you." I clutched her hand tight, relishing the feel of her skin against mine. "Prove that you will *live* for us. Live for *me*."

Just as always, Yvaine made me wait. And wait.

Lugh had completely shut down. His tears stopped. All he did was continue to hold his sister's hand. It was the only thing he could do for her.

I leaned down and whispered in my loved one's ear, "If you don't wake up, I'm going to break your new sword in half and throw it over a cliff. You hurt me, Yvaine. So, how can I continue to look at that beautiful weapon when your as equally beautiful face isn't the one wielding it?"

Silence.

My forehead against hers, I groaned, "Yvaine." There were no more words to give. So, I gave her all that I had left. I placed my lips against hers.

My hand was clutched tight. "You threaten my weapon and then kiss me? What kind of elf are you?"

I pulled away to find blue eyes staring back at me. They were as pure as the daytime sky and just as open. "A sexy one," I said, unable to deliver the line without choking on my relief.

She granted me a smile. "I can't argue with that."

"Yvaine!" Lugh lunged between us and held his sister tight.

She returned the gesture with vigor. "I knew you wouldn't let me down," she said.

Lugh laughed, his own relief obvious. "Yeah, well, you're heavier than you look. It took me a while, but I found help."

"Help? Why not just use a healing spell?" she asked, confused. She sat up and gazed at the daytime sky, instinctually searching for golden beasts.

"We don't…" Lugh began.

"The reversal spell took everything from both of you. Magic and blood." I placed my hand on Lugh's shoulder. "You only survived because Lugh thought to release the magic that's been stored in the dagger for the last thirteen years. It was able to heal him and keep you alive long enough to find Alon. But nothing more. It's gone." I took my loved one's hand again. "I'm sorry."

Tears gathered in her eyes, but they didn't spill. "If it was the cost for living, then it was worth it. You did the right thing, brother."

Lugh nodded, pleased by his sister's words.

Yvaine released her hold on us and stood. We reached out to her, but she held up her hand, leaning against the tree. "I just don't understand why the ancient ones thought that half-breeds were a good reason to bring magic back. What difference could it make?"

Alon chuckled, and we all suddenly remembered he was there. His body had taken root in the soil. "Common and Fae together is powerful magic. It is the transition from darkness to light and from light to darkness. It is the bridge between peoples. A bridge of choice and freedom. Of goodness." *Of peace.* "Only when there was peace among peoples could magic be returned."

"Interesting," Lugh commented.

Yvaine didn't share her brother's understanding. "Hmph. Well, that's ironic, considering that we *lost* our magic to bring back everyone else's."

The spriggan smiled and reached into his leafless branches. He held up a long blonde strand of hair in the sunlight. "I believe this is yours."

Yvaine approached and stared at the hair. "You're giving it back? Why?"

"It's not mine to give. Only the caster can give their magic."

"Magic?" Yvaine plucked the hair from his grasp, yet the branch stayed, growing outward.

Excited, Lugh said, "'A caster's magic is stored, not only inward, but outward as well. Magic can be found in a lost tooth, so long as they possessed magic at the time.'" Lugh hugged Arlen, startling our massive friend. "The spell book told me that long ago, but I didn't know what it meant until now." He took Yvaine's hair and examined it in the sunlight. "You can have your magic back, sis." *The spell book told him that?* Somehow, Lugh had earned the book's respect, and it changed masters. I chuckled, knowing that Dearil had his grimoire stolen by a novice.

Yvaine took the long strand back, her eyes questioning. "You said that only the caster can give their magic. The elves told me that it could not be given," she told Alon.

The spriggan's branches reaching higher than before, he said, "The elves are wrong about a lot of things."

Yvaine approached me, the expression on her face foreign. "What's wrong? This is good. You have magic," I said. *Why wasn't she happy?*

Yvaine leaned forward for what I thought was going to be an embrace, but instead, she stole my bow. "Hey, I was only trying to get you to wake up. I wasn't actually going to break your sword," I explained, worried for my weapon.

She picked up her sword and cut my bow's string, too impatient to unstring it properly. "Yeah, you were. But that's not what I'm doing." Concentrating, Yvaine whispered quiet words to the golden hair. It lengthened and thickened, until I questioned if it was hair anymore. She looped the ends and hooked them on the bow, commanding it to grow and shrink as she wished.

Yvaine placed the bow in my hand. "I give you the remainder of my magic, Cole. If anyone deserves light in their life, it's you." She wrapped her arms around my waist and kissed me, though I was unresponsive, shocked at what she'd done.

"You can't do that! Take it back!" I shoved the weapon at her, afraid.

Yvaine backed away, smiling. "It's too late. It's already given. Why don't you give it a try?" she taunted.

I looked to Lugh for help, but he had the same smile on his face. They were certainly related.

Unsure, I nocked an arrow and aimed for the dark tunnel. "Sit lux vivere."

The bow's magic came to life. Amethyst light shone, even under the sun. I loosed the arrow, and it took the light with it, carrying it down the dark tunnel and banishing the shadows within. This time, no one could stab me afterward. Because now I could see. Now, I had light.

"*Let light live.* A perfect first spell," Yvaine said.

And it was a first spell. I had taken magic, stolen it all my life. It had felt good to have that power, but it never gave me the feeling it did now. With my family's light a part of me, I felt whole. I dropped the bow and gathered Yvaine in my arms. The magic seeped from my pores, swathing her in everything I had. Everything she had given me. And it only grew in strength. "I love you, my kind and selfless woman. How can I ever make it up to you?"

"I can think of a few things," she teased.

"Oh, please spare me. Since you guys are being gross, I'm going to take a nap. Haven't slept in days." With that said, Lugh went to the center of the open meadow and laid on his back, too warm from the sun to care about the snow beneath him.

"That actually sounds like a good idea. Join us?" Yvaine asked, her eyes full of joy.

I nodded, and she ran toward the sun, laying down beside her brother. Arlen joined soon after, allowing the siblings to nestle into his fur.

Curious, I asked Alon, "Why are you rooting here? Your home is in the bramble?"

With a voice thick with sleep, he answered, "There's no reason to hide anymore." And indeed there wasn't. The spriggan's roots grew long and deep below the snow. His branches grew high, inviting both Common and Fae to rest within his new foliage. But we weren't Common or Fae anymore. We weren't the *Conscius* or the *Caecus* either. We were all something entirely new.

We were the definition of goodness.

Placing the bow over my shoulders, I removed the flute from my waistband and fingered a new hopeful melody.

Joining my family, the four of us looked up at the sun. We appreciated its warmth and beauty, knowing it was no longer something to fear.

Respice Finem

Acknowledgments

Readers, thank you for imagining.

Imagination is what makes humanity extraordinary. I look forward to each publication, knowing there are those out there experiencing the world through my eyes. And hopefully inspiring other's imaginations, as many have inspired mine.

Thank you to my family. There are four people out of the billions on the planet who I can truly rely on. They give me the strength I need to strive for more each day, and I am grateful to have them in my life.

Thank you, Plato, renowned philosopher and writer, for your wise words. Your memory lives on in those who turn their souls to the light.

Author's Note

This novel was inspired by a short story I wrote in elementary school when I was just beginning to discover my joy for writing. I was very much into action-packed novels and badass characters at that age (and still am). I drew inspiration from my own life and created a story about a young girl defending her little brother. It became a handwritten, crumpled piece of paper found many years later in an old box in our parent's basement.

Next, is the original unedited draft for the story that would later become *Bloodline*.

My brother was about to die. It wasn't right. He just turned 4. The man I had grown to hate in just a short amount of time held the knife in his hand, but he had a gun a short distance from him. I was about 5 feet away from it, but I couldn't move. The man with the knife had paralyzed me with some sort of drug. I don't even know how I had received it and that scared me. But I couldn't give up! I tried to force myself up. To fight for my brother. What if I'm not strong enough? What if I fail and my brother dies? All because I'm too weak. But I kept trying. Although I was paralyzed I had never felt my body more strongly. I felt the muscles burn, my bones crunch from the struggle, the screaming voice in my head telling me to give up. Then I felt it. The burning and adrenaline coursing through my blood, working its way through my body.

Just as the man was about to plunge the knife into my brother's heart, I had his gun in my hand and against the man's head. The look on his face gave me a jolt of confidence. It was a mix of surprise, anger, and a little bit of I'm screwed. Although I had the gun to his head, he still had the knife against my brother's skin, ready to spear him. He seemed to notice me glance at it. This made him smile. "Let my brother go you bastard and maybe I'll let you live."

"Why don't you put the gun down like a good girl and I'll let you and your brother go?" We all knew that was a pile of crap. He wouldn't let us go. As soon as I put down the gun he'd finish my brother and go for me next.

"No. It's my way or the highway you son of a bitch." This time he didn't argue. He just stared at me, measuring my expression and what he saw there frightened him. I don't know what my face looked like, I couldn't feel it, but it must have been pretty damn screwed up for his reaction. He slowly pulled the knife away and let my brother go. My brother ran to embrace me, but I couldn't at the moment, so I pulled him behind me. Then the man's expression changed. It went from fear to the most extreme terror any expression could pull off.

"See ya in hell." I pulled the trigger, smiling all the while.

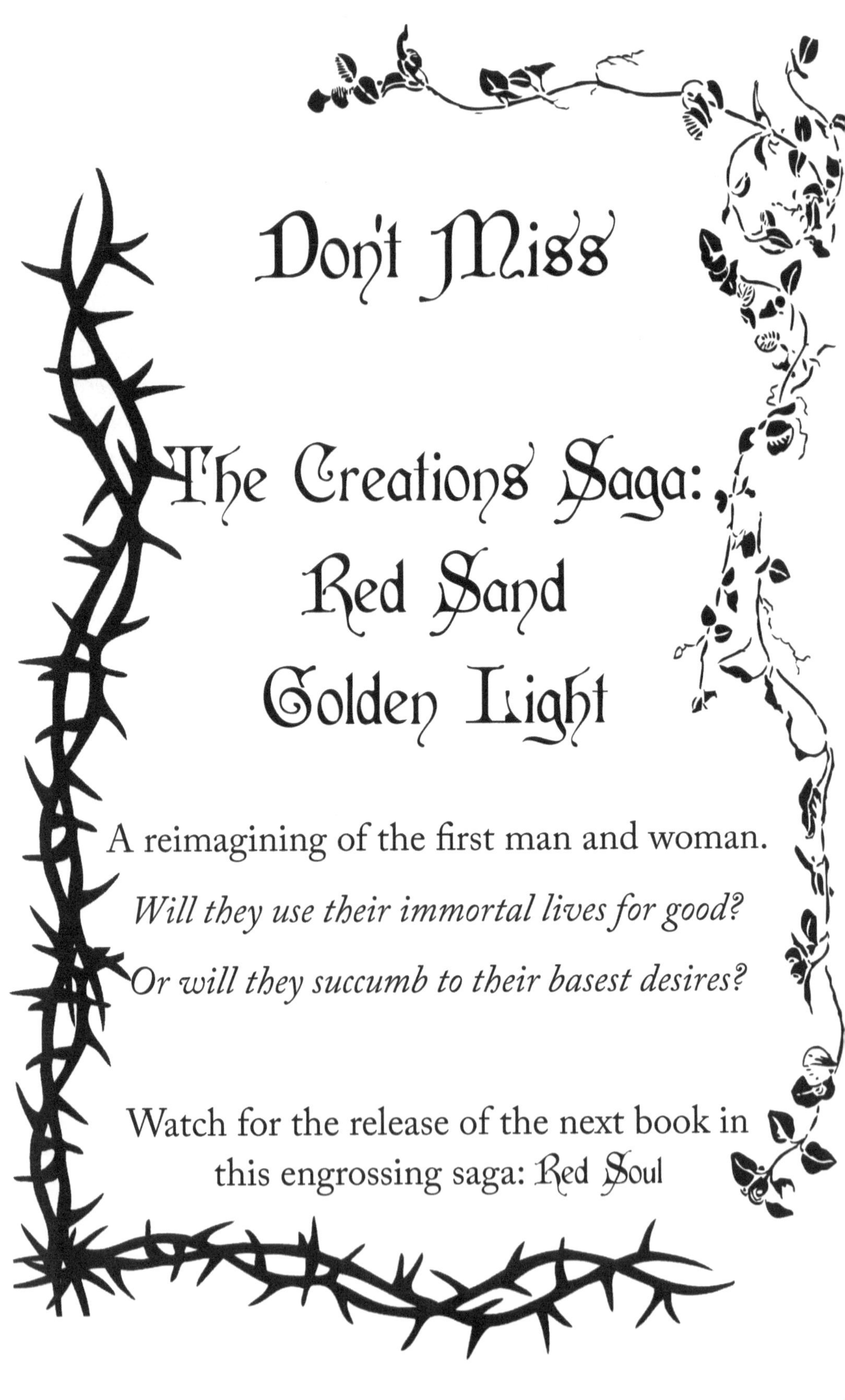

Don't Miss

The Creations Saga:
Red Sand
Golden Light

A reimagining of the first man and woman.

Will they use their immortal lives for good?

Or will they succumb to their basest desires?

Watch for the release of the next book in
this engrossing saga: Red Soul

About the Author

Award-winning author, Anne MacReynold, believes our universe holds magic that we have yet to comprehend, and wields this power of thought in her writing. Not only do her philosophical views weave themselves into her stories, but her life, as well. Anne continues to find happiness with her family and animal companions in Alaska, a place that still displays the natural beauty that is the Earth, and a home that allows her to spend time with those she loves. Anne proves that sometimes the simplest of lives can be the most fulfilling.

Follow the author's releases at annemacreynold.com or on social media:
Facebook/WriterAnneMacReynold
Twitter/AnneMacReynold
Instagram/AnneMacReynold

www.ingramcontent.com/pod-product-compliance
Lightning Source LLC
Chambersburg PA
CBHW061341190726
48288CB00005B/1545